ANNIE
AND THE
WOLVES

Also by the Author

Novels
The Spanish Bow
The Detour
Behave
Plum Rains

Nonfiction
Searching for Steinbeck's Sea of Cortez

ANNIE AND THE WOLVES

ANDROMEDA ROMANO-LAX

Published by
Soho Press, Inc.
227 W 17th Street
New York, NY 10011

Library of Congress Cataloging-in-Publication Data
Names: Romano-Lax, Andromeda, author.
Title: Annie and the wolves / Andromeda Romano-Lax.
Description: New York : Soho, [2021]
Identifiers: LCCN 2020020023

ISBN 978-1-64129-316-7
eISBN 978-1-64129-170-5

Subjects: LCSH: 1. Oakley, Annie, 1860–1926—Fiction.
2. GSAFD: Biographical fiction. 3. Science fiction.
Classification: LCC PS3618.O59 A84 2021 I DDC 813'.6—dc23

Interior design by Janine Agro

Printed in the United States of America

10 9 8 7 6 5 4 3 2 1

To my sisters: Honoree, Eliza and Nikki

Homo homini lupus [Man is wolf to man].
Who in the face of all his experience of life and of
history, will have the courage to dispute this assertion?

—SIGMUND FREUD, 1930

ANNIE
AND THE
WOLVES

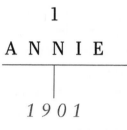

1

A N N I E

1 9 0 1

S he woke to the shriek of the whistle and the squeal of brakes. Three in the morning, yet the sleeper car was flooded with sparking, shuddering light.

In that bright silver moment as the trains collided, she felt herself lifting from the bed, time slowing as it had always done at the bottom of a breath when she lined up a shot. She was floating, her gowned body surrounded by twinkling glass and feathers, every barb aglow. Then she slammed into the wall. A blast of pain raced across her pelvis and up her spine. Too much to bear.

Annie Oakley thought, *Away.*

And then she was.

ANNIE WAS ON HER BACK, laid out on a piece of canvas within sight of the toppled train car, a wool blanket over the bottom half of her body. For the moment, no one attending to her.

Turning her head, she could see other passengers from the demolished show train being escorted, limping and stunned, toward an upright stock car that had been turned into a makeshift hospital, its large panel doors open and dozens of people crowded inside. Other wood-sided cars had been reduced to splinters, their contents thrown into the swampy North Carolina lowlands alongside the tracks. Outside were cowboys, Indians, train crew, all trying to help. A bison from the show stood in a ditch, unharmed, its massive beautiful head turned toward her, backlit by the yellow dawn.

The sun was rising. Hours had passed. But it had not felt like time passing. She had skipped from the moment of the crash until now, like a stone across a pond.

She rolled to one side and cried out in pain, attracting the attention of a man in a gray cap who was pointing a rifle at the head of a downed horse. The man hesitated and looked Annie's way while she stared past him, wanting to help the creature, but it was useless. Moving even a few inches had brought her to the edge of a blackout.

The horse was on its side on the ground, ribs moving with uneven, quivering breaths. The man settled his shoulders and aimed the rifle again.

Pearly smoke, that burning acrid smell, and her thought— *No!*—but she knew it must be done, and done well. Eyes closed, she listened and counted. Three shots. A pause. Four more. She felt her anger rise. *The placement must be exact for it to be merciful. It shouldn't take so many shots.*

She opened her eyes and saw the man step a little way down the tracks toward a second, equally lame horse. It was one of her favorites: a dark chestnut with a white blaze down its face. This time, it was as if the rifle were being placed on her own forehead, the steel muzzle set between her own eyes. Skipping forward had been no reprieve; it had only brought her to the next terrible place. She closed her eyes, felt her heart slow. Again, she thought, *Away.*

And she was. Back on the train just as the light filled the sleeper, just as everything turned a glimmering silvery white. She felt herself floating, falling, knowing.

It is trauma that sends us away, but there is pain also where we land.

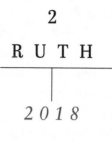

2

R U T H

2 0 1 8

Friday

R uth was just out the door for her speaking engagement at the local high school, laptop bag over her shoulder, when the delivery truck pulled into her driveway. She paused with a hand on the knob, fresh fall Minnesota air filling her lungs, watching as the man in brown shorts approached.

She wasn't expecting a package—was she? Hope was dangerous, but she couldn't hold back a smile as he handed over the box.

"Something good?" he asked.

"Possibly."

Taking it, she noted the Vermont return address and heard the soft slide and thud of what could be a rare journal, more than a century old and certainly improperly packed. But she wasn't about to rebuke the sender. Not when he was trusting her with this, Annie Oakley's own words, unknown to any scholar.

The sharpshooter had left behind an unfinished autobiography and some everyday correspondence when she'd died in 1926, but little else of substance written in her own hand.

Ruth's last email exchange with an antique collector who called himself Nieman had ended inconclusively. He'd agreed to send her a few scans or mail select photocopies on the condition that she understood he was in a hurry, with a large-scale purchase planned pending the journal's authenticity. She promised to take a look, despite his refusal to provide any details on how the item had come into his possession.

Context matters, she had replied. *The more you withhold, the less reliable my analysis will be. Also please keep in mind that an original provides much more information than a photocopy. I'll work pro bono; that isn't the issue. But I can't do much without quality source materials.*

The journal was only the first step. Nieman had gotten a glimpse of a letter and wanted to purchase an entire set of rare correspondence, all of it somehow related to the journal in terms of content, about which he had offered only meager clues.

Your call, she'd responded, trying to play it cool. *I have some time this week. Next month is busier.*

It was a lie. Aside from the speech she was giving to a history class in thirty minutes—make that twenty—Ruth had nothing scheduled for the rest of the year, aside from trips to the chiropractor and putting her house up for sale.

Watching the truck back out, Ruth tried not to wish or want too much. She ran a hand through the curled ends of her auburn hair—styled, for once—trying to prolong this feeling of well-being. She was wearing a corduroy jacket she'd ordered online and her luckiest blue-stitched cowboy boots. She'd removed the knee brace she normally wore under baggy sweatpants in order to squeeze into jeans she hadn't bothered to take out of a drawer for months. She felt the warm sun on her face and smelled burning leaves.

History is well and good, but the present is worth noticing, too. Remember this. For a few lovely seconds, time didn't matter.

But as soon as the delivery truck was out of view, it mattered again. No time to slice through the layers of fibrous brown packing tape. Definitely no time to make sense of journal entries.

She should be able to summon some patience, considering she'd been stuck with no new leads for several years.

Ruth unlocked the door and hurried to the kitchen counter, planning to leave the box there. Then she spotted the kitchen scissors, sticking out from her jar of wooden spoons.

Just a peek.

She ran the point of the scissors down the flap and pulled. Inside she saw bubble wrap. *Bubble wrap!* Nieman should have known better. Through the plastic she saw a color: burgundy edged with dark brown. The real thing. Not a set of photocopies. She wouldn't have taken the risk, but he had, and bless him for it.

Her fingers reached to pull the wrapped journal out of the box, but then she caught sight of her watch. She was due in Holloway's class at 2:05. The walk, about three-quarters of a mile from the end of her road, down a trail and to the back entrance of the public school, took a fit, healthy person fifteen minutes. For Ruth, it would be twice as long.

She felt her stomach flutter with joy at what she'd received, overlaid by nerves about being late. She shouldn't have opened the box, but she was too excited to feel any regret. She reached into the ceramic dish next to her mail basket, grabbed the key to her Honda Fit and proceeded through the garage door before reason could stop her.

Door open, laptop bag on the passenger seat, thumb drive with her slideshow ready as backup in case her own computer was wonky and it was easier to use Holloway's. Garage door up. Seatbelt. Key in the ignition.

Maybe today. It had to happen sometime. Why else had she put off selling the car, once she'd broken up with Scott and had no one else to drive or even halfheartedly maintain it?

Because you're going to want to drive again. You're going to be ready at some point.

The hatchback didn't look anything like the small Subaru sedan she'd smashed up. This was new and bigger, silver, ridiculously clean. Well, of course it was clean. It had less than fifty miles on it.

Her hand gripped the gearshift without taking it out of park. She touched her toe to the gas pedal just to feel the positioning—no surprises—then placed the slippery bottom of the boot squarely against the brake. Quick glance at all mirrors. Another squeeze, preparing to shift into drive. Out on the dead-end road, there wasn't a single car or pedestrian to worry about. *Look forward.* Look right, even though there were only woods that way; still, there could be cyclists or walkers coming from the trail. Look left. Right one last time.

Ready.

Then she saw it all at once. New Year's Day. The bridge, the car with its hungover driver braking too fast on the icy road ahead of her, the guardrail.

She knew what would come next—the vision, terror-fed illusion, whatever it had been. She couldn't let her mind go there, or her body would follow into a full panic attack.

Heart in her throat, Ruth yanked her foot off the pedal and her hand off the gear shift.

"Oh, god," she sputtered.

She took a deep breath as her mind slammed that door shut just in time. She fumbled with the seatbelt, hands shaking, desperate to be free of the strap. She would move slowly, tricking her body into a state of calm. She would gather up her things and exit the garage without drama. She swallowed and inhaled again. As she opened the door, she checked her watch. Ten minutes to two.

Now you've done it.

AT THE SCHOOL, RUTH HURRIED toward the metal detector, eyes focused on the yellow banner beyond: WE LOVE OUR VISITORS / HORIZON HIGH. But the seated security guard called her back.

"Quick look at your ID and you'll be on your way."

"I don't have anything on me."

"You don't have a faculty ID?"

"I'm not faculty."

"But I've seen you around here, haven't I?"

"My fiancé teaches here." She'd barely spoken the words before regretting them. Scott wasn't her fiancé anymore. It just slipped out sometimes.

"Another official ID from this list, then. You can't enter the school without one of these. Plus, you have to sign the visitors log."

She hadn't brought anything except her laptop and keys. In her flustered state leaving the garage, she'd forgotten her purse.

Past the security station, classroom doors opened and teenagers spilled out, the halls echoing with squeaky footfalls.

"I'm running out of time," Ruth said. "Is there something we can do?"

From the corner of her eye she noticed a student, maybe sixteen or seventeen, standing behind her: dark hair, tall. Skinny jeans and a collared plaid layered over a graphic T-shirt, jacket hanging from one hand. The guard gestured for him to go around Ruth and show his school ID, but the boy remained where he was.

"That's okay," the boy said. "I'm not in a hurry."

"Oh, sure." The guard laughed. "You just want an excuse to be late for class. Tell 'em you were stuck behind a terrorist." He added for Ruth's benefit, "This isn't the airport. We can make jokes."

"But you can't make exceptions."

"No, ma'am."

So she was not only late, but apparently a "ma'am" at thirty-two. Wonderful.

Ruth asked, "Can you at least get a message to Mrs. Holloway for me?"

Making no move to rise from his chair, he gestured back outside. "Main visitor center. South side. Past lots B and C, then swing a left past the bus zone. Guard there can send someone to hand-deliver a note, but she probably won't see it till end of the day."

At the beginning of the year, she'd given herself until December 31st to make a professional appearance—anywhere. When Jane Holloway issued the invitation in September, Ruth knew this was the easiest way to finally check one item off her Rehab Resolution List. Someday she'd work outside the house again, and the last two years, terrible as they were, would be sealed away, moved into deep archival storage.

But that was *someday*. For now, she'd settle for much less: just one good, purposeful, dignified hour.

From among the scattered students still milling around, pocketing gadgets or fumbling with backpacks, a familiar figure emerged.

"Scott!" she called out. "They won't let me in."

He paused, squinting. New sweater, same old glasses.

"Jane Holloway's looking for you."

"I know. I left my wallet at home. I don't suppose you could vouch for me? All this new security . . ."

"Tell me about it." He approached, calling to the boy in line behind her. "Reece, get going. You're late for your next class. And hey, you weren't in calculus."

The boy slid his school ID out of a tight back pocket and handed it to the guard. "Did I miss anything?"

Scott's most detested question, Ruth remembered.

"Did you *miss* anything? Oh, no—we were just hanging out. Besides the quiz and the chapter review." He turned to Ruth. "I'll send someone to tell Holloway you've got a hitch. And Ruth—sorry. I'd drive you to your house if I could, but my own class is starting. You can take the shortcut, right? Ten-minute walk?"

Reece was still lingering, fists crammed into his tight pockets. "I've got a car."

"That's all right," said Ruth.

"No, really. I can drive you."

She glanced at her watch. "It's okay. You get to class."

"It's, what, three minutes by car?"

Surely he couldn't just leave campus without permission. "That doesn't seem . . . weird to you?"

"Weird is good," he said.

Scott frowned at Reece and gestured toward Ruth's laptop. "Do you have a scanned ID in your files? Passport, maybe? I might have put that in a folder for you when we were . . ."

Planning to go on vacation. Thailand or Vietnam, they'd never decided.

"Maybe. It takes about ten minutes just to boot this thing up."

"Ten minutes?" Reece said. "That's messed up."

Scott shook his head. "He's right. You've got to get that into the shop."

"Defrag it, at least," Reece said. "Free up some space on your hard drive."

"You're both right." The computer shop was fifteen miles away, not on any bus route from this side of town. Nothing was easy or quick these days. "I'll get to the mall this weekend."

Scott must have heard the catch in her voice. "Reece here could do it for you, after school. Hire him for a house call. He's a whiz at that stuff."

"I don't know—" she started to say, but Scott wasn't listening.

"Reece, you know the cul-de-sac on Pine Street, behind the school? She lives in the A-frame."

"All right, all right," Ruth said, in a tone that meant, *Stop. It's my life now. You were liberated from the landscaping and recycling and laptop fixing.* Maybe he was trying to reconnect. Still, this wasn't his problem. It wasn't appropriate for him to give out her address, though she hadn't objected last spring when he'd sent over a pair of students who mowed lawns and cleaned windows.

"Scott, thank you for your concern. You should get to your class. And Reece, nice to meet you, but you're late, too."

"Holloway's my last period," Reece said. "I can tell her they won't let you in."

Resigned, Ruth took a deep breath and really looked at the teenager standing on her side of the guard's station, refusing to walk through. "That would be a big help. Thanks."

He was six inches taller than her, long arms jutting out of rolled-up flannel sleeves. There was a black infinity symbol on his forearm. Maybe a real tattoo, or maybe just a temporary pen-inked doodle.

She spotted it and, for a moment, couldn't look away. *So familiar.*

The nape of her neck tingled. She didn't know this kid, but she'd just had the sudden urge to step forward, lean in, tell him something. Something important. Thankfully, she stopped herself. But what had she wanted to say?

Blink, she told herself. *Blink and breathe.*

Maybe seeing her ex again *was* a bad idea, as Dr. Susan, her first therapist, had said. Running into him could've tripped some switch in her brain, even though she was nearly mended now: stable, rational, mostly delusion-free. Or maybe this was just the price for having sat behind the wheel of a car. Or for having gotten too worked up about the journal.

Hell, maybe it was all three, too much adrenaline filtered through an injured brain slowly remolding itself—a process that could take years, all the doctors said. She recorded every incident and setback on her kitchen calendar. Full-on, visually detailed attacks, plus the lesser surges of anxiety. Ripples emanating from a distant splash.

"You okay?" the boy asked. "You look dizzy."

Without thinking, she took a step toward him to see if he smelled familiar; he did. But it was only stale cigarette smoke and a hint of deodorant spray. Most teenage boys smelled like that.

She was tempted to say, *Don't smoke*, but that was none of her business. What she actually wanted to say was, *I thought you'd quit*. That made even less sense.

"No, I'm fine. You should get going. Thanks for telling Mrs. Holloway for me. I'm heading home and will come right back, but the class will be halfway over by then. Can you give her this, so she can have the slideshow up and ready?"

Reece took the thumb drive, nodded and started down the hallway until he was side by side with Scott. Then he swung around and walked backwards. "So, should I come fix your laptop later, then?"

Scott looked back over his shoulder, also awaiting her response.

It wasn't so much that she wanted to please the man she'd almost married and then lost. She just wanted to reassure him and, more important, herself, that she was okay now. Not afraid or obsessed or stuck, not imagining things, not falling apart. All that was over.

"That would be fine," she said. "Anytime."

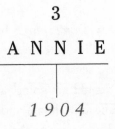

3

ANNIE

1904

Annie would never forget the first headline: August 12, 1903, from Kansas, the *Salina Daily Union*: ANNIE OAKLEY'S DOWNFALL—COCAINE BRINGS THE FAMOUS RIFLE SHOT TO THE DEPTHS. Another, two days later, from Delaware: ANNIE OAKLEY STOLE TO BUY HERSELF COCAINE. The third headline was from North Carolina: ANNIE OAKLEY IN PRISON.

"How could they, Mr. Fraley?" she asked the first of two lawyers she and Frank had hired when they'd decided to sue all fifty-five newspapers. "They're such bald-faced lies. I don't see how they'll defend themselves."

"They'll say they got it off the wires. A woman using your name, or something close to it, was arrested. That part of the story is arguably accurate. How could reporters be sure it wasn't you?"

"But that's ludicrous. Anyone could have seen that poor wretch wasn't me."

"They'll say they had good cause to believe it, with you being in the entertainment business."

"Not *that* entertainment business."

"Most juries don't know the difference between burlesque and sport shooting in a traveling show or exhibition," Mr. Fraley said.

"Anyway, they'll say they couldn't stop the presses. They'll say it wasn't malicious and caused no damage. And when that doesn't work, they'll go back to the beginning and make the jury think maybe those stories had an ounce of truth, or that even if the stories were completely wrong, they *could* have been true."

"You're saying they'll attack my character."

Frank reached over and touched the back of Annie's hand. "They'll find nothing to attack."

Frank's comment should have calmed her, but it had the opposite effect, because even Frank didn't know everything. When they'd become acquainted—she, a tender fifteen-year-old who could have passed for twelve—he'd thought she was the most unsullied, untouched, innocent woman he'd ever met. If he knew everything, he would think less of her. He would study their relationship anew, seeing reasons for the disappointments they never discussed. At the very least, he would pity her.

"I understand your point of view," Mr. Fraley said to Frank, "but it doesn't matter. They'll make her wish she'd just accepted an apology and never bothered to sue. It's a lawyer's job to wear people down."

That was eight months ago. She hadn't liked the lawyers, Misters Fraley and Paul, in the beginning. But she respected them now. They'd been right about everything. The defense lawyers and the newsmen, who didn't appreciate her counterattack against the yellow press, had done all they could to stifle her determination. Already she was more tired than she'd ever been in her life, and this was less than a year into the lawsuits, a process her lawyers predicted could last four to five years, even longer.

"You'll get through this," Frank said. "Look at all you've overcome in this decade alone."

He didn't understand that the wear was cumulative. Of course, it shouldn't have been. One was meant to get stronger, to learn from every crisis, to build an ever thicker shell. That was indeed how the first half of her life had felt: an accretion of layers, a stoicism, a set of tricks for dealing with stage-door Johnnies and everyday boors, another set of tricks for holding off the competition and demanding one's right to remain in the limelight. But since . . . when? . . . perhaps early in her forties, something had changed. Frank would always blame the train crash. It was an easy event to point to. Everyone could see the pain caused by broken ribs, a twisted back. No one could doubt the physical toll.

But Annie knew it was an entire series of blows, none of which could be entirely separated: first, the accident and the tricks it had played on her mind; next and unrelated, but equally injurious, the malicious headlines; and finally, the trials themselves. Each by itself might have been mere nuisance, a bee sting. The sum total was something else: a swarming attack. This was what it meant not only to age, but to fall from grace. To have your face pushed down in the mud, or worse.

At her very first trial, in Scranton, the defense lawyer had taunted her. "You're the woman who used to shoot out here and run along and turn head over heels, allowing your skirts to fall."

"I beg your pardon," Annie replied without emotion. "I didn't allow my skirts to fall."

At that moment, she'd allowed herself to look out at the jury, expecting sympathy, moderation and intelligence. But the first among them who caught her eye had none of those traits. He was a pale, narrow-faced man with poorly cut hair, a slack jaw and black eyes, staring right at her. He seemed to be looking for signs that she was part of the underworld, a drug fiend, a performer in a "leg show" or something equally ridiculous. Annie stared back at the man as long as she dared, expecting him to blink and look away. But he wouldn't. Instead, he noticed her looking and leered—a fleshy-lipped halfway smile. She leaned back in her chair, heart pounding. He looked familiar, but so many of them did. Maybe it was the mouth. Maybe the beady gleam of his eyes.

She could imagine his hands on her wrists. She could imagine— *remember*—his smell. The man she'd never forget. The man who wasn't a man at all, but an animal.

The defense lawyer asked her again, "Didn't you turn handsprings?"

"I am the lady who shot, but I didn't turn handsprings."

Later, her lawyer would say that she looked unflappable. But she hadn't felt it. She'd barely managed to find the words. Her heart had trilled so fast, it felt as if she'd had a pigeon caged inside her ribs.

The first trial had been in November. Now it was April. But even after those months, as she found her way to the farthest edge of the dark train platform, that juror's face remained with her. Thirty-three years had gone by since the chapter of her childhood about which she seldom spoke. The juror shouldn't matter, but he did. There were dozens more trials still to come. People whispering. Men staring, assuming.

She tilted her hat low over her eyes in the hopes that no one would recognize her as she waited for the train doors to open. She had an all-day trip home to New Jersey ahead. But she didn't want to go home, even with Frank waiting there for her, already knowing the first argument they'd have. She had an idea that would upset him: Europe, a quick trip to get away from it all. The trials were unevenly spaced—sometimes only weeks apart, more often months. The steamer would take a week or longer, she might spend ten days in England or the continent, and finally another week back. With Frank if he truly understood. Alone if he didn't.

Perhaps she would find a spa, some place with hot springs and minerals that would leach away whatever was ailing her. Perhaps she'd find a doctor. In America, she didn't dare buy cough syrup or a tin of herbal tea, lest the reporters would twist it into more evidence that she was a drug addict. In Europe, she could see someone confidentially. But would that help?

She checked the train station clock. *Why must everything run late?* But it wasn't yet. She was simply getting anxious.

She pulled up the edges of her collar and tugged the lapels of her heavy wool coat, trying to create a barrier against the cold that no one else on the platform seemed to feel. They were all dressed for spring. She was shivering, but perhaps that was because of the meals she kept skipping. On many of these trial days, she fasted, too upset to eat.

A European doctor. Perhaps he could give her something for her ailments.

She had occasional headaches. But that wasn't enough reason to consult a medical expert. Really, what bothered her most were the images that flashed through her mind. They'd started three years ago at the time of the train crash, the full terror and strangeness of which she'd confided to no one. But after several months of unhealthy rumination, she'd gotten control of them. Her life seemed to be on track. She'd appeared as herself in an East Coast stage drama that, while hackneyed in terms of plot, was successful enough to run for several months. At one performance, she'd fallen from her horse. The press enjoyed that—any chance to see her fail. She'd avoided injury, but she had to admit that her mind had been wandering. She'd been thinking about the crash, or more specifically, the minutes after. And with even more intensity, the minutes before, working her way backward through increasingly vivid reencounters with every sensation before the collision, looking for the limit to her strange immersions in those prolonged and exceedingly lifelike moments—a limit she hadn't yet found.

And then came the ridiculous Hearst lies, completely unrelated to anything that had happened before. Just another bit of extremely bad luck. The recovery she'd made over three years was now without purpose, for this had stalled her career yet again. She had gone forward a step and back two—more than two, because sources of unresolved bitterness had been dredged back up, a black scum painting the lining of her defective soul. The images began to return, fed by anger, frustration, the parallels between the worst moments in her life and this one: having no control over a man who would ruin her. She felt pursued by inappropriate thoughts, a muddled temptation to indulge the memories, to deepen the pain, as if pressing on a bruise or reopening a barely healed cut.

On the train platform bench closest to her, someone had left a folded newspaper. *The Saint Louis Chronicle*. She didn't want to read the paper. Hearst owned most of them—*Washington Evening Star, Detroit Tribune, Baltimore Sun, Chicago Examiner, New York Daily News*. They'd all printed filthy stories about her. Career-destroying lies, and that was no exaggeration. Annie never wanted to read a newspaper again.

A man approached, studied her from head to foot, gestured toward the bench and accepted her tight head-shake. She would not sit. When he did finally lower himself with a grunt onto the bench, she became aware that he was in an even better position to ogle her from behind.

The train doors weren't opening. She needed to be away from the foul-breathing man. She didn't want to be here. But she didn't want to be in New Jersey, either. She didn't want to be anywhere, except perhaps in a city where no one would recognize her, in a city where someone might be able to help her deal with her nerves—and her rage.

She could hear the man behind her, rustling the paper and then merely breathing, too heavily. She would not turn around. She would not move away. She was waiting to get on the train, that was all. She had managed to perform on stages and under bright lights and in open fields and in the center of enormous race tracks for audiences of thousands without feeling vulnerable, but now every set of eyes burned into her.

She had to be stronger, but how could she be? First the train crash, then Hearst, and now this: daily humiliations on top of pain, both physical and mental.

The predator can spot weakness.

The world was full of wolves.

THREE WEEKS LATER, SHE WAS standing at the rail of the steamship, still more than twelve hours from Liverpool. Ridiculous to look this early for signs of land this far out. But it had been a long crossing, especially because Frank had not accompanied her. Equally distressing had been Annie's need to keep her identity hidden in order to avoid any attention from the American press. Whenever presented to anyone aboard the ship, she referred to herself as Mrs. Butler. *Phoebe*—her birthname—*Butler*. None of it a lie. She didn't like telling lies.

And yet today at breakfast, her identity almost had been revealed. The captain, speaking to their entire table, had asked if she might demonstrate her shooting skills, from the deck.

"I brought no arms," she said without smiling.

"I'm sure we can find something. We have a number of sport shooters aboard . . ."

She leveled her gaze at him. "It's Sunday."

"Well, that's the best day for leisure."

She shot him a dark look.

"Pardon me," he said, and changed the subject. Well, at least he got the hint, and yes, they could believe she was pious if that meant they left her alone.

As she stood to leave, he apologized and mentioned that there would be a small church service to attend after breakfast, if that appealed. It didn't. She begged off, claiming a headache, and went first to her cabin for a warmer coat and then to the deck.

She avoided a cluster of lounge chairs where a trio of women were gathered and chatting, and instead picked the last seat in the row, one chair down from a woman who was peering through binoculars in the direction of distant seabirds.

"I see you've decided against the captain's offer as well," the woman said when she lowered her field glasses. Now Annie recognized her. She'd been at breakfast and had some sort of European accent, maybe German. She was in her twenties and rather somber: black coat, black hat, voluminous checked scarf that hid the bottom half of her small pretty face.

"I prefer to be alone," Annie said. Not meaning to be sour, she added, "I don't mean without the company of another woman, like yourself. I just . . ."

"It's all right. I understand."

"And you? No interest in the prayer service today?"

"I'm not Christian."

"Oh. I see."

"You?"

"I was raised Quaker," Annie said. "Mother taught us we didn't need a church building or any particular set of prayers to feel the presence of God."

"Then we have a different heritage but are of a like mind," the woman said. "I'll leave you to your own peaceful thoughts." She picked up a thick book with a blue cover, the title too small to make out. Annie didn't read much herself, and never without effort. A lifelong failing.

Noticing Annie staring, the woman said, "It's about trafficking."

"I'm sorry. I didn't mean to intrude. And I don't know what that means, actually."

"Of humans."

"White slavery, then."

"That's another term for it."

"I hope it's on the decline?"

"Not with the increasing flow of people into cities and from one country to another. I'd say it's only bound to get worse." The woman smiled and reached across the empty chair between them to shake hands. "My name's Giselle."

"Phoebe. Phoebe *Ann.*" This was ridiculous. She was no good at false identities—even partially false ones. "It doesn't sound like light reading."

"It isn't. I'm preparing for a conference."

"In Liverpool?"

"Berlin. After that, I'll return home to Hamburg. Last month I was in Delaware. Do you know they lowered the age of consent in Delaware from ten to seven? How could a seven-year-old girl provide consent for anything of an intimate nature?"

Annie was speechless.

Giselle said, "I'm a social worker, but I have the good fortune to travel for these sorts of women's events." She leaned forward in her deck chair. "Should I know who you are?"

Annie thought, *When Thomas Edison made a film of me shooting, you were probably no more than five years old.* "I'd rather you didn't, to tell you the truth."

"It's just . . . the captain seemed to imply you're famous. Are you sure you haven't done something exceptional?"

Annie didn't like people who overvalued themselves or wore their achievements on their sleeves. For professional photographs, she had to gussy up, but how many medals did anyone need? She'd recently had a trunk of them melted down, the proceeds sent to charities.

Taking the question seriously, Annie said, "I've earned an honest living since I was a child. I've always put food on the table. I don't think that's exceptional. But it's always mattered to me."

"I take it you're not married."

"I *am* married, actually. But that's never changed my desire to be independent, financially or otherwise."

Giselle sat back, satisfied. "Well that's refreshing. He must be an unusual man, your husband."

"He is," Annie said, feeling an unexpected lump in her throat.

That should have been enough of their mutual prying, but Annie didn't have any of the props that Giselle had—binoculars, a book—behind which she might look occupied. All week, she'd stayed in her cabin whenever possible, passing the time by embroidering two new skirts. She didn't mind embroidery, but enough was enough. She needed to ride a horse, walk with a dog into the woods, or even this: simply converse with a person, but only the kind of person who wouldn't talk about trivial things.

Annie asked, "So you work with people who are . . . or were . . . ?"

"Rescued. I work with young girls, mostly."

"How do they do, later in life?"

"Some do very well. And some don't."

"Why the difference?"

"I wish I knew. People can have the same set of experiences, and some sail onward while others sink. But what I see most often is girls who seem perfectly well, who appear productive and even gay. You find out later they're not the same people underneath." Giselle must have caught the shift in Annie's expression, because she added, "It isn't all so discouraging, I promise you! It's one reason I travel to meet other women—to be instructed and encouraged. Have you heard of Bertha Pappenheim?"

"Sorry."

"She's unified most of the Jewish women's organizations in Germany. It's even more impressive if you know her personal history. Before she discovered activism, she was a very sick young woman. Paralysis, loss of speech, not to mention the nightmares and hallucinations she suffered!"

Giselle turned back to the topic of Pappenheim's published writings and organizing triumphs. Annie knew she was supposed to be interested in that part—women's rights, labor issues, various kinds of reform. But she couldn't resist asking, "The hallucinations, what were they caused by?"

"Hysteria, supposedly." Giselle wrinkled her nose apologetically. "It's a ridiculous, overly generic diagnosis—a way of ignoring women's real complaints, most of the time."

"Did they perform surgery on her?" Annie had heard of that, as well as strange manipulations involving a woman's intimate regions.

"Nothing so drastic. She was treated by a Viennese doctor. But here's the curious thing, which I find hopeful in my line of work. He gave her no medicines. He didn't bathe her in ice water or confine her with straps or do anything to her physical person."

"Then how was she cured?"

"They talked."

"About?"

"Whatever emotional upset was producing her symptoms, which made them vanish entirely."

"They only talked?"

"That's all."

4

RUTH

When Ruth stepped into the house, a 1970s relic with a moss-covered roof, surrounded by black spruce and balsam fir trees, her landline was ringing. She got to the phone on the fourth ring. It was Jane Holloway, calling to apologize for the security hassle.

Ruth reached for her purse. "I can be back in fifteen minutes." There would be time for a few slides at least, and then she'd leave Holloway with the handouts she'd prepared. Better than nothing.

"Let's reschedule instead. How's next Thursday?"

"Let me see." As if she had some packed agenda to check.

"And as long as we're starting over, I have a second class I'd like you to speak to, the same day. They're younger, not as familiar with the time period, but now I'll have time to get them ready."

It was gracious of the teacher to pretend this redo was an enhancement, allowing Ruth to maintain her dignity.

After another round of apologies, Ruth microwaved a cup of tea, grabbed an ice pack and went outside, lowering herself into an Adirondack chair on the porch. Once she started reading the journal, she would ignore everything else. If she didn't ice, she wouldn't sleep well tonight, and here, on the porch, there was sun, at least, one of autumn's final gentle days in advance of a long northern winter.

The cold had just worked its way through her pants and into the muscles around her leg when a car pulled into her driveway and the boy stepped out. He called to her, "I told you it was only three minutes by car."

She looked at her watch. "School can't possibly be over yet."

"Soon enough. Holloway let us go to the library. I told her I was helping you with your laptop, so she said I could take off a few minutes early, plus give you this."

He held up her thumb drive like a winning ticket—but for what? She couldn't imagine why anyone, never mind a teenager, would be so interested in paying her a call.

"You want to work on the laptop now?"

"Nothing better to do."

He was still carrying his jacket. He'd taken off his flannel and tied it around his waist; underneath was a close-fitting, bright purple T-shirt that said ROCKETS. She noticed that he was thin, but not scrawny, as she'd thought. And he didn't slouch. He had the confident, conscientious, shoulders-back posture of someone who performed. Thespian crowd, maybe.

"You don't have homework?" she said.

"Only the most boring stuff."

Boredom she could understand well. Ruth had been in the hospital for several weeks, then home with a cast and in too much pain to do anything for months. With a broken body and a brain clouded by meds, she had found little to do but doze with television on in the background: *The Crown* at first, then sitcoms and finally cooking shows—the only two possible outcomes being whether the dishes were delicious or inedible.

Scott had recommended Reece. Holloway likewise knew he was heading over to help her and evidently thought that was normal and positive. Ruth didn't feel uneasy in Reece's presence, she just felt . . . a surprising familiarity.

"We haven't even talked about how much you charge," she said as he stepped up to the porch.

"Fifty dollars. My standard fee for a tune-up."

"That's not much."

"It's easier money than making espresso, which I also do."

"So you've worked on laptops before."

"If I hadn't, would you want to hire me?"

When she hesitated, he smiled. "It's really easy, actually. You could do it yourself. Start with a utility to remove unwanted files and extensions—"

"Okay. I'll stop you right there. Fifty dollars is fine."

She removed the ice pack, started to stand up slowly, and sat back down again, surprised by the pain. She knew how she looked: eighty years old instead of thirty-two. This was ridiculous. But that was always her thought, and it never helped. She took a sip of her tea and prepared, pushed herself up to a standing position again, then went inside the house, gesturing for him to follow.

A HALF HOUR LATER, REECE was running the defrag from the kitchen table she'd half-cleared for his work while she did the dishes, trying to look busy until the chore was done and she could see him out. The journal was where she'd left it, on the coffee table in front of the couch.

He stood up and wandered toward the nearest bookshelves, which lined the kitchen as they lined every other room: presidential biographies, American Indian wars, Victoriana. She waited to see if he'd pull out a book, but he didn't. She remembered the feeling from when she was younger, trying to find the right corner of history to step into. There was just so much, most of it unapproachable and seemingly irrelevant. Then you found one person or event, tugged that single thread and waited to see if something tugged back.

She asked, "How much longer will this take?"

"Hard to say. Could be thirty minutes."

He started to pull something out of his pocket—his phone, she assumed. He would lose himself in YouTube, Facebook or Instagram, probably. Instead, he pulled out a Sharpie marker and started rubbing his thumb against the cap. A nervous tic.

"I think we're wasting time," he said.

Why had he just said that?

"I think so, too."

Why had *she* said that? The words were out before she could think, but now she found herself frowning, embarrassed, as if an enormous burp had just slipped out.

Ruth wanted to add, *If we're going to work together, you need to think historically, whether it's the distant or recent past: technological changes, social context. And you have to stop smoking. Your body is a temple.*

She heard her inner monologue and thought, *Work together?* She didn't even know this kid.

And, *Your body is a temple?* That wasn't even a phrase she used. It was bad enough to have a senseless thought. Worse to have one in a voice that didn't seem like your own.

She pointed at his shirt. "Rockets—is that a band?"

"Cheerleading, although the other guys call it 'tumbling' to save their reputations. It's a gymnastics alternative that some of us started because we refuse to run around to really bad music with smiles on our faces. The senior who founded it graduated, so I took over this year. It's a stupid name, but we're not bad."

"You're a cheerleader?"

"Cheerleaders were all men once."

True. She knew that. "But Rockets isn't your passion?"

"It's not high art. But it's something to do for an hour. Which still leaves the rest of every day to be bored."

"Is there anything that *does* interest you?"

"Used to be dance," he said. "Ballet, modern."

"Used to be?"

"Also computers. But that's like saying you like some type of car when what you mean is you want to go somewhere. What I mean is, I don't actually care about the car. I don't want to code or work for Google or Microsoft, which is what teachers assume, just because I can optimize a laptop and I like to look things up. Sometimes I think I hate the Internet, actually, but I can't stay off it, because I'm just looking."

"That's normal."

"No, it's not." He squinted. "I'll have my fingers on my phone like I'm supposed to be searching for something, but I don't know the right terms to type in. You know? There's this feeling, like I was just about to do something. Just about to find something out. But I've already lost it."

"Have you ever described that feeling to anyone? Maybe a school counselor?"

"At school they'd just say I have ADD, like I'm not paying attention, or OCD, because I can't stop wanting to search."

"And your parents? What do they say?"

He rolled his eyes. "My mom likes me to take zinc."

"Does that help?"

Ruth detected a hint of a smile. No words were needed.

One of Ruth's arguments about not being ready for kids any-time soon had been that she didn't know how to talk to children. Teens were even harder. To which Scott had replied, *You don't have to talk most of the time. You just have to listen.*

"I like to solve problems," Reece said. "But I don't have any good ones at the moment. I mean, obviously, I don't know what I don't know."

"Okay," she said, sympathizing. And deciding.

"Okay what?"

"I've got a problem, or maybe a puzzle, which could be a hoax. But I'm really hoping not." She took a deep breath. "You might learn something interesting."

RUTH PULLED THE BUBBLE-WRAPPED PACKAGE from the box, shaking her head. The journal should have been wrapped in glassine or tissue paper, then further supported by firm boards and cushioned so it wouldn't slide in the box, to start.

"Reece?"

They'd relocated to the couch in the living room. Now he looked over her shoulder, studying the plastic-wrapped book in her hands.

"Yes."

"If you ever send a very old, rare journal to someone, don't wrap it in non-breathable plastic. With big temperature changes, you're asking for condensation."

"I will absolutely remember that. What are we waiting for now?"

"We're reminding ourselves that research takes time, no matter what nervous collectors or greedy dealers might want to think."

"Right."

Reece had taken the Sharpie out of his back pocket and was holding it between two fingers, restlessly tapping his knee. *Ticka-ticka.*

"Just a second," she said.

Ticka-ticka.

"Shhhh."

Ticka-ticka-ticka-ticka.

Ruth placed a hand over Reece's in order to stop the sound. He tensed in response.

Maybe he didn't like being touched. Or maybe he was just a

weird kid. In a swift, martial arts-like motion, he flipped her hand over—not roughly, but with firm intent—and held her wrist—still gently—and tugged her arm to his knee. He pulled off the Sharpie lid with his teeth. He set the tip of the black marker on the soft underside of her forearm.

When she didn't yank her arm back, he started drawing. In less time than it took to breathe, she had an infinity loop matching his own.

When he'd lifted the pen, she withdrew her arm and rubbed her wrist.

"Why did you do that?"

"I don't know." He looked as surprised as she did. "Because you told me to."

"Just now?"

"No, before. Or . . . later?"

"What do you mean, 'later'?"

"I'm not sure."

She tried to summon indignation—it wasn't right for a guy to reach out and grab a girl or woman. But this had felt more like another tic than a real attempt to subdue her, and besides, his own alarm had preempted hers. He was rattled, and whether or not it made any sense, she wasn't. Almost as if she'd expected it.

She pulled her arm into her sleeve. "Okay."

"Sorry."

"Let's forget about it."

"Yeah."

She really wasn't the teen-mentoring type.

"Just don't do that again."

RUTH OPENED THE JOURNAL GENTLY, her fingers barely touching the edges.

The first page was written in German: heavily slanted cursive; ink faded to a light brownish-purple.

"What is it?" Reece asked.

Her reading of German, a grad school requirement, was serviceable but rusty. The first words that jumped out at her referred to ears and eyes, myopia and mild deafness, and beyond that, problems breathing. She'd have to use a dictionary to confirm, but not until she'd had a chance to skim further. The writing was hard to read, penned in a consistent hand, but dense and embellished, with long tails on the letters.

She skimmed five or six pages, turned another page, and sat up straight.

Two capital letters were written at the top of the first page: "ZN," followed by compact paragraphs of handwriting—in English this time.

With effort, Ruth started to read aloud.

The mind . . . has an uncanny way . . . of saving us from unendurable pain.

Sometime after three in the morning, there is a sound of screaming brakes, and then the two locomotives collide, sending her flying across the narrow train compartment.

Ruth could picture: North Carolina. And the time: 3:20 A.M.

Nightclothes billowing, she seems to float: the pink- and gold-striped wallpaper gleaming behind her, her gown and the wallpaper and the entire railcar glowing as the train topples.

Reece's breath was loud in Ruth's ear. "You can't go any faster?"

"No." She returned to the script.

One car topples off the tracks, dragging the next in apparent slow motion, resisting gravity, like feathers drifting, falling slowly, light shining between each perfect white barb.

There. Hovering. Luminous. There.

She is lost for a moment in the memory . . .

"What is it?" Reece asked.

"It looks like an account of the train crash, 1901."

"Annie Oakley's train crash?"

Ruth hadn't explained anything to him prior to opening the journal. "How'd you figure that out?"

"Holloway told us you were going to be talking to our class about Annie Oakley. We had to read her Wikipedia page."

Ruth continued studying the slanted letters, which closely adhered to the ruled lines, also handwritten: a ledger that could have started out bound or as loose sheets, bound later.

She didn't need to grab her phone or a file or a book off the shelf to make the comparison. She was already sure, because she had seen Annie Oakley's rounded, inelegant scrawl enough times. The sharpshooter was deprived of an education in her early years, a fact that shamed her. Ruth knew that this dense and formal cursive wasn't Annie's.

That was a problem. But only the first.

Ruth looked at the handwriting again: in places it looked more like hand-penned classical music than like handwritten prose. The little a's and e's and o's were so small and tight that they were completely filled in with ink. The d's looked like quarter notes. No one wrote like that anymore. To Ruth, it seemed elegantly European.

"It looks old," Reece said.

"Possibly."

"How would you know for sure? Test the paper? The ink?"

"Both. And you can also study the text itself, looking for individual words or phrasings that give hints about culture and time period. If you have an author in mind, someone who has left behind other indisputable works—"

"You can analyze the handwriting," he interrupted, excited.

"—but it's easier than ever to fake handwriting digitally, so you shouldn't rely on that. And you can use stylometric analysis to search for patterns in punctuation or a preference for particular words, but only if you have a known sample for comparison."

He started to drum his fingers on his thighs, restlessly awaiting more information. "I don't really get that word: *uncanny.*"

"It means strange."

"Sure it does. Uncanny valley. That's a term used in robotics. But who says that? *Uncanny?* Did anyone say that back in Annie Oakley's time?"

Reece's phone sat on his thigh, the screen darkened, but she could feel his fingers wanting to go to it again, not used to delaying gratification or tolerating uncertainty. Ruth had stopped reading.

"Head-on train collision. Ouch," Reece said. "Did she die?"

"I thought you read her Wikipedia entry."

"Skimmed. Maybe not to the end."

Ruth fought the urge to scoff. "No, she didn't die. She lived twenty-five more years. But it was a devastating accident. It led to the Wild West show's eventual downfall. A hundred and ten horses killed. Injuries to performers. Huge financial loss." Silently, Ruth reread the page from the top. "Fuck."

Reece was smiling, amused by her profanity. There was nothing to smile about.

"*She,*" Ruth said.

"Yes?"

Ruth closed the book, fingering the velvety cover. "It's not a journal."

"What do you mean it's not a journal? It's old. It's handwritten. With ink."

"It's not *her journal.* It's written in the third person. *She.*"

"Yeah, I know what third person means. But that doesn't mean it's not a journal. It could be *someone's* journal."

"But not hers. Annie Oakley didn't write many letters. She authored only one unfinished autobiography. A more candid, first-person journal would have been a significant find."

"And this isn't significant, why?"

"Because," Ruth said, "it could be someone's ridiculous novel, handwritten and sandwiched between notes that have no relevance. It could be anything. The sender's email was antfarm@aol.com."

"Ant farm? Kinda weird."

"The AOL part is weirder. Who on earth still has an AOL address?"

"That's an excellent question." Reece's fingers crawled toward his phone. "First, tell me: What's AOL?"

Ruth shook her head. Not now.

"Annie's own words," Ruth muttered under her breath. These weren't Annie's own words. Nieman—if that was even his name—had deceived her.

In graduate school, where digital sleuthing had become all the rage, Ruth had learned about the recent discovery of a lost diary of David Livingstone, the explorer in Africa. Written with berry ink that had faded to illegibility, the old pages were stored away, practically forgotten. Then a scholar from the University of Nebraska—*Nebraska!*—realized he could use high-tech spectral scanning to render the faded ink visible, revealing a completely unknown side of the explorer.

"People aren't honest when they're speaking or writing to others, only when they're writing for themselves," Ruth said. "Finding or decoding an authentic diary—something the public was never meant to see—is what a historian dreams about. This isn't that."

"It could still be something interesting," Reece said. "It could be an account—an *honest* third-person account that Annie Oakley gave to someone, like a reputable newspaper reporter."

"And that would be less valuable, but still neat."

"Just 'neat'?"

"Unfortunately, I don't think that's what this is."

"That's just your hunch."

"Yes. But it's a highly informed hunch."

"So you're not going to read the rest?"

"Of course I will. Even as a complete hoax, it might hold some interest. At the very least, I want to know why this guy Nieman sent it to *me*."

"Did he ask for anything in return?"

"Only my time—and not much of it. He's on some sort of deadline."

"Hmmm."

Reece's phone squawked.

"That would be my dad."

"He must be expecting you home."

"No, it's all right." He looked down at his phone. "A friend stopped by the house. Well, not a friend, really. This guy, a new Rockets member. Hopefully not coming by to quit." Reece looked up. "Can I use your bathroom? The laptop should be ready to restart soon."

"Sounds good. Down the hallway on the left."

In the kitchen ten minutes later, Ruth wrote out a check as Reece closed the laptop lid.

"If it ever takes more than ninety seconds to boot up, just give me a call." He nodded toward her phone and read his number aloud, watching as she punched in the numbers. "Aren't you going to give me yours?"

Ruth hesitated. "That isn't weird?"

"No. How else am I supposed to find out any news you have on the journal?"

"There may never be news."

"Come on, you promised I'd learn something interesting. Are you a historian or a member of the overprotective parents' committee?" Reece reached into his jacket pocket for something—oh yes, that nasty cigarette habit. But he didn't light up yet. "Hey, why did you lie about Mr. Webb?"

"Lie?"

"You told the guard he was your fiancé. But everybody knows

Mr. Webb is single. Last year, he joked about not having a date for the prom."

"I misspoke. We were engaged a long time ago. Anyway, Reece, please don't mention that or the journal to anyone."

"I won't," he said, holding out his phone to her. It was a deal, evidently. She entered her details and pressed "save."

5

REECE

The sophomore they'd been calling Kale, like the vegetable, was on the porch and just about to leave when Reece got home. Another few minutes and they would have missed each other completely.

"How's it going, Kale?"

"Caleb."

"Sorry," Reece said. "I didn't know the nickname bothered you."

"It was a freshman thing."

Reece held the door open, but Caleb refused to enter first, following only after Reece passed him into the house and down the hall toward his bedroom. For his part, Reece was still distracted, mulling over his discussion with Ruth. He hadn't told her everything. He'd tried to muster the nerve, right at the end, but faltered and failed to tell her he recognized her, and not because they'd ever met.

He'd also given her that line about zinc, and she'd bought it. Just from the look of her house with its untended yard and all those boxes inside, along with the dust and the gloom, he could tell Ruth was a fellow depressive.

In the bathroom—first stop for any snoop—he'd opened her dark-wood, apothecary-style cabinet with its twenty or so tiny drawers. He'd found some interesting items, not only single keys and fortune cookie slips, but prescriptions filled and not taken. (Fill date from over a year ago, expiration date passed, and yet the bottle of lemon-yellow pills was three-quarters full. Bad patient.) *Reminder to self,* Reece thought. *If you ever stop taking your meds, don't be so obvious about it.*

He'd also found three white bar-shaped pills—Xanax—in a separate drawer. They were nestled against the dark, sweet-smelling wood like eggs in a nest. The lemon-yellow pills hadn't called to him, but these did. The only other thing he'd ever stolen was eyeliner in fifth grade, because he'd wanted to try it out but was too embarrassed to pay the cashier. *Just one. Or two.* But leaving a lone pill would only call attention to its missing partners. Reece pocketed all three.

It wasn't like him to have done that. He wasn't into tranquilizers or antidepressants—not even the ones personally prescribed for him. It bothered Reece even now, fingering the pills in his pocket as he passed his own bathroom on the way to his bedroom at the end of the hall with silent, morose Caleb still walking behind him.

"Actually, I gotta use your bathroom," Caleb said.

"Make yourself at home. I'll wait for you in here."

In his bedroom, Reece stood by the window, checking his phone. For what? That was the perennial question. He hadn't gone out with anyone for over six months, which eliminated one entire category of possibility and distraction. Aside from a new exchange student who'd shown zero interest, the pickings at Horizon High were slim. Nothing to be done about it.

Reduced libido was one of the side effects of the prescription Reece was taking—though, of course, depression itself wasn't great for sex drive. His parents certainly believed in medication, and he didn't want to burst their bubble, which had been stabbed mercilessly already. Summer had been shitty for everyone.

By September things had started feeling better. Classes starting, everyone busier, and at least a few dinners when Reece's father forgot to stare meaningfully into his eyes and ask, "And how are you feeling *today*?"

In truth, he felt good, but also on edge, keyed up. Two or three days ago, Reece had started sensing it: something was coming, forcing him to be on high alert. He'd had trouble sleeping. His scalp tingled; when his mother noticing him scratching, she asked if he needed dandruff shampoo. He kept thinking he had to pee, but then he'd try and nothing would come out. If he told anyone, they'd think he had some kind of venereal infection. For obvious reasons, he knew that wasn't the case.

Reece found himself reading headlines with greater interest. North Korea ready for a nuclear attack? Zombies spotted somewhere? Not according to the *Minneapolis Star-Tribune*.

He kept studying faces and expressions, wondering if anyone else noticed anything unusual. Finally, this morning at school, he saw a woman with a limp and blue cowboy boots out of the corner of his eye. Then he got a closer look at her face. And he knew. Forget history class. He'd stepped back and stared. It *was* her.

Reece knew her name without asking. *Ruth*. He thought he needed a clever plan, but it all fell into place: her forgotten ID, her shitty—sorry, poorly maintained—laptop, and as always, the helpful interference of his math teacher, who never failed to involve himself in things that weren't his problem. No complicated stalking necessary.

Reece remembered her from the dream, looking at him—from above, to be specific—worried, giving him instructions. What else? He needed to calm down and make himself remember—*let* himself remember—as much as he wanted to forget.

Some parts of the dream were pleasant, even blissful. Others, not at all.

The setting—Griffin Memorial Hospital—was likewise not so congenial. Worst of all was the face of his mother crying when he emerged from sleep, groggy and half-drugged, barely able to focus on her anguished lament while he tried to hang on to that confusing dream, which had seemed of utmost importance, even then.

Reece tried not to think about the day of his hospitalization or the embarrassing family fallout, only about Ruth's spoken message in the dream: *It didn't work. Draw the symbol. Don't give up. Be firm. And just—be honest, Reece. I'll believe you.*

But that was dream Ruth.

Real Ruth had been another story: indecisive, suspicious, the very last person to trust Reece. Then again, she didn't seem to have the information dream Ruth had. Which was, at least partially, his fault. He had to get a handle on his own dream and tell her everything he knew, even if it was confusing. He wasn't like Caleb, a timid rabbit who thought you could hide behind a bush and be safe.

"Hey," said Caleb, pushing the bedroom door open.

"You can sit down if you want," Reece said, pointing at his made bed.

"That's all right."

Reece waited for Cal to explain himself. If he was coming by to quit the Rockets, it would sabotage their routine.

"So," Reece said, beginning to lose patience.

"Is that a poster of a male model hanging over your bed?"

"Dumb shit, that's not a male model. It's Sergei Polunin. I thought you knew something about dance."

No reply.

"Unreasonably gorgeous," Reece said, "but he's an athlete. The Royal Ballet's youngest dancer, but he crashed and burned a couple years later. Supposedly he's more stable now." In response to Caleb's frozen expression, Reece softened his tone. "I can text you the link to a great documentary about him."

"Not my thing."

Reece really wasn't in the mood. "Polunin's girlfriend is a beautiful ballerina, if that helps."

He didn't know if Caleb was trying to get across annoying homophobia or fake bravado. All of it seemed like a cover for something else. He'd heard how much Cal/Kale/Tool/Caleb had been harassed at school. It had started freshman year, and it probably wasn't Caleb's fault. He seemed confused. Like an easy mark. And he still hadn't explained why he was here.

"Look, is somebody bothering you at school?"

Caleb coughed into his hand, sat down on the edge of the bed, then thought better of it, standing up with his hands crossed over his crotch. Absurd.

"Then what?"

Caleb pulled his phone out of his pocket and barely looked at it.

"Look," Reece said. "We need you in the Rockets. You're good. And more important—sorry—but you're short and light." And graceful, which Caleb probably didn't want to hear. Most guys couldn't tell where their arms and legs were, flying through space. They bumped into other people just walking down the hallway. "The show's coming up soon. We're counting on you."

It was going to be a halftime spectacle for the last football game of the season. After that, they'd do an end-of-semester holiday thing and then gear up for talent show in the spring. But this was the important one with the big crowd: jocks, parents, alumni, people from town. It would be held outside on the football field. A welcome change from the stale auditorium.

"Besides," Reece said, trying another strategy, "it's a fun group. Mikayla is going to start training with us. Didn't you go out with her last year?"

Caleb tucked his chin into his chest. "Not really. One school dance."

Mikayla was meek, but also tiny: definite potential to replace Caleb as a flyer. Reece had to keep his options open, but he wasn't going to make it that easy for a member of the team to quit. And maybe Caleb was here for something else. Sometimes they asked questions about math, which Reece was good at. Other times it was about Reece's suicide attempt, especially if they were thinking about their own early-exit plans.

Reece thought about the red marks he'd seen on Caleb's neck last year. Caleb claimed they were hickeys. If so, that was one wild weekend. To Reece, they'd looked more like rope burns. But maybe that was only his own morbid imagination.

"You played soccer last year, right?" Reece asked. "Why'd you stop?"

"Injury, at first. It healed, but my parents still said I couldn't do after-school activities until I got my grades up."

"But zero hour's okay?"

Caleb laughed for the first time. "They're fucking amazed I get out of bed at all."

"But you know that next week we have afternoon practice, too? It's only a week, though. Just for the show. But you gotta be there, or our choreography will fall apart. If you *do* have to stop coming, for any reason, tell me ahead of time. All right?"

"Why do you care so much about this show, anyway?"

"Because I do."

Caleb squinted over Reece's shoulder. "I gotta run. You got a cigarette?"

Reece walked toward the bedpost where he'd slung his jacket and dug around slowly in the pocket, thinking maybe Caleb was just trying to get up the nerve to say more. As he pushed his fingers around the lining, he stared up at the Polunin poster and thought about school—not the time-wasting, low-bar school he attended, but the early college private school with the national-caliber dance program that he hadn't gotten into. He'd been crushed.

Luckily, he hadn't googled how to slash your wrists properly. He'd ended up with only three faint scars, bare white threads against the pale skin of his wrist, which he now kept hidden under a wide leather band with metal snaps and faux Navajo styling.

They say you can't erase the past. But you can accessorize it.

Returning to school in September after that act of despair, he knew he faced a choice: give up on dance or find a way back in. Taking over leadership of the Rockets had been the right move. Coaching others had given Reece a way to stop thinking about himself and to be reminded, watching novices, that repeated failure was necessary in life. *Get over it.*

That was why this show mattered, even if Reece wasn't going to spell it out to a guy like Caleb. Because you had to start somewhere.

Reece withdrew the crumpled pack and handed it over. Five cigarettes.

"Keep it. I'm trying to quit. You need a ride home?"

"No, I want to walk."

"All right. Offsets the unhealthiness of the smokes." Not really, but whatever.

Reece didn't feel guilty adding to Caleb's smoking habit. It was the least of the guy's problems. Underclassman, small for his age, pretty face, bad grades, former jock desperate enough to try tumbling, butt of the other jocks' jokes, not enough attention from his parents, too much attention from creeps.

Reece asked, "Didn't I see you get a ride from Vorst the other day?"

"That asshole? Are you kidding me?"

Vorst was the volunteer coach who hung around the Rockets' practices. They weren't allowed to use the gym equipment at all without him, but he didn't know a thing about their act. Most of the tumblers just learned to tolerate him without engaging.

"So why did I see you near his car?"

"You saw me *keying* his car."

"Wait, really?" Reece laughed. "You messed up his car?"

That made Caleb half-laugh.

"My mistake," Reece said. "Anyway, the offer's still good. I could give you rides home from afternoon practice, if that helps."

"Maybe," Caleb said, serious again, all the light gone out of his face. "But I like to walk."

Out on the front porch, where they said their goodbyes, Caleb lit up a cigarette, blew out a stream of smoke and with it, a mumbled confession. "I might not be at school some days coming up."

Reece shook his head. "Staying home isn't the answer. Whatever's going on, my advice, and I mean this, is to show up. Just come to school and lay low. I promise you, if you're gone, people will talk about you more . . ."

"I don't care if they talk."

Of course he did. Everyone did. "Then *what*?"

"Then nothing."

Reece sighed. "Then I'll see you at practice tomorrow. And Caleb, if you're getting hassled by anyone I know, especially if it's someone in the Rockets, like Gerald and his friends . . ."

"I know it's no big deal. They're just joking."

"No. If you're feeling hassled, then they're being dicks, and I want you to tell me."

Caleb didn't answer, but Reece had to assume that was it. Sometimes you just had to ride out a reputation or grow beyond people's limited expectations. Already, Caleb looked and sounded a lot different than last year's freshman "Kale."

Back in his room, Reece texted Ruth, since the sun was setting and she might have already finished the rest of the journal. No answer.

He had an English assignment to do. But an argumentative essay about the politics of gerrymandering seemed so much less interesting than trying to find out whether someone was committing a historical hoax.

He did a little online browsing. As it turned out, Ruth McClintock no longer taught at the local community college, and though she had published a few academic papers about the 1800s, she didn't seem to have a book out anywhere.

That had been ridiculously easy.

He texted her again. **Have you read it all yet?** It was like he had another underclassman on his hands, someone to encourage and take care of. And she probably thought she was doing *him* a favor.

An hour passed with no answer. People over twenty-five had no manners.

6

RUTH

When Reece was out of sight, Ruth stood slowly, hand on her hip, ready to go back into the house, still thinking of the journal entry's first line: *The mind has an uncanny way of saving us from unendurable pain.*

Well, yes and no. During her own accident, Ruth's mind hadn't protected her with gauzy, soft imagery or any sense of slow-motion serenity. Instead, it had flooded her with fear and terror, then gut-punched her with a confusing hallucination.

Comparing her own traumatic experience to Annie's was a senseless distraction. She should be thinking only of Oakley herself, once a strong, independent girl from a humble background, not only talented with guns but a survivor. In her teens, she started beating men at shooting matches, and from there she kept going, rising to the very top of her domain, in control of her own image, determined, unstoppable.

These were just some reasons Ruth admired Annie. But none of them adequately explained why Ruth, as a third-year grad student, had suddenly become interested in the Victorian sharpshooter, abandoning her first subject—a study of Western photographer Edward Curtis.

She was even less sure why a healthy academic interest had—after

her car accident two years ago—turned into a life-altering obsession. Whatever the reason, Ruth knew it was complicated,
because all of her life after the accident was more complicated.
The past, present and future had buckled together like the accor-
dioned front of her car where it had caught on the barrier of the
Fifteenth Street Bridge.

Ruth didn't expect this journal to answer all the big questions,
but one answer, for now, would do.

*The mind has an uncanny way of saving us from unendurable
pain.*

Ruth wondered if her own mind was protecting itself from
something best forgotten.

RUTH TOOK OUT HER CONTACTS, slipped on glasses and
changed into her comfiest U of Iowa sweatshirt. She tugged an
elastic off her wrist and pulled her hair through it into a ponytail,
her default for long days and nights of concentration alone.

Then, from her perch on the couch, she went back to the start,
transcribing the parts she'd read to Reece and then continuing,
taking in each new sentence slowly.

*It was a warm fall night. This was in the Carolinas, a place
in the American South, she informed me. Her husband
was in another car, up late exchanging stories with some
other performers. The train's windows were open, admit-
ting a deep perfume that she had been savoring just before
she nodded off.*

*Now that perfume was replaced with an acrid smell, the
mournful whistle and the shrieking brakes, the catapulting
motion as her body left its narrow bed, train car aglow,
white light, feathers.*

*When her recall slowed, I prompted her: Did she see
actual feathers, or was she just making a comparison with*

the appearance of the slow-falling train cars? Could she better describe this experience of floating? How long did this last?

She didn't answer. Her eyes remained opened, unfocused. Her body, tense at first on the couch, finally relaxed. I didn't intrude but watched her agitated right hand, set limp and trembling against her waist.

She wanted to stare, she told me. She wanted to remember: tens of thousands of feather-filled glass ball targets—hundreds of thousands—shot in a lifetime. She saw the moment this way, a moment of weighted silence, a moment of dazzling light.

A perception of slowed time. One that she could slow further yet through force of attention.

And finally, a sense of acceleration again, of the oncoming train or the past rushing up to swallow the present, in that moment before everything sped up, before things hurt. In that great rush of pain, she breathed deeply, as if gathering up some kind of diffuse energy, and skipped forward, like a stone across a pond.

"How so?"

"Like I might land, and sink, or skip yet again. In any case, I am moving forward, purposefully but without any control. I understand that it's the trauma, that it makes one want to flee the danger. I've thought about this, you see."

I didn't interrupt, even while sensing she had moved from memory to self-diagnosis. There is a temptation, especially among intelligent women, to play the doctor, when what is truly necessary is for the patient to surrender and speak without the need to impress, charm or disguise.

"You are on the train."

"Not any longer. I removed myself. To a spot where

I could see the wrecked train and the rescuers starting
to shoot the first injured horses, the ones that had been
removed from the first of many stock cars."

"This was upsetting?"

"Terribly. First, to see them injured, and then to see that
man doing such a bad job of putting the horses down. It
upset me enough that I suddenly found myself back on the
train."

"Back on the demolished train?"

"No. On the train as it was before, just prior to the crash.
I'd only skipped from one sort of pain to another, and then,
when this second place was equally upsetting, I returned
to where I'd been. But now I knew exactly what would
happen next. Soon enough, I'd be on the other side once
again, but slower if I did nothing to accelerate it, hours
after the accident, hearing the horses being put down again,
knowing precisely how many shots it would take . . ."

"Remarkable. Of course, you know there are explanations for this apparent clairvoyance."

"I am more than able to distinguish fact from fantasy.
I'm not interested in explanations, and I'm not interested
in clairvoyance. I simply accepted that I had slipped or
skipped forward somehow."

She was becoming combative.

"You're taking notes?"

I explained that it was part of the method and that I
would never use her real name in any notes, private or
public. This mollified her, because she continued.

"I'd done it before. Moved forward or slowed time
down, or at least had the sensation that it was advancing
or slowing. The former, when I was in an unpleasant situation as a child. Removing myself, as I believe many people
have done, in situations of discomfort or shame. But never

so vividly and completely. Never to a second place as bad as the first."

"Many people do this, you believe."

"Maybe more women than men. I haven't done a study of it. I hoped that you or someone in your field might have."

"Dissociation."

"If you'd like to call it that."

"What would you call it?"

"Survival."

I pressed her to continue, and she explained how she recovered after the accident and how, during this time, she kept returning to the experience, reliving the brief wonder and deeper terror of the crash. I informed her that the revisiting of the event is a common response, a way of working through it, as if the mind has an unfinished task. It was a classic fixation, a traumatic neurosis created in the moment of the accident.

She listened and considered, but did not seem reassured or compelled, as if this exercise were mere child's play and she had not yet arrived at the memory she truly wished to discuss. She reviewed the other details of the crash, but only because I asked, with less enthusiasm and without the emotional changes I have come to expect.

Willful ignorance, denial, the refusal to accept what lies buried in the subconscious—these are the very producers of illness. But I was beginning to suspect that this ZN might not be a typical hysteric. She admitted to only one physical symptom, though her reticence to talk about it was a powerful indicator. Unlike a typical sufferer, she did not seem to experience any great relief upon divulging details of either her hallucination or the accident itself. If there was any neutralizing of the episode, or discharging of the imprisoned emotion, she did not seem to experience its benefit. Having found some facility in repeatedly reliving the train accident and its immediate precedents, even while it pained her to do so, she became even more fixated on remembering further back, before the crash. With equal vividness, she insisted.

"How so?"

"I'm accustomed to repetition and practice, and this was target practice of another kind. I kept going, trying to find my way into moments before the accident, knowing that if I could inhabit the minutes before, the hours and even days before, there might be no limit. I had seen something—done something—that I had not realized was possible, and now that I knew, I couldn't leave it alone."

It was only now that I sensed that her case was not only one of traumatic neurosis, but perhaps a spontaneous neurosis that had existed before that. The fixation was elsewhere. The train crash had only reminded her of it, or had triggered an associated fear or frustration, even while she insisted its main role was providing her a capacity she'd never had before: this increasingly controlled "skipping or sliding," as she understood it.

I asked when the hand shake had begun.

"About a month after the accident."

"Not immediately after."

"Absolutely not."

"And does that later period correspond with any emotional upset?"

"No. Only with the effort of visiting the past. The strain of it, mental and physical, perhaps even spiritual, I'm not sure.

"The effort of remembering."

"No, of visiting. I haven't gone far. I've not mastered it yet."

I noted that she had, in every instance, refused to use the

words "remember" or "memory." For her, the only accept-
able terms seem to be "visit," "inhabit," "relive," "episode."

I told her that remembering should be a healing process
overall, not a physically injurious one.

A knock at the door. We'd run out of time, a fact that
seemed to inspire her to greater candor.

"I am not remembering, Doctor."

"If I'm to help you, I must ask you to be more clear."

"I'll try."

She looked relieved, at last, and just as quickly, tense
again, still holding back.

I told her we could examine her symptom and her conflict in greater detail, but I had another patient waiting and
a full schedule. If she didn't plan to be in our city for long,
the options were limited. The last time I dealt with a patient
with her sort of nervous problems, we met twice daily for
many months.

This provoked nervous laughter. It seems a distinctly
American trait, to believe every problem can be solved overnight.

On leaving, she was anxious about how we would continue with an ocean between us.

"I can recommend analysts in your country. The method
in America may not be precisely the same, but at least you
might find a professional confidante."

"Impossible."

"You could extend your stay abroad."

"Also impossible."

"That leaves only corresponding by mail, if you're
willing to be candid in your letters."

"I'll try. But if I say everything without consideration,
you may stop me. Sometimes, I want to be stopped. More
often, I don't. If someone . . . an expert, a doctor . . . told

me I must not keep doing this thing, that I must stop or surely I'd lose my mind and my health, both, then maybe I could stop."

"And this is why you've come to me: To ask if you should stop confronting your past?"

"Yes."

"I can assure you, I'm the last person to advise you to stop. It's only by reliving the past that we are relieved of it."

7

R U T H

ere, Ruth turned the page and saw, rather than the continuation of the narrative, a page written in German.

"Oh," she said out loud, a single disappointed syllable that hung in the air like the dust motes dancing in the slanting autumn light before settling onto the scratched oak floor.

The journal's sudden return from English to German had thrown her out of the trance in which she'd spent the last hour. Not only the switch in language, but also topic. Now she read about an unnamed patient with trouble breathing, another with ringing in his ears.

She turned the next page. The handwriting was the same, but the tone impersonal and the details dull.

Ruth read about a third patient with respiratory troubles. And fourth with sinus headaches, just as her own headache was coming on, because the handwriting took considerable time to decipher, the unfamiliar words refusing to give up their secrets as easily due to the additional barriers of a second language and medical terminology.

"Too bad," she whispered. She didn't even have a cat with whom to share the frustrating news.

Her phone dinged. She picked it up, hoping—what, exactly? It wasn't like Scott had texted in ages. But it was Reece, barely home and already bothering her. For the moment, she ignored him.

Ruth closed the journal and rose from the couch, went to the bathroom, walked to the kitchen and filled a glass of water. She was in such a distracted state, she couldn't remember if she'd just taken two ibuprofen in the bathroom as she'd intended.

There is a sense of acceleration again, of the oncoming train or the past rushing up to swallow the present, in that moment before everything speeds up, in that moment before things hurt.

Ruth thought of her own accident, that moment that had seemed to last forever: careening toward the car in front of her, then swinging away as she braked. The certainty that her car would crash through the barrier and slide off the bridge—and then everything speeding up again, all too fast. Sirens and faces. The rescuers, the bystanders. None of them knowing what she had experienced, what had run through her mind just when she thought she was about to die: out of nowhere, an image of Scott, injured and bleeding. All this time later, she'd told only her two therapists. Scott had never found out.

Ruth walked back to the bathroom and opened the bottom left drawer of the apothecary cabinet, the first piece of furniture she had ever bought herself after she'd moved back into her mother's house, as an unsuccessful attempt to add her own adult personality to a home that would never truly be hers. The tightly fitted drawers had to be tugged in order to open. Surely she would remember having done that if she'd already taken the ibuprofen?

Ruth found herself staring at the cabinet with its five rows of drawers, remembering what she'd first loved about it: how it kept everything separate, taming the random items inside. Every pill bottle, memento or extra key had its own small dark wood-scented space.

You like old shit, Kennidy would have said.

You simply appreciate pretty things, Scott would have said.

Compartmentalization, her grad-school buddy Joe Grandlouis would have said—would still say, if Ruth ever called him, something she'd been meaning to do for ages.

What's wrong with that?

Nothing—until it can't be done anymore.

Ruth's mom, Gwen, wouldn't have said anything at all. She didn't notice when new things entered the house, when her daughters were troubled, or even when her youngest daughter, prone to substance abuse, had gone into her bedroom and not come out for nearly twenty-four hours.

"All of you are right," said Ruth as she twisted off the bottle's lid and shook two orange caplets into her hand. She stared at them. Had she just taken these, or had she only been *thinking* of taking them? Luckily, they weren't Vicodin or Xanax or any of the stronger medications off which she'd mostly weaned herself. More important now was the question: How could we expect to remember what had happened in our lives two or even twenty years ago when we weren't sure what had happened a minute ago?

"A few more can't hurt, in any case."

She swallowed the pills.

MEMORY WAS FICKLE, BUT THIS journal was clearly not just about memories, not just about trauma, though that was how a Viennese psychoanalyst would see it, of course. It was about clairvoyance, maybe more.

Back in the living room, Ruth continued reviewing what she'd read, thinking of Annie's train crash, her own car accident and what Annie had disclosed to the man taking notes.

Ruth thought about the birth of psychoanalysis. Had that been in the 1890s? No, 1880s, she was fairly certain.

She tried to picture Annie Oakley, just under five feet tall, reclining on a couch in her long skirt and black boots, waist pinched by a severe corset, long brown hair fanned out on some fussy little bolster or pillow. She was thinking about Annie's various trips to Austria and Germany—where she had supposedly shot the end of a cigarette held by the German Crown Prince Wilhelm II, at his request—and whether the sharpshooter had mentioned anything about scientists or cures of any sort. It was highly improbable, but not impossible.

In his email, Nieman, as he called himself, had presented the journal as "Annie Oakley's true account, in her own words." If he'd asked for money, Ruth would've been suspicious. Instead, he expected answers and insights, quid pro quo, claiming urgency. He was willing to share materials no scholar had ever seen, but only because he needed her help ascertaining their authenticity. He didn't mention why he'd chosen Ruth for this task or how he had gotten her contact information, though of course it wasn't hard to track anyone down these days.

His instructions had been: *Read it first. I don't want to color your impression in any way. Then email me and I will send you my questions. Answer the questions and I may be able to provide you with more documents—a letter collection, which I haven't properly seen and can only obtain after a significant investment, which I won't make unless your answers suggest it is worthwhile.*

Ruth wanted more pages, the continuation of Annie's therapy sessions, if that was what these were.

Annie, what next? Where did you go?

Of course, she still didn't know if it was the real Annie Oakley, whose name had never once been used. But the other details pointed all too obviously: sharpshooting, feather-filled balls, the train accident, Frank, and—though they weren't explicitly named—the Wolves.

When I was in an unpleasant situation, as a child. Removing myself, as I believe many people have done, in situations of discomfort or shame.

The unnamed analyst had put his finger on the sensitive spot:

a *"spontaneous neurosis."* A *"fixation"* that preceded the traumatic neurosis of the train accident, by many years.

This either was someone meant to be Annie, or it was Annie.

Therefore, to make things simple: *Annie.*

But only for about seven pages.

Then, no more.

RUTH WANTED TO READ THE journal from the beginning again, to look for more clues to the analyst's identity that she might have overlooked. But first, quickly, she texted Reece, just to be polite and perhaps slow the arrival of the next slew of messages. His most recent had been: **I looked up Uncanny. Commonly used in AO's time. Not a red flag after all.**

Now she texted back: **Good job. How'd you figure that out?**

Google Ngram.

Good. Did high-schoolers use that? It wasn't flawless for establishing word popularity over time, but it would do.

You don't think it's a reporter's account, but given she's describing accident and you said Wild West show sued the train company, maybe written up by lawyer? Testimony?

Better than the reporter theory. Ruth smiled and replied, **Not impossible, based on the part we read together.**

Ruth hadn't yet decided how much she'd share with Reece, but already, her inclination was shifting. She hadn't written anything in a year; she'd been out of teaching for twice as long. Since her breakup with Scott, she'd had no one who would walk in the door, ready to hear about her latest discovery. And besides, the kid was desperate in the same way she'd once been desperate. To be a part of something. And perhaps to get away from something else.

Ruth texted, **The rest makes it clear. He's an early psychoanalyst.**

OK! So. Freud?

Not Freud, I don't think, but will investigate all options.

A minute passed before Reece replied. **Wiki says AO was a famous hysteric written about by Freud. Is this her?**

Let's not go calling anyone a hysteric, thought Ruth. But she wasn't going to thumb-type a lecture on the misdiagnosis of women in the late 19th and early 20th centuries.

Different AO, she texted. **That's a code name for Bertha somebody.**

Reece had the answer quickly. **Pappenheim. From Vienna. Never mind about Freud. Wasn't her therapist. But . . . AO, not Annie Oakley?**

Coincidence. This journal calls her ZN. A code. One letter back. Bertha P became Anna O. This Annie Oakley became ZN. If it's real.

Easy code.

No one guessed who Bertha was for decades as I recall, so OK code evidently. Not our problem.

Weird coincidence, two Annas.

Not so weird, Ruth replied. **Many women named Ann/Annie/ Anna in this period.**

But two AOs?

Let's not get stuck on that.

It was something that Scott might have said to her, or even Dr. Susan, except that Ruth's psychotherapist would have used the term "apophenia," the false perception of connections and meaning in the presence of unrelated phenomena. One was supposed to ignore that little echo in one's head, or the tingle, or the voice that said, *This! Pay attention to* this! Fortunately or unfortunately for Ruth, historians were pattern seekers. Yet it was equally important to remember: a pattern was only a tool for discovering truth, not truth itself.

Reece texted, **When can I read the rest?**

More to find out first. Which wasn't an answer. **Bye.**

She pulled her laptop closer and composed a quick, neutral greeting to Nieman, thanking him again for entrusting her with the journal. Then she got to the point.

You mentioned the seller allowed you to see one letter from the collection you're thinking of buying. I presume it is a letter from "ZN" to the doctor, to continue their relationship by correspondence, as he suggested. Do you intend to include it? Is the analyst not named or addressed? Do you have anything else that connects Annie Oakley directly to this journal? I wouldn't want to waste your time by offering an uninformed opinion if you have another document that will answer the question or at least narrow down the options. With the letter as opposed to the journal (if I am correct in my hypothesis regarding its presented authorship), we would at least have known handwriting to examine and compare.

Ruth hadn't been sure about the last line, which was really just a cheap bid for him to cough up the letter so she could see it firsthand. Just as she'd told Reece, handwriting analysis was an ever-weaker tool in the digital age.

It seemed ridiculous to push forward with more research until Nieman got back to her. Was he testing Ruth by withholding the letter, or was he intentionally hobbling her efforts?

He was hiding something, she decided. But who didn't hide their most treasured secrets? The woman in the journal, "ZN," hadn't seemed forthright; the analyst wasn't either. He hadn't told his anxious new client that he believed her experiences to be pure hallucination.

And Ruth? In the depths of her illness, she had lied on a regular basis.

RUTH PUT ON THE KETTLE, selected an Earl Grey tea bag and stood with the spoon in her hand, staring at the sugar bowl on the counter, still wondering why she'd been chosen to receive this journal. Why had it shown up today, not two years ago, when Ruth had needed it most? Why in the presence of this young stranger as stubborn and argumentative as Kennidy, her own kid sister, had been?

Perseverating was often associated with post-traumatic stress disorder, especially with certain types of brain injury. She had talked through strategies with Dr. Susan Joy Hovsepian—or Dr. Susan, as Scott and Ruth had always called her—such as setting a firm time limit for thinking about any given topic or image. *By which I don't mean dwelling on something for a week, Ruth. I mean ten minutes. Use a timer.*

THREE YEARS EARLIER——

8

RUTH

After the accident, everything had changed for Ruth—not only her work and her intimate relationships, her daily routines, her body and her brain, but even the way she saw the world. Her life, formerly quiet and mostly fulfilling, had been turned inside out. But it would be wrong to say that life before the accident had been trouble-free.

Her mother, Gwen, was in her final months of terminal breast cancer when Ruth dropped out of grad school in Iowa City and moved back home to Minnesota to be with her. Even before she started dating Scott, the only good thing that happened that dismal winter and spring, Ruth had come up with the idea of salvaging part of her unfinished dissertation about Annie Oakley and converting it into a slim, nonacademic book.

Scott encouraged her. *It'll be good for your CV. Maybe it's your way into a museum job.* Her adjunct teaching certainly wasn't paying the bills. *It doesn't have to be brilliant. It's just a good old story about a historical figure people already like, told in a fresh way.*

None of that seemed convincing enough once Ruth was in the office of Laura Boyd. Was the editor stifling a yawn, or was the sun in her eyes? They were seated around a small round table in a room dominated by enormous picture windows framing a reed-edged pond. It was a fall day: brilliant blue sky, dazzling light bouncing off every glass and metal surface. Ruth looked across the room to the editor's corner desk, above which hung family photos, two diplomas and a shot of Boyd herself next to a canoe and a Labrador retriever.

"Tell me again," the editor prompted. "Why does this book matter *now*?"

Ruth took a sip of water, as if she'd only been warming up. "Gun culture. A new Annie Oakley book will deepen our understanding of American gun culture."

The editor was gazing out the window at a flock of geese taking flight from the pond. For the first time, she settled back in her chair and looked at Ruth with real, unhurried interest.

"Tell me more about that."

It was one of several themes in the book proposal, but here, in person, Ruth could expand and improvise in response to Boyd's cues. The editor was familiar with Oakley's fame as a celebrity performer and her cheerful go-get-'em reputation, familiar to Americans since the inaccurate and irrelevant 1946 musical, *Annie Get Your Gun*. But she hadn't known about Annie's work as a serious gun advocate. She hadn't realized how fervently Oakley had promoted the use of firearms to women—up to twenty thousand of them—as a way to protect themselves.

Boyd asked, "Did you know Eleanor Roosevelt packed a pistol?"

Ruth hesitated. "She was amazing, wasn't she?" Ruth had once seen a photo of the First Lady's gun permit. She wasn't convinced that this meant the first lady carried or shot a gun frequently, but she knew gun-rights advocates enjoyed thinking it was so.

They talked at length about Annie's early years, when she was already a traveling performer. But only briefly about the years before that. When Ruth mentioned Annie's troubled childhood, Boyd's eyes didn't light up.

"I think people overemphasize the importance of childhood experiences," the editor said. "It's tiresome after a while, don't you think? Everyone's had hard times, especially in the old days. We have a book about Lincoln coming out next spring. Did you know his father rented him out as a servant? 'Ten to thirty-one cents a day,' evidently. To do whatever people wanted. Log-splitting, farm work, whatever. Lincoln's own words: 'I was a slave.' "

"That's . . . surprising."

"Yes." Boyd beamed. "A slave! But here's the thing. He rarely talked about it. In the book, we give it maybe a quarter of a page. His father was domineering, semiliterate, didn't want Lincoln to get an education, and I wouldn't be shocked to find out he knocked him around—and let the neighbors knock him around, too. I mean, if they were paying, right?"

Ruth took another sip of water.

"Kidding," her editor said. "Where Lincoln's involved, everyone gets way too serious. That's the problem with most popular history: *too serious.*"

The press was publishing less about the Civil War and Native Americans, even while they'd added some coffee-table-size books on historic gardens and pioneer cooking. They were even beginning to package books as gift sets: a small baking book sold with a miniature cast-iron pan, a book on early American brewing sold with a set of mason-jar drinking glasses. Ruth had a creeping suspicion Laura Boyd didn't really care for history at all—neither the public nor the personal kind.

"In our forthcoming book," Boyd continued, "the slave comment isn't the jumping-off point to explain how Lincoln became Lincoln. People grow up. They get over things. It's just a *brief* anecdote."

Ruth pictured Abe Lincoln's somber face. She'd like to read more, actually, about whether Lincoln's views on slavery and his willingness to go to war might have owed something to this early experience, or what he'd been thinking when he'd chosen to use that word, "slave," knowing how it would resonate with the day's most pressing controversy. But Ruth also knew better than to question a point emphatically made by the woman who would decide whether to publish her.

So the door to childhood trauma was closed, and they were back to straight gun talk again, navigating together as they reviewed the presidential assassinations during Oakley's lifetime: Lincoln, Garfield and McKinley. One could say that Americans' fascination with guns and the belief in solving problems with physical force had led to some unfortunate consequences. One could also say that guns were part of America and had always been. Ruth would tie this fact to the uplifting story of a well-known woman with a positive outlook, someone easy to admire.

Responding to Laura Boyd's unmistakable leanings, Ruth used words like *empowerment*.

The one word she never used was *revenge*.

RUTH WROTE THE BOOK CHRONOLOGICALLY, unsatisfied with the childhood years, the part that interested her the most and Laura Boyd the least. The material was scant. Born in 1860, Annie—born Phoebe Ann Mosey—grew up in western Ohio, the fifth of seven surviving children. Following overexposure during a blizzard, which led to pneumonia, her father died. Soon after, Annie started trapping. At the age of eight, without permission, she lowered an old gun from the wall of her family's cabin in order to shoot game. Legend had it she was a bizarrely talented shot from day one. Annie continued hunting, feeding her family and selling extra game to a local buyer. It wasn't enough.

Annie was sent to the Darke County Infirmary, a poor farm where the superintendent and his wife liked their young ward, but not enough to keep her. Annie was then lent out to a farm family, new parents who needed help with child-minding, pumping water and all the other chores of farm life. They promised to pay and educate her, promises never kept. Instead, they beat her. Whipped her. Possibly worse.

The Wolves. That was what Annie had called them just before her death in the autobiography she'd never finished writing. One source suggested that Miss Oakley was just trying to protect them "kindly." Not so. There was no reason to believe that Annie felt the need to be "kind" or forgiving of the couple who had abused her. Other early biographies failed to mention this part of Annie's life at all.

Two years or a little more. Age nine to eleven or twelve. Those were the years that Ruth refused to allow to pass in a single sentence or a sparse paragraph.

How do you write about what you don't know, what you can't prove?

Ruth found herself dwelling on what was known and unknown about the Wolves, imagining those early episodes. Driving back and forth to her job as an adjunct at the community college forty minutes away, she caught herself daydreaming at stoplights, playing imaginary scenes like a movie in her mind. The false promise of fifty cents a week and an education, the lonely Ohio cabin, the infant Annie was made to care for, the endless physical chores, the beatings and whippings that left scars on her back, the blizzard in which Annie was made to stand outside shoeless, the despicable woman who turned a blind eye to her husband's cravings.

Sexual abuse—if that was what Annie had experienced—was both tragic and arresting, a car wreck you couldn't help but stare at but that made you sorry when you did, because the images would never leave you. At the same time, Ruth already knew her editor was uninterested in this aspect of Annie's story, as well as any other part of the story not in service to a simple inspirational theme.

There were two small foundations and a limited number of American museums that referred to Annie Oakley. On their websites and in their most visible public interpretations, some made mention of the Wolves. Some did not.

Ruth decided to tackle the question directly. She called Laura Boyd.

"How's this," Boyd said. "Cover the childhood episode, keep it very short, and name the Wolf. Most of the older biographies don't, isn't that right?"

"Because it's not certain. A few names have been suggested, none a perfect fit."

"Then give readers the options."

"You're not worried about me naming an innocent man?"

Boyd laughed. "Five years ago, I would have been worried. But the culture has changed. Men who are still living and famous are being called out on social media all the time without evidence. You're talking about naming a possible child abuser who has been dead for, what, a century?"

"Possibly a hundred and fifty years."

None of Ruth's best guesses satisfied her, and she started to explain to Boyd about a man named Boose or maybe Bosse, another named Rannals or maybe Reynolds, and an entirely different family named the Studabakers, just to start.

"Ruth," Boyd interrupted. "You're losing me in the weeds here, which doesn't bode well. These men are long dead. Their great-grandchildren are long dead. One did something, another maybe didn't, or perhaps nobody did anything that wasn't considered normal behavior. Weren't plenty of young girls forced to chop wood and carry buckets of water in those days?"

Ruth tried to keep her voice level. "It went beyond that."

"Okay, and the parts that 'went beyond.' I'm sorry. Men take advantage. They always have. Isn't that common as well?"

"It is. That's the point, I think. The 'common' thing that

Annie suffered made her who she was: an uncommon woman fueled by . . ."

Ruth was about to say "rage," but she stopped herself. She had no proof of rage. She was projecting, letting Boyd's loose standards erode her own scholarly self-respect.

"Okay," Boyd said. "We're getting somewhere. The woman she *became*. Annie Oakley was abused—maybe. But it doesn't matter who did it. I'm rethinking my earlier suggestion. You're not sure, so let's not name him at all. It's a little late for justice, don't you think?"

The conversation ended in a series of banalities that dribbled off into the discussion of photo research, marketing and publicity, Instagram and Twitter.

By the time Laura Boyd hung up, Ruth's phone was hot against her cheek. Whether or not Annie was angry, Ruth certainly was.

Why *did* she have to know—and name—the Wolf? Why did she have to understand why Annie herself hadn't named him? Why did we have to know anything at all?

Ruth shouldn't have been surprised that people were losing interest in history. They didn't even care about truth in the present.

She had to stop herself before this internal rant and its rhetorical questions soured her on research altogether. Ruth cared. Maybe she hadn't cared doggedly enough about other things in her life, but she cared about this.

FOR THE MOMENT, RUTH PRESSED forward, digging into the middle years, for which documentation was more plentiful. The challenge here was making the familiar fresh. The public liked the Annie they already knew. Ruth felt she was gently renovating a house with historically sourced materials. It was more a form of carpentry than construction. And it was certainly not demolition. No one—certainly not Ruth's editor or publisher— had begun this project intending to surprise or upset any reader.

In graduate school, Ruth had enjoyed brainstorming with like-minded colleagues. When she'd gotten a call in November from her old friend and doctorate peer Joe Grandlouis, now a visiting professor at the University of Washington, his voice brought back the memory of not only the two months they'd dated—a poor match, though not one she regretted—but also the pleasure of academic camaraderie.

Joe, as it turned out, was calling with news. His wife, Christine, had given birth to their daughter Reka: healthy, six pounds two ounces, "as ugly as her father."

"Oh, come on," Ruth said.

"Well, only for the first day. Then we saw some improvements."

Joe knew he was good looking. A bear of a man, tall and broad-chested, who wore his shiny black hair in a long braid down his back.

As Joe told her, he was finishing an article on Chief Sitting Bull's role in the Wild West show, a performance allowed by government authorities after the leader and medicine man surrendered to US forces almost a decade after defeating Custer at the Battle of Little Bighorn—or Battle of the Greasy Grass, as Joe and other Plains Indians preferred to call it.

Joe wanted Ruth's perspective on the closeness of Sitting Bull's relationship with his fellow performer Annie Oakley. A minor point that affected no more than a paragraph, but something he didn't want to get wrong. He was on the fence between two interpretations: one, that Oakley and Sitting Bull had been genuinely close. Or two, that the acquaintanceship was struck up on a whim and deepened, but only slightly, by circumstance.

"Theory one," Ruth said, "Sitting Bull chose Annie as a replacement for the daughter he had lost, according to the Lakota tradition of adopting to replace lost family, gave her the moccasins supposedly made by his daughter, was truly and deeply impressed with Annie's shooting skill. Relationship of mutual respect. 'My dear, old, faithful friend,' Annie called him later in life. You know all that."

"I think I already know theory two," Joe said. "Same meet-cute start—the chief was impressed by her shooting the first time he saw it—but the rest was mostly marketing, for both of them. Watanya Cicilla."

Ruth had to agree. "The 'Little Sure Shot' honorific—if that's even the proper translation—couldn't have been bad for her image, and maybe the benefit ran both ways."

"So that's what you're saying in your own book. You're going for door number two. Colleagues of convenience, nothing more."

"Lacking better evidence. Even if it's not as good a story."

"You're right. It's not a good story. Well, maybe this call was just me procrastinating. But there's always the sense that you're missing something that would turn things upside down and bring these old dead guys to life."

"Don't I know it."

"Maybe that's just authorial self-sabotage. And dirty diaper avoidance."

"Exactly," she said. "So, tell me about new babies. Do they really never sleep?"

"Better than I do."

She understood that, as well.

THE DEADLINE LOOMED AS RUTH wrote about Annie in her forties, beginning with the famous train accident in 1901, after which—anecdotally—Annie Oakley's hair turned bright white.

Ruth had a dream one night of the forty-one-year-old Annie standing alongside a train track next to a toppled, derailed car. She had aged overnight. She was ashen-faced, thin-lipped, haunted. Staring. Trying to tell Ruth something.

You can't go forward without going back.

Or was it, *You can't go back without going forward?*

Maybe she had said both. It was all a blur, suffused with the smell of smoke and something sour, like urine, the product of animal panic. As far as Ruth could recall, she had never remembered a smell from a dream before.

In the dream, Ruth felt she was doing something wrong, that she was disappointing Annie somehow, and that very disappointment seemed to make Annie fade, her outline blending with the rising smoke, even as she continued muttering something that Ruth couldn't hear. She tried to go toward her, stepping over the railroad tracks with great effort and the sense of being held back, the motions syrupy and slow.

She heard Annie speak again, even more faintly, from behind a veil of smoke or fog or simply time: *Open the cabin door.*

Ruth woke up, heart pounding, trying to hold on to her memory of the dream, the feeling of frustrated movement and also guilt that she wasn't doing what Annie had begged her to do. Ruth didn't believe in ghosts, but she did believe that time itself, like many a historical script, bore faint traces and echoes of what had come before and been effaced.

All our stories were like that: our passing joys and sorrows just the latest scratch marks on the Möbius strip of time and space that must of necessity be endlessly recycled.

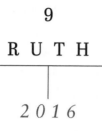

9

R U T H

2016

That fall, as her deadline loomed, Ruth felt sure her biggest error had been in not understanding young Annie, of having been too afraid to understand. It explained her sense of remorse but not her anger, a physical heat in her belly. At times, driving home from the college after classes she'd once enjoyed teaching, her hands on the steering wheel began to shake. She had to clench the wheel more tightly to make them stop, even when she wasn't thinking about the book—even when she wasn't thinking about anything at all. Where had those sudden surges of anger come from?

Ruth had been dating Scott for eight months. He kept several changes of clothes at her house; he'd brought over his guitar, an electric wok, his own vacuum cleaner after hers broke. He'd nursed her through the flu. He'd dedicated multiple weekends to emptying her late mother's basement of junk—a job that even now was far from done, but at least they'd made a dent in the piles. He was undoubtedly a good guy. And far from stupid.

"I have to ask," he said one night after they'd cleared the dinner dishes and opened a second bottle of wine, when Ruth confessed that she was starting to feel the vise grip of writer's block and didn't understand why this book was giving her so much trouble.

"Were you sexually abused as a child? Or later? Anything like that?"

She paused. There was no reason to pause.

What Ruth *had* experienced as a teen—one of her mother's drunk boyfriends aggressively flirting with her, another exposing himself from the bedroom doorway—hadn't seemed like assault or anything close at the time. It was just gross. Ruth had been in high school when those incidents occurred. She had her own escape route planned by then: college, dorm living and no plan to come back to this town, ever.

Ruth hadn't thought about Kennidy then. She tried not to think of her little sister, rest in peace, now. Scott hadn't asked about what *could* have happened to either of them, given their mother's oblivious, neglectful parenting. He'd only asked if she'd been abused or assaulted.

The answer was simple.

"No."

"Okay." He smiled and reached across the table for her hand. "I just thought I should ask."

It was a cold Wednesday night in October when they made the decision. They'd fallen asleep on the couch together watching a movie, and after they woke up and looked at the clock, Scott slumped toward the door, where he struggled into his shoes and coat.

"You can just stay," Ruth had said.

"Would love to. But I left my laptop and my grade book at the apartment."

"It's so cold out."

"Only getting colder."

"You should always bring all your work stuff here. Just in case."

"But there's always something."

"Bring it all over, then," she said, zipping up his coat for him, standing on tiptoe to kiss his neck and tug the collar up around his ears. "Every last book and poster and extension cord and lemon zester."

"I don't have a lemon zester," he said, giving her one last return kiss. "I might have a garlic press, though. So, I empty the apartment, and then?"

"And then stop paying rent, obviously."

Three days later, he moved his final belongings: half into her house, half into the garage until they sorted things out. When Ruth saw Scott unload the gun from the trunk of his car, she started.

"You have a gun?"

"Two. Something I do with my brother. More target practice than real hunting, just because we're getting lazy." He tried to hand the rifle over to Ruth so he could unload the weightlifting set he'd brought on his final trip.

When she took a step back, he tilted his head, curious, but he didn't withdraw his extended arms.

"This make you nervous?"

"A little," she said, though she didn't know why. She wasn't against shooting. She wasn't even against killing animals.

"Wait a minute," Scott said as a smile spread across his face. "You're telling me you're writing a book about the nation's most famous sharpshooter and you don't know how to shoot?"

"When I was writing papers about Edward Curtis, I didn't know how to take great photographs, either."

"But that's different. You studied him for . . . a year? Maybe two? You've been into Annie Oakley ever since."

Scott's smile kept getting bigger, which annoyed her. She didn't want to be annoyed. He was moving in. It was a special day they'd experience only once.

"I grew up in a family of women. Then I went off to college and grad school."

"In Iowa. People in Iowa hunt."

"My friends weren't weekend hunters. All right?"

He walked the gun over to a corner of the garage where he'd been stacking tools and sports equipment. "Hey—sorry. I was just surprised. I didn't mean to push your buttons."

"You didn't," she snapped.

"Let me rephrase that. I didn't mean to be a jackass. Better?"

"Much better. And maybe you did push my buttons."

Inside the house, they emptied several boxes. But Ruth still couldn't get the exchange out of her mind.

"So actually," she said as they stood side by side, unwrapping drinking glasses, wads of newspaper accumulating at their feet, "my mom dated a guy who had a gun. And I didn't like him. She was always bringing home guys like him. This one lived with us for a couple months. He was a creep."

Gwen had been a phlebotomist at a blood-plasma donation facility, drawn to hard-luck cases, which in her line of work, walked through the door on a daily basis.

"What kind?" Scott asked.

"What kind of creep?"

"No, what type of gun did he have. Rifle? Shotgun?"

"I don't remember. It just made me uncomfortable having the gun in the house, given the regular bouts of chaos. He kept it locked up. I was grateful for that."

It wasn't like she'd never told Scott about her mom's spells of depression, which meant days sleeping in a dark room. The guys who came and went. And her half-sister Kennidy, a full ten years younger than Ruth, a bit of an attention-seeker, prone to trouble— all of it worse when alcohol or other substances were involved.

The unpacking had slowed. The small dining table was cluttered with dishes and duplicates—the extra blender, the extra toaster—that they would have to donate or sell. The inherited house was bigger than Scott's bachelor studio, but it was still modest. There wasn't room for all the stuff he'd taken the trouble to haul over. Maybe this would be more complicated: making space, sharing everything.

"My sister always managed to get into things," Ruth tried again. "If there was leftover beer in the garage from some big holiday stock-up, Kennidy got into it."

"What teenager wouldn't?"

"Not just that. If my mom had leftover Vicodin from the dentist, Kennidy found it. If a guy Mom was dating had a new bag of golf clubs—"

"Golf clubs?"

"Yeah. If a guy had golf clubs we weren't supposed to touch, next thing you knew, one was in the back of my car and we were going for a drive."

"This sounds like a story."

Scott had mentioned ordering pizza. They were both hungry and eager to pick out a movie.

"Just . . ." she started to say, and then thought better of it. It wouldn't sound like much. "She attacked a garden gnome with it. Raised a ruckus, as our mom would have said. That's all."

Even as she tried to laugh it off, the smell and the sounds came back to her: Marlboro Lights, Foo Fighters blasting from the only speaker that worked, the headlights bouncing through the dust as they followed the old gravel road.

Ruth was home from Iowa City, just for the weekend. Kennidy was seventeen. They went driving with the music and the smokes and red plastic cups of whiskey between their legs. And the golf club, which Ruth didn't know about until they reached their destination: a cabin in the woods, close to an hour away. Ruth knew Kennidy was angry with whoever lived there, but no more than that.

Lukewarm 7 and 7s. Country roads past hayfields, and a mystery destination. Bad idea, obviously. But Ruth was trying to make up for the gulf that had always existed between them. She'd hoped her little sister would open up, ask for advice, promise to lay off their mom—anything.

Kennidy directed Ruth along the drive with little explanation and, on arrival, told her where to park, under a tree away from the cabin, partly hidden. Kennidy got out, grabbed the club from the back seat and started swinging at the ceramic gnome on the stoop, which toppled and crashed, then at a drainpipe that dented on impact. A little light was on inside. Ruth saw the figure move behind a curtain—a man, no question about it. Slow-moving and slightly stooped. Not a young guy. Through the window, she could see the blue flicker of a TV set. Tacked next to the door were two team pennants: the Twins, whose logo was everywhere in their town, and another Ruth didn't recognize, because she was bored by spectator sports, baseball especially: a blue jay.

Now, ankle-deep in piles of packing material, holding a casserole dish she didn't know where to store, Ruth had fallen silent. She hadn't said anything about the cabin or the man inside. She'd left off at the silliest part on purpose: the lawn ornament, the swinging golf club.

"That's all?" Scott asked.

"I was just glad she never got her hands on a gun. Because she didn't exactly know how to deal with her emotions."

"Well, I think I should take you to a range once and let you fire a few rounds, just so you know that it's not something to be scared of. That's number one."

She nodded. Surely with Scott, it wouldn't be scary. It would just be normal. Safety-conscious, even.

"And number two, just so you know. Golf clubs don't kill garden gnomes. People do."

"Yes. Exactly."

RUTH'S LOVE LIFE THAT FALL was fine—great, even. Her work life wasn't.

She got an extension. Ruth estimated that she still had a quarter of the work to go. Oakley was born in 1860 and died in 1926. Ruth got bogged down at 1901.

Boyd finally told her over the phone, six weeks before the extended deadline. "New isn't really what we need, here, Ruth. Frankly, if you gave us an updated version of the Riley book, we wouldn't be unhappy."

The problem, once Laura Boyd read the partial manuscript of Ruth's slim Annie Oakley biography, wasn't that she thought it was an unacceptable mess. The problem was that she thought it was fine. To Ruth's surprise, the editor sent the manuscript out for preliminary review by a handful of experts, with a fuller review to follow. In the meanwhile, Boyd simply wanted Ruth to fast-forward to a polished conclusion.

"I can't," Ruth told Scott on a winter night a week before Christmas. They'd planned to fly to his parents' house in Chicago on the twenty-fourth and stay just past New Year's. "I can't pretend to be enjoying the holidays when I'm supposed to be finishing this thing."

They were on the couch, supposedly relaxing—Ruth with her laptop while Scott deleted emails from his phone.

"Why don't you put that away," he said. "I'll rub your feet."

"I know you have to go to your parents'."

"I do. But you don't."

"I feel terrible. We already bought my ticket."

"It's changeable." Scott always refused to catastrophize with her. "You just need time alone, without interruptions. You are so *close*."

"Maybe," she said, feeling around for the slightest optimistic inclination. It was there.

On the wall across the room hung an early Christmas present Scott had given Ruth, hoping it would motivate her in the weeks leading up to her deadline: a framed photo from an auction site.

The image showed Annie Oakley from behind, with long wavy brown hair, a tiny nipped waist, a voluminous skirt that ran to her calves, and thick leggings that continued down and over the tops of sensible black shoes. A gun was set over her shoulder, pointing behind her as she looked into a handheld mirror. A favorite trick. An odd photograph. Aiming backward.

Backward.

It had given her a little shiver, even then—a good shiver, she'd thought at the time. At the very least, a strange and memorable one. Ruth could imagine looking back on this moment years from now, thanking Scott for his refusal to turn small problems into big ones.

It was fallacious to see history as a clear series of turning points, evident to the people living in the heat of those moments. But at the same time, it sometimes *was* possible to feel it: history happening, like a warm current of water passing beneath a swimmer's treading feet, or about to happen, like a swell building at sea. She had that feeling now.

She asked, "But what'll you do for New Year's?"

"Dad will fall asleep on the couch. I'll make my mom a grilled cheese sandwich. We'll try to watch some TV countdown, but she'll keep getting up to fold laundry and probably miss the ball drop."

"That sounds bad."

"Not really. My folks aren't going to be around forever. Midnight's just midnight. And you'll give me something good to read when I come back."

IN A WEEK, RUTH COVERED only two more years of Annie Oakley's life, but that wasn't important. She'd broken through the bottleneck, she knew she could finish in just a few weeks more— and all because of Scott's steadfast support.

Now would be the perfect time to express thanks, and Ruth

knew exactly how. Neither of them liked her mom's house. It was finally time to sell it and start their life together fresh.

That afternoon, while others were stocking up on New Year's Eve liquor and snacks, Ruth was in the basement of her mother's house. There she found all the documents she'd barely glanced through in the grief-blurred weeks after Gwen's funeral: a sagging banker's box with old rental agreements, canceled checks, mortgage documents, inspection reports and printed emails between Ruth's mother and the neighbor, Van, from whom Gwen had first rented and eventually purchased the house. The emails at the top of the pile all involved haggling over the health of the septic system.

The irony wasn't lost on Ruth. These sorts of documents, when related to a historical figure of importance, were captivating clues to lifestyles long forgotten. Locate them in the present or recent past, and they were tedious.

Ruth looked at the date of the first email again: 2013. That was odd. At least a year before the house had changed hands, they were debating the septic system's age and the house's value. Ruth's mother hadn't even thought of buying it until 2014 at the earliest, when she already had cancer. Van had lowered the price $25,000 below its true value—a bargain inspired by generosity. But if the neighbor had meant to be generous, why did he seem so argumentative and petty in his emails? If he was doing a supposed favor that he'd initiated, why did the sale seem shadowed by acrimony?

Every document confirmed it. The house was quietly inspected, appraised, and purchased not during the year Ruth's mom was diagnosed with cancer—the story Ruth had always been told—but a year earlier, in 2013. The year Kennidy had died.

Maybe, then, Ruth was remembering incorrectly, and their neighbor's act of generosity was not a gesture meant to help soften the blows of cancer, but to mitigate the loss of a troubled child.

Ruth wanted it to make sense.

But it didn't.

Because negotiations for the house sale were too early even for that: July 2013. Summer, not fall. They predated Kennidy's death by three months.

WHEN SCOTT CALLED ON NEW Year's Eve from his parents' house, Ruth didn't mention the inconsistencies she'd found, though they troubled her. When he asked what her plan was for the next day, her last one to herself, she said, "Everyone else will be sleeping in with hangovers. I'll hit the grocery store while it's empty."

The next morning, despite having avoided any kind of holiday binge, Ruth felt less than clearheaded. She awoke several times, and finally, at 4 A.M., she went back to the banker's box, flipping through the emails again for something she'd missed, like a more personal note explaining why Van had decided to sell. Her search only yielded more questions.

Ruth went for a morning drive in the country—8 A.M., no souls around—with a travel mug full of coffee and a muffin on her lap. She headed northwest without thinking and got off Highway 68, turning down a county road and taking it for a while, then turning left at another county road, then a right. Random zigzags. Big squares. Endless numbered roads.

She'd enjoyed drives like these when she was a teenager with a brand-new driver's license: flat pavement, no traffic, big sky, plenty of time to daydream. But she wasn't just daydreaming this time. She was trying to remember that summer night with Kennidy, just months before her sister killed herself and—as she now knew— just a month before Gwen had bought the house for an artificially low price from a man who didn't seem likely to be generous. The events themselves were odd and closer in time than she'd realized. But it was her late mother's strange legacy of obscuring certain dates and specifics that bothered Ruth most of all.

Ruth kept driving, looking for a certain stretch of hayfields, a particular gravel road, a familiar oak tree. But she couldn't find any landmarks. All county roads looked the same. It had been dark, and they'd been drinking. Nothing stood out to her now.

Later, she would remember this moment and question whether the problem had been her need to search or giving up on that need. Because she had, in fact, let it go. She put the problem back in its box, something that—when her mind was sound—she had always been able to do, though not with complete ease.

Driving back toward town, Ruth tried to clear her head of foggy images and the week's worries. She still had grocery shopping to do. After that, she might have a productive afternoon of writing.

Focus, Ruth.

But still her mind slid: first to Kennidy, and then to their mother and to the house again. A cost and timing equation that never balanced.

It was 11:26 on the morning of New Year's Day, just one day before Scott was due home, when Ruth's mind slid to that equation a final time only seconds before her wheels locked into their own alarming skid on the ice at the Fifteenth Street Bridge, requiring her to pump her brakes, trying to avoid the fishtailing of the car heading toward her.

Red Toyota, one man inside, still hungover from a party the night before.

Red.

No way to stop.

It happened too fast for her to store the memory for proper retrieval later. Ruth was informed by police that the other car had been blue, not red. She couldn't even get that detail right.

What she did remember was a vision of office towers rising on the far side of a frozen lake. That meant her car had swung to face north before spinning again, hitting the south guardrail, splitting the edge before stopping, caught before falling, nose tilted down. What she remembered was the sound of the bumper tearing off and undercarriage scraping, metal buckling, all of it deafening, and her own panic.

Not the water. Please. No. Don't drop into the water.

The doctors told her she had either lost consciousness by that point or had been in such a state of shock she couldn't perceive with accuracy at all.

Traumatic images become fragmented, they had told her. In states of high terror or stress, during combat or rape or extreme physical trauma, the prefrontal cortex of the brain shuts down. Chemicals surge.

You can't go back without going forward.

It didn't work.

The fear circuitry, especially the amygdala, takes over. The hippocampus is impaired.

Be firm, be honest. I'll believe you.

You can't go forward without going back.

Short-term memories aren't stored properly. Spatial and time information—sequencing—is altered.

Don't walk away, Ruth.

Open the cabin door.

They told her: you may have a sharp memory from just before, but what you think you're remembering during the accident isn't reliable.

But it sure seemed reliable to Ruth, especially after the panic and all the voices in her head quieted, especially when her frenzy of thoughts funneled down to just one. *Not the water. No, no, no.* Foot on the pedal. Hands on the wheel in front of her, the air bag not yet inflated. And then the perfectly clear image of Scott.

It wasn't, as her therapist suggested after the accident, because she had been thinking of Scott just before impact. She'd been thinking about Annie Oakley. She'd also been thinking about her sister and her mother and her own unfinished work.

At that moment, she *was* in love with Scott, in that comfortable way that allows us to take the person we most need for granted. He was so reliable, so faithful, so integral to her recent past and her much longer future to come, that he didn't take up much space.

But then he was there, in front of her, in the car now filling with a cloud of air bag chemicals, as close as the shattered windshield, which was impossible to see clearly in comparison with Scott's face.

His eyes were wide and his mouth was slack, like he'd just received hurtful news or a physical blow to the stomach. His neck and the front of his button-down shirt were white, and then the shirt wasn't white, and it was horrible—more horrible even than what Ruth was experiencing. Her experience was completely unreal, impossible to assimilate. His experience was the real one, the undeniable nightmare.

No, no, no.

None of it made sense. He wasn't in the car. He was at his parents' at that moment on New Year's morning. He was five hundred miles away. He was safe.

No matter how many times they would tell her the Toyota was blue and although she knew the half-frozen lake that she barely missed falling into was blue and the slice of sky that might have been glimpsed later through the door pried off by rescuers was blue, none of that matched the vision she'd had on impact with the guardrail.

No, no, no.

Her shoe pushed so hard into the brake pedal it felt like the bones in her foot would break. Her arms locked hard, trying to press her entire body back into the seat even as she felt the car tipping downward.

She had never wanted something so clearly, so purely. She wished to stop the fall from happening, to be anywhere but here. And she felt sorry—for all she had taken for granted, for all she had missed.

And with that longing, the image of Scott's face. The flash of color. Not blue at all. But *red red red*.

1 0

RUTH

D r. Susan Joy Hovsepian had been the first therapist to whom Ruth had confessed the disturbing image she had seen of Scott back when they still lived together. Dr. Hovsepian suggested it was connected to either an urge or a persistent thought that presented itself as an urge.

At Dr. Susan's recommendation, Ruth attended a Harm OCD group therapy session. Listening to other people talk about wanting to stab their mothers or drop their babies on their heads did not help Ruth understand her vision of Scott suffering and bleeding. The intrusive image said nothing about her relationship with Scott or her desires, real or imagined—in fact, it said the opposite. Ruth did *not* want to see Scott hurt.

There was one possibility that seemed obvious, if only to Ruth: that she wasn't fantasizing or imagining at all, but glimpsing a future event.

"Have you mentioned this to Scott?" Dr. Susan asked during the private session, which took place in early March, three months after the crash.

"No."

Dr. Susan made an approving sound, lips pressed shut.

"You think I shouldn't tell him, then?"

"What do you think?"

"I think it would scare him."

"Why?"

"Because it would either mean that he's going to be seriously hurt in some way we can't predict or that I'm batshit crazy."

Dr. Susan hummed again with closed lips and touched her platinum hair—a "tell" the therapist indulged when she disagreed with the use of a word or phrase.

Ruth said, "A lot of people believe in future predictions of some sort. Premonitions, dreams that serve as warnings . . ."

"A lot of people?"

"One person in ten. Something like that."

"You seem to be doing a lot of online research. We've talked about limiting your screen time. You're still having headaches, yes?"

"Fewer of them."

"Your brain needs rest."

"It also needs answers."

"You've identified a difference between yourself and the others in the group. They understand they are imagining things that haven't happened, that *don't need* to happen, as much as they struggle with intrusive thoughts about these imaginary situations. Whereas you, Ruth, are seeing things you can't easily distinguish from reality."

Not the point. If it *did* turn out to be reality at some point, then she wasn't having a hard time distinguishing.

"And that," the therapist said, "brings us back to something we've discussed before, which is schizotypy."

"You're saying I'm schizophrenic."

"These issues may exist on a continuum. Some forms of schizotypy are benign, like religious experiences or even simple creativity." Dr. Susan smiled. "I'd like you to continue attending the Harm OCD group."

"I'm not going to harm Scott!" Ruth hadn't meant to yell. "I'm not even anxious about it."

Dr. Susan leaned back in her chair. "It concerns me, actually, that you're *not* anxious about it. We also need to consider PDFTBI. That stands for psychotic disorder following traumatic brain injury."

"Psychotic?" They had just been talking about continuums and creativity. "I definitely don't think I'm psychotic."

"People get stuck on the label. Which is why it's more helpful to talk about managing your symptoms. Besides that image, is there anything else that flashes into your head with regularity? Particular voices, words?"

It was a ridiculous question. Of course words were always flashing through Ruth's mind. She read and wrote for a living, constantly turning phrases around in her head, probing them for deeper meaning.

You can't go forward without going back.

Dr. Susan pressed her. "Voices?"

It didn't work.

I'll believe you.

Open the cabin door.

Dr. Susan pressed again. "Specific words? Phrases?"

Ruth was getting increasingly uncomfortable with Dr. Susan's line of questioning. "I think I need a second opinion."

Dr. Susan smiled again, but there was no light in her eyes. "That's never a bad idea. I'd be happy to give you a referral."

DR. PADMESH TALKED LESS AND prescribed more. Ruth went through two rounds of antipsychotics and was on the third, clozapine, without having told Scott the whole truth—what she was seeing and how often she was seeing it, despite any type of therapy.

Meanwhile, their relationship was foundering, despite Scott's optimistic talk about "post-traumatic growth," a catchphrase he'd picked up from Dr. Susan, which Ruth did not appreciate.

Instead of feeling like hope, it felt like pressure. Ruth was supposed to be a *better* person for what she'd experienced, with a greater sense of perspective and a zest for life's simple pleasures. They were supposed to be closer as a couple, positively *ecstatic*.

Scott proposed in April, eager to plan a wedding ceremony while his father was still well enough to attend, and for that reason she'd given in. But second thoughts were close behind. She couldn't walk down a grocery-store aisle, much less a church aisle—and that wasn't even the point. Scott didn't know her well enough to have made such a momentous decision. Since the accident, she barely knew herself.

During the months neither of them recognized as the end, she often felt an argument brewing the moment he came home. One day, seven months after the accident, Scott had barely walked in the door, beat from a long day at school. Ruth started to explain how William Randolph Hearst, the famous newspaper magnate, had allowed an outrageous false story to run in his papers, claiming that Annie Oakley had stolen some clothes in order to fund a drug habit. The story went viral.

"First, Hearst tarnished her brand," Ruth said, following Scott as he dropped his backpack and laptop bags in the hallway. "Then, when she went after him in court, he sent a private detective to her hometown to dig up dirt on her—anything he could use to undermine her legal case."

"Can I just use the bathroom first?"

"Of course," she said, but she hung outside the bathroom door. When he came out and headed toward the kitchen, she tagged behind. "So, Hearst goes digging. Which doesn't actually turn up anything, because she really was a prim and proper lady, but it was classic intimidation."

Scott pulled a beer out of the fridge. She gestured for him to hand her a bottle, but he didn't.

"Isn't that risky with the clozapine?"

She shrugged. Fed up with the side effects, she'd stopped taking the clozapine, and was nearly off Vicodin and working hard to quit Xanax, a withdrawal process that was far from easy because it exacerbated many of the symptoms—anxiety, tension, paranoia, irritability, intrusive memories—that had pushed her into taking too much of the tranquilizer in the first place. Scott had no idea.

"I thought you wanted to write more about her childhood. That you'd underplayed the stuff about the Wolves."

"This leads back to the Wolves. He was another Wolf. I think that battling him for six or seven years could've led her to reappraise her entire life."

"Should I order takeout?"

"Are you listening?"

"I'm trying. I've got forty-seven tests to grade. I missed lunch because we had an incident with a senior who was acting up, making threats. They searched his backpack."

Backpack searches happened every month. Serious threats happened at least once a semester. "Can I finish?"

"Sure," he sighed.

"So, here's the amazing thing. Annie Oakley is famous in the annals of American libel law because she won so much money. Hearst even pressed for new legislation to stop her."

"That's great," Scott said, waiting, phone in one hand and grease-spotted restaurant menu in the other.

"But here's the key. As much as she won, she didn't make a profit. She and Frank probably *lost* money in the long run. Sometimes Frank or Annie's nieces would travel with her, but not all the time. She must've spent a lot of time on trains, not able to perform, not able to do much else—and even when there were months between trials, she couldn't jump into a new production.

That was how much it mattered to her. To be right. To get back at Hearst. To reclaim her reputation. To undo that feeling that must have gone all the way back to the Wolves, back to her two years essentially being a slave with no control over her mind, her body . . ."

Scott was studying Ruth's face. "Are you still taking the clozapine?"

Sometimes Ruth thought he preferred her drugged to undrugged, because drugged, she couldn't work. She couldn't search, focus, persist.

"You're usually groggy when I get home," Scott said. "Right now, you're wired."

"Being groggy sucks."

"I'm sure it does."

"Can I please finish what I'm trying to tell you? So that at least I have it straight in my head when I try to write it up tonight?"

"Tonight? You're not supposed to be working at all."

"I still have a chance to finish this book, if I can get my head straight."

Scott set down his phone. "Ruth, are you taking the clozapine?"

She looked away. "I don't need it."

"That's what the kid at school said when they asked why he'd gone off his antidepressants. That he didn't need them anymore."

"Maybe he didn't."

"But then again," Scott said, pitch rising as he lost patience, "he started making threats against kids who'd bullied him. You don't know when a kid like that will act up."

"I'm not going to 'act up.'"

"I didn't mean that. I'm just worried you'll suffer in ways you don't have to. Those attacks, and the feeling you're dying—"

"The clozapine isn't for the panic attacks."

"What's it for, then?"

"They're not even technically panic attacks."

"This is new information. Do you want to explain?"

"Not when you sound like that."

"How am I supposed to know what's going on in your head?"

"Trust me, you don't."

"Well that sounds like a great recipe for a relationship."

Scott glanced at his phone on the table, but he didn't pick it up. It was the wrong time to order takeout. The wrong time for just about anything.

His next comment feigned interest. "What did Oakley's husband think of her vendetta?"

"Vendetta?"

"She'd made her point. The whole country must have known after the first retractions and the first trials that she wasn't a drug fiend. Hearst was punished. But she kept going."

"Why shouldn't she have kept going?"

"Because it didn't change anything. It only continued to cost her."

"Because it was justice."

"Was it?" He asked again, more gently now. There was no malice in his voice. "I have a feeling that Frank Butler might have wished she'd given it a rest."

"He was amazingly supportive."

"Yes, supportive enough to want her to be happy. I know he wouldn't want to see her waste a good part of her life due to an unhealthy obsession."

"Why are obsessions only unhealthy when women have them?"

"I think all obsessions are unhealthy."

"Well, Frank didn't see it that way. I'm sure about that." She knew no such thing. She just wanted Frank to be extraordinary— for his time, for any time. "Anyway, you don't know anything about Frank Butler."

"I know that . . ." He stumbled on the next words. "I know that he loved her."

At the sound of her normally stoic fiancé choking up, Ruth didn't keep debating. He'd won the argument, but there was no prize in it.

SCOTT SEEMED TO THINK THEIR ending was inevitable, but to Ruth, it felt more like a roulette wheel that could have stopped in just a slightly different position, changing everything.

Two months after their last big argument, Scott went on a cycling trip with his brother. He could have come home an hour sooner, an hour later: all of it might have changed. As it happened, he walked in just as the realtor was on her way out.

Scott stood in the entryway in black bicycle shorts, calves painted in mud, smiling. He was handsome and fitter than ever, still tan from his long rides over the summer. Ruth was plump, pale, achy and hobbling. They had diverged. But that wasn't the issue.

Scott stepped aside to make room for the agent's peculiarly unfriendly exit. When the door closed, Scott said, "So? Good news? Bad news? Did she do a market evaluation?"

"No."

"Isn't she the one you're going to use?"

"No. She was my mother's real-estate agent, five years ago."

"Wouldn't that make her a good choice?"

"Not necessarily."

"But she knows the house's flaws already, right? Its charms, I mean." He was still smiling.

Ruth finally met his glance squarely. "I wasn't asking her to sell the house. I was trying to ask her if she remembered—about the timing. About why my neighbor sold the house so cheaply."

There were more words, more questions, a few choice expletives. Ruth couldn't remember them now. Her eyes had fixed first on the pulsing vein at Scott's temple, and then on the bike pump in his hands. He was the gentlest of souls, but he looked like he wanted to swing that pump and crack something. He didn't, of course. Scott never let his emotions get out of control. But his words were harsh.

"You decide. Give me one sign, one reason to hope we're not actually wasting each other's time, being civil roommates rather than real partners, building a life."

"You want me to decide between Kennidy and my mom, and you?"

"Kennidy, your mom, Annie Oakley, Hearst, book deadlines, fucking up your meds—"

"Excuse me?"

"—obsessing over past questions, imagined mysteries, projects that will never end. Between filthy boxes and old papers—"

"Between all that and you?"

"Between all that and *us*, Ruth. The past, or the present."

NOW —

11

R U T H

2 0 1 8

Friday

When the kettle whistled, Ruth started and looked down at the spoon, clutched in her fist like a dagger, protecting herself . . . from whom? From what? Only her own disobedient body and mind. She had been so lost in thought that she'd forgotten why she was standing here next to the counter—making tea, ruminating, killing time in hopes that Nieman would see the email and get back to her so she'd have more information to work with.

Ten minutes was what Dr. Susan had prescribed her as a time limit for rumination. But Ruth deserved more than that, considering she'd gone several months barely thinking about the past at all. There was one good thing about that: she'd had no horrible attacks lately.

Ruth leaned against the kitchen counter, sipping her tea as she stared at the calendar on the far wall. All of October, and the only date marked was the minor incident she'd had behind the wheel of her car. But she hadn't seen the worst. She'd remained in control, even retained consciousness. That incident barely counted.

Perhaps it was because she saw Scott so rarely and was otherwise removed from most reminders of their time together. Or maybe it was because her brain was so starved of any stimulation. Surely she could stand the smallest dose now.

When the phone rang, Ruth's heart quickened. She'd included her phone number in the emails to Nieman. At last, they could cut to the chase.

"This is Ruth."

"Hi." Scott cleared his throat. "It's me."

"I know. How are you?"

"Hey, listen. I know I'm not supposed to call you out of the blue, per Dr. Susan's recommendations."

She frowned. "I don't care about that."

Even though a call from Nieman would have promised possible new revelations, she wasn't disappointed. She turned to look at the boxes lined up along one side of the living room. The labels were written in his neat, square script: GRAD SCHOOL FILES.

Another, unlabeled box contained old sweaters. She knew because she had opened it and worn his baggiest, spruce-green sweater around the house, amazed that it still harbored a faint scent of campfire smoke from the last time Scott had worn it. Did he know that she sometimes still lifted his old clothes to her face, searching for any scent that would bring her back to their happier months?

"Hello?"

"I'm here," she said.

"I thought it was time for me to come and pick up my boxes. I'm sorry for leaving them this long."

She could hear the contrition in his voice, the misunderstanding. He assumed she was annoyed.

"It's no trouble. Believe me, my own boxes take up more room than yours do." She was looking at one now, at her feet.

"Are they in the garage?"

"No, living room. The garage is too damp. I moved a few I was worried about. Just some little ones."

"You shouldn't be moving boxes. You shouldn't have to deal with my crap at all. I'm sorry."

"Don't apologize. I know your place is tiny. We agreed on a year. I really don't mind."

"Ruth, it's been a year. Officially, as of a few weeks ago. I actually meant to email you back in September, but the first weeks of school are always crazy. Seeing you there reminded me."

Her heart sank.

"You're a really good teacher, Scott. I always told you that."

"Yes, you did."

"You're a really good *guy*. I wish—"

"Honey." He caught himself. "Ruth. I know. It's all right. About the boxes. I did promise to get them out of your way this fall. I re-signed my lease, and the place hasn't gotten any bigger, but there's no point putting it off. Let me just find a friend with a truck and I'll email you."

"Really, no hurry."

"No, it's gotta get done. Hell, I should toss half that stuff. The past just weighs a person down."

She summoned her courage. "You don't ever have second thoughts?"

He let slip a soft, strangled note of exasperation. "Sometimes I do. And then I remember how every fight ended the same way. They just got louder at the end."

He waited a moment before adding, "I'll be in touch about the boxes. Have a good night. Really."

"Good night."

THE CALL FROM SCOTT HAD left Ruth heavy-chested, like she was coming down with the flu.

If those feelings had overwhelmed her a week ago, she would have resorted to putting on some old movie she'd seen a dozen times, accompanied by too many beers and culminating in a sad late-night stagger off to bed. But she couldn't keep doing that. She had to engage her brain, or she would just keep spiraling downward.

She rallied. On to Vienna.

The Austrian capital was the most untapped lead to follow, a place about which Ruth knew next to nothing. That blankness, at the moment, felt like a relief.

As for early analysts in Vienna, there were indeed more than a handful. The easiest ones to track had belonged to a discussion club run by Freud, and the master himself was easiest to start with, because scholars had done a good job of listing all his analysands—psychoanalysis patients—both the well-known and those who had hidden, for a time at least, behind pseudonyms.

Ruth reviewed over forty and felt confident Freud hadn't been involved with Annie, but even so, she emailed herself dozens of database links to his writings for more leisurely perusal later. *Repression, denial, projection, sublimation.*

Nearly all of Freud's archives had been open for public inspection since 2000. There were still a few restricted items—the strangest, a letter from his mentor Josef Breuer, sealed until 2102. Often, items were sealed for several generations, but waiting 177 years after Breuer's death definitely counted as strange.

It was Breuer, as it turned out, who'd invented the talking cure, not Freud. He was the one who'd counseled Bertha Pappenheim, "Anna O.," and Freud was associated with her only because the two men had co-published the book that included her case, *Studies of Hysteria*, in 1895, more than a dozen years after Bertha had stopped being a patient.

Drilling down into Breuer's life was a little trickier. The Library of Congress had his papers, 425 items in all, mostly correspondence, and included as a subset of the Freud collection. Ruth felt a pang of sympathy for this mentor who was so quickly eclipsed by his protégé. Ruth could find no listing of his analysands, besides the famous Pappenheim, a Jewish woman descended from an old and wealthy Viennese family.

Still, Ruth did locate one felicitous detail: scholars mentioned that Bertha, a polyglot whose "hysteria" often prompted her to jump from one language to another, often insisted on speaking English. Clearly, this presented no problem for Breuer.

The details of poor Bertha's case were disturbing. Her physical and mental distress was severe: paralysis, hallucinations. Breuer's goal was to lead his patient toward a catharsis as she expressed previously repressed emotions. This therapeutic talk, which Bertha herself called "chimney sweeping," proceeded not randomly, but backward, moving from the present day to the source of Bertha's most disturbing images.

There was no guarantee a method like Breuer's would work. But then again, a woman who was desperate and unable to confide safely in the people she knew best might be willing to try anything. Ruth considered this from her seat at the kitchen table, where she'd been writing up her notes for the last hour. As the whole yard within view of the table turned slowly dark and her windows turned into dim mirrors, she felt the presence of possibility.

Ruth wrote an email to Mariette, a researcher friend based in DC who was well versed in the history of psychology, asking for her insights into Breuer's known analysands.

It was time to cook dinner, something Ruth skipped all too often until she found herself suddenly ravenous and gave in to an unsatisfying frozen burrito or can of soup. This time, she resorted to something even more pathetic: a bowl of overly sweet granola. Because she wasn't quite done yet.

All roads seemed to lead to Breuer, especially patient notes referring to lungs, ears and eyes. He'd become an analyst only by chance. Conventional doctoring and physiological research had been his real trade, as Ruth discovered while perusing online

mini-biographies. He'd demonstrated the reflex nature of res-
piration, discovered the function of the semicircular canals and
published twenty papers on physiology, many quite long.

Ruth felt a bubbling-up of gratitude for Nieman. She'd initially
been disappointed by the eighty-some pages of non-Annie material that filled most of the journal, but she should have known
better. Documents, like archaeological artifacts, were most valuable *in situ*.

The granola was gone, leaving speckled milk at the bottom
of her bowl. Still hungry. She shook the granola box—empty—
and contented herself with sipping the milk. She was several
days overdue for a trip to the grocery store, but as long as she
had anything at all in the house—cheese and crackers, a few spotted
apples—she'd keep putting it off. Grocery store aisles had started
seeming long after the accident.

It didn't matter. Food didn't interest her. The manuscript did. If
this journal was a hoax, its maker had definitely planted as many
links to Breuer as one could. Then the best way for Ruth to assist
Nieman was to provide negative evidence: that ZN couldn't be
Annie, the analyst couldn't be Breuer, or both.

1 2

R U T H

Saturday

Ruth didn't remember falling asleep, but she had, with the
laptop on the couch near her feet. She opened her email
and found the best possible morning gift: a message from
Nieman.

Dr. McClintock,

I have good reason for not being able to share everything I
have at this juncture. Forgive me if that seems coy, but I really
have no choice.

Nonetheless, I hope you will be able to help me with the
following.

My questions are:
1. Who is the analyst? Do you have prior knowledge of Annie
   Oakley visiting and corresponding with such a person? I
   find nothing mentioned in the standard biographies.
2. The source provides little information about precisely
   where the papers were originally found, except a street:
   Hassgasse, and evidently from there the papers went to an
   unspecified museum that "did not have room." The source,

whom I know only via a username, has decided to sell them now only because he is cash-strapped. This story seems suspect even in its generalities. Can you posit a provenance and chain of custody?

3. I am preparing to invest to the whole of my means into this project for personal reasons. Do you believe it's possible to help me make this investment decision in just a few days? I am not technologically savvy. My prime collecting days preceded the World Wide Web, and while I've kept up with a few websites here and there, I have no doubt someone your age knows tricks I don't.

It was true. If Nieman were technologically savvy, he would've found Ruth's CV online and seen that she wasn't a "doctor" in any sense; she hadn't completed her PhD. Yes, he needed help, but at least he'd recognized it and made his questions plain.

Ruth was almost ready to write him back, expressing her first hunch about the analyst's identity. But as long as he'd mentioned it, she googled Hassgasse. It meant "Hate Alley." Really? That didn't seem likely to exist.

When Ruth took a break for email, she saw a new message from her grad-school friend. *Thank you, thank you, Mariette.*

Easy question, easy answer, Mariette wrote. **Breuer didn't do analysis after Anna O.**

It was hard to believe that Breuer could have invented the very foundation for modern psychoanalysis and then immediately abandoned it. He was the one who'd made "Anna O" famous. The one who'd mentored Freud, not the other way around.

Ruth replied, **You're sure there wasn't a single analysand after Anna O? Is it possible he simply isn't known for his later cases?**

Mariette was still online. She answered quickly.

I'd say it's common knowledge. My own view is that Breuer regretted his first experience dealing with a psychoanalytic patient.

The case had rattled Breuer, but he would have had time to recover. He met with Anna O.—Bertha Pappenheim—from 1880 to 1882. The first session with Annie or "ZN" had to be later than 1901, and probably no sooner than mid to late 1902, given Annie's recovery time after the train accident. An exact date would help.

Coffee mug in hand, Ruth decided to comb through the non-Annie parts of the journal again. She had been tired during her first reading. She might have missed small clues while straining to decode Breuer's handwriting.

LONG AFTER SHE'D STOPPED CHECKING the clock, fueled by a peanut butter sandwich at midday, some apple slices and cheese at dinner time and a bowl of ice cream hours after that, she came across a barely legible date she'd overlooked in the notes of the medical patient just following Annie.

The twentieth of some month—either a 1 or a 7, meaning either January or July. The patient notes referred to respiratory troubles exacerbated by summer allergies. So it was July, then. And the final numbers in that date—1904—were certain.

Ruth pounded the table with her fist. Then she sat, stunned, realizing she had what she needed: not one kind of negative evidence, but two, and this latter piece was the more concrete.

First of all, Hate Alley in Vienna wasn't a place.

Second, in 1904, Annie was battling William Randolph Hearst in court, busy traveling from trial to trial. This was the very last item Ruth had researched before setting aside her book altogether—the last finding she'd ever tried to share with Scott. It had seemed like a key puzzle piece then; it was even more important now. Ruth had read everything she had in print and digital form about the Hearst trials. She was certain Annie wouldn't have left America at such a sensitive time or chosen that year to confide weakness to anyone.

Ruth allowed herself a peek at the clock: 1 A.M. For one amazing, distraction-free day, she had almost begun to believe something incredible, perhaps even disturbing and wonderful. She'd swum far from shore to a place her feet could no longer reach, and luckily, she had turned around just before it was too late.

Ruth went into the bathroom and washed her face, feeling jumpy, nerves jangling. She wasn't going to fall asleep soon, meaning she wouldn't wake up early either. Better to write the email now, so that Nieman, several hours ahead of her, could read it first thing, and she could sleep in, without guilt or distraction.

She decided to be blunt.

The email began:

Mr. Nieman,

To answer your last question first, you can save your money.

After which she explained each reason for her doubts.

RUTH WENT TO BED FEELING triumphant, like she'd closed a book on two years of professional and personal failure, defeating the loudest of her demons. She could be the old Ruth again: skeptical, unsentimental, not prone to hyperassociation, wishful thinking or any more serious delusions.

Hate Alley? *Really.*

She was once again the person Scott might have married, had she not screwed that up completely. He had seen her at her worst, fueled by book-deadline anxieties, then made paranoid by her family's own confusing history, then temporarily insane—also cranky and fat—by her car accident. If only he could see her now, able to come to a quick, logical conclusion, able to set a fruitless project aside, he would know she was back to her earlier, healthier self.

She fell asleep, mind on that confusing, futile desire: to go back to a simpler time, even if it meant she'd never received the hoax journal in the first place.

And then, nine hours later, she woke with a start.

I could be wrong.

I could be overcorrecting.

Ruth had no logical reason for thinking she'd made a mistake. It was only a feeling.

I missed my chance.

And not just that.

Something bad is going to happen.

1 3

CALEB

Sunday

Caleb knew where Vorst lived because they'd stopped there once—an old house in town, stuck between an even more decrepit A-frame and some woods, near the school. Vorst ran in—"You sit tight," with a wink that made Caleb uncomfortable—to grab two six-packs and an electric heater for his weekend place outside town. That cabin, at the end of a long gravel road surrounded by hayfields, was always cold.

Luckily for Caleb and unluckily for the asshole, he had slipped up that one time. Now, the old guy's house, with its trim lawn and its stupid bird feeders, was a magnet. Caleb rode past on his bike, hat pulled low and hoody cinched tight, peddling fast, hardly able to think past the pounding heat in his head, trying to picture exactly what he would do.

He'd daydreamed an elaborate kidnapping and torture scene, the kind of thing you saw in movies, but that would require getting physically close, which was the last thing Caleb wanted. It would also require help—a vehicle, friends or at least one trustworthy sidekick, none of which he had. Caleb hadn't told anyone about Vorst, and couldn't bear to, not even the smallest admissions, like when Reece asked if he'd gotten a ride from the retired coach the other day.

Caleb had lied without thinking. He'd even told Reece that he'd keyed Vorst's car. That was stupid. What he'd meant in his own fucked-up head was that he was *thinking* of keying the car. He was always like that, thinking instead of doing, and even his thoughts never made sense.

So much of it was his fault, and now this was, too: having no one to help. No backup, no sidekick, no ideas, only too much time to pedal around, waiting for someone else to solve the fucking problem for him. Well, it wasn't going to happen. He passed the coach's house, did a sharp U-turn, put in headphones and rode by again.

Caleb was so lost in thought staring at the tan house as he approached a fourth time that he didn't notice the pickup truck barreling toward him. The truck swerved to the other side of the road to avoid him; Caleb corrected his course and returned to his own side and went even farther, up and over the curb onto the grass of a neighbor's yard, almost crashing, foot out to catch himself and then back on the pedal, bike still upright. Still pedaling.

It was all over in an instant, but Caleb was covered in sweat, his heart thumping a million beats per minute. He kept going, mouth open, stupid look on his face. A few minutes later, another car passed. Was that Mr. Webb, his math teacher?

It would not be good to be seen in this neighborhood by anyone, but especially by Mr. Webb, who always had that soft, good-guy look on his face. That could be harder to take than the teachers who never looked at you at all. He always asked too many questions. *How are you holding up? Getting into a groove this semester?*

Caleb had no plan, only a feeling inside him that kept building every time he saw Vorst at school, every time he remembered last spring, every time he remembered last week in Vorst's car.

He'd spent all summer pushing the spring semester out of his head. He was good at that, convincing himself that certain things had never happened, that he wasn't the kind of person who would have done any of that.

As long as no one ever found out, as long as there weren't reminders or consequences, he could go days without thinking about it at all. Hell, think of all the things guys managed to forget about, from breakups to war. His stepdad sure didn't seem to remember much about his Afghanistan tours.

Then last week, Caleb had seen Vorst standing next to Mikayla at tumbling practice with his arm around her. From across the gym, Caleb froze. He watched Vorst's hand, patting her shoulder, pulling her closer. He knew that hand. He knew that sideways hug. He knew the look on Mikayla's face, too: uncertainty, yielding to toleration, maybe even some kind of awkward gratitude.

It was an out-of-body experience.

She's next.

Mikayla had gone with Caleb to the spring dance and confessed only at the end, after they'd both spent a pathetic night barely dancing or even talking, that she hadn't really wanted to go. Not with him or anyone. She'd just been too shy and nervous to say no. The fact that Caleb might have done the same thing in her position didn't make it any less humiliating.

She'd said, "Don't hate me."

He'd said, "Of course I don't hate you."

In the school gym, when he first spotted Vorst sidling up to her, he should have done something. He could *still* do something.

But only in his imagination, evidently. Just last week, when Vorst—with whom he hadn't talked in months—offered him a ride, Caleb accepted, thinking it would be a chance to say something that would give the old pervert a reason to worry.

Caleb kept waiting for the right moment, trying to untangle the words in his head and prepare his voice so it wouldn't crack or tremble. He leaned hard against the passenger door until Vorst pulled onto his street. When the car came to a stop at the curb, Vorst reached out and set his hand on Caleb's thigh. That was all it took. Caleb tensed but couldn't move, paralyzed.

"You know what people will think if you say anything," Vorst said, as if the coach could read Caleb's thoughts.

Caleb reached for the door handle.

"First, they'll think you're a liar," Vorst said. "Second, they'll think you're a fag."

Caleb pushed the door open. Without looking back, he heard Vorst call out, "Have a great weekend."

CALEB KEPT RIDING, DOWN ANOTHER road past a trailer park and beyond, to the farthest edge of the woods, where only homeless campers and the most desperate weekend partyers hung out. He dropped his bike and sat next to the remains of an old campfire littered with beer bottles. He pulled off his backpack and extracted the stuff he'd been holding on to since May.

Months earlier, he'd burned most of the photos he'd lifted from Vorst's cabin during his final visit. He'd thought they'd be useful as evidence or blackmail. But then he'd taken them out in the privacy of his bedroom and looked at them, feeling sick, and realized his plans wouldn't work. Vorst wasn't in the photos. There was no proof of where they'd come from. The first time Caleb felt any measure of relief was when the corner of that first photo had turned black and orange, curling as it flamed. One by one he'd burned them, releasing the shame and the evil, leaving nothing but black-gray wisps.

Caleb wasn't a natural blackmailer or even a quality witness. He wanted the past eliminated. He wanted no one to see the kids in those poses. He wanted to help those spirits be free.

But there was one photo he couldn't burn: the one of the

skinny girl sitting on the brown couch in jean shorts and a halter top. Her eyes looked like the barely dressed and fully naked kids' glassy eyes, and she was pretending to smile. All the other kid photos were all mixed up, but there was an entire separate shoebox of stuff that had belonged to this teenage girl.

Vorst had mentioned a daughter who had died the same year he'd retired. *Drug overdose. Don't ever mess with that stuff, Caleb.* That was a joke, considering Vorst's love of pills and liquor.

Vorst talked about her enough to make Caleb feel uncomfortable, because he kept going on about how they were the same. Sometimes it was positive. *She loved soccer, too. And 10Ks, working her way to a not-bad half marathon. That girl could run.* Later it would turn negative. *She wouldn't listen, either. Wasted every opportunity I gave her.* But there was one thing he said about her and never about Caleb: *She was getting fat, though. Can't do cross country if you're fat.*

The girl in the photo was definitely not fat. She had the twiggy legs that all serious school runners had, and a chest that was nearly flat, two small bumps that barely wrinkled the striped cloth of her halter top. With the pictures of young girls who were nude, Caleb did his best to look away, but since she was dressed, he let himself look.

This girl had a different last name according to the papers in the box, but that didn't mean she couldn't be the coach's daughter. Did the girl know what her father did for fun? Caleb hoped not. That would be truly fucked up. Maybe it was better she'd died.

He looked at the photo one more time.

He opened the skinny notebook of hers that he'd taken, so full of her messy cursive and doodles that he didn't even know where to start. Folded inside were five or six printouts. One was a list of scholarships to apply for. Another was a short college application essay, barely a page, on "the person I most admire." Man, the cheesy shit they made you do. But he read her essay in full because he'd sat on the same couch with the same dead smile pasted on his face, and he felt he knew her.

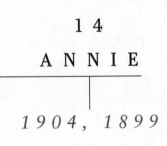

14

ANNIE

1 9 0 4 , 1 8 9 9

Write *everything down,* Herr Breuer said at the end, bidding farewell after their short meeting in Vienna. *Your dreams, your memories, any apparition or fancy.* That's how they would continue the "cure" they had started, according to the doctor.

He hadn't been easy to find based on Giselle's description: respected older Jewish physician. Even Giselle's report of a newspaper photograph she'd seen—dark, curling beard; high, balding pate; dark, kind eyes—failed to bring the target any closer. Half the men in Vienna's coffeehouses matched that description! But then Annie remembered something else Giselle had said. The sympathetic doctor was also an ear, nose and throat expert. She inquired at a local health clinic and by early afternoon held the correct private address in her hands.

Just two hours later, Annie walked out of the good doctor's office and down the streets of Leopoldstadt, toward the Danube, feeling exposed, jittery, tired—and free. She hadn't told him everything, but he had given her permission.

It's only by reliving the past that we are relieved of it. She must not forget.

Now, weeks later, she is in America. Life is tranquil at first, but only until she returns to the trial schedule, spending too much time in courthouses, train cars and hotels.

One night, alone in the Midwest, she resolves to obey her doctor's instructions and strike up their correspondence. On a piece of hotel stationery, she describes a frustrating experience on a New York subway car. She sets the letter aside.

She begins again, describing the recurring dream, in which the Wolf comes after her: through the Darke County Infirmary, into town, and from there into the woods.

This is probably the sort of letter Herr Breuer wants, and because he wants it, and because she knows it is a trifle—not the important thing, not the *real* thing—she doesn't send it right away. The letters, undated, have begun to accumulate. Is she even writing for him, or only for herself? Both, she decides.

The good doctor has said that she doesn't need to stop what she's doing. He must know about the mind's mysteries. When she is brave enough to be candid, he will know even more.

But first, she must understand herself: What are the boundaries of the possible? There is only one way to tell, the way she has done everything that ever mattered—by practicing. By working toward ever farther targets. Alone.

SHE SLOWS HER HEART. SHE knows that picturing the white light and falling feathers returned her to the toppling train, but she hasn't yet connected the right colors, images or sensations to other places she feels she must visit. One night that resembles all the others—yet another dinner of beef and tepid mashed potatoes served to her under a silver dome in another hotel room on a main street within walking distance to another courthouse—Annie closes her eyes and stops trying so hard to understand. Instead, she simply goes where she is taken.

She smells fresh earth and spring buds. She feels the soft picnic blanket under her hand, the warm earth under her outstretched legs. She hears the voices of her friends Emily and Lillian—not as close perhaps as female friends should be, but she is grateful for their company. They offer her a sandwich.

"Yes, please, Lillian," she says, dry lips parting.

Lillian answers with delight: "Our lady speaks! We thought you might be nodding off again. Was the walk too long?"

Emily adds, "We were just talking about the dreaded milestone: turning forty. You're the youngest—more than a year to go, isn't that right?"

Eyes still closed, Annie allows the sensation of her body to grow and sharpen, blood flowing, nerves awakening. Even though it's 1899—of this she has no doubt—she can still feel a bit of her older, hurting body within this younger, healthier sack of self she is temporarily inhabiting. She is aging herself prematurely by traveling to the past. Her hip registers in firm detail the contours of the hard ground. When she inhales deeply, her lungs ache. She has never skipped backward so far or felt so many physical sensations so clearly.

Opening her eyes, Annie looks at her friends, with whom she has shared many jokes about the way they're all aging. Emily likes to complain about her round stomach and wide rump; Lillian, about her turkey neck and the feathery lines forming above her thin upper lip. They're blind to their own beauty: the sparkle in their eyes, the blush in their rosy skin—and she was blind to it, too. But now that she's begun to experiment with time's slippery properties, mortality seems more real, just around the corner for everyone you know and maybe you as well, should you accidentally skip too far.

"Annie," says Lillian, seeing her friend's eyes well up. "What's wrong?"

"Nothing. The walk was splendid. I could go twice as far."

They finish their tea, pack and walk up a grassy hill in search of a hidden century-old burial ground.

"Do you think," Annie asks her friends, "that the tribes of this area thought much about revenge?"

Lillian says, "Against whom?"

"Against us, of course."

"For what?"

"For stealing their land."

Did Annie just say "stealing"? Other times, she has said "taking," or simply "settling."

What does that mean, *other times*? She had the impression earlier that this vivid, embodied visit was a first, but perhaps it isn't. Another thing she must keep in mind: her progress is neither predictable nor linear.

Lillian laughs with inspired delight. "But ladies, the Indians did have their revenge on white men." She pauses before delivering the punch line. "Tobacco!"

The hill is steep, but Annie plants her next steps squarely, enjoying the brisk, fresh air, which never fails to infuse her with optimism. Being with Lillian and Emily reminds her of all the times they've discussed the plight of women and how best to change the world. Emily favors getting the vote. Lillian prefers quiet philanthropy. Annie herself has found pleasure in teaching women to shoot, for self-protection and to instill a confidence that might spur excellence in all things. But what if she did it on a bigger scale? What if she taught not just a few girls and ladies here and there, but thousands? Maybe that's the best way to banish this bitter melancholy, the midnight sickness that strikes without warning. Think of what other women do: go on marches, break the law, starve themselves. Maybe it just takes a cause and a focus on the future to obliterate the poisonous past.

But these are not the thoughts of later Annie, revisiting this place. She is losing herself in this picnic-day Annie, *becoming* her, the line blurring between herself now and herself then, the double-exposure that Annie has seen in falsified photographs, including ones meant to make people believe in ghosts.

Is she a ghost? No. But she does believe in them.

They follow a line of trees past a copse, pausing at the edge of a field. Emily thumbs a booklet purchased from the Buckeye Paranormal Society about local ghosts and graveyards. There is supposed to be a stone wall and some kind of marker.

Lagging behind, Annie says, "Tobacco aside, it's hard to imagine Indians not wanting revenge." She feels satisfaction in the very shape of the word, the first syllable preparing the top teeth to graze the bottom lip, the second drawn out, as score-settling often is.

They've crested another hill and are just about to turn back when Emily spies in the distance, at the bottom of the grassy slope ahead, a pyramid-shaped pile of stones.

"There is a strong spirit there," Emily says. "A century has done nothing to diminish the pain."

"It will be *our* pain walking all the way back up this hill," Lillian complains.

But Annie feels it too as they walk down: the pull toward the bottom, toward the stones.

"She's waiting for us," Emily says.

Lillian's eyebrows lift. "Now you're giving me the shivers."

"*She?*" Annie asks. "Not a whole tribe?"

"Just one woman."

"We've come this far," Annie says. "Let's finish it."

At the bottom, they nervously sidle up to the stones, but the silent rocks tell them nothing. Emily pulls out her paranormal tourism guide and begins to narrate. An Indian girl was buried here, captured by white settlers.

"Kept as a slave, for the purpose of the white man's pleasure. Poor girl. Probably wished they had shot her instead." Emily closes the booklet and stares at the rocks. "Well, that's one way to injure a soul. And what more is a ghost than a permanently injured soul?"

Annie hears Lillian's response as if it were muffled, coming to her through a long tube. She crumples, hand over her chest.

Lillian crouches at her side. "Is it your heart?"

The pictures come all too quickly, too clearly. One woman, an entire fort of men. The futile call for mercy, the responding laughter, the physical degradation, slim legs kicking as they drag her along the inner stockade path, first by her wrists, then by her hair. This young woman, hardly older than a child, huddled in a corner of a dark room, the smell of whiskey pervading, more men entering to watch.

"I can see her," Annie says.

She remembers her own experience inside the cabin—and worse, inside the woodshed—with the Wolf. The suffering remains undiluted. Pain and trauma make time leap in certain places and stick in others.

Annie thinks: *A future of teaching women to shoot—yes, it's worth doing. But it isn't enough.*

Annie knew how to shoot when she was a child. It didn't stop the Wolf from taking advantage of her. Neither did it stop her, at times, from blaming herself for not having escaped his clutches sooner.

"Poor girl," Annie says, but she is no longer talking only of the Indian captive.

She had a gun all those years ago, but she didn't use it. To purposefully injure another person was beyond the capabilities of her docile child's mind. But she is a child no longer.

1 5

R U T H

An old pickup truck rattled down the street. Ruth had already seen it go by twice.

Ruth was expecting visits from both her home inspector and her real-estate agent—a welcome distraction from checking email, as she'd done obsessively all morning. Though she'd followed up last night's email with several new ones, telling Nieman she'd been too hasty in dismissing the journal's value, it was too late.

His first reply was terse. **Return journal asap. I will compensate you for the postage. Thank you for your effort.**

She tried one more time, emphasizing the desire to talk by phone.

He replied: **Your job is done, and I have no doubt your initial evaluation was correct. I believe in following one's instinct. You've followed yours.**

But I didn't, not really! She'd only followed the most conservative, limiting possibility out of fear.

At the sound of the pickup slowing in front of the house yet again, Ruth put on tennis shoes and a light jacket and went outside. The driver stopped. Ruth saw only a mop of strawberry blonde hair until the woman brought her face closer to the window.

"Is this Pine Street? I couldn't find a street sign."

"Yeah. You lost?"

"I'm helping a friend move. You're not Ruth, are you?"

The word didn't register for a second. "Move?"

"Well, just a couple boxes. For Scott—Scott Webb. I have a truck, so . . ." She paused to open her door, clambered down and came around the front of the pickup, hand extended. "I'm sorry. Margot."

"You teach with Scott?"

She tilted her head. "No."

They both turned toward the sound of the advancing car. Margot's face, which had been pleasant and pretty even while forcing an awkward half smile, turned radiant at the familiar sight of Scott, swerving fast into the spot behind Margot's bumper. She dropped Ruth's hand and trotted over to meet him just as he was shutting his car door.

Together, they walked to the edge of Ruth's yard, where Scott hurried through introductions. "Margot, Ruth. Ruth, Margot."

"We met," Ruth said, forcing a smile. "She has a pickup."

"Yes! She has a pickup. I could have done it in a couple trips. But then there are my extra tools, the skis . . ."

"Always more than you think," Margot said.

"That's true," Ruth said.

Ruth showed them inside, trying to keep her attention focused on Scott instead of Margot, but she couldn't help it. She noted the crisp white blouse beneath the barn coat: stylish. She noted a cross pendant dangling at Margot's neck. Scott was agnostic. She noted the manicured, painted nails: Scott had confessed that long nails didn't appeal to him. Too dragon-ladyish. But then again, those were the things men said when they talked with women and didn't admit that a cute ass and a pretty face could make up for a number of mild fashion disagreements, and even some religious ones.

But Ruth wasn't going to ask. Anytime she caught Scott's eye, she could see his inward wince. He'd meant to show up first and explain.

Margot glanced around the cluttered margins of Ruth's living room and box-lined hallway to the seventies-era bathroom. "You are going to be *so* glad to have this stuff out of here."

"Yeah, well," was all Ruth could manage.

When they were in the garage, Scott remembered. "The old television."

"It's worthless. I need to drop it at the recycling place."

"I think there's a fee."

"You don't have to do it."

"It's heavy, Ruth. I'll take care of it."

Margot leaned in. "Isn't there a service that will pick it up for you?"

Thankfully, Margot waited in the pickup truck when Scott did his final load.

He had the wide-screen television in his arms when Ruth spotted another small box with Scott's initials on the side.

"I guess there's always gonna be one more thing." Ruth picked it up and heard the contents shift. "Oh."

Rifle already at his apartment. He had a revolver in a lockbox, too—somewhere. This was the extra ammunition.

Ruth leaned against the inner wall of the garage, feeling a ping in her bad hip and an answering tightness in her chest.

Scott set the television at his feet. "You okay?"

"I can't believe this. It seems like yesterday we were moving your stuff in."

"Same time of year."

"How did this happen?"

"Ruth," Scott whispered back. "It wasn't my choice."

She made an effort to stand up straight and blink her vision clear. "I'm putting the house up for sale again."

"Good. It's a lotta work, I know."

"How are your parents?"

"Dad's more or less the same. We have him in a facility, finally."

"And your mom?"

"Adjusting. She doesn't want to admit her life is easier now. Makes her feel guilty, and guilt's not healthy."

"So, what do you say to her?"

"That life throws us challenges. And that she shouldn't feel bad about thriving just because Dad can't."

They continued to take a moment in the damp, dark space, each glancing toward the open garage door to make sure Margot wasn't within earshot.

"I'm sorry, Ruth. For today."

"Guilt isn't healthy, right?"

Scott shook his head. "Feeling guilty and feeling sorry aren't the same thing. I haven't done anything wrong. But I'm still sorry that you're alone."

Ruth felt a knot in her throat. "You got a haircut." She knew he would hear the tremble in her voice, but she had to say something. "It looks good. And new glasses, finally."

"Just this morning, in fact," he said, sliding them down his nose and back up again.

Ruth couldn't help but ask. "Is it serious?"

"She'd like it to be." He started to say more, then checked himself. "I didn't mean for this to be so awkward. I should've emailed you this morning, as soon as I realized I had Margot and her truck to help out, but I didn't think you'd check email on a Sunday."

Was he kidding? That was about all she did nowadays.

"It's okay," she said.

"You're sure?"

"Of course I'm sure."

FOLLOWING SCOTT'S DEPARTURE, RUTH FELT the sharp claw-ends of depression pressing at her skull. She couldn't let them dig in. It was only 11 A.M., the entire day yawning before her. It would be too easy to spend the entire day revisiting every memory of her relationship with Scott, every mistake and wrong turn.

Ruth wanted to know how Nieman had found her. She wrote a quick email to her most sympathetic contact at one of the two major Annie Oakley foundations—an older woman named Sophie who was a distant cousin of Annie. Ruth asked if she or another foundation board member, Lila—the closest living Annie Oakley descendant, now in her nineties—might have shared Ruth's contact info.

Then, just for good measure, even though it was a long shot, Ruth phoned her old friend Joe. No answer. She left a message. The truth was, she really just wanted to hear a friendly voice.

She remembered her first date with Joe: the first of two good men in a row she'd walked away from. At least she didn't attract the bad ones.

They'd met at a history-department mixer. She'd asked a question about his heritage. He offered to show her. The next Friday, he picked her up at the edge of campus and they walked five blocks to a bar called McDougal's. They went inside, ordered beer, played darts, swapped stories about dissertation advisers. At first, she'd thought he was a little big, a little sloppy, but he kept making her laugh—even when he disagreed with her about some historical or political point—and with every laugh, she saw him differently. His bulk became comforting. His chipped incisor was charming. The mischievous way he narrowed his eyes made her melt. Only at the end, when they were making out against the brick wall near the entrance to her apartment building, did she take a breath and remember to ask. "Your heritage? What was that about?"

"I'm half Irish."

"Oh, come on." She punched him on the shoulder. "But what about the other half?"

"Sorry, that part's not dating at the moment."

She didn't understand then, but she got it later. He was sick of all the grad-school women who pursued him for his "exotic" qualities. He refused to be anyone's guide or guru, and he was certainly no suffering silent type—though he did, on occasion, smoke a peace pipe. So as far as he was concerned that year, he was Irish. Take it or leave it.

Well, on her mother's side, Ruth was Irish, too.

Now, standing in Gwen's old kitchen, Ruth reheated a half cup of coffee while staring at the scratches on the cupboards and the peeling edge of laminate on the cheap countertop. This house wouldn't be easy to sell.

"Okay," she said, slugging back the acidic coffee, the mess of her romantic past still tugging at her, but not as strongly as the physical mess she couldn't ignore. "Back to it."

Ruth gave herself a deadline: all boxes out of the living room by 2 P.M. The bedroom closet was already overstuffed. There were only two places to put them: garage or basement. Easy choice.

Moving boxes slowly wasn't like actively puzzling over history. Instead of occupying her mind, it freed it to wander, and not in a pleasant way.

Why had she written such a definitive email to Nieman? Why hadn't she waited? But she knew why. Because the uncertainty in her brain had felt like a cold draft. She'd wanted to slam shut one of the only doors she could.

IT WASN'T EVEN LUNCHTIME, BUT Ruth wiped her dirty hands on her jeans, entered the house, grabbed a bottle of beer and drew herself a bath.

Toes up on the edge of the old tub, beer bottle precariously balanced atop a metal soap dish, she stared down the length of her legs just under the water's surface. She noted the untrimmed nails and stubble, the fish-belly-white curve of her calves and that one long, jagged scar up her left knee and thigh. At least it was visible. She could point and say, "It hurts there, for obvious reasons."

Not so with the aching places in her heart.

You decide. Between all that and us, Ruth. The past or the present.

Ruth felt her foot, balanced on the far lip of the tub, suddenly jerk. As if in slow motion, she saw it bump the metal soap dish. The beer bottle, only half full, tipped over and fell with a rich *sploosh* into the bath.

Surprised, she half-grunted, half-laughed. At least the beer hadn't spilled onto the floor. The brown bottle was still sinking and settling, nudging her calf. But then her leg jerked again, hard.

Not good. Not right.

You can't go forward without going back.

She tried to calm down and breathe, focusing on the cooling sensation of the air coming in through her nostrils, the gentle swell of her belly as the breath made its way through her body, bringing love and calm and kindness.

It didn't help. Her leg jerked a third time, as if an electrical current had traveled through it.

It hadn't happened for months. But it was happening again now. Her teeth clamped. Her arms tensed. She knew what would come next.

Every time, her vision fuzzed and her ears rang. Intense fear flooded her. Her blood pressure plummeted. From the outside it looked like a panic attack, but it wasn't. Panic attacks weren't usually based on a real threat. Her attacks were more like shock, the response to something real.

They were always the same, varying only by degree, but Ruth had never had an attack in the bathtub. As her fingers grasped uselessly at the tub's slippery edge, Ruth's rear end slid forward and her feet rose higher, her shoulders and neck now submerged and her lips sputtering. The bathwater itself seemed to fizz and pop as her vision darkened at the edges.

Grab the tub.

How long could you last under water without drowning? She'd never lost consciousness completely, but she'd lost the ability to control her limbs beyond a stiff-armed flail. She'd slid off a couch once and another time fallen to her knees. But this time, she knew she was in danger. No one would find her. No one would haul her out and pump her lungs.

Grab the tub.

Ruth knew the image of Scott was coming and that when she saw it, her body would shut down. Her fear of water brought it on even faster: *No, no, no. Don't let the car drop.* And then, as before, Scott.

He was in front of her. But this time, he looked different. He stood calmly with his hands on his waist, shirt cuffs rolled up, feet planted on short clipped grass with white lines—a sports field. He was staring off into the distance, peering through—she noticed only now—new glasses, the square-lensed ones she'd just seen this morning. She'd never noticed that detail in the vision before.

Then he squinted, starting to look worried. He lifted both his arms and waved them in the air, signaling to someone to either look his way or to stop. The vision had begun only seconds earlier, but now it would proceed as it always did, toward the end she didn't want to witness.

"Don't fight it," Dr. Susan had told her.

But she had to fight it. She knew it was her responsibility to understand, to keep watching. But she couldn't bear it. In that moment, when she thought her own life might end, Ruth couldn't think of a single time when she'd sacrificed herself for anyone.

If she loved him, she would see more, she would bear more. This had always been the test. She had failed and would fail again, because she was selfish.

Ruth felt water enter her nose and she choked, coughing, hands scrambling again for the rounded tub edge. She fought for air. She didn't want to see, but her inner eye remained open a moment longer. She saw his confused expression. His lips mouthing words that she couldn't make out. His chin tucked into his chest as the impact sent his whole trunk backward and the color spread. Red.

She managed to squirm and roll to one side, knee pushing, shoulder against the tub bottom, left side of her body above the water surface, only her right ear submerged now as she took panicked, gasping breaths, alternating with coughs. She wouldn't drown. She had air enough to breathe, air enough to scream.

"No!" she finally managed to shout.

Then he—it, that future day—was gone.

RUTH STARTED TO LEAVE THE bathroom—wet towels strewn everywhere, stripped-off jeans and sweatshirt left in a sopping pile on the floor—but then went back, riffling through her apothecary drawers for anything that would take the edge off. No luck, only the expired bottle of clozapine, taunting her. It wasn't what she needed anyway.

I'm not psychotic.

She didn't think she was suffering post-traumatic stress disorder, either. *Pre-traumatic* stress disorder, maybe. That was how it felt.

She got an ice pack and curled up on her couch, where she slept two hours and woke up feeling like Robinson Crusoe washed up on a beach, face planted hard against the sand, half-drowned.

Ruth looked at her phone: nothing from Scott, Joe or Sophie. Instead, sixteen new texts from Reece, who didn't know the whole research project was over. She'd already told Nieman the journal was fake. She'd send it back by way of express mail first thing tomorrow.

Reece's last message: **Any news?**

So I've made a mistake. Possibly.

With the journal?

With everything.

I'm a good listener.

It's a long story.

My barista shift doesn't start until 4.

I have a home inspector coming over.

That takes?

Two hours maybe. She paused. I just have to let him in. I don't have to stay.

Meet up at the north entrance to Rovers Run.

That was the wooded path popular with dog walkers, beyond the school's sport fields.

She was about to say it was too far; her knee and hip already hurt from all the moving of boxes she had done, plus the thrashing in the tub.

But Reece didn't even wait for her reply.

Text me when you're there.

1 6

REECE

"You can't just leave without answering me," Reece's mom said as he yanked a jacket from the hook near the front door. She'd followed him into the hallway, still holding her cell phone, ready to call the therapist's office and set their first family appointment since his "attempt."

"I'll think about it," Reece said.

"That's what you've been saying for a month."

"I'm busy."

"Not too busy for your hobbies."

Hobbies? Was that what she thought his upcoming show was, a hobby? If she'd ever paid attention, she'd have realized it was the only thing that kept him moderately sane.

"Fine. Don't come to the Rockets show, if that's what you're getting at. Skip it."

"I didn't say we wouldn't come," she said, following him onto the porch. "And Reece, this isn't a zero-sum game. We're on your team. You know that, right?"

"I know what's best for me," he said, without looking back.

He didn't ask to borrow the car. The place he planned to meet Ruth wasn't far to walk, and he didn't want to owe his parents anything.

Talking wasn't always the best idea, his mother should realize. If he opened his mouth at a family session, he was bound to say what he thought, which was: it *was* their fault, actually. Not their fault he'd cut himself—you could never blame that final step on anyone but your own fucked-up self—but their fault that he'd gotten so depressed. Last spring, they'd sabotaged him. To get into the senior-year performing-arts program, he had to audition. New Hampshire: yes, it was far, the timing was lousy and money was tight. But they could have taken him or let him go alone. Instead, they'd talked him into option B, the video audition.

The official program instructions said that video and live auditions were weighted equally. The unofficial chat groups run by prospective and admitted students told a different story.

He replayed his last argument with his father.

"How do you know?"

"Because I looked it up."

"The application instructions don't say there's a problem with video."

"Dad. I'm not a moron. Why don't you ever believe me?"

"Show me where it says you're penalized for sending in a video."

"You have to read between the lines. No one ever comes out and says you can't get in with video. They say you have to make an *impression*. You have to prove to them it's worth paying to fly or taking a crappy bus all night because you really want to go to their school. You have to give a shit."

"We're just worried you're putting all your eggs in one basket."

That was the heart of the matter. They'd never thought he might get in, but they *said* they didn't think he could afford to waste a week of school, especially so close to midterms. Besides, they were too cheap, and on top of that, they were ridiculously, maddeningly allergic to any kind of risk.

Well, now they'd gotten a glimpse of how risky hopelessness could be . . .

Reece had gotten so worked up, striding fast while replaying the argument in his mind, that he arrived at Rovers Run five minutes early. When he saw Ruth walking slowly up the trail, he felt his whole body relax, yearning to hear something that would take his mind off this shit town of people with no imagination.

Don't disappoint me, he thought.

"SHE THOUGHT SHE COULD SKIP or slide forward, like a stone across the pond," Ruth told him. "The trauma of the train crash exaggerated something she'd already experienced. And her fury at the events in her past made her determined to control it."

They were on the trail, not entirely alone, with strollers behind them and dog walkers ahead, out enjoying the brisk air and the bright-yellow blaze of aspen trees interspersed with the trail's dark evergreens.

"This is good news. So why do you look worried?" Reece responded.

"Because I wrote Nieman last night and told him the journal was probably a fake. I didn't think Annie would risk going to Europe in 1904."

Reece waited for Ruth to say more, but she had the expression you saw on kids' faces when they walked out of a test knowing they'd bombed it.

Reece took a deep breath. It was time. "There's something else we need to discuss. I had a weird dream this summer."

Ruth acted like she hadn't heard him.

"You were in the dream," he said, "talking to me. You told me to draw the infinity symbol on your arm. It felt like a premonition."

"Wait. How could you have known then it was a premonition?"

"I'm not sure. Obviously, I'd never met you before, but you were there."

"Why didn't you tell me?"

"Oh, you mean when you didn't even want to give me your phone number? That's when I should have expected you to believe in my dream?"

When she paused, Reece assumed she was about to apologize. Instead she said, "I have visions, too. They started two years ago. The most recent one"—she looked at her watch—"was two and a half hours ago."

Then she told him about the ordeal in the bathtub, just around lunchtime. And about the car crash, when the visions of Mr. Webb had started. That part was definitely news.

"Wow," Reece said. "You almost drowned today. You weren't going to mention that first? Or the premonition, either?"

"I was updating you on the Annie research."

"But maybe your violent vision of the near future matters more."

"They're separate issues," she said, brow furrowed. "I think."

"Okay, great. I'm glad you're keeping everything neat and tidy. Do you separate all the foods on your plate, too?"

A golden retriever bounded over to them, friendly and slobbering. Ruth knelt down and let him push his furry head into her chest. When the owner called the dog away, she remained in the crouch, one knee down on the muddy trail. Reece realized he was supposed to do something. He hurried to her and grabbed her elbow to help her stand.

"Are you wearing pajama pants?"

"They're the only dry pants I had left due to the . . . bathtub incident. Or at least, they were." Her knees were soaked through. She groaned as he helped lift her to an upright position.

"Maybe you need to try harder in order to see the whole vision clearly," Reece said. "I don't know. Relax?"

"I take tranquilizers sometimes. But I haven't lately. I haven't taken any prescription meds for a while."

He became uncomfortable as he watched her expression change. She'd noticed her Xanax was missing. But one confession was enough for today.

She rubbed her eyes. "As I've started to see more of it, it feels like I'm dying. My body shuts down."

"But maybe only because you're fighting it."

"Reece, did you hear what I said? It feels like *I'm dying*."

This was his chance, the perfect segue. "Okay, but I was telling you about my dream, remember? I was at Rockets practice with seven teammates. We were all in our purple shirts."

How could he explain? That image of those seven people couldn't have existed back when he'd had the dream in June, but it had become real. He had *made* it real.

"Go on," she said.

"It was a good dream at first. Then it got confusing."

Ruth pulled her phone out of her vest pocket. "Sorry, it's the home inspector. I've got to answer this."

Even the paranormal couldn't compete with a text, evidently. Probably his fault for being so mush-mouthed.

When she'd finished texting, she asked, "In your dream, did you see . . . Mr. Webb?"

"No, but you were there trying to tell me something. To write the symbol on you. And some less clear directions, like 'talk to me' and 'keep trying' and 'be patient with me.' You said, 'It didn't work.'"

"What didn't work?"

"I don't know."

"Think, Reece."

" 'Don't smoke.' "

"Don't smoke?"

"You're upset when you say it . . . or maybe you're laughing?

One of those stressed-out panic laughs. Look, I can't explain everything, this isn't like some movie premonition: 'Go back in time and buy AT&T at twenty-eight dollars.'"

She didn't smile.

"And?"

"I can't hear or see all of it. Sometimes when I'm calm and focused, I try to replay it in my head, hoping I'll remember more. Maybe if I weren't on so many meds, I'd dream it again. They say you get a strong rebound effect that triggers dreams when you go off."

"Meds?" she asked.

"Antidepressants."

She nodded. Maybe she was still remembering that zinc comment he'd made. Or maybe she *had* noticed the missing Xanax.

"They work well for you?"

"Too early to tell. Anyway, the dream was a one-time thing. Like an NDE, near-death experience. Maybe that's what you and Annie had, too."

"Mine wasn't a near-death experience," Ruth said. "Those are supposed to be peaceful. Mine was terrifying."

"Mine *was* peaceful—but only at first. I wanted to see it, to go toward it, like Annie wanted to get out of that train at the moment of collision. But I couldn't make sense of it, because I didn't know the people yet, or the situation."

"But you just called it a near-death experience."

"Yes."

"That implies you were *near death*, or you thought you were."

"Yes. This was when I tried to kill myself. Last summer."

Ruth stopped in her tracks and took a step sideways away from Reece, but the path was narrow, bounded by shrubs and chest-high grasses on one side and a chain-link fence on the other.

"Oh." Her voice had gone cold. "Your poor parents."

"Well, I wasn't thinking of them at the time."

"Obviously."

"They found you?"

"My dad, yeah."

Reece waited for her to start walking again. Instead, she turned around and gestured that she was going back toward her house.

"Hey, it was stupid, I know," he said, stunned by her stony response. "But I had reasons."

"Not good ones."

"You don't know that."

"I do." Her face was white, but her neck was flushing red. "I told you that my little sister died. I didn't tell you how. What she did hurt people, and yes, I'm angry about that. And she's not here, so—"

"So, you're going to yell at me," Reece said. But he lowered his voice, because he got it now. "Okay, I'm sorry. About your sister."

Ruth was standing still on the trail, eyes closed. Her pajama pants, wet at the knees, sagged. The hair around her face was damp and sticking to her cheeks.

"I'm sorry, too. You're helping me, I know. I haven't always been the best at . . . receiving help."

"Which you warned me about," Reece said. "I mean, future you. *Keep trying*, et cetera."

"That was smart of me. It's just . . . any memory of my sister disorients me. I don't mean just emotionally. I mean physically. Like, vertigo."

"You were close."

"That's the problem—we weren't. I think if we had been, she'd still be alive."

"Sorry." Reece looked at his feet.

"It's strange," she said, opening her eyes again. "Even with everything else happening, I keep obsessing over my sister. Knowing it's too late to help her doesn't change the fact that I still want to. It feels like a physical tug, pulling me back to the year she died. My brain keeps skittering back to these dark corners."

"Maybe the corners matter," Reece said.

Reece came forward and almost touched Ruth's wrist, but he didn't want to scare her. This time, he just gestured to her arm, which was hanging at her side—wrist turned toward him, the infinity loop visible, only slightly faded. Three days had passed. She could have chosen to scrub it off, but she hadn't.

He wanted to tell her about the moment he'd started feeling woozy, looking down at the mess he'd made, the blood pouring from his arms and turning the electric-blue rug in his bedroom black. His most desperate thought had been: *I'm so tired of myself. I'm tired of not mattering.*

And then suddenly, he'd felt arms around him. He was surrounded by bodies, by the smell of clean sweat; he could feel hot breath and hear laughter. They were in a huddle, he and a half-dozen people, all wearing the same T-shirts. Purple.

He'd designed the Rockets shirt based on that memory. Or he'd had that memory based on the Rockets shirts he would design later?

"For whatever reason," Reece said, "that day, I leaped forward into what seemed like a better moment with a group of people and this intense feeling of belonging. But it didn't last long. It's like my brain was saying, 'Here's the buzz,' and a few seconds later, 'Here's the hangover.'"

But that was wrong, too. It didn't feel like a false high followed by a crash. It felt like ultra-reality: the greater truth behind some curtain normally kept closed. "And on my way back to that moment, I passed through a cloud of something else. Something bad, somewhere just down the stream of time."

"Something bad. Explain."

"Panic. Everyone pushing and a few people falling. It's all a blur. But in the dream, I know. Something's gone wrong. And it's not so much a surprise as a feeling, like *Here it goes.* Like I've been waiting for it. Like we've all been waiting for it, including you."

"And I'm there."

He couldn't tell if she believed him.

"Yes. And you're giving me instructions, like I said."

Ruth's face was unreadable. "Okay."

He couldn't tell if she was upset or just distracted. Pulling her phone out again, she said, "It's the inspector. There's a problem. I have to get back to the house right now."

"Listen. Please. We've had a similar experience, Annie included. We thought we were going to die and started heading toward the light."

"I didn't see any light."

"The proverbial light, obviously."

"If all it took to experience what we did was a person in a traumatic moment and heading toward the proverbial light, then this would happen a lot."

Reece wished she'd stop fighting his every suggestion. "Maybe it does. But most people who have a near-death experience head back to the past. They review the events of their life like a slide-show, right? *My life flashed in front of my eyes*, et cetera." He didn't mention the endless Google searches and really bad You-Tube videos he'd watched on this, just to help him see a pattern. "They go back the way they came—toward the beginning of their lives, not the end."

Ruth was squinting at him.

"The three of us went forward, for whatever reason," he said. "We were *pulled* forward by fear or hope. You wanted to be with Scott, and then you were. I wanted to feel something—surrounded, accepted. And I was. Annie wanted out of that train, and the next thing, she was with a horse she loved. But in all three cases, the good moment turned bad fast, so we didn't get to that peaceful, happy part before waking up in the hospital room or train. We just got bounced back."

Reece still couldn't read her expression. He was helping her make sense of her experience. Why didn't she look happier?

He tried one last time, "This ability . . . Annie Oakley did something with it. She used deliberate practice to learn to control it."

"I need some time to think about this."

"You need time? We don't have time." Dream Ruth had told him that. "I'm tempted to stop taking my meds. To have the dream again, to figure out—"

Ruth interrupted, "Don't go off your meds. I don't want to be responsible for that." Then she turned and headed back toward her house. For someone with a bad knee, she was walking fast now. Reece called out to her.

"You know that point in the movie where someone has superpowers but doesn't own up to it and you want to shout, 'Let's go get the bad guy. Get the helicopter. Call the White House.'"

Ruth called back without looking over her shoulder. "In those movies, no one has to deal with home inspectors."

1 7

RUTH

"Follow me down here, if you don't mind?"

Minutes later, Ruth and the inspector stood in front of the water heater, or rather, in front of a stack of folding chairs in front of the water heater. To the side were additional obstructions. Peering into the gloom—and only now, Ruth realized she should have replaced the dead lightbulb over their heads—Ruth recognized a broken vacuum cleaner, an old wooden sled, suitcases that dated to the 1950s and stacks of cobweb-covered canvases from the year Gwen took a community college oil painting class.

"I'll need to get in there."

"Closer to the water heater, you mean."

"And behind it. As well as around the furnace, in all the crawl-spaces, the attic, the garage. Nothing can be closer than two feet to the walls. Didn't your realtor explain?"

"About staging, yes. And baking cookies to make the house smell better."

The scent of mildew hung in the air. Half the basement was shrouded in darkness. Ruth could sense the inspector's smirk. The time for baking cookies was not near.

Ruth squeezed past the folding chairs and started to tug at one of the surprisingly heavy suitcases, but the inspector shook his head.

"You've got a big job to do. We'll need to reschedule."

SHE EMAILED NIEMAN TO ASK if he had a street address so she could use a package service instead of USPS, and also whether he could supply a phone number for tracking and insurance, et cetera. She hoped she might be able to track him down that way, to reopen the dialogue she'd never meant to shut down completely. But still, he did not reply.

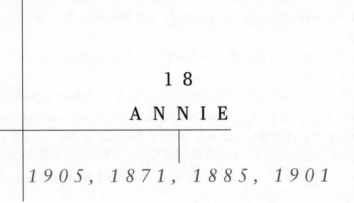

18

ANNIE

1905, 1871, 1885, 1901

At times, anger feels like the only force guiding her. It takes her back to the Indian graveyard again and again until her frustration is so great it's like a dam breaking.

Finally, she opens her eyes in the place of her greatest pain and sorrow.

She sees yellow grass, a wagon track, and the Wolves' cabin, but only for a moment. As quick as a candle snuffing out, the scene vanishes. Then she is elsewhere: back in the present, or a few years before that, or sometimes at an in-between point—the 1880s, when she was in her mid-twenties, working for Buffalo Bill. When she finds herself at this pivot point, she is comforted slightly by the familiarity of the tents, the sounds and the smells, the presence of Sitting Bull, her friend and confidant. But her young womanhood is only halfway as far as she needs to go.

Annie can't attest to how many times she is delayed or diverted. She can't count her journeys any more than a dreamer can chart every foggy shift in a long and tortured dream. She knows only that she has gotten close many times, yet never quite close enough, to do what she intends.

At one point, she describes this taxing time-skipping in a new letter to Herr Breuer, trying to capture the sights and sounds of the dreamlike world that is no dream, a kaleidoscope of disoriented moments.

Rereading her own confused prose, penned in her childish handwriting, she forces herself to consider the matter again. She ponders the question of responsibility. With this new skill of hers, shouldn't she be able to act out of something beyond personal rage? Shouldn't she try to do something purely good in the world?

THERE IS ONE NOTABLE ATTEMPT, one notable failure.

It occurs to Annie that she should be able to prompt herself, if she can only steel her mind and execute her task with clarity on a day not so very far back in time. She will write a simple letter and make an attempt at changing the course of events. This is not only a civic duty, but a personal one. She is from Greenville, Ohio; the assassin was living elsewhere in Ohio; their president, Mr. McKinley, was from Ohio. It's all still recent, still very much talked-about, and perhaps still malleable—if time and history are like muddy roads after a rain, soft at first and only hardening later.

In the brief letter, which she mails care of general delivery to the man's parents, she uses her real name, hoping it will catch his attention. She says that she knows his plan, that he must renounce violence. She does not explain how she knows.

Signing with a flourish, she feels she has fulfilled her obligation, though it does not give her the expected satisfaction. Perhaps, deep down, she knows it can't be so easy.

When Annie returns to the present day, 1905, she makes inquiries.

McKinley is still dead.

Leon Czolgosz has still shot him.

But not when she assumes—not in June, when Annie is quite sure the assassination took place—but rather later, in September. She asks a stranger on a train. She asks a man selling newspapers.

Still not convinced, she asks Frank, when she gets home later that evening and they sit down late to dinner—the first time they've seen each other in more than a week.

Her appetite is off, as is Frank's. Neither of them touches more than a few morsels on their plates. She presses Frank on the point: surely, if the assassination had happened . . .

"Well, of course it happened. What do you mean by that?"

"I only mean that I was sure it happened in June. And didn't they hang him sometime in July?"

Frank sets down his fork. "How can you forget? He was electrocuted in October. The very same day of our train accident, in fact. The date is seared into my memory."

"Oh," she says.

"You look pale."

"It's just . . . why should it be the same day?"

Is it some form of punishment for trying to change the past, a message from dark angels, thumbing their noses at her, warning her she's already gone too far?

"No reason," Frank says, picking up his fork again. "Pure coincidence. I'm only surprised you've forgotten. But there's something else I want to discuss with you."

She's seen this moment coming. She's dreaded it.

"It was just under two years ago," he starts carefully, "that we sat down with Fraley and he warned us that we were embarking on a road that could take many years to travel. I believe he said four."

"Or five."

"But it seems it will take longer than they first imagined. Our accountant would like to meet with us, the first of the month."

"I'll be away."

Frank looks down at his plate. "Of course."

"Well, why wouldn't I be away? I have a trial on the third. I don't have time to talk to accountants."

Frank picks a piece of gristle off his plate. Annie hears a scuffling near their feet.

"Please don't feed the dog under the table."

"The trials and the accountant are related issues. We're losing money on this, Annie."

"Money isn't the point."

"Money isn't the point, *up to a point*. We can't let your quest for revenge bankrupt us."

"Quest for revenge?" She pushes her chair back, ready to stand. She doesn't bother to point out that nearly all the money she is squandering—if it indeed could be called squandering—is hers. She's earned it.

"It's not logical," he says. "You've won most of the trials so far. Nearly everything you do in your life, Annie, you *win*. But a person can win and still lose, don't you see that?"

Under the table, Dex barks. He almost never barks.

"You've spoiled him rotten while I've been away. He climbs up on the bed now!"

"Why shouldn't he? If I had company . . ."

"Fine, get another dog. Get as many as you'd like."

"I'd rather have a family."

"*We're* family."

She starts to tremble. Even though she curls her fists under the table, the shake becomes stronger. They haven't spoken of this for fifteen years, and then only once, in the Wild West show days, lying side by side in bed, in her performer's tent in the dark, where she didn't have to see his face. They'd had an argument about their plans, and she explained—but not really explained—that she wasn't ready to be a mother. Would never be ready, and also possibly couldn't be. But she didn't want to discuss medical issues. Her anatomy was her business. They were talking about love and desire, or its lack. Not everyone is made to be a mother.

"Don't make me talk about it anymore," she'd said to him, turning away.

"But you haven't talked at all. You haven't made it possible for me to understand."

He almost left her the next day. She is sure of it. He skipped breakfast, wasn't in attendance at the two o'clock or the seven o'clock shows. She didn't see him at dinner, nor back in the tent at 10 P.M.

In any traveling show, there are temptations. Men who drink night after night and play cards and gamble. Beautiful women, in the show and in the crowds. Frank doesn't drink and claims not to gamble, though he perhaps wagers occasionally. As for women, well, Frank is handsome. Women find his Irish accent and his dark eyes charming, even now. He'd have no trouble finding a new partner in life. He was married and separated before they met—yet another thing they never, ever talk about. He could easily marry again.

"Annie, you don't look well. Give me your hand."

When she doesn't, Frank bangs the table, making the silver jump. "You think I'm talking about money or my own needs, when you're the one making yourself ill with all this!"

She whispers, "I saw a doctor."

"I know! Another month spent away from me. As if that's what our marriage needed. As if that's what *your health* needed. Whatever advice he gave you, it was the wrong advice, because you've looked worse every day since coming back from that ludicrous trip."

She grips the edge of her seat and tugs it back toward the table, to indicate her willingness: she won't leave the room. She's trying to listen and be reasonable. But she's also trying to hide her spasming hand under the table.

"You can't hide what's happening from me," Frank says. "I don't know if it's the trials or some other preoccupation or some dangerous medicine that Austrian gave you."

"He gave me nothing," she says, almost too quiet to hear. "Only permission."

"What kind of blasted permission?"

"The permission you'd like to withhold from me: to face my past, my long-ago past, from before we met."

"Face the past? You can't even remember four years ago, when the president was assassinated!"

Frank looks down at his mostly untouched food. He calmly picks up the plate and places it on the floor. Dex bolts out from under the tablecloth, glances once at Annie, then at Frank, who nods. The dog covers the plate with his curly mop of a head, gorging with abandon.

"Frank!"

But she knows she has controlled many aspects of their household up until now. A man will rebel, in big ways or little ones.

"Are you corresponding with someone you knew before me?"

"Oh, Frank." If he is talking about men—lovers—she's had none besides him. She may have beaten him during that first shooting match, but he won her heart and has kept it, always.

He looks disappointed to have those simple possibilities shot down. Still, she thinks she can soothe him. She says, "You used to write me poems, do you remember? I always loved your poems."

He won't look at her. His gaze remains fixed on the dog, sitting proudly next to his master's chair.

"I have a request," he says. "I don't need to know what you're doing—what you're taking, what you're drinking or what strange thoughts you are indulging. I don't know why your hand shakes so badly you'd be challenged to hit a target. I just want you to stop."

"I won't stop the trials."

"Then the other thing. Stop doing whatever is making you like this."

Dex is looking up at her. She pats her leg. He won't come. She pats it again and whistles. A small growl, so soft she might be imagining it, sneaks out of his throat.

She can't believe it. No loyalty. Perhaps she's overestimated the power of fidelity—in man *or* beast. Or maybe the dog senses something too. Maybe she looks—smells—different, the experiments making her strange.

"I will stop," she says finally, "and I will explain, because I love and respect you, because I love everything we've created together." She stands up, dropping her napkin on the table, glaring one more time at Dex, who no longer knows her. "But only when the time is right. Only when I'm done."

1 9

C A L E B

Monday

Holloway was asking him a long question, the beginning of which he'd missed because he was half asleep. It ended, "She argued for equal pay and even for having women in combat, a wildly uncommon position in the late 1800s, yet she wasn't an advocate of the vote for women. Any opinions about why that might be?"

He had rested his cheek so hard against his palm that he was sure there was a red handprint on his face now.

"Caleb?" she asked again.

"What?"

"Did you do either of the readings about Annie Oakley to prepare for Ms. McClintock's visit?"

"Yeah." He hadn't read the academic paper. He hadn't even read the Wikipedia entry. And he was stuck now, entirely distracted, fixated on the name Mrs. Holloway had just pronounced clearly: McClintock.

That was the last name of the girl. The one in the halter top with the dead eyes. But she looked about fifteen or sixteen. Of course, the photo was probably five years old. She might be twenty now. A history expert at twenty-one. Well, that was pretty good.

But she was also dead, supposedly, before she would have had a chance to become an expert at anything. Maybe Vorst had just said that, because he'd cut her off. Disowned her. He seemed the type of guy to do that, just as he'd suddenly gone cold on Caleb— thank God—after the summer.

Holloway came around the front of the desk and leaned against it, refusing to move on and pester another student. "The second reading I assigned referred to Oakley's 'subtle subversion.' She was a conservative lady in the Victorian era, in terms of her outward appearance, but also an iconoclast. Other examples of this, Caleb?"

"Sorry, what's an iconoclast?"

Everyone was staring at him now, enjoying the stalemate.

"An icon smasher, a skeptic," Holloway explained and then, sympathetic to his confusion or else wanting to make his idiocy clear to everyone watching. "She was a rebel, Caleb."

She was a rebel.

That was what the halter-top girl had written in her one-page college application essay, in reference to the woman she admired. Both of the women, actually. And it made sense that she was now a history expert and that she had broken off things with her creepy dad because she, too, wanted to be a rebel.

Holloway said, "Tell me one thing you know about Annie Oakley or you get a zero for the day."

Caleb crossed his ankles under the desk and pushed back his bangs, searching his memory for details from the essay. "Okay, so people think she gave in and lost the shooting match to the guy she married later, but that's only in the movie version. In real life, she didn't throw the match at all. She didn't lose on purpose to anyone, ever."

Holloway sat back on the edge of her desk. "All right. So, you read a little . . ."

"Oh, and some people thought her brother taught her to shoot, but in later interviews he said that wasn't true. She taught herself.

Even her brother didn't know why people added that lie, but I think it's because no one could imagine a super-young girl would be so talented and such . . . an iconoclast, I guess."

Holloway laughed. He'd never heard his teacher laugh before. "I didn't know she had a brother, and none of that was in the assigned readings, but that's great, Caleb. Thank you for participating."

His heart was beating fast. Holloway moved on to somebody else. Everyone was still staring at Caleb, but he didn't give a shit. He was in his own head, going over what he'd just found out. The McClintock girl in the photo who had supplied him with those details was alive. Vorst's daughter or not-daughter was alive.

He felt like he'd gotten incredible news about some celebrity who'd disappeared years ago and had suddenly resurfaced. No, that was stupid. She was a real person, someone who used to live—maybe still lived—right in this town. It was more like he'd just found out a friend hadn't died.

Caleb thought of the essay again, and its writer. The girl had started out talking about Annie Oakley and all the things that made her unique, special and tough. But then by the end she was talking about her sister, because it was her sister who knew the most about Annie and talked about her all the time. And then the girl did the bait and switch that you probably always had to do in college essays, where you seemed to be talking about something from a book and then ended up talking about something from your life, and you got soft, you tried to make the reader cry, because if he or she did, you'd probably get a scholarship.

The woman I most admire who isn't famous or long dead is my sister. We don't always get along, and I used to be mad at her for moving out of state. But now I realize there are two ways to get back at your enemies. You challenge them in a shootout or you flee. The fleeing makes sense, especially if you go someplace where you'll have a good life. Success is the best revenge, right?

And even if you have future battles, you have to heal first, gather up your strength.

Annie Oakley got away. My sister got away. She's in graduate school now. Our mother doesn't think I'll get into college. She wants me to work and live at home next year because she thinks I'll just waste our money and the experience. But that's not my plan. Even if I don't go to college, I'll still move away from here.

Everyone was standing up, sliding textbooks into their backpacks. The girl in front of Caleb pushed a handout in his face. "Hello?"

He hadn't heard the announcement.

"What do we have to do?"

The girl shook her head—*pathetic*—but she was smiling. "Answer these discussion questions and come up with a new question for Ruth McClintock when she comes next week. She rescheduled, so now we have to do more work."

"*Ruth* McClintock?"

"The author," the girl said, "The historian who's coming." Under her breath she whispered, "And the teacher knows you're high, asshole."

"I'm not."

Ruth McClintock.

He felt like he'd lost something. Kennidy—that was the name on the essay—might not be alive after all. Okay. Easy come, easy go.

But for some reason, it wasn't. He walked out of the class and didn't make it to the next, just went to the bathroom and stayed there as it filled with people and emptied again. He sat in a closed stall and hoped no one would look for him while he let the news sink in. He set his elbows on his knees and pushed the heels of his palms into his eyes.

She hadn't gotten away.

Caleb didn't know why he'd spent all this time half-believing she was Vorst's daughter. She wasn't his daughter. There were no snapshots on the fridge, no framed pictures of her on the walls, only framed yellow newspaper clippings of Vorst himself at track meets and football championships. What kind of father hung up pictures of himself and hid his daughter's in a drawer? She was something else to him, for a longer time than those other kids maybe, and that was creepiest of all. Why that box contained no naked shots he didn't know, but he knew there had been naked pictures. Vorst always took pictures. Maybe she—like Caleb—had made an effort to find and destroy them. That was another way they were alike. They wanted no reminders of the shitty times. And if that were true, he should honor her by getting rid of the other things he'd found, like her notebook and all the crap stuffed inside it, including her essay.

But it might have been the last thing she'd ever written, the last thought she'd tried to share with anyone. Was it okay to erase that?

Kennidy hadn't made it and had probably known she wasn't going to make it, not to college or anywhere good. Words were cheap, and words in assigned essays were the cheapest. She was saying shit people wanted to read, though he knew she'd loved her sister. That part was real. She'd loved her sister and had known she was disappointing her and had known she'd never get away. If you had all the pieces, the essay and the photo and the smell of licorice candy in your nostrils and the memory of Tang and cheap vodka still burning in your brain, you could tell.

2 0

R U T H

Again the next day, Nieman did not reply.

Monday morning. Fresh pot of coffee. Pens and note-book on one side, manila folders on the other, laptop on with multiple windows open: 1870 census, footnotes by Riley, map of Preble County.

It had been a long time since Ruth had taken out her file dedicated specifically to all the possible Wolf identities. She reviewed the sources of her previous confusion, the multiple names and identities that editor Laura Boyd hadn't wanted to hear about, because to her, one bad man was the same as any other.

Not to Ruth.

Biographer Glenda Riley had said the Wolf was "generally believed to be a member of the Studabaker family." But by whom, and according to what evidence?

Ruth's own suspects, hardly unique among the conjecture found online, were as follows: an old man named Boose, some-times spelled Bosse, or his son-in-law, a young Civil War veteran named Rannals, sometimes spelled Reynolds. Spellings were noto-riously inconsistent in those days.

Ruth had plenty of secondary sources, all guesses made by others over the years, but as for primary sources, she had only one: an 1870 census document in which a ten-year-old named "Mosey, Ann" was listed as part of an extended "Boose" household. This same year, Annie was not listed as part of her biological mother's household, miles away.

According to this document, farmer Abram Boose had a wife and a four-year-old child, but he also had a second orphan helping out—a thirteen-year-old boy named Solomon. When Annie talked or wrote about the Wolves, shouldn't she have mentioned her fellow survivor? By all accounts, she never did. Reynolds had a wife and a baby, and most likely they lived in a separate cabin on the same farm. A couple with a baby would need help most of all. If the extended family split their orphan laborers, they might have sent the girl, Annie, to deal with the baby and kept older, stronger Solomon in the main house.

"James Rannals" was probably the Wolf. It was a fair guess, the one that felt almost but not completely right to Ruth.

There was one more outlandish option that Ruth couldn't ignore because it had been mentioned by other respectable writers. Boose or Reynolds could have lent Annie out to their neighbor, as was frequently done. Close by, on a neighboring farm in Preble County, there were two families, most likely related, with the surname Wolf.

Ruth didn't like the theory. It was pure conjecture; Annie was never named on any document associated with the extended Wolf family. And it was too neat, almost over the top. Because if the Wolf was named Wolf, then Annie hadn't hidden her captor's identity. The secret was no secret.

But a woman always kept secrets about these things, or so Ruth thought. Especially one as insistent upon control and propriety as Annie Oakley. It was one of the reasons abuse continued and nothing ever changed.

RUTH SPENT THE AFTERNOON HAULING items up from the basement, tagging bags for donation pickup, stacking freebies at the curb and digging through drawers that might contain photos worth saving or documents in need of shredding, avoiding still the opening of other boxes and those two oddly heavy suitcases, one held shut by a flimsy lock.

Still, Ruth was not disheartened. As the piles grew, she felt a momentum building. She was astonished by the sheer amount being flushed out of previously ignored closets and corners. The human propensity to collect and lose track of what one has collected had often delighted Ruth as an aspiring historian. Just last year, in a barn, a family had discovered a crate of letters covered in mouse droppings from the famous suffragettes Susan B. Anthony and Elizabeth Cady Stanton. It had been moved several times and camouflaged for decades by the other clutter surrounding it: books, magazines, tools and old furniture.

See? Things are found all the time. You can never be sure.

But Gwen McClintock wasn't Susan B. Anthony, nor was Kennidy McClintock Annie Oakley, Ruth mused, opening an old desk drawer to find only more canceled checks and a slew of pink "while you were out" phone messages, blackened with frantic doodles—who bothered keeping those?—that no one would ever want to read or store.

She had already closed the drawer and was turning to go, desperate to have a break from the dank basement. But then she turned back.

If those were messages to a historical figure, you would have made sure to read every one. Her finger slid under the bronze pull. She opened the drawer.

That message on the top, taken for Gwen by a receptionist at her phlebotomy job, was from "the school." The message read: *Expecting you at meeting tomorrow 9 am next Mon re: Kennidy, urgent.* The next two messages were variations on the theme. The principal at Horizon High had been trying to reach Gwen several times that month of May. A fourth slip said: *Missed you at meeting, urge you to reschedule.*

Gwen avoided Horizon High. She would have used work as an excuse. Ruth's best guess was that Gwen never attended those school meetings and possibly never returned the calls, either. But that hadn't stopped her from doodling on the pink notes themselves, tracing over the phone number of the principal's office. In one place, she'd traced and retraced the number *8* so intently that the pen had broken through the page.

2 1
R U T H

Tuesday

All day Ruth reviewed her notes and tried to avoid checking her email, then gave in. *Just one more time. He'll reply. But Nieman hadn't.*

She decided to call Joe Grandlouis again. She felt guilty the moment he picked up. A baby was crying in the background. She could hear Joe's wife offering to take over while Joe went to an upstairs office and closed the door.

"I'm really sorry," Ruth said. "I didn't mean to interrupt your evening."

"No, no. I got your voicemail from last weekend. I just . . ."

"No explanation needed."

"Actually, I was looking for the original letter before I called you back. I finally found it."

"Letter?"

"I'm sorry. New-parent brain. Haven't slept much in the last couple months."

"Poor thing. How's Reka doing?"

There was an awkward pause. "Reka is two years old. The one keeping us awake was born six weeks ago."

"Oh gosh. I'm sorry. Two years old, already? Congrats. On the second one, I mean."

"Thomas," he said. "Named after my dad. Got there before Justine did."

That was Joe's sister Justine, who was engaged but not yet married. They'd always been in a playful rivalry over who would have the first children, to be named after both of Joe's deceased parents. At least Ruth's brain was working well enough to remember that story.

"Thomas," Ruth repeated. "Sorry, Joe. I've been in kind of a time warp since . . ."

"I'm the one who should be apologizing. It's still tough, I take it?"

Her throat tightened.

When she didn't answer, Joe said, "I'm glad you've got a good guy to lean on, or I'd be worried."

In the background, Ruth could hear the sounds of Joe shuffling around his office, the metallic rattle of a filing cabinet being yanked open and banged shut.

"Okay, so I do have it somewhere. From the guy, Bert somebody. That was your question, right? If I'd sent someone your way?"

Ruth was so sure it was someone like Sophie—an organizational contact—rather than a friend, perhaps because she expected a friend to dash off an email letting her know, but that was Joe for you, even before having kids.

"Bert Nieman?"

"I don't think that last name is right. But definitely Bert, yeah. This was a long time ago. Let me think: over a year and a half. Minimum."

"Did he send you an old journal?"

"No, just a couple typed pages, like a story." Another drawer opened and closed. "I took it to be fanfiction."

She wished he would stop rattling around and just explain.

"Okay," he said after the last drawer banged shut. "You know about my Sitting Bull essays."

"Plural? I know the one you were writing that mentioned Annie. You asked me for help with it a long time ago."

Joe went on to explain that before the second baby brought his productivity to a standstill, he had managed to publish several more essays that he hoped would one day work as a collection.

"One was about Sitting Bull's prophecy about Custer and his men. Another was about Flying Bird, a young warrior who had premonitions of his family dying in another battle, which later did happen. But the interesting parts of his visions were the cityscapes and things that sound like skyscrapers and high-speed cars, described a century earlier than they existed—that's the stuff readers want to know more about. As you'd expect, the Flying Bird essay was the one that brought the cuckoos out of the forest."

"And Bert's a cuckoo?"

"He sent me this. Hold on. I'll call you back in thirty seconds."

Moments after disconnecting, the images arrived to Ruth's phone: photos of what looked like two typewritten pages, crinkled and stained. She magnified and puzzled over it.

Yellow—

I focus, trying not to lose sight of the yellow grass and the worn wagon track leading up to the cabin, but I know the man I'm hunting isn't there. I'll wait in ambush, as long as I can. Any moment he might come down the road, returning from town in the wagon, bones weary from his trip. Alone.

When the view in front of me begins to flicker like a guttering candle, I focus harder. I try to ground myself more deeply in this place, smelling the wet ground, fallen apples, chimney smoke rising above this familiar stand of woods, from the cabin beyond. But it's not enough. I've arrived at the wrong moment. Despite the bitterness that has brought

me to this place, despite my clear desire and undeniable
rage, something remains undecided.

And because of my hesitation, there is no other explanation, the yellow grass begins to fade. I can no longer feel the
frost-hardened ground under my feet.

"Give her water," says a voice that doesn't belong to this
time or place.

Not yet . . .

My vision darkens before new images come to replace
the old, the smell of apples still in my nostrils, but fainter.
My ribs ache.

The familiar voice again. "You'll see. She'll be fine."

Giving up, I open my eyes and accept where I've landed,
seated on a dark red rug opposite the Chief in his private
performer's tent. A young Indian woman kneels at my side,
encouraging me to sip from a tin mug. It must be a pivot
point or a sort of hole I fall into on my way to or back from
where I'm trying to go.

Bringing forward a piece of hair, I expect to see gray. It's
brown. The backs of my hands are unblemished: the hands
of a girl in her twenties, not a tired forty-one. I'm wearing
one of the Wild West show outfits I sewed myself. Sitting
Bull's finest eagle-feather headdress hangs on a peg on the
far tent wall. If Cody enters and finds me here, he won't see
anything out of the ordinary. If Bill and Sitting Bull and I
are all together, this must be 1885 or thereabouts.

I've tried telling Sitting Bull many times before what will
happen to him five years from now, after he's left the show
and gone back to his people. Perhaps he has refused to
listen. Or perhaps the future and the past can't be changed,
only seen. I don't know. Perhaps the uncertainty itself drops
me here, like a pigeon shot out of the sky.

"The future and the past are our two most difficult

battles," Sitting Bull says. "They are not battles we are always meant to win."

Everything is both fragmented and familiar. Yellow. The smell of apples. Our most difficult battles.

I tell him that I can't get back to the right time. I can get to the cabin, with the She-wolf and the baby. I can creep through the yellowing grass and pause outside the window. The Wolf isn't there. He's just left the house. He hasn't returned.

I become immaterial when I try to linger without purpose. I am stuck and exhausted with the effort. And when I come back, my body hurts and my foolish hand shakes.

And meanwhile, here at this place where I've landed, a mallet rings against a stake. A show horse whinnies. Here, tents are going up. Life is moving forward.

"I can't arrive at the right moment," I tell Sitting Bull.

"What is the right moment? What is it you want to do, daughter?"

I can feel myself raising the gun, sighting down the barrel, feeling the power of life and death in my hands, thinking: run.

"I'll decide when I'm there."

"But you have been there, Watanya Cicilla. You've looked into the Wolf's eyes. You've smelled his fear. Did it make a difference?"

This wasn't something Nieman had shown her.

Ruth wasn't done reading, but her phone rang and she brought it to her ear.

"I didn't get through all of it yet," she said.

"He didn't want to send me the whole document, just a badly typed sample. He said the original was handwritten, but he didn't share that. Everything about him sent up red flags, most of all the fantasy element of Annie Oakley somehow having visions or whatever is supposed to be happening there."

"What did you tell him?"

"One, that even in terms of fiction, I wasn't convinced."

"Wait. Did Bert say this was fiction?"

"No. But I didn't like him. He was cagey. It seemed like he wanted to pick my brain without giving anything in return. And when I started questioning some of the Oakley stuff, he came back telling me I wasn't an Oakley expert, that he'd find his own."

"So, you sent him to me."

"Are you kidding? I was trying to save you from him. This was—yeah—February of last year. You were just home from the hospital. I mentioned your name so that he could look up your publications." Ruth had only two journal articles and a published conference paper to her name, but she appreciated that Joe considered them worthy of mention. "I didn't give him your email or phone number or anything, and I certainly didn't encourage him to reach out. So, wait—is this guy bothering you now?"

"No," she said. Nieman—or Bert, or Bert Nieman?—had been willing to mail only a typed, out-of-context excerpt to Joe Grandlouis, a young history professor with an impressive CV of publications online. Later, he'd decided to entrust the full journal to her, an unemployed Oakley scholar of no renown. Maybe she was simply the last logical possibility. Or maybe she was the most logical possibility.

Googling Ruth's name, he would have easily found an announcement about the forthcoming Annie Oakley book, back when it *was* forthcoming, on the university press website. He also might have found a newspaper article detailing Ruth's crash. Maybe he knew what she had in common with Annie Oakley—a serious midlife accident, to say the least—and thought she'd be vulnerable to a hoax. Or perhaps he'd gathered that her circumstances were the only reason she might have a sufficiently open mind.

"He *has* been in contact with me," she told Joe. "He sent me a journal—not fiction, or that's not how he presented it. And he has something more I want. Some follow-up letters he hasn't bought yet."

"But he didn't show you this letter or whatever it is?"

"No."

"What's he asking from you?"

"Nothing."

"What's the problem, then?"

"Well, actually, he's dropped out of touch before I got to see all that he had."

"That sounds like good news. Anyway, if he was trying to pawn off something extremely dubious, he's barking up the wrong tree. You're the last person to believe in some cockamamie story about Oakley and Sitting Bull and visions."

But what if she was exactly the person who would believe?

She wanted to tell Joe so much, but she only said, "I've changed, Joe."

But Joe was off on his own tangent. "Hey—those horrible scenes I used to write about the women and children at the camp just before the Battle of the Greasy Grass, and Custer setting up nearby so they could terrify them and take them as prisoners? I used to get off on that stuff."

"It was why we broke up," she said. It had come to her in a flash: how his insistent dwelling on graphic details had soured their very last road trip together. It was just hours after they'd visited one particularly grim Native American historical site together that they'd called it quits.

"What?"

"We broke up, that summer before my last year in grad school. After an argument about just that: glorifying morbid historical details."

"That's not why we broke up."

Joe was always so certain about everything.

"Anyway," he said when she wouldn't argue with his statement, "it's true you never liked the dark stuff. Or you'd take one tiny hit, the same way you'd take one hit off a roach—a little American slavery, a little bit of Auschwitz—and pass it back, quick. You'd talk about the stuff that didn't scare you, because it was already a cartoon in your head. But the deep-dark shit, no way."

"If I were you, I wouldn't refer to Auschwitz as a cartoon."

She tried to say it in a lighthearted way, but that wasn't how he received it.

"Don't talk down to me, Ms. McClintock. You and I both know what happens to genocide that's already been processed and monetized by Hollywood so many times that it doesn't give modern people nightmares, when it should."

There was a tense silence, not even a crackle over the phone line. For a moment, Ruth thought maybe Joe had hung up. But then she heard the squeak of his office chair, followed by a sigh.

"Ruth, I was only trying to say that I'm the one who has mellowed out. I get it now."

She waited, still holding her breath. This was a new Joe—one who stepped back from the brink.

He asked, "You know John Greenleaf Whittier?"

"Vaguely."

"Poet, mid-1800s. He has a poem that goes, 'The great eventful Present hides the Past; but through the din / Of its loud life hints and echoes from the life behind steal in . . .'"

"Echoes. Yes."

"More than echoes. Friggin' howls. But do we subject people to that? I think about the stuff I used to write, and then I think of Reka and Thomas. I think of the readers who might have their own kids. It feels wrong to pull some of those emotional strings. It's too easy to make people squirm and hurt. Easier than making them think."

"You're right."

"I am? That's a first."

"And you were right back then, too. Maybe it should hurt sometimes."

"Tell me more." She could hear the smile in his voice, trying to find his way back into a less prickly conversation. But this was serious.

Ruth said, "You said I couldn't be a historian if I couldn't stomach all the bad things that human beings did to each other. Maybe you reveled and ranted a little too much. But I . . ."

She paused. Why *had* they broken up again?

She could picture Iowa, on the roof of her apartment in the heat of a summer night, with Joe, smoking and drinking cheap red wine. A disagreement not about history, but about her own sister. Kennidy was having a bad time. Joe thought Ruth should talk her sister into an extended visit. Ruth was wary. Kennidy always seemed angry with her, contemptuous even. On top of that, Ruth needed her own space. She needed to contain the chaos of Gwen and Kennidy and everything she'd left behind. Whereas Joe was the opposite, open to conflict and complications.

They had fought then. They had kept fighting about other things, but that late summer disagreement had set the pattern. When Kennidy died, in October, they were done.

"You thought I could help her . . ." she started to say to Joe. The image was so real, suddenly. She could see the Iowa stars overhead. She could feel her lip at the edge of the tin cup. She could smell the cheap grapey wine. "But I didn't face things. I looked away."

Just as she had during her visions of Scott. As she had so many other times in her life.

Silence. That was how it was on the phone with Joe: the silences could be long.

He finally asked, "You all right?"

"Yeah."

There it was, retrieved from forgetfulness. Carried up from the basement archive of abandoned memories.

They'd broken up because of Kennidy. Or rather, because of Ruth's reaction to Kennidy and her problems, her need to shut down and close out everyone, especially Joe. It disturbed Ruth that she'd remembered this so inaccurately, that it was something Joe could have told her, if she'd ever asked. Before the accident, she wouldn't have asked. She hadn't wanted to know.

"Jesus, I'm a selfish bitch sometimes," she said.

"Easy."

"No, I am. I have been. First into the lifeboat, that seems like my motto."

"But don't lifeboats have room for, like, sixteen or twenty people?"

"Damn it, Joe."

"Okay," he said, then more softly, "Okay, okay. I know what you're saying. You know how many of my cousins overdosed or killed themselves? Five. Another two in prison. Am I glad I moved away? Hell, yeah. Do I feel like shit for moving away? Hell, yeah."

Ruth waited for him to say more, but when he didn't, she took a deep breath. "Anyway, your Sitting Bull essays. And the thing Bert sent you."

"Right. You were the one to tell me two years ago that Sitting Bull wasn't really Annie's mentor. You told me that your sharpshooter and my chief possibly weren't all that close, beyond the pet names."

"Back then I thought they weren't."

"And now?"

"Now I'm open to other interpretations."

"Oh, great. So now you think I should have listened to the guy?"

"Wait. *Listened?* Do you mean literally? Did you actually talk to Nieman?"

"To Bert. Yeah. He sent me the letter first, physical mail. I called him when I couldn't make heads or tails of what he'd sent me. But it was hard to understand him."

"Foreign accent?"

"No, throat cancer. He didn't explain that when he first reached out to you? He told me plainly he was dying, stage four, and that was . . ." Joe paused and whistled. "Shit. That was a year and nine months ago."

THEY TALKED JUST A FEW minutes more about Sitting Bull and the moccasins he had given Annie Oakley, the ones made by his daughter. While Joe talked, Ruth stayed quiet, thinking.

The ones he'd worn at the Battle of Little Bighorn, Custer's Last Stand—the battle Sitting Bull had predicted because he'd had a vision just weeks earlier.

The moccasins he had worn during the battle. The very same ones Sitting Bull had given to Annie Oakley, another seer—and maybe more than just a seer.

It was starting to click, even as they finished the call, but Ruth wasn't ready to tell Joe everything. She needed to read the rest of what Bert had sent first. Joe wouldn't understand the context of that letter fragment he had. He couldn't possibly guess why Annie Oakley would have written it, or to whom.

Ruth read the end of the extract, squinting at her phone.

"You've looked into the Wolf's eyes. You've smelled his fear. Did it make a difference?"

"I can't remember."

"You've been looking into his yellow eyes all your life. You cannot arrive there because you are always there."

Riddles are not what I want, only his counsel. He is the only person in whom I can confide. Not Frank. Not any of my nieces. Only this old Chief, nearly as lost in my world as I'd be in his.

"*I need him to hurt,*" I say.

"*He is hurting.*"

"*I need to feel him hurting. I need him to run.*"

"*And so he runs. But you are the one who gets no rest.*"

Reece? You around?

He didn't immediately reply. Unusual.

Sorry for yesterday. But I have big news.

Still nothing. He must be away from his phone. Maybe he was working at the café.

Reece, it isn't just clairvoyance or neurosis, either.

She'd tell him in person, the thing they should have come out and admitted from the start.

It's time travel.

2 2

R U T H

Heading outside to meet her ride, Ruth saw a man hammering the new FOR SALE sign into her yard.

"Whoa, whoa," she said, hurrying over to stop him, but the chore was already half done. He'd excavated a hole near the curb on the property adjoining hers. Van, her neighbor, had just come out as well.

"I'm really sorry about this. Hi—Ruth. Gwen's daughter." She held out her hand. "We haven't really talked since I took over my mom's place, but I think I came over to your house once when I was about twelve."

Her hand was still awkwardly extended. "For a class assignment. Oral history. You told me about your family's Minnesota roots, how you used to own this whole street and all kinds of farmland."

He looked at her hand for a long moment before taking it and then squeezed her knuckles in a tight, dry grip that hurt a little. "Of course, I remember."

He'd been handsome once, she could tell, but he made no effort to smile or appear neighborly now. He wouldn't look her in the eye. He just kept looking at the hole in his lawn, his jaw moving as he sucked on a piece of hard candy. She smelled licorice.

"I'm sorry about that," she said. "I don't know how they made the mistake. Unless you're selling your house, too? My realtor keeps saying they'd love to tear down both our houses and put new four-bedrooms up and down this whole street. But I suppose that might be good for you—don't you own those empty lots across the street, too?"

He said nothing. It was amazing, actually, his ability to sit there showered by questions and not bother answering.

The man with the excavator tool stood looking at the both of them, offering no apology.

More tersely, Ruth said, "The realtor knows my address—obviously. They shouldn't have done this."

"Well," Van said. "I'm sure this fella here can fill it back in. Can't you?"

"No problem at all."

"All right. Good." Van turned away. He was already walking back to his house, his hands shoved into the pockets of his satin baseball jacket. An old guy, but lean and strong, like an aging cowboy.

This was the man who had sold her mother the house at a below-market price. He could answer Ruth's questions. She had never thought of just knocking on his door, because for her, answers came from archives, from documents, preferably not from people—especially not ones who wouldn't look her in the eye.

She should knock on his door another day and try harder. But right now, she was intent on getting to the café right away to meet Reece.

Still, Ruth's eyes lingered on the neighbor as he walked slowly back to his house: stiff gait, lean frame and bony shoulders, the sheen of his blue jacket with gray cuffs and, just when he turned sideways, the flash of an arm patch—almost impossible to make out at this distance—featuring a blue bird and a red maple leaf.

THEY RETREATED TO A CAFÉ table in the far back, next to a low bookshelf full of old board games with boxes split at the seams. Ruth caught Reece looking at the mess with the same disdain with which he'd contemplated her garage full of poorly stored crap. He tried to dress sloppy—flannel shirts, long bangs—but was in fact a perfectionist, compulsive and neat.

Also, possibly, he could hold the occasional grudge.

"You're not upset, are you?" she asked.

"Why would I be?"

"Our walk," she said. "Maybe I didn't respond with enough empathy when you told me about what happened to you last summer. I wasn't as attentive as I should've been."

"No. That's fine."

A teenage girl with an apron was passing close to their table, pushing a broom. "Reece?"

He looked over his shoulder. "Five minutes."

Reece had placed a tiny notebook and pencil on the table, taking extra care to line up the pencil next to the pad so it wouldn't roll away. Next to it, he had one of his Sharpies. His phone was conspicuously absent.

On Ruth's side of the table was the printout of what Joe had shared with her, from the "pivot point" Annie kept returning to while trying to reach the Wolves.

"You go first," he said, gesturing to the pages on the table. "Read what you've got."

She could see he was excited, even if he wouldn't admit it. After she finished reading the letter fragment, Reece clapped, reciting, "'And so he runs.' Go get 'em, Annie."

"But those aren't the final words. The final words are about her not getting any rest. She's not at peace with what she's doing. I'm afraid to say it out loud. If you were . . . anyone else, I wouldn't say it."

"Anyone else being . . . ?"

"An editor or a fellow researcher. Frankly, any adult." She leaned forward, whispering. "Do you realize that my tentative belief in this basically spells out the end of my career as a historian?"

"Do you have a career?"

"Touché."

Reece slid the printout closer, skimming it. "I don't know, I'm sure that as an academic, you could still write articles about the fact that Annie *thought* she could time travel. That's the safe way to put it."

"Exactly. And I could point out that when H. G. Wells wrote about a time-travel machine in the 1890s—Annie and her generation weren't unfamiliar with the concept—his character went into the future. Nearly a million years into the future. To talk with happy vegan dwarves. Whereas when a woman like Annie has a chance to time travel, she goes—"

"To the past."

"Yes, to a realistic, traumatized past. Goodbye, time machine, that was a lark, and we don't even need machines to travel through time if trauma will do the trick. Hello, dawn of psychoanalysis and the recognition that the past won't leave us alone. The distant future is trivial by comparison. And then we have the rise of the modern, time-obsessed novel: Proust, just four years after Annie went to Vienna, if she did, and then there's Woolf's *Mrs. Dalloway* and Joyce's *Ulysses*—"

"But then you'd have to read *Ulysses*."

"Who says I haven't? And I could do analyses in terms of gender, different modes of scientific thinking, cultural concepts of time, the synchronization of railroad time and the adoption of Greenwich Mean Time in the late 1800s, the anxiety of the individual in the face of industrialization—"

"But you're not going to."

"No." Ruth looked down into her coffee cup. "I don't think I could tolerate burying the truth of Annie's story under that kind of academic avalanche."

"Good. Because there's no time to waste," Reece said. How many times had he said that now—two, three?

The girl with the broom was still hovering, sweeping under the table next to them. She mouthed the words, "Reece. Two minutes. You're in big trouble." He ignored her.

"My guess," Ruth said, pulling the printout back to her, "is that it's a letter, even though the friend who gave it to me didn't recognize it as such. I mean, obviously it could be a diary entry, too, but Breuer had suggested she send letters detailing any 'hallucinations' as a way to continue their sessions over distance."

"Do you think Breuer answered each time?"

"We don't know. If she was on a roll, he may not have had to say very much. A good analyst mostly listens. By this point, Sitting Bull isn't encouraging her to keep making trips into the past. Or at the very least, he's being ambiguous. So she has two mentors: a Viennese analyst who isn't above giving advice but thinks she's imagining her experiences, and a Lakota medicine man who believes everything she's experiencing but won't tell her what to do."

"Could Sitting Bull see into the future, too?"

"He saw the Battle of Little Bighorn, but in an abstract way: white soldiers falling like grasshoppers from the sky. That supposedly spurred Lakota warriors on to beat Custer. Sitting Bull may have seen his own death, too, which didn't stop it from happening. Maybe the difficulty is in interpreting these visions."

"Or maybe the visions simply don't change things."

"Maybe."

A couple sat down at the small wooden table next to them.

Ruth whispered, "You think it's okay that we're talking about this here?"

Reece looked around. "This is exactly the kind of stuff that gets talked about here. I have to listen to it all the time."

"But won't people think—"

"That we're planning a multiplayer RPG or outlining our plots for NaNoWriMo? Yes, that's exactly what they'll think."

"Okay," Ruth said, trying to emulate Reece's nonchalance. "So she's physically present. People can see her and talk to her. She believes she can take action in the past."

"But should she? The butterfly effect and all that."

Ruth shook her head. "Not that. It's more that, from the perspectives of morality and mental health, should a person really go back and seek revenge?"

Ruth didn't know the answer. Joe had once told her about First Nations' attitudes on revenge—a concept they didn't use, exactly. It was more a question of rebalancing things. But this was easier in a closed community or where there was real justice. It was harder when your enemy was distant or institutions failed. Revenge was a last resort, and it might have a terrible price. The question for Ruth was, who paid it?

None of that interested Reece at the moment. "I want to know the mechanics," he said. "I'm starting to think that when trauma bounces someone forward toward another trauma, it's like a laser hitting a mirror. The person bounces back."

Ruth nodded slowly. "But that's just the *how* of it, not the *why*—or the *why us*. Maybe we're focusing too much on what's happened to us—my car accident, Annie's train crash, your suicide attempt—and forgetting to think about what *kind* of people we are."

"And what kind is that?"

"Did your parents make you practice dance as a kid?"

"Actually, they tried to stop me. So you're saying we're obsessive."

"In Annie's day, they just called it hard-working. But yes, we're prone to intrusive thoughts, compulsive searches. And on the upside, discipline, perfectionism. You said you were always like this. I might've had a touch of it, but it definitely took over my life after the accident. The physiological side could be the other part of what allowed us to travel this . . . route, I'll call it, that doesn't exist for everyone."

Ruth was beginning to see it, finally, as a nearly physical thing: a path discovered, like a game trail, and then reused and worn deep. Sci-fi and the supernatural weren't her thing. History was.

Ruth did a quick search on her phone and showed Reece a picture of the Natchez Trace in Mississippi: a path used by animals and Indians, and later robbers and slave traders, dug amazingly deep by travel alone, so that, with the trees bowed overhead, shading the trail, it looked almost like a tunnel or chute.

She scrolled to a particularly haunting image. Through that chute flowed bodies, hope and terror. It was only a trail, no people, but the forces of history—millions of footfalls, a single-file progression of the greedy, the unlucky, the unwilling—were visible in its distinctive, hollowed-out shape. "Maybe misery digs the deepest groove of all."

Reece said, "I've read about certain Native visions, the kind they saw after sun dances. They would cut themselves and dance to exhaustion."

"That's right. You and I shot forward and then slid back after experiencing fear. Like the Lakota sun dancers, Annie was willing to suffer in order to see more. She marched back and forth again and again, to keep the route open and even lengthen it. She said that she had to relive the physical pain of her train accident many times before she started seeing an earlier past."

"How many times have you had your vision?"

Ruth had to think. "Maybe a dozen, but the recent ones are the most detailed. When they first started happening, I did whatever I could to shut them down. And then I stopped seeing Scott. Being away from him may have reduced my triggers."

"So," Reece said, "Annie Oakley was willing to put up with

pain. She was supremely athletic. She already knew breath and pulse control. She was no stranger to fasting. Drugs and alcohol, not so much?"

"Make that none. Teetotaler."

Reece kept ticking off his mental checklist, "Extreme focus. Deliberate practice. Visualization."

"Of colors," Ruth said, her mind filling, as soon as she said it, with a sudden scarlet flash. It had never rocketed into her mind like this—a quick pulse, invited—because she had never allowed it. She had fought it with every ounce of her being. She added, "The white of the oncoming train light. The yellow of the grass by the Wolves' cabin."

"Purple," Reece said quietly. "The first thing I ever saw was a comforting sea of purple."

"Red," Ruth said. "Red red red."

Ruth closed her eyes. Across the room, the hiss of the espresso machine started up. Next to them, a couple was talking softly. Farther away, a chair scraped against the wooden floor. She noted each sound and let it go, still seeing, behind her closed lids, that singular color.

"But as for the rest of it," Reece said, "how far her time travels went and the consequences—for that, we need the rest of the letters. We have to get in touch with Nieman. Look at this." When she opened her eyes, he pointed to his small notebook. "You're a historian. You need to talk to him the old-fashioned way."

"Believe me, I want to. But he won't give me his phone number."

"Antfarm." Reece smiled, turning to a page filled with his neat, tiny script. "That's where I started. There's an Ant Farm and Myrmecology Forum online. But I didn't think that was it." He turned to another page: all caps, tiny letters, rows of checkmarks. "Ant farm, as in *antiques farm*. Like, an antique shop that's near a farm, or in a barn. Sounds like Vermont, right? Maybe he's the owner."

"Nieman is a collector—a buyer. Not necessarily a seller."

"Aren't a lot of buyers also sellers? If you buy enough crap, at some point you end up also selling it. Seems like a vicious cycle to me."

"Not vicious and not crap—we hope," Ruth conceded. "But you can't just phone every antique shop in Vermont."

"No. I could only call one hundred forty-two of them, so far. I got the names from the Vermont Antiques Association Directory. There was no Bert Nieman listed, but I figured it could be a pseudonym, so I'm just going to keep dialing and asking around."

"That's great, Reece."

"It will be once it works. What's your next step?"

"I sent another email to Sophie, my foundation contact. Leaned on her a little harder. The foundation has closed files, and I want to make sure we're not missing something there."

The café door opened and two girls entered, bringing a gust of cold wind with them. It smelled of late fall: moldering leaves, a touch of rain, the promise of snow. Reece glanced their way with a worried look on his face. Ruth expected his eyes to track the girls as they slowly made their way to the counter, still talking, phones in their hands, but his gaze stayed on the slowly closing door, sensing something—the same thing she was sensing. That stark familiarity. The urgency.

"Red," whispered Ruth, smelling the cold fall air. She was starting to see it. She was *letting* herself see it.

"Purple," whispered Reece.

Neither of them noticed the woman approaching their table until she was there, standing right next to them. Sixty-something, gray hair pulled back, solidly built, arms folded over an apron with the café's name.

"I don't mean to interrupt whatever word game you're playing. Meet me in the back office, honey. If you don't mind."

When Reece didn't stand up to follow, the lady turned to Ruth.

"Listen. I don't know if you're a family friend, teacher or what, but I'm friends with his mom, and we're doing everything we can to keep him focused and out of trouble. A job helps with that." She gave Reece a thin-lipped nod. "He knows the rules. No phone, no wandering off to use someone else's phone, no wandering off to sit in a corner with a friend. And now this. I'm stumped."

Ruth stood so she was eye to eye with the woman, who seemed to be blaming her for Reece's behavior. A moment ago, this corner of the café had been cold. Now it was blazing hot. She tugged at the zipper of her fleece vest, desperate for air.

The woman said, "This was a place where he could get away from electronic screens and work on the impulse-control issue."

"*Was?*" Ruth put a hand to the back of her chair to steady herself. She was tense, and she didn't think it was due to being confronted by a stranger.

"I'm sorry," Ruth said, aware her words were slurring. "I didn't mean to distract him. I assumed his shift was"—she closed her eyes—"done."

"He's a bright kid," the manager said, but it sounded like the words were coming through a long tube. "But three strikes, you know?"

Three strikes, Ruth thought in echoing slow motion, counting them out. *One, two . . .*

"I'm just going to sit down, if you don't mind." The chair was suddenly too far away. The floor was better: cool, comfortable, quiet.

She saw the lady's face, and Reece's looking down at her from above.

Ruth wanted to be alone so she could do what she always did. *Try to move past it.* But then she remembered: *There's no reason to rush. Watching isn't going to hurt you.*

Just as they'd always tried to tell her in those Harm OCD sessions, the ones she thought had nothing to teach her. *Suppression will only make it stronger. Thought isn't action. You aren't doing this thing. You aren't really there.* And she wasn't in a bathtub, either. During the attack yesterday, she'd seen so little.

Be curious. No, more than curious. Confrontational. *Demand to see. Demand to understand.*

She tried to think of the bravest person she knew. Joe came to mind. She wanted to save Scott. But she wanted to *be* Joe.

Ruth tried to block out the faces above her, all the people in the café, surely staring at her by now. She closed her eyes and attempted to stay with the image.

She was cold, with wind on her face, and squinting at something: a figure, prone on the ground, face down, head covered from behind by a hood. She could see only the slim hips: could be a boy or a girl. The jeans and shoes offered no clues, either.

And then Ruth's view took in the tall golden grass on all sides of where the person was lying—or hiding. Beyond it, where the grass ended, there was a strip of shorter, patchy, trampled grass, and beyond that, a white line. Then, ultra-short green grass or Astroturf. It was the school, no question: wilder parts unmown, the transition of shorter grass where people walked, the manicured football field.

Near the edge of that field stood Scott, waving his arms. His expression was one of concern. The white shirt. The red shirt. That image again, but starting earlier. Filled in with more detail.

She saw Reece, his silhouette familiar to her now, in the distance, standing next to the bleachers, surrounded by other kids his age, all in purple shirts. But maybe she was seeing that only because he'd described it for her. Maybe she was seeing him because even now, in the café, Reece was talking to her, asking if she was all right, if she needed water or fresh air.

She was suggestible. Everything was getting mixed in: all the possibilities, all her anxieties. Look, there was her own neighbor, the one with whom she'd just had the one-sided conversation about the hole in the yard. He stood only fifty feet from Reece. Everyone was here, it seemed.

Visions couldn't be trusted in all their details, could they? You brought your own experiences into them, projected your culture, your personality or your emotions. Sitting Bull's vision: soldiers, *falling like grasshoppers from the sky.*

Two people could see the same thing and interpret it differently. The Lakota people had prophesied a "black snake" coming to their lands. Modern-day activists in the Dakotas believed that black snake was a proposed pipeline. More than a hundred years earlier, poor Bertha Pappenheim, "Anna O.," had prophesied a black snake, too. For her, it was associated with the death of her father.

But Ruth wasn't seeing grasshoppers or a black snake. Her vision was more like a dream or crudely recorded video, shaky and blurred, but with recognizable figures and faces. She had to see them. She forced herself to pan across the sport field and see who was shooting and being shot, looking for clues as to when this was happening.

Keep watching. But the vision was quickly fading. Ruth tried to store up everything she could, tried to look around again, like a swimmer underwater, running out of oxygen, trying not to break through the surface until the last possible moment.

As she tried to hold on to the vision, Ruth's blood pressure plummeted and her ears filled with roaring static. She knew how she looked, lying there, pale and sweaty, eyes dilating like a drug addict having some kind of fit. She struggled to lift her feet and felt her heels knock against the legs of a chair until she managed to prop them up higher, on the seat. That was better. She felt the blood return, and with it, the image faded, her heart speeding back up to normal.

"I'll call 911," the manager said.

"No, she's had these attacks before," Reece said. "She had one just yesterday. Isn't that right?"

Ruth nodded her head, eyes still closed. Two days in a row.

That had never happened before. Normally they came weeks apart.

"It'll pass," Reece said. Give it to teenagers to take blackouts in stride.

The manager asked, "Are you sure?"

Ruth managed to open her eyes fully. "I'm fine. Just let me rest a minute."

"I still think we should call," the manager said.

"No." Ruth reached a hand up and let Reece pull her into a sitting position. "No ER."

"See? I'll drive her home," Reece said. "She'll be more comfortable there."

"Okay," the manager said, eager to be relieved of any responsibility. "And Reece, this doesn't change anything. Leave your apron. You may be doing a good deed, but this is still your last day of work."

2 3

R U T H

He helped her into his car, moving a pile of library books from the passenger seat to the space at her feet.

"Are you going to tell me what you saw?" Reece asked.

"I'm still trying to get my bearings, Reece. I feel fried. Like I just walked up and touched an electric fence."

"Sorry."

They rode in silence and were turning into her neighborhood when Ruth nudged a book with her toe and, opening her eyes, said, "Shirl Kasper's biography of Annie. You read this?"

"Kasper doesn't believe Annie's hair turned white after the train accident. She says it turned white suddenly weeks later, for unexplained reasons. Maybe the stress of jumping forward or back did it. You said you felt fried. In her session with the shrink, Annie said it was physically painful, and he noticed the shake in her hand. Maybe it takes a while to develop control. But maybe there's also a limit to how many times you can have visions or time travel."

"Which means you have to pick your battles and make the most of each visit."

Ruth sat up straighter, eyes on Reece. "Okay. I saw a figure in the grass. Someone lying down, maybe hiding, facing a green sports field, where Scott was—or will be—standing."

"That's all?"

"That part was the clearest. Then I saw a lot of people next to the field and in the bleachers. But I think by that point I was becoming suggestible. The sounds in the café were bringing me out of the vision. But I did try harder this time, Reece. I did. And I think it's possible to see more."

WHEN THEY PULLED UP TO the house, Ruth spotted something on her front stoop, a white package gleaming in fading evening light, and a lockbox hanging from her doorknob.

"I wish it were from Nieman," she said, squinting. "But I'm pretty sure it's from my realtor."

Reece scooted down in his seat. Ruth followed his gaze toward the neighbor, who was currently ambling toward the curb where the sign had been mistakenly planted. They both watched as he pushed at the half-fixed hole with his foot, then bent to pat a dislodged chunk of turf back into place, trying to repair the damage.

She whispered to Reece, "Why are you hiding?"

"I'm not hiding. I just don't want him to come over and make small talk. He's an asshole."

"You know him?"

"Of course I know him. Rockets, remember?"

"But Van is retired."

"He volunteers, which makes him the worst kind of coach. Too much time on his hands. We don't need his help, but they won't let us use the gym or any of the equipment without a sponsoring adult."

"So he helps out the Rockets?"

"Mostly he gets in the way trying to help or just stands and watches, being creepy, and for that, they give him plaques and Applebee's gift cards."

She still felt she was misunderstanding. "So you don't like him."

"*Like* him? Van Vorst? He's a fucking pedophile."

"That guy? My neighbor? You're messing with me."

"Correction: pedophiles don't always act on their urges. Coach Vorst does. He's a fucking sex offender. He just hasn't been caught."

"He goes after young girls?"

"And guys. The shy kids, the misfits. All I know is what I've seen in friends' texts. He's an equal opportunity offender, evidently. Maybe he just chooses whoever won't talk."

"The school shouldn't let him get near kids, then."

"Right. But I don't think he has a police record or anything. Rumor was that he was asked to retire early. So he's officially off payroll to satisfy parent complaints, but then kids graduate and parents move away and everyone forgets. Then he returns to volunteering. What's to stop him?"

They were still sitting in the car, both of them hunching as the engine ticked and cooled, watching as Vorst walked slowly back to the far corner of the house, where he fiddled with an empty bird feeder hanging from the branch of a spruce tree.

"Don't say it," Reece muttered.

"What?"

"That he can't be that bad a guy, feeding birds and all that."

"I wasn't going to."

"Even Hitler loved dogs."

"I bet."

"And was a vegetarian."

"Noted."

Ruth had no idea what to do with this new information about her neighbor. Had her mother known Van Vorst was a creep? Were the stories true? She didn't think Reece would spread that kind of gossip carelessly.

"His family settled this area back in the 1800s," Ruth said.

"Good for them."

"Homesteaders. They used to own this whole street and some farmland near here, too." She remembered the homework assignment and going over to his house to interview him during the first week of seventh grade. It was her history teacher's bright idea, once she learned Ruth lived right next to the man descended from a well-known local pioneering family.

Vorst had told her how the woods had looked before there was ever a school or subdivisions. When she was young, she'd loved the forest, its quiet depths and magical light, but it seemed more threatening once she reached adolescence and came to equate shadowy places with people who might want to do her harm.

She remembered sitting on Vorst's couch. The scratchy fabric made her legs itch. He was only a foot away with the scrapbook on his lap. She could smell the licorice on his breath as he talked. Gradually he inched the scrapbook closer until it was balanced on one of her thighs and one of his, which made it harder to scoot farther away. The vinyl of the cover stuck to the skin of her bare leg.

That's all he did. He didn't touch her or say anything provocative, but maybe men like him rarely did on a first visit. And Ruth was sure on that day, sitting next to him on the couch, that there would never be a second. She kept wishing she'd worn pants instead of shorts so the scrapbook wouldn't stick to her thighs, making her aware of her own body, her own trickling sweat, her physical self, which was changing, awkwardly and imperfectly.

When she was standing at the door ready to leave, he said her name and she turned. He was holding a camera. "Take your picture?"

She wanted to say no, but she couldn't. It was just a photograph. He wasn't standing close to her. He wasn't even forcing her to smile.

"If no one had bothered to take those pictures from my parents' day, I wouldn't have a scrapbook to show you. You said you like history? I do, too."

That made sense. And then she had opened the door and walked down the path to the sidewalk and turned left, eyes down, still uncomfortable but embarrassed to feel that way, blaming herself often that year for being uncomfortable for seemingly insufficient reasons.

When she got home, Ruth told her mother about the encounter. The details of what she'd said eluded her now. That Vorst had acted strangely? That she didn't like him taking her picture? That she didn't like his licorice breath? It didn't matter. All she remembered was her mother's response.

"You're not being nice."

Girls were supposed to be nice. And adults could do no wrong.

"Did you thank him?"

"I think so."

"You think so?"

"No—I mean yes."

"You don't sound sure. When you get an A+ on that report, you go show him. And thank him properly."

The oral history came back with a C–, which might as well have been an F. Ruth had never gotten anything but A's before.

"I never liked him," Ruth told Reece now.

"A minute ago, you were shocked when I said he was a pervert."

"I was and I wasn't. I felt something before and I didn't want to put a name to it. I think I've been telling myself to ignore it for years."

They watched Vorst retreat into his house, pulling the door closed. The action-sensor light over his porch went out. Ruth sighed, and Reece sat up straighter. "I wouldn't even want to live next to that guy."

"Me neither," Ruth said. "You got another couple hours free?"

RUTH CARRIED IN THE WHITE package, stuffed with flyers, another clear package with additional real-estate info, a brown envelope with no return address, and a card from the realtor, who had shown up at 6 P.M. Ruth had forgotten about the appointment. Did she want to sell this house or didn't she?

Yes. More now than ever.

She looked at her phone: two missed calls. "Nothing from Nieman."

"I'm going to find him for you," Reece said. "We're going to talk to him."

"Correction," Ruth said, opening the mystery envelope first. But it wasn't good. "It's a prepaid express envelope for the return of the journal, and a note, but not from him."

It was written in a light, uneven hand:

He'd like the journal back immediately, please. Sincerely, Hetta.

"From a woman." Ruth showed Reece. "Wife? Sister?"

Hetta had added in an even shakier hand, as if she were in a hurry or simply battling her own self-censor: *This was a blow to him. He has stopped work on the project.*

"He stopped," Ruth said, "because of me. He had good questions about provenance and possible chain of custody. And we didn't even get that far. Because I stopped him from looking."

"And why did you?"

"Because . . ." She hadn't tried putting it into words before. "Because I thought I could go back and have the healthy mind I used to have, the life I used to have, if I resisted believing in anything farfetched."

"Ha!"

"What's so funny?"

"You wanted to go back in time. So you resisted believing that another person—someone you've been studying for years—could go back in time."

Ruth let that statement soak in, turning it around in her mind.

Reece added, "You can still help Nieman, though. Give him solid evidence. Get him back in the game."

Ruth sighed. "Right. And then we have this."

The realtor's note was friendly enough, given the gaffe. But she did give Ruth some firm instructions. *I heard from the inspector he needs to come by a second time, which sets us back, but we're ready and agreed on the listing price unless he finds something you haven't already disclosed. I've left some tips on house preparation ahead of showing, and I have some more papers for you to sign. Let's keep pushing this boat out to sea! Best wishes, Jan.*

What followed was a laundry list that exceeded what the home inspector had already told her. Ruth knew she had a lot of stuff to move, floor space to open up, walls to reveal.

Jan had written, *Applies to your home in particular: we have lots of buyers concerned about mold.*

"I don't see anything about not storing things in the garage, as long as there's a cleared zone so they can see the interior walls," Ruth said to Reece. "Want to earn fifty bucks?"

"If we're talking three hours or less, sure. After that, I have to get home."

She dropped onto the couch and opened her laptop. "Okay, let me check my email first."

Reece remained standing. "I hear that's a great way to get started on any horrible cleaning project."

Ruth patted the cushion next to her. "No, you're going to like this. It's from Sophie, my foundation contact."

First, I'm sorry to inform you that Lila Walters passed away last February at the age of 94. I thought you would have seen it in the newsletters.

"Who's Lila?"

"Lila Walters," Ruth explained. "Like Sophie, she is—*was*—related to Annie Oakley. High up at one of the foundations. I missed the obit entirely."

It was the end of an era. Ruth had always wanted to interview

Lila, but Lila had always refused and Ruth had taken no for an answer too often. No longer.

But on to happier news. I'm in Minneapolis to talk to some non-profits about foundation funding, and Wednesday I'll be seeing a friend at the Mayo Clinic in Rochester. I believe that's three hours from where you are? Care to meet for dinner? You asked me a question, and I'd like to answer it, but not by email. It's complicated. In any event, I thought it would be a pleasure to finally meet.

"That's tomorrow," Ruth said. "She wants to have dinner. I think she knows something."

"About our journal?"

"No telling. Maybe just about restricted materials. I think she's tempted to share."

Ruth tried to muster energy in light of this good news—and not just out of the blue, but from a potential ally, practically a friend. A road trip. She hadn't driven outside town limits in ages.

Scratch that. She hadn't driven at all.

She no longer drove.

And she had the inspector coming a second time on Wednesday. Of course, she could cancel. But Ruth recognized the signs of self-sabotage and knew the house should have been sold and vacated ages ago.

"I'll do it. But it's going to be hard," she said, noting the bus schedule: ten hours, a transfer in Minneapolis.

"Getting to Rochester? *That's* hard?"

"As hard as cleaning up this disaster of a house."

"We've got that part covered."

"I'm just . . . really tired."

The attacks always drained her, but this last one had come close on the heels of the previous one, plus she'd allowed it to go on longer. She shut the laptop lid fast and stood up, not wanting Reece to see her hand trembling.

In the bathroom, she washed down some ibuprofen with water

and found herself gripping the sink, staring into her reflection. It looked wrong, like her eyebrows were a touch too high, a shadow at her chin too dark, her whole face blurry. The lighting in this bathroom had always been terrible, but this was something else. It bothered her again that she couldn't find her last few Xanax at the moment she most needed one.

She eased herself down to the floor, where she remained for several minutes. When lights began to strobe behind her eyelids, she opened them wide again and hoisted herself to a standing position. She splashed herself with water, leaving splatter all over the sink and mirror.

When she came out, Reece had already prepared a plate of Ritz crackers, a dollop of peanut butter, another dollop of cream cheese, a small mound of raisins and two limp, nearly white sticks of celery. It looked like snack time for toddlers at a nursery school.

"It was the best I could do before you got distracted with all the boxes and crap," he said. "You need to eat something."

It didn't look appealing, but she swiped a Ritz into the peanut butter and found to her surprise that it hit the spot: sugar, protein, carbs, salt. She'd probably needed this back at the café.

"Thank you," she said.

"You know, I think this may be the first time you've said that."

He dipped an albino celery stick into the cream cheese and added a line of raisins. "May I? Here's what I propose. You get to Rochester and be back by Thursday."

"Why Thursday? The house inspection is Wednesday, but I don't have to be here for it."

"Thursday because you rescheduled your visit to Holloway's class, remember?"

"Oh, shit."

She kept forgetting things. Her ability to think clearly was in serious doubt.

"Listen," he said. "You go to Rochester, squeeze this lady for everything she knows, come back Thursday before Holloway's class, and I promise to bring you Nieman's real name and phone number. Right now, let's make your house less like a reality show about hoarders."

It was a kind offer, especially the cleaning part. If time travel really were possible and common, everyone would skip past these things: house sales, physical and mental rehabilitation, waiting for your ex to marry and have children with someone else.

"Maybe I'm wrong about everything," she said.

"No one's wrong about *everything*."

"Maybe the journal is a big joke, and I'm just projecting everything from my own life onto Annie Oakley, like the idea that a woman her age would suddenly have a crisis that made her revisit the darkest chapters of her life."

"If all that's just your imagination going into overdrive," Reece said, "why does Sophie want to meet with you?"

24

CALEB

Wednesday

Tuesday, Caleb hadn't gone to school. When texts started arriving from Reece asking why he hadn't shown up for Rockets practice, Caleb ignored them. He was alternately thinking about someone else and trying not to until it got so bad he wished he could jam a stick through the spokes of the wheel of his consciousness just to stop it.

He was still thinking about the Kennidy girl, who was related to the historian coming to talk to their class. Maybe the woman knew that her sister had been deep in Vorst's clutches, which could've had something to do with her eventual overdose, though of course the coach didn't see it that way. Maybe the woman knew nothing at all. Caleb's parents sure didn't.

Caleb wanted a sign, any sign. He wanted someone to tell him what to do, how to deal with the scream bottled up in his chest, ready to explode.

After school yesterday, he'd come home and argued with his stepdad, then gone straight to his room, where he proceeded to ignore the outline he was supposed to write for Mrs. Holloway's World History class on top of the new assignment they'd just been given to get ready for Ruth McClintock's upcoming visit. Already, Caleb was behind on the imperialism paper by two weeks.

After Holloway had started the timer on partner discussions in class, Jared, the football dude on Caleb's right, said, "I dunno. Imperialism's bad, I guess. I'm writing about that."

"You got an iPhone?" Caleb asked.

"Yeah. So?"

"So, it's made in China? At the direction of overlords based in California."

"I'm not writing about China. Maybe England or something."

"Never mind."

Caleb still had a minute left to talk—he couldn't fault Jared for stealing all the time—but the truth was, he wasn't clear on the topic, either. From what Caleb understood, imperialism was about subjugating other people for your own benefit. Which is basically what any human being did, if he could. You either stood on top of people or they stood on top of you. Nations were made up of people. And empires had been around forever and always would be. Pretending otherwise wasn't just phony, it was infuriating.

But anyway, that had been two weeks ago. Anyone who gave a shit and wanted to pass had had their topic approved and had begun their research. Now the class—minus Caleb and one or two other fuckups—had moved on.

On Friday, the girls in the front row had been obsessed with whether they needed to use Roman numerals or if they could just use bullet points, and how many spaces to tab. As they peppered Holloway with these questions, Caleb was already zoned out.

Outlines were harder to write than full research papers. You had to understand your whole topic before you could think in an organized enough way to boil it down into an outline—because spitting out ideas as they came to you and seeing where they went was easier than boiling them down into a series of organized little points. How could he know the points he was going to make before he made them? Why didn't teachers get that?

Last year, in history class, he'd gotten away with doing the whole thing in reverse. Step one, type until you hit page three, five, whatever. Second, look for sources that might back up the facts or opinions you've already typed. If you're really stuck, make them up.

Third, when you're basically ninety percent done, outline. Fourth, write the short proposal paragraph—that thing Caleb was supposed to pitch verbally and then hand in during week two rather than week twelve—because now you know what you've said and therefore it's actually semi-possible to pretend you are planning to say it.

In other words, do the whole thing exactly backward, because that was the only way you ever knew anything, not when you were in the thick of it, but when you were looking back and almost done.

The system worked with teachers like Mr. Philbin, who would give you a C even if the whole thing was two months late. But Holloway was different. She really believed in this outlining shit. Caleb was going to fail her class. But that hardly mattered, considering he wouldn't be around by the end of the year.

These were the facts Caleb was reviewing as he sat on his unmade bed, looking up at the ceiling. No wonder he couldn't figure out what to do as he biked past the asshole's house over and over. The steps—how he'd gotten himself into this situation, what he should do about it, what would happen if he did manage to hurt Coach V—were like the outline. It didn't come out of his head all in order, one detail at a time. He wasn't ready to think that way.

Thinking clearly, starting at the beginning, made him sick. It forced him to remember the first time Vorst had given him a ride. He'd praised Caleb for his soccer skills—which frankly, weren't that impressive, since Caleb had started soccer late compared to all the other kids, who had played since they were four or six.

Vorst had commiserated about Caleb's parents—sticklers about grades, uninterested in anything else in Caleb's life. Fall semester, freshman year. Caleb hadn't made any friends. His mother didn't defend him against his stepdad's constant criticism. They told Caleb that he didn't have a clue about anything, that he was bound to be a failure. They told him to focus less on sports—it's not like he was all that talented anyway—and more on getting his homework done.

Caleb had said, "I'm the one thinking about the future. Like athletic scholarships."

Caleb still remembered Vorst's expression that day: indignant on Caleb's behalf.

"Listen. In your parents' day, college cost a fraction what it does now. No one can afford it without sports or music scholarships. At least you're trying to think ahead. You're smarter than your parents, Caleb. They just can't know that."

The coach was smooth. Some guys didn't like him, but others, like Caleb, did, especially as the weeks went on, and the coach gave him more playing time, praised him, offered him rides every couple days. Then Caleb injured his hamstring. Even though he was getting better and able to run again, they still dropped him from the team.

Coach V talked him into cross-country running: easy at first while his hamstring healed. Not with the team, just the two of them, or more often, Caleb alone, on trails outside town where the early snow was packed down. Vorst would drive him, drop him off at a trailhead, drive to the far side of the trail system three or four miles away and be there waiting.

"Feels good to be out there, doesn't it?" Vorst would say, waiting in the warm car, with Gatorade or juice, or after the first few times, a can of beer. "You know, some people won't run a single mile unless they get a medal or a T-shirt for it. But we're different."

They stayed parked and kept talking. Another beer. "Don't worry. You deserve it."

Caleb hadn't eaten much lunch, and the run had left him woozy. The beer went directly to his head.

Coach V was on a roll. "Doesn't matter what anyone thinks. Live your own life." He offered him yet another beer, and Caleb didn't want it, but once it was in his hand, he didn't know what to do other than finish it. Before he dropped Caleb at his house, Vorst even gave him a piece of hard candy to cover up the smell. "And when you're back in shape, we'll get you started on looking for college scholarships. My daughter was going after some good ones, right before she passed away. I've got some contacts. Personal recommendations are essential these days. No letter from a coach, no free money for school."

And then there was that day in late January when Caleb got into Vorst's car parked at the empty trailhead and didn't say anything when Vorst asked him to do what Caleb did, which was practically just sit there. It was just a favor. An exchange.

The engine was on. The heater blew noisily. The windows fogged. It was over in minutes, and that was good. It was easier to just do it than to try to get out of doing it. Vorst always got super quiet right after. That silence, and the absence of pressure that followed, were a huge relief. If it had always been that quick and easy, that wordless and painless, Caleb could have put it all behind him. Even now, he believed that.

But it wasn't that easy. The next time was at Vorst's out-of-town cabin—still winter; the cabin was miserable until they'd picked up that portable heater—when he drank the nasty Tang-and-vodka screwdriver that Vorst gave him, knowing what Vorst had put in it. Because here was the fucked-up thing: people at parties got roofied without knowing. But Caleb had taken the drink completely aware of what was in it: "Just Ambien," Vorst had said. "Enough to take the edge off."

When Caleb hesitated, Vorst said, "I know you kids take this stuff at parties. It's just like having two or three drinks. You can handle three drinks, can't you?"

Vorst put a movie on starring the guy who did the Buzz Light-year voice, but this was a Santa Claus movie, which was harder to pretend to watch than *Toy Story*. At one point, Vorst went to get something from the cellar and was gone for a strangely long time. Caleb went to the bookcase where other videos were stored, trying to be chill—though chill was the last thing he felt—hoping there'd be something less awful to watch.

Below the videos were several drawers, and without thinking, Caleb opened one. And there were the faces, staring up at him.

They were girls and guys close to his age and a little younger, sitting and staring at the camera with glazed expressions or sleeping—sleeping *off* something, more like, on the couch that was already familiar to Caleb. A few were naked. Not actually doing anything, not involved with any other person or in obscene poses or anything, but nude. That was the word his mom used when she was trying to sound artsy. God, why was he thinking of his mother at this moment? She could never find out about any of this. He felt the burn of the drink in his throat. Some of the kids were really young.

Compared to stuff Caleb had seen online, raw and outrageous from the first second a window popped open, this was nothing. But it didn't *feel* like nothing. It felt like opening a trapdoor down into a cellar and seeing there was a real person, small and quiet, sitting in there. Why did it freak him out so much? Because that was porn. It wasn't real.

That was what they told you—even your own damn stepdad when you found his ancient magazine collection, when he sat you down and forced you to listen. "Don't get confused. It's not real, buddy." As if that were a bad thing.

Not real was okay. Good, even. This was real, and he didn't like it, and he didn't know what to do. On top of that, the Ambien was kicking in and with it, the sleepy unreality that was normally a preferred state to being in the cabin, sober.

Caleb listened for any sound that indicated Vorst was coming up the stairs—nothing—and opened the second drawer, hoping to be persuaded somehow that it wasn't *like that*. There was an explanation.

The entire second drawer, deeper than the first, was filled with USB flash drives—black, yellow, silver—more than Caleb had ever seen in any one place.

Now, *this* was a collection. Caleb stared. Thousands or tens of thousands of digital files or images, possibly. They could be normal pictures—Vorst was always carrying a camera from one sports practice or event to another—but Caleb didn't think so.

Now what?

It wasn't like Caleb had said, even once, "Take me home now."

It was easier to think he had brought this all upon himself than to admit that it was all Vorst and it wasn't just their secret and Caleb wasn't the first.

You're a fucking idiot, Caleb thought. Not: *The coach is a predator.* Not: *Van Vorst is a criminal.* Only: *Caleb, you're not even special when it comes to this.*

And then there was the separate shoebox in the back of the drawer, dedicated to the girl with the halter top. The girl who had died, who must be the same person Vorst called his daughter but really wasn't—not that it made anything better.

"Everything all right?" came Vorst's voice from the stairwell.

Caleb hurried back to the couch, heart in his throat, sounds of the Santa Claus movie only a little louder than his own ragged breathing.

"Get comfy," Vorst told him.

"I'm comfy."

"No, I mean, take your jeans off. Heater's on. It's not cold anymore."

Caleb's policy was to say as little as possible, not to agree or disagree, just to go into that place where you could pretend later that nothing had happened. Without talking, there were fewer details to remember. After ten minutes, when Caleb became too sleepy to keep his eyes open, it was a relief.

Caleb woke up later, only a little nauseated, but also confused and sore in ways he'd never been sore, in ways that wouldn't let him entirely forget, though he would try. Vorst had crossed a line.

There was something set loose in Vorst that weekend: bravado, maybe, knowing that Caleb's parents didn't know where he was, weren't paying proper attention, didn't seem to care. Things changed. It wasn't a matter of forgetting an awkward two minutes or a half-remembered session on the couch. That had always been embarrassing and humiliating. Now it became something more. Caleb couldn't find a way out.

Vorst no longer praised Caleb or commiserated over the stupidity of Caleb's parents. He taunted Caleb, making him feel like he'd started whatever it was they were doing. After all, he'd chosen to sleep over for a full weekend.

"Remember when you were fighting with your parents, and I let you stay?"

It was on a Sunday after spring break when Caleb woke up ten hours after he'd gotten woozy from sipping the Tang. Not an hour, not the length of a movie, but a whole day, gone. That freaked him out.

He told Vorst he wouldn't do it again. The rest, okay, but not that. Not something that put him fully under.

"But I don't like it the other way," Vorst said, studying him like he was a jigsaw puzzle, "when you're awake at the start."

Caleb shrugged his shoulders, waiting.

"She didn't like it either," Vorst said after a while. Caleb didn't ask who *she* was. "I showed her a party trick. I can show you, too. It feels good. Like a natural high without the hangover."

The trick was making him black out. The next time they were in the cabin together, Vorst leaned against his chest, crushing him, and Caleb felt one hand grip his neck, and only then did Caleb understand. He'd heard of the choking game, but he didn't know if this was the same thing. He didn't know for sure that he would wake up at all.

Later that night, when Vorst was carrying some bags out to the car, Caleb bided his time—"Gotta go to the bathroom before we drive"— then ran back inside before Vorst had the chance to lock the door. Caleb went directly to the drawers where he'd seen the photos of kids. He took some, started toward the door, then turned back and grabbed some things from the shoebox—the girl-in-a-halter-top shoebox—stuffed it all in his backpack fast, all without thinking, and then, with his heart in his throat and his backpack clasped to his chest, joined Vorst outside.

"Here, let me show you how to check the oil," Vorst said, like he was his dad or something.

"Uh, yeah. Okay." Heart beating like a jackhammer.

It didn't matter what they did inside that cabin. It didn't matter that Caleb had two big red thumbprints turning into bruises on either side of his neck. The coach was living in his own world, whistling away, filling his bird feeders and checking the oil in his car. Fucking amazing.

The next day at school, someone made a joke about the hickeys on Caleb's neck, and the joke spread fast. Caleb helped it along, adding his own fabricated details. If people wanted to believe he had some phantom nympho girlfriend, that was fine as far as he was concerned.

Summer was around the corner. The next weekend, Caleb told Vorst that his parents were taking him on a trip. He never just said, "I don't want your hands on me anymore." He certainly never said, "I'm going to tell the school and my parents and the police." The final week of school was the hardest, but he made it through.

Over the summer, they didn't see each other. Caleb grew four inches and packed on weight and for the first time could wear a men's shirt in size small without swimming in it. He was still scrawny for his age, but nothing like he'd been as a freshman. He thought about what Vorst said about the girl who wasn't really his daughter, "She was getting fat," as if there couldn't have been anything more disgusting. Caleb wasn't fat, but he wasn't reed-thin anymore, either. He'd always known that muscles could be a form of protection from other guys his age. He'd never realized that they could also be protection from an old pervert who liked kids who looked like they were twelve years old.

"You're looking like a man, chum," his stepdad said that first day of school. Caleb rolled his eyes, but he also felt like he'd just made it across a river filled with crocodiles.

The first week of school, the coach seemed to ignore him. *Good.* But that didn't mean Coach V was ignoring everyone.

Mikayla. She's next.

That was where Caleb had to stop. He couldn't think about much beyond that. If he could have taken the actual gray mass of his brain out of his skull and scrubbed it with a stiff wire brush until his nerves burned and his eyes bled, he would have.

So, fuck Holloway and her outlines. Caleb didn't care about Roman numerals or bullet points. He didn't want ordered thoughts and sharp memories. He didn't need pro and con or before and after.

If he just went with the flow, it looked like this:

He wanted Vorst gone. No longer on this earth, but having suffered before departing it.

That was the uncensored version.

And only now that he'd said it—admitted it—maybe he could work backward and figure out the right steps to make it happen.

2 5

ANNIE

1905, 1869

Annie opens her eyes and sees the rutted track leading past trampled grass to the old house and knows she has arrived. This is the right place and the right time. Autumn of a familiar year. The oak tree shades the western side of the house. There is no swing hanging yet from its thickest, blackest branch. The white paint on the old house is fresh. A dog barks once and then yelps, silenced inside the house by an unkind hand. The oak's leaves are red and curling: October, maybe. The baby was born in summer. He'll be three months old now.

Annie creeps carefully, head low, rifle tucked close to her chest, stalking. She half-expects to see her own figure coming around the side of the house, carrying firewood or peeking out of the kitchen window. But that makes no sense. She's never collided with herself before. The wagon is gone, but a thin spiral of smoke curls above the chimney.

It's like dreaming all night of thirst and then waking and tipping a pitcher into a cold, clean bowl and preparing to dip one's hands into that beautiful, fresh water. That moment of intense thirst will soon be quenched, need and satisfaction just a hair's breadth apart. Is that what she'd always loved about hunting? The promise of satisfaction, as close as the pull of a trigger? Or did she simply love that it was something that she was good at, that put food on the table, that made her feel safe and strong and like everything would turn out fine? But it didn't turn out fine, even with a gun. Even with the talent she had, even with her confidence in herself, which this man—this beast—had almost managed to destroy.

But what does she plan to do now? Try as she might, she hasn't been able to face the thought squarely. Her body is telling her: *walk softly, don't be seen.* Rifle ready. Resolve firm. She brings the gun even closer, presses it hard into her flat chest. From inside, she feels so much like a woman—a woman of some forty years—that she keeps forgetting this is the body of a girl: arms thin, ankles narrow, long brown hair in a single braid almost to her waist.

For a moment, the recognition of her own bodily youth scares her. But there's no reason for fear. She's never been weak, even as a girl of nine or ten. She's just been confused and unaware. For years, she blamed herself for not standing up to him. It sickens her to remember him moaning and pressing into her, whispering in a hoarse, oddly high-pitched voice that she liked his attentions, that he wouldn't keep coming back except that she was such a little tramp. He accused her even as his dribble ran down her trembling, pinned leg and into her skirts. He claimed that she liked it more than he did. In time, he became even more bold, asking the question out loud. "Do you like me, girl? Do you?" He yanked her head back by the hair until she answered, not with what he wanted to hear, but only with a gasp. That seemed to be enough. He just wanted to hear a voice, any voice. "I'm so lonely, Annie," he said once, catching his breath as he lay, collapsed on top of her, not yet fully spent but resting, panting. She lay, stiff and silent, waiting for him to remove his bulk so she could slip away, caring not one whit for his so-called loneliness. Then she felt him harden and start again.

And the She-wolf knew. She *had* to know. Especially when,

just as they were stoking the fire the first time or the tenth, he told Annie to follow him out to the woodshed—said it right in front of the She-wolf, as she put away her sewing and shifted the baby's crib closer to the fire—and they did not come back for an hour, carrying a handful of kindling. Once he fell asleep lying on top of her. Her toes started to tingle inside her too-tight boots; she was losing feeling in her legs, but still he didn't move until hours later, when he woke with a start and stumbled out of the shed with her trailing behind, silver light marking the path. She hated everything at that moment: even the creaking oak tree, even the full moon that had risen over their heads, tracking slowly across the cold sky. Everything went about its own business, pretending not to see. That was what she had learned, living at the house. In the end, nothing and nobody cared.

Except, perhaps, for one person: Mrs. Edington, the lady who ran the infirmary in Greenville and had loaned Annie out as a laborer to the strangers in the first place. But it didn't take much for the Wolves to fool her. Annie had seen a letter arrive from Mrs. Edington, and a few days later, saw the He-wolf bent over a piece of paper, scribbling a half-literate reply. No doubt he told her that Annie was getting her wages and being taught to read and write. No doubt Mrs. Edington believed him. One day, Annie would escape back to the poor farm where she'd be taken back in. But not yet, and meanwhile every day was an eternity.

Creeping up to the cabin now, Annie remembers it all. Biting her lip to stop her teeth from chattering, she stalks closer, wishing for the world to be quiet for her, to aid her quest. Her boots silently grind the dry leaves into frost-speckled mud. Everything is dying with the season. One more pathetic old man won't shift God's balance terribly much.

Then suddenly, the little cabin's door swings open. A woman stands there, hand over the front of her shabby checked brown dress, drawing in a breath of welcome surprise. "Oh, Phoebe Ann."

The Missus takes a step forward, hand raised over her brow. It's a bleak autumn day, clouds streaking by, but still bright compared to the shadows of the dark home. "I'm so glad you're back. Come quick."

Annie hesitates, trying to match this moment to what she pictured, and that is the problem. She never pictured it in enough detail. What to do about the woman, the baby and the mutt, who runs out the door and past her now, stumpy tail wagging, happy to escape the nag who hit him just moments ago.

Seeing her balk, the woman misunderstands and calls out reassuringly, "He's gone to town."

It doesn't feel right to call her the She-wolf in her own cabin, as the thin-faced Missus bustles from woodstove to narrow kitchen table, hurrying to fill two chipped mugs with water from the kettle. "I saw you'd taken the rifle. I was afraid you were gone for the whole day."

Annie doesn't know how to answer.

"Even if we need the grub, even if he told you to stay out for a good spell," the woman says, "I'd rather have your company. Jack was crying so long and hard I really thought he was going to stop breathing. I tried everything you do, but he wouldn't quit. Walking and rocking and cold air until he was gasping and every bit of my milk was gone, so I wetted the cloth with sugar water for him to suck on, and I even went looking for that little blue bottle the doctor gave us . . ."

She is rambling without a breath, as if she won't get it all out otherwise and she can't decide if she should laugh or cry. The woman's whole body is trembling with what she has almost done just to make the cabin quiet again. It's hard not to throttle a child who is screeching in your ear and punching your sore breast with those mad little red fists. "But you know, I think someone in this house went and drank that solution? I guess my husband has trouble sleeping, too." And she laughs again, the most unnatural, unmusical laugh Annie has ever heard: a stuck window forced open, screeching.

But here's the thing that Annie forgot. The She-wolf did not, in fact, despise her. Did not, in fact, always mistreat her. Even the He-wolf, bad as he was, didn't always do wrong by her. It's been hard enough to remember the pain and the sorrow. It's equally hard to remember this: that Annie felt, at moments, that she could almost belong here, if he would just stop the worst of what he was doing.

Does a sheep ever refuse to run from a wolf, not just from the paralysis of fear, but from stupid hope?

That thought makes Annie angrier, and the rage, turned inward now, makes her confused. She knows what happens when she gets confused. The face of the She-wolf fades. The view of the cabin flickers. The smell of apples lingers. Darkness falls.

"Give her water," says Sitting Bull's gentle voice.

2 6

R U T H

The Greyhound bus would be leaving at the undignified hour of 6 A.M., and while Ruth was gone, the home inspector would be coming. It would be smart to go to bed early, but Ruth was too wired to relax. Reece had left last night at 7 P.M., having done as much in three hours as she could have done in a day, moving items so fast Ruth barely had time to classify them.

When they took breaks, Reece showed her videos of his Rockets team rehearsing. He apologized repeatedly—*we don't have this move down yet, we're missing two of our guys here*—but he needn't have bothered. It all looked impressive to Ruth: all those young bodies flipping, lifting, balancing, rolling and jumping back up, unhurt. Reece showed her a few still shots, naming some of the members: *Gerald, Caleb, Courtney, Justin, Raj.* She asked about one child who seemed too tiny to be a high schooler. At first, Ruth thought she was a boy, with her close-cropped hair, thin arms and flat chest. *That's Mikayla. Her parents are from Kenya. She can't weigh more than ninety pounds. Flyers are hard to find. She subs for Caleb when he blows off practice.*

Reece's mood soured then, but just as well—there were more heavy boxes and small pieces of furniture to move, music blasting again. Then he went home, leaving Ruth to manage another round of sorting on her own.

Dinner hour, with a chance to do more online research, was her reward, with more housework to follow. The house was quiet with Reece gone. The frozen burrito turned slowly in Gwen's ancient microwave.

Before Ruth had told him not to bother anymore, Nieman had asked in his email, *Could you posit a provenance and chain of custody?*

She knew the word "posit" of course, but she'd never looked it up. *Synonyms: To speculate, conjecture, imagine . . .*

Well, of course she could *imagine* a provenance, if that was all he'd wanted.

In recent decades in Vienna, apartment renovations had turned up a number of surprises, like the eight hundred Holocaust-era cardboard boxes of documents found in an empty apartment in 2000. Whether hidden or in plain view, war-era documents continued to emerge, especially as real-estate values skyrocketed and new owners and contractors opened doors, pulled up flooring and drilled holes through walls.

Josef Breuer, still her best guess as the author of the journal, had died in 1925, years before the Nazis gained power. However, Ruth reasoned, his papers must have gone somewhere—and not all to the Library of Congress archives, which had only 425 items related to him, far fewer than the library's Freud archives, with over 46,000 items.

According to a genealogy website, the oldest of Breuer's children was Margarethe Schiff, born in 1872 and dead in 1942—murdered, as were other Breuer family members, in the camp at Terezín outside Prague in what was now the Czech Republic.

Using digitized public-access records on Holocaust victims, Ruth did a search on Margarethe, unsuccessful at first. But then she found her in the database, thanks to the National Archives in Prague, with the correct spelling of her first name—Margarete. Off to one side of the webpage were statistics on others who had traveled to Terezín with her: 1,008 deported. Only 38 survived.

There was an image of her death certificate with the cause of death, written in uneven block letters: *Suicid*. No *e* at the end, followed by the German word: *Selbstmord*. Ruth clicked on the image to enlarge it, studying the fancier signatures in old-fashioned script not dissimilar to the handwriting Ruth had been studying in the journal. Ruth couldn't help but think of these self-satisfied, monstrous concentration-camp doctors and bureaucrats wielding their fancy pens. *Assholes*.

There, too, were the specifics of her transport and her last known residence: *Vídeň 2, Haasgasse 8*. This was the street the seller had mentioned, but someone along the way had misspelled it. Not *Hassgasse*, or *Hate Alley*; not *Hasengasse*, or *Hare Alley*, but *Haasgasse*.

The seller hadn't been lying. It had only been a typo, just as there had been an error in various spellings of Margarete Breuer's name, which was why one had to keep digging and never look away.

Ruth copied the Vienna address into Google Maps. There was the neighborhood where Breuer's grown daughter had lived until her deportation on Transport IV/9. There was the place, not far from a royal park and the Danube, where Breuer's records of his visit with Annie Oakley might have been passed down to his daughter and carefully stored, perhaps even hidden. There was the residential address on a small lane where the journal—as well as any letters that the doctor had received later—had been forgotten and found again. Hypothetical at first, more likely with every detail found—a knowable, understandable thing.

Unlike, say, Ruth's own sister's life and suicide.

Type Kennidy's name into a search box and you were rerouted to celebrity stories about the famous Kennedy clan and the suicide of RFK's wife, Mary, in 2012. Never mind that Ruth's mother had insisted on spelling her daughter's name in an uncommon way.

It made no difference. Kennidy McClintock, daughter of Gwen McClintock and sister of Ruth McClintock, hadn't done anything worthy of fame, or lived in a police state that kept an obscene number of records, or died in an era tragic enough to inspire massive digitized documentation efforts. But that didn't mean she hadn't suffered. Only that she had suffered mostly alone, leaving few traces—or at least few that Ruth knew about.

But then again, Ruth had never wanted to look.

RUTH WAS IN A CLEAN, beige-and-white-walled room, sitting on the floor and staring into the calming geometry of metal tubular chair legs, the underside of blond, Scandinavian-style furniture. Beyond the chair legs: a blank wall. She was in the university library, no question, using a cell phone in violation of library rules. On the end of the line was her mother, Gwen, talking to her in a calm tone. But Ruth felt dread. Something was wrong. Something involving Kennidy.

"Mom," she kept trying to say, but her mother wouldn't listen, and now Ruth remembered why she was so desperate to get through to her, so that her mother could check on Kennidy in her closed bedroom so that something might be done before it was too late.

"*Mom.*"

The phone call hadn't gone the way it should have. Her mother hadn't listened. She hadn't forced open Kennidy's door. When Ruth's phone rang again the next day, just past noon on a Monday, Ruth felt the wrongness in her gut. The caller ID said Gwen, but the voice at the end of the line was a friend of Gwen's from work, helping to make the first phone calls while Gwen stood by, speechless and in shock.

"Come home, Ruth. Your sister . . ."

Now Ruth opened her eyes. She'd fallen asleep on the couch doing her Holocaust-era research. The clock on the wall read only 10:35 P.M.

The garage still awaited her. She returned to the chilly space, no longer enlivened by Reece's playlist. She didn't have to do any more sorting tonight, but the items she'd most avoided before now called to her. There were hatboxes full of costume jewelry, knotted chains and dead watches. She didn't want most of it, but she knew this was her last chance to find the odd item or two that would bring back memories of Gwen dressed up, trying to look her best.

Ruth's mother had been stolen from her at the worst possible time. A mostly healthy woman should not have died at the age of fifty-one. Ruth blamed her mother's bad habits: junk food, smoking, zero exercise. And she blamed Kennidy, the very embodiment of chaos and dysfunction. Or she *had* blamed her. Now things were looking more complicated.

Ruth stared at two gray suitcases, heavy and moldy-smelling, that had once belonged to her late grandfather. It was just like her mother to hide things rather than deal with them. Chances were, these hideous old suitcases contained her grandfather's old clothes. Unless they held Kennidy's.

She pulled a chair closer, old light fixture flickering overhead. The suitcases were brown in normal light. Now, in the bluish glow of the fluorescent lights, they were an odd shade of green, like a cold, algae-tinged lake. A color that called both "dive in" and "beware."

To Ruth's right was an old nightstand with a broken leg. She'd had Reece put it into the "don't-know" pile because of its drawers full of miscellany: old concert ticket stubs, playing cards and matchbooks. In the back was a pack of ancient cigarettes, one of many Kennidy would have hidden around the house. Ruth gave it a sniff, pulled out a bent one and lit it up. Another dose of masochism. First, it tasted like how the rest of the basement-stored furniture smelled, like mouse droppings and damp plywood, but then the tobacco got burning.

And there it was: the smell of college parties. The smell of Kennidy and their drive to that cabin in the woods on a warm night, though the trees weren't fully greened yet, so it wasn't quite summer, but almost. That night when Kennidy had taken the golf club out of the trunk and started swinging.

Ruth, buzzed and squinting at the figure of her sister in the headlights, had called out to her through the window. "What the fuck, Ken?"

"What the fuck *you*. Are you coming?"

"What are you doing?"

It was clear what she was doing: wreaking havoc. Making a point.

"Why? Ken—come on."

Kennidy shouted in the direction of the cabin, "Come out, you fucking coward! Give them back!"

So this person had taken something from her sister. She could've at least explained.

"Help me," Kennidy said, squinting into the headlight beam toward Ruth, not waiting for a reply. She went to the door and pounded on it, screaming curse words. Seconds passed, time extending and dissolving and twisting, reshaped by panic and the alcohol coursing through their veins.

Ruth missed the moment when the door opened briefly, but she saw her sister bending to pick up something scattered just beyond the headlights' reach. Kennidy walked back to the car, head down, hands pushing something into her back pocket.

"What was that?" Ruth asked when her sister slammed the door.

"Nothing."

Ruth backed out fast, spitting up gravel, barely missing a tree. They bounced down the driveway, back toward the main road.

"Put your seat belt on at least. Damn it, Ken, I mean it!" Ruth was busy scanning the country road ahead for police cars that might be sitting on the dark shoulder, waiting to pull them over. She was begging her own brain to sober up.

When they'd made it a few miles with no one following, Ruth asked, "I take it an ex-boyfriend of yours lives there?"

"Something like that."

"Does Mom know about this guy?"

"Pretty much."

"You gonna tell me about him?"

"I would've, if you'd gotten out of the car and helped."

"What was I supposed to do? Break windows? Clobber the guy?"

"Maybe."

"So you're saying I failed some test."

"Yeah. You failed. We both did."

"But you got what you wanted," Ruth said. "What were they, pictures?" She was guessing. Who printed photos these days? Nearly all the ones Ruth had were on her phone. And hadn't Ken's generation grown up with more warnings than her own about the perils of sexting and images ending up in the wrong places?

Ruth asked, "Why'd you let him take photos of you in the first place?"

"I didn't know."

"You didn't know?"

"Not really."

"So you were drunk, high, or passed out." Ruth was starting to feel protective, but no less mad. "You realize worse stuff can happen then having your photo taken, if you're regularly passed out around this guy. Right?"

Kennidy muttered, "We haven't had *sexual intercourse*, if that's all you're worried about. I'm not even his type, exactly. Too fat, for one thing."

"Oh, Jesus Christ."

"It doesn't matter. I'm not taking my clothes off for him anymore. We're done. And anyway, I have the pictures."

Ruth's irritation was making her drive too fast. The last thing they needed was to get stopped by the police. "You know that he could still have digital copies, right?"

As soon as she said it, Ruth wished she hadn't. But she was just so fed up at her sister's naïveté, among other things.

"Turn around," Kennidy said.

"I'm not turning around. What do you think, you can get his laptop and his phone *and* his cloud login?"

"Believe me, he doesn't know how to use the cloud. He doesn't even have a laptop. His computer is this enormous desktop thing that's almost as old as I am. Anyway, he has some other stuff of mine."

"Clothes?"

"School stuff. Notes. Some things I'm working on. It's mine, all right?"

"Kennidy, don't go back to that guy's place." Ruth wasn't as worried about a physical fight as much as she was about her sister patching things up with the creep. "Forget the making up and breaking up. Forget the fireworks. All of it."

"See?"

"See what?"

"Your voice."

Ruth looked over at her sister. Ken had closed her eyes and slumped far down in her seat. "The judgy 'you could do better, Ken,' voice."

"You *can* do better."

"See?"

"See what?"

"Mom doesn't say that."

"She doesn't think you could do better?"

"She doesn't think I can do anything."

Ruth banged her hands on the steering wheel. "I don't know what you want from me. Mom isn't nice to you but she doesn't judge? *I'm* being judgmental? I don't even know what I'm judging, or whom."

"Or *whom*," Ken said. "Oh my god, really? Or *whom*?"

"*Which douchebag*. Is that better?"

"People don't say that anymore."

"They don't say what? *Whom* or *douchebag*?"

Kennidy shot her a withering look. "Either. Here, stop at the gas station. I've got to pee."

Minutes later, her face appeared in Ruth's window. "You can take off. I called a friend to pick me up."

"Which friend? I'm not leaving you here. You're still drunk."

Kennidy walked back the way she'd come, toward the door of the twenty-four-hour gas station, calling over her shoulder, "And you're still a bitch."

With that word ringing in her ears, Ruth stubbed out the cigarette and looked around the garage. She shoved the old pack into her jacket pocket and leaned over to lift the suitcase lid. As she did, she felt her eyes fill, not for Kennidy at first but for their mother, who had arranged this little sarcophagus with care. In place of questionable, disjointed memories were concrete, indisputable objects.

On top was a dress Ruth had never seen before, probably from some homecoming dance. Below that, a soccer uniform. Next, a pair of jeans that had provoked a family fight, because Kennidy had been sent to the mall to buy her fall school wardrobe and spent it all on this one overpriced item, then barely wore it.

Below the clothing were several sports trophies and yearbooks from freshman and sophomore year. A thin spiral-bound notebook had a handful of handwritten poems followed by mostly blank pages. Behind that was a daybook from Kennidy's junior year, the last year she'd completed: mainly homework assignments, but also lots of personal scrawl in the margins, little symbols that no doubt provided clues to that week's party, missed period, weight gain, weight loss or hookup. In place of heartfelt confessions there were only codes and scribbles.

Apparently, Kennidy hadn't kept a traditional diary, as Annie Oakley hadn't. The lives with whom Ruth's own life was interwoven seemed to resist straightforward, reliable narratives or any kind of disciplined diarist's impulse. Maybe most lives were that way, neither assured nor shame-free enough to risk leaving a trail for just anyone to follow.

That didn't mean Kennidy—or Annie—had taken everything with them, however. Maybe they were just choosy about with whom they shared their secrets.

You tried to tell me before, but I wasn't listening. Tell me now, Ken.

The second suitcase was locked, but the lock was so flimsy and rusted, it flew open the moment Ruth kicked it.

This one had fewer personal items, more correspondence and random detritus.

There was a manila folder with envelopes—some addressed to Kennidy, some addressed to Gwen or, more bureaucratically, to PARENT/CUSTODIAN OF, most opened and a few still sealed. According to the postmarks, some had arrived after Kennidy's death.

And then there were two Polaroids. Kennidy was on an old brown couch in a room Ruth didn't recognize. Eyelids heavy, possibly drunk or stoned, wearing a neon orange bikini top and denim shorts. She was thin, but her pale belly bulged slightly over the shorts because they were so small. Her legs were open, and her head was tipped to one side, gaze fixed on whoever was taking the photo. It looked like a badly done modeling shot of a teenager trying to look sexy or trying to please someone who'd told her to look sexy.

You know that he could still have digital copies, right? . . . Don't go back. Forget the fireworks.

When had Kennidy ever passed up fireworks?

It was already two in the morning. Ruth gathered up an armful of reading material: assignment book, poetry notebook, sealed envelopes and everything else she hadn't had time to study properly. With luck, she'd get three hours' sleep, then spend most of the day on a bus with little to do and nowhere to turn, except toward a past she had always ignored.

2 7

RUTH

The driver was late. The bus station was only six miles away. Ruth's bag was already outside at the curb.

"Are there any advantages to your post-accident condition?" Dr. Susan had asked.

"Advantages?" Ruth had wanted to throw something at her therapist at that moment, but the room was bare of any stone sculptures or other convenient projectiles. Smart lady.

But now, all these months later, waiting for her ride, Ruth thought about it again. Back in grad school, she hadn't been the best at asking for help. Now, she couldn't avoid it. Which was how she'd met Reece, by letting him optimize her slow laptop. It was why she regularly wrote emails and placed calls, asking for strangers to help her search even when she didn't know exactly what she was searching *for*. Bad manners for a historian.

While making her coffee that morning, Ruth had left a voicemail for an archivist she'd never met at a Vienna museum she'd never visited in a manner that suggested urgency, as if a person thousands of miles away had nothing better to do than to brainstorm on her behalf. She'd gotten the idea last night, after staring at Margarete Breuer's last address before deportation on Google Maps. The Sigmund Freud Museum was close to where Margarete had lived; that would be the place to try if nothing else panned out. But Ruth didn't really think that a set of confusing documents in English with no mention of Freud himself would end up there. She was betting on the Jewish Museum of Vienna, only a mile from Haasgasse 8.

According to Nieman's seller, the items had been offered to an Austrian museum many years ago. For lack of room, supposedly, they hadn't been kept. A foreign archivist wouldn't necessarily have recognized the "ZN" of the journal or made the Breuer connection if his name wasn't present in the pages.

Now, as Ruth stood in the doorway, watching for her ride, the call came in from Vienna, where it was just past the lunch hour.

Ruth suffered through an embarrassing introduction using her terrible German and was then transferred to a young archivist by the name of Franziska, who spoke English beautifully. When Ruth explained what she was looking for—proof of a journal or letters that had been brought to a museum, possibly theirs, but which hadn't stayed there, the archivist was helpful.

"The documents were found in a former Jewish residence, but made no mention of Jewish citizens?"

"They were written by an American named Annie Oakley who might have visited Vienna to see a psychoanalyst, whose daughter was Margarete Schiff," Ruth said. "It was in her house, I believe, that the documents were found. Certainly, the analyst and his daughter were both Jewish."

"Yes, but is his name in the letters, clearly?"

"She might have addressed him at the top of each letter. But maybe not clearly. Or perhaps not using his proper name, if she was trying to obscure their relationship."

"The problem is quantity," the archivist said. "People bring us hundreds of thousands of documents from their cellars and attics, whether it relates to the war or is something older that was only hidden away during the war—anything they find. This is no exaggeration. The Nazis kept fifty million records on seventeen million people. We have an obligation to decide what should be stored or sent to a more logical repository in Austria or anywhere else in the world, and what should be digitized, and in what order. Something could be here but not yet processed."

"No, the originals aren't there. I believe they ended up in the US, with a private buyer."

"That can happen if they seem to have little local relevance. If the clearest element was the author, and she was American, and especially if the documents were pre-Holocaust by many years, they might have been offered to someone who could do something with them—a museum, a library, a descendant."

"I was hoping you'd kept a digital copy before sending it onward."

"Unlikely. Even for digitization, there is a waiting list. Though sometimes we might log a donation before passing it on. Letters, you say?"

"Yes." Ruth gave the list of names or abbreviations that might appear in it: Annie Oakley, AO, ZN.

"And I don't have proof that there are letters going in the other direction—that the Vienna recipient kept copies of his replies, in other words. But in any case, his name is Josef Breuer."

The archivist paused. "There's a name I recognize. I can tell you, certainly, that anything in his name, especially if it had American significance, would have gone to the Library of Congress. They have a finder's aid for his correspondence, online."

"Yes, I'm aware."

"And they don't have a Breuer-Oakley folder?"

"Absolutely not."

"That's a shame. Before you go, let me just try Breuer for you." In the background, Franziska typed and hummed pensively, then grew quiet. Under her breath, the archivist said, "Bugger."

"Is something wrong?"

"We used to have something, but the original was sent away, destination unknown, and we don't even have a digital copy, just an internal note."

"Please, tell me."

"It's logged as 'Condolence card, Mrs. Annie Oakley Butler to Breuer Family, 1925.' I'm guessing this was after Josef Breuer's death, yes? But our museum received it only in the 1980s, before we had a proper reopening of the archives. We've been a start-and-stop operation many times through the wars, unfortunately."

Outside, the car pulled up. "That's excellent, Franziska. Thank you."

"I'm sorry it couldn't be more."

"It's worth more than you realize. I'm immensely grateful."

IT WAS A TINY THING, but it was everything. For Ruth, it was a set of leads: the Breuer family was put into contact with Annie Oakley in 1925, thanks to a card she'd sent upon Josef Breuer's death. Having received her address, they might have decided to return Annie's letters to their proper owner at that time; if they were tardy, they would have missed Annie herself, for she died in 1926, and Frank died of grief only weeks later. From there, the letters could have gone anywhere.

Or perhaps the Breuer family didn't return Annie's letters, but instead kept them stored through the Holocaust and later. That meant whoever had donated the condolence card in the 1980s had also donated or sold the 1904 letters, which might not have had Breuer's name on them at all.

Anything that could narrow the search—time windows, possible reasons for donation—made it more plausible to establish chain of custody.

But none of it mattered so much as this new proof that Annie Oakley had indeed known an obscure physiologist—and briefly, psychoanalyst—from halfway around the world named Josef Breuer. She'd known him well enough to note his death. To reach out with condolences to his family, despite being near the end of her own life. Which made a certain odd journal's authenticity less preposterous.

Annie knew Josef.

From where did belief come? It started out as small as a seed: information, a feeling, or both. It didn't take much. But it did require nourishment, attention—a kind of love, in other words. You had to love to believe.

Ruth had always advocated for skepticism in all matters. She hadn't thought to be skeptical about her own skepticism. How could she really know what she knew, when so much that was essential could exist out of her field of vision?

THE COST OF HIRING A private car had seemed excessive. Less so, after Ruth got on the bus and a man slid in next to her— large, grizzled, smelling of a long night spent drinking whiskey. She didn't blame him for not being clean or being tipsy. She blamed him for insisting on talking to her, mile after mile. The only trick that worked was burying her face in her reading, pantomiming complete absorption.

Ruth couldn't choose to simply gaze out the window unless she wanted a long discourse on her seatmate's struggle with his bad back and the fact that those jet contrails you saw in the sky were really chem-trails being laid down by the government to control the population. Also, the Holocaust had never happened.

That last part was ironic, considering that between reading the pages in Kennidy's notebook, Ruth had emailed a quick thank-you to the kind Vienna archivist, whose very job involved digging through mountains of Nazi extermination records. Ruth couldn't imagine a more difficult assignment, or so she told herself before regretting her self-deception. If it were harder to think about the Holocaust than her own dead sister, she wouldn't keep looking at her phone, hoping the pleasantly chatty Franziska would follow up.

On a global scale, the Holocaust was overwhelming. But the thing was, Ruth McClintock had played no part in it. Not even a tangential role, like that of the quiet shopkeeper or non-Jewish neighbor who, in the late 1930s, hadn't spoken out against the Nazis. Americans loved weeping over tragic Holocaust movies, just as Germans were among the world's greatest fans of early novels featuring Indian braves. Joe Grandlouis had accused Ruth of exactly this: indulging in the darkness of history, but only as long as it was distant, as long as it was something in which her nearest and dearest had not been complicit.

The hardest part of thinking back to Kennidy's high-school years wasn't realizing that her sister was endlessly sad; it was that she'd been, once upon a time, briefly happy. In her freshman year, when she was fourteen, Kennidy had started the school year with optimism, eager to leave eighth-grade drama behind. That carefree spirit lasted about three months. In the margins of Kennidy's assignment books, Ruth read the shorthand notations that hinted at boy crushes, a countdown to soccer tryouts, and names of BFFs who came and went: Jessica and Brittany and Piper, girls who had scrawled their own messages next to Kennidy's, as if every page was a banal yearbook in miniature: *Never change*, *YOLO* and *Class of 2014!!!*

And then there was Christmas: *Ruth here 23rd. Snowmobile trip or x-c ski?*

Ruth didn't remember renting a snowmobile—not even the mention of it. She didn't remember skiing. Her memory of Christmas featured hitting a bar that night with some former high-school friends—anything to get away from the gloom of the house and her mother's heavier holiday drinking.

On the 27th, Kennidy had written only *Mall.*

Ruth hated the mall. Unless she was returning an ugly sweater from her mother, she would have skipped that outing.

From that particular winter holiday, Ruth could remember only one fight with Kennidy, in which she blamed her sister for constantly baiting their mother. Ruth had never had a hard time getting along with Gwen. She'd signed her own sick notes from the third grade on, earned her own "allowance" at side jobs since she was thirteen, and lied as necessary, omitting whatever her mother wasn't ready to hear. *"She's easy to handle. Just tell her what she wants, Kennidy!"* That was the unfortunate truth about Gwen. She was both narcissistic and easily distracted. She didn't ask questions. She didn't expect deep conversations. She didn't book her daughters their first gynecology appointments, broach topics like sex or drugs, or review college catalogs. She was a mother who could be easily handled, as long as you didn't actually need anything from her, whether it was a signed permission slip or a heart-to-heart.

Ruth had opted to parent herself. Kennidy was a different story. She wanted lots of hugs as a toddler and got into more arguments as a teen. She'd accept conflict over being ignored. She'd find someone to demonstrate affection if Gwen didn't.

On the 29th, *R left.*

On the 31st, *Joey party with Troy, watch out new year here I come.*

Ruth wanted to ask their mother, *"Do you even know where Ken's going on New Year's? She's only fourteen."*

She wanted to say to herself, *What was so goddamned important that you had to go back to campus on the 29th? You couldn't have stuck around three more days? You couldn't have taken Kennidy skiing or gone off to a cabin just by yourselves to drink hot chocolate and play board games? You couldn't have been the one to take her to the mall?*

And these were the relatively easy parts. When things got

harder by late sophomore year, Kennidy seemed to have turned to poetry. There were poems about desert dunes and moonlight, coyotes and hawks, railroad tracks and broken factory windows, Arctic landscapes and Atlantic hurricanes, though Kennidy had never been north or east of Minnesota. And there were even more poems about mystery girls—repulsive or waiflike and sad but potentially lovable—who were clear stand-ins for how Kennidy saw herself on any given day.

On the margins of the next-to-last assignment book Kennidy would ever keep, there were numbers: *106, 103, 99*—the last with a big smiley face. On November 5 of her sophomore year, Kennidy weighed less than a hundred pounds, a dubious achievement that Ruth doubted anyone had noted, except perhaps to praise her for it. She was on the soccer team and was a long-distance runner. Being leggy, slim and flat-chested was de rigueur. Even when her grades slipped, her sports participation remained strong. Which might have explained why the mentions of Troy and Joey and Jordan and Collum all petered out or become mere enigmatic abbreviations—*Fri out w P, Fight w JW*, hearts filled in or crossed out—and were overshadowed by sport and workout notations.

Now there were calendars with running mileages. Finish times. And also meetings: *Coach V 3:30.*

The first mentions made sense. He was a coach. She was into running. But after a while, just as the other friends' initials had faded from mention, so did the numbers indicating mileage times. Still, there was *Coach V, 4:15.* Weekends, too: at 5 and 7 P.M. or just the name—no time of day, just an asterisk, or an exclamation mark.

And more and more, just *V*.

The codes became more enigmatic yet, not even words, just symbols: stars, plus and minus signs. Ruth thought back to her own adolescent journals and all the symbols she had used to stand in for late periods, hangovers, covert kisses . . . and more than that. Ruth was deep into an assignment book from Kennidy's junior year now. There was also a senior-year assignment book, but it was almost entirely blank, except for one fall weekend marked for a retake of the SAT. So she had still been hoping to go to college even then, just weeks before she went into her bedroom and never came out.

Ruth went back to the junior-year yearbook: that was when things had happened, what it all hinged upon. The notations that spring were especially dense: *V, V, V.* Until May, when they stopped.

Why, Kennidy?

Ruth's stomach clenched, fighting motion sickness from the bumpy ride and the smell of the man next to her and the imagined smell of someone else—licorice hard candy.

Ruth had gone to his house, too. She had sat on his couch. She had pressed her sweating legs together tightly, feeling the sticky surface of the scrapbook against her knees, and she had leaned away, against the armrest of the prickly couch, disliking his unwanted attention. He hadn't tried anything, not a handshake, not a hug. He had sized her up correctly. He had known not to try, or maybe Ruth was giving herself too much credit. Maybe he simply didn't try that first time and would have later. Ruth felt she would have known how to resist him, but perhaps she was wrong.

Why, Kennidy?

But she knew exactly why, because they'd grown up in the same household. Children needed love, and not just when they were small and cute, but even when they were older, changing and often unlikable. That was when they needed it more than ever.

V, V , V.

And then finally there was no V.

Full stop.

Sometime after this, Ruth had visited home. She and Kennidy had gone drinking and driven to that cabin in the woods. Ruth remembered the golf club, the garden gnome, that blue sports pennant tacked next to the door. She remembered Kennidy stalking off: *"And you're still a bitch!"* But that had been after riding in the car for a sullen and silent forty minutes—time they might have talked, even if it had hurt.

Ruth wished she could have those minutes back, every one of them.

2 8

R E E C E

Reece's mom had scheduled the family counseling session without his blessing.

"If you come, great. If you refuse to come, your father and I will go anyway," she said, putting away groceries while she talked. "Mondays, four o'clock. Your afternoon practices will be all done by then, right? We thought it would work out for everyone."

She hadn't asked whether or not he wanted them to come to the big show on Friday. Despite his outburst the other day, he hoped they were smart enough to know that he really did want them there. But if they didn't come—well, *that* would certainly be fodder for discussion on Monday.

Did that mean he was going on Monday?

He groaned, closing his bedroom door.

He didn't want to talk about last year. He especially didn't want to have to replay last summer: the moment he did it, the temporary relief and enduring dread, waking to shame and confusion in the hospital.

From outside the door, he heard his mom ask whether he was planning to join them for dinner.

"Already ate!" he called back, a bag of chips under one arm and a bottle of root beer under the other.

If the family therapist forced him to, he would talk. That was the problem! Not that he would sit and glare and say practically nothing, but that he'd explode.

I shouldn't even be at this shit school.

I would have been earning college credit while I was still in high school.

I could have been on the East Coast already!

Oh yes, Reece would give that therapist an earful.

Right fingers scrolling while his left hand dipped into the greasy potato-chip bag, lips stinging lightly with vinegar and salt and pleasurable indignation, he summoned his evidence. He looked again at the program's admission page, which showed that the average admitted entrant had lower PSAT scores than he'd had. And he'd had a 4.0. Grades and scores were not the problem.

Maybe a clinical expert would agree with him. Maybe she'd tell his parents that they'd sabotaged him. Itching to go before the judge—*therapist*, rather—Reece opened the photos section on his phone and scrolled back to the videos he hadn't replayed in over half a year: among these, the two videos he'd sent into the school as part of his failed application package.

He stared at the first unplayed video, thumb hovering.

He wanted to see himself dance, wanted to be back in that moment when everything was still possible. And at the same time, he expected some measure of disappointment. Of course, the video would be shitty quality. It couldn't compete with an in-person audition.

The school had asked for one solo performance plus one group. For solo, he'd had Gerald record him in the school gym doing a much-simplified choreographic number inspired by Polunin's "Take Me to Church" video, featuring the Ukrainian dancer storming around an empty barn to the sound of Hozier's hit song. Reece winced, realizing how many other applicants might have sent something similar. But he'd been full of hope last spring. At the time, he hadn't worried about doing something trite.

Reece wiped salt and grease onto his jeans and gripped the phone with both hands. Did he really want to do this? It wasn't like he'd never watched the video before he uploaded it to the program website. But that day last March seemed like years ago.

He pressed play and the sound started up, his friend's whisper audible for the first few seconds in the background—"Come on Gerald, shut up now, this is serious"—and there Reece was in the corner of the screen. Capri-length nude tights, no shoes, bare chest. Muscles more visible because he'd been leaner last spring.

It started slowly with him on his knees, head down and swaying, face hidden by dark shaggy hair until he pushed it back. Then he lifted himself up on one hand, one leg extended, foot pointed.

Collapse back onto the floor. Upward thrust of the chest, as if a hook through his sternum were hoisting him up toward the ceiling.

All good so far, as the music got going.

Then the pace picked up. He leaped, spun, dropped to the floor in plank position. Okay, a little sloppy, but it was the switch in tempos. He was just getting going.

He pushed up, rigid plank again, and flipped over, chest up, one clean line from toes to head. Taut—or it was supposed to be.

In his defense, the move was harder than it looked.

Reece swallowed hard.

In the video, he pulled his knees to his chest. Scowled. Emoted. Jumped again and swung around and leaped, using all those early years of ballet training which clearly . . . weren't enough.

The video was just over three minutes. He was only a minute and forty seconds in.

Reece watched his younger self repeat the moves with slight variations and no improvements. His leaps were nothing like

Polunin's. His attempt to appear artfully pain-stricken just looked like a temper tantrum on the floor.

Worst of all was the unchoreographed slip—a poor landing that turned into a skid—around 2:10. Reece closed his eyes. The song was still playing. He couldn't watch anymore.

When the video was finished, he opened his eyes and exhaled loudly through his nose.

Not good. Understatement of the year.

Had his ability to judge skill changed that much in six months? Why hadn't he realized that this video hadn't been the right thing to submit?

Okay, he thought, shaking his head. So that was one video. Better to aim high and fail—right? The application committee must have understood that.

For the second video he'd had limited choices, given that he hadn't danced in a group since the start of high school. Instead, he'd asked another friend to record a short Rockets performance featuring half of the group. With luck, the tumbling and acrobatics, incorporating some dance moves, would be less shockingly bad than the solo video.

Reece pressed play.

This video had fewer surprises. It wasn't shockingly bad. It also wasn't shockingly good.

Reece watched his own moves, nodding without satisfaction. Raj flipped off Gerald's shoulders and then did some hip-hop moves. Justin and Vanessa did a half-modern bolero-flamenco hybrid that didn't quite fit the music but always captured the audience's attention.

All fine, especially for a high-school performance, but nothing special.

We just don't want you putting all your eggs in one basket.
We're just not sure you're ready yet.

They'd been at least partly right. He'd have to give them that.

Which didn't mean he didn't still feel cheated, somehow. It would take a while to get over this. And no, he didn't want to talk to a therapist about it.

The routine still playing in the video was so familiar and dully adequate to Reece that his mind began to wander, eyes taking in what was happening along the edges of the screen.

Two other Rockets members were visible at the back of the gym behind the main performers, clapping in sync, keeping the energy high. And there, farther off to one side, alone but not entirely alone, was Caleb. He'd started hanging out at practices and performances that spring, not yet a member, only watching in the beginning. But that wasn't the weird part.

The weird part was the look on his face—a thin-lipped grimace.

Vorst was directly behind him, his entire head visible above Caleb's. Reece had forgotten how much shorter Caleb had been, just last spring. Vorst had a hand placed on each of Caleb's shoulders and his fingers were digging in, like he was pressing him down into the ground. Caleb made a shrugging motion and started to turn and pull away, but then he didn't. Vorst had him rooted to the spot.

Maybe Caleb had been talking during their performance, not that anyone would have cared with the music blasting. Maybe Vorst was pressuring Caleb into staying to watch in support of the team and for his own benefit. Maybe they'd just had some sort of argument and this was the aftermath.

Reece's attention went back to Caleb's face. He enlarged the image. Caleb took a breath and held it, eyes shut, like he was at the doctor's office waiting for a shot.

Reece's homage to Polunin had meant to show deep pain, but none of it had worked: not the dancing or the contrived facial expressions, either. He hadn't been able to fake agony. He'd just looked like an idiot.

Caleb's agony, by comparison, was clear as day. The guy looked like he might puke or spontaneously combust.

It didn't mean anything, necessarily. But Caleb looked desperately uncomfortable, and Vorst was right behind him, standing too close. Was Vorst closing his eyes, too? Reece did *not* want to imagine the old coach was grinding against Caleb, in a public place no less, but it wasn't impossible.

That image would take a while to process. Then what?

2 9

R U T H

Sophie had arrived at the restaurant early and taken command in a preferred corner next to a fireplace with bread and olive oil already on the table.

Without getting up, she called out, "Ruth!"

"Sophie."

They reached out to clasp hands, appraising each other. Sophie looked younger than Ruth had expected, with a burgundy-colored asymmetrical bob, a black turtleneck and chunky silver jewelry. Ruth had done her best—long skirt with a belt, yoga-style soft blue wrap top—but she still felt underdressed. Then again, she'd been on a bus all day. As Ruth allowed Sophie to pull her into a full hug, she hoped she didn't stink.

"Sit, sit," Sophia said. "Do you want the booth side? Would it be more comfortable?"

Ruth had tried to suppress her hobble on the way in, but Sophie had still noticed.

"No, this is fine." Ruth smiled brightly.

Sophie was already studying her menu. Ruth did the same, scanning the specials without noticing the words, suddenly uncertain why she was even here. She had enough on her hands: Kennidy's papers and mementos, so much still to be read. Scott's future, and Reece's too, so much still to understand. The rest might be nothing more than a silly wild-goose chase.

A waiter appeared as soon as Sophie raised her finger. "Bring a second pinot gris. Unless you want something different?"

"Maybe just water to start."

"Water and the pinot gris. If she doesn't want it, I'll make it disappear." Sophie laughed. In a stage whisper, she added. "It has been a shitty, shitty day. Pardon my French. And please tell me you're not vegetarian."

Ruth took the cue. She ordered a steak, medium rare.

There was no need to guide the conversation, thank goodness. Sophie had an agenda.

"First, I have to tell you. I was on your committee."

Ruth was confused at first, thinking back to her grad school, dissertation days. "Committee?"

"The university press," Sophie explained. "They bring together their own people and some outside experts. The foundation was contacted, no surprise. I was happy to do it. Usually, these committees are confidential, but in this case, the book isn't coming out now—I'm so sorry about that—so I don't think it matters anymore." She paused long enough to take a swallow of white wine. "The point is, I thought it was a good manuscript. A good start, anyway. There was nothing . . . inaccurate, objectionable . . . and that's what the press wanted to know. The greatest damage is done by biased people with no interest whatsoever in plain facts."

Ruth waited. This was no high praise. Fair enough.

"On top of that," Sophie said, "I know you were hamstrung. I know you'd been trying to get more information from Lila for some time. She ran a tight ship, to put it kindly. And so, your email to me."

"Yes."

The waiter arrived with salads. Ruth hadn't ordered one.

"Caesar dressing—their best. Do you like Caesar?"

"I love Caesar." The only correct answer.

Sophie waited for the waiter to withdraw. "But like I said, shitty day. The Minneapolis meetings were not a success. Everything I'm going to tell you tonight is confidential. Do I have your word?"

Sophie lifted her glass, and Ruth followed. They clinked.

"All right, then." Sophie leaned in close again. "This goes back several years. Business side first: the foundation has lost a lot of funding. I was here in search of new sources: 3M, General Mills, Target. I wanted to go home and show them we don't have to rely on Mr. LaPierre for everything, and with Lila gone, it's easier to come out and say it: good riddance. But I misjudged. Beyond a few historical societies and small museums with Western themes, there aren't a lot of organizations that care about Annie Oakley right now. We got a little too dependent, I'm afraid."

For all the time Ruth had spent researching Annie's life, she hadn't paid attention to the logos that showed up at the bottom of the foundation screen, if there were logos at all.

Mr. LaPierre. The pieces finally clicked. "So the NRA doesn't want to support you anymore?"

"Frankly, they were always lukewarm. What do they care about history? But Lila charmed them." Sophie took another sip of wine. "As for me—I was about done by the time Sandy Hook happened, and Wayne gave that awful speech blaming video games and the media, no tears shed for the children themselves. But then the very next year, the NRA opens its museum of sporting arms in Springfield, Missouri—that's practically our neighborhood. It's certainly our people. Plus, they've got three of Annie's guns on display there. To outsiders, we look cozy."

For half of the bus ride, Ruth had rehearsed how she would begin to tell Sophie about Nieman, the journals, Vienna. But it was becoming clear that Sophie's own confidential story didn't converge with anything Ruth had come to ask or say.

Sophie sighed. "The upshot is, some problematic materials

have gone unseen in order to not ruffle feathers, and all for what? They've already cut their donations by sixty percent. And to keep the rest, we have to continue Lila's legacy, oversimplifying what Annie Oakley stood for. If I can find new funders, I'm staying on the board. If I can't . . ."

She paused with her fork in the air, and then set it down, salad uneaten.

"Sophie, I'm so sorry." Ruth waited as Sophie steadied herself, eyes clearing. Ten seconds, twenty, still waiting until it was the right time to push for more. "You were saying. Problematic materials?"

Sophie dipped her hand into the purse next to her chair, brought out a tablet and set it on the white-cloth-covered table. She tapped it on, entered the password with one swift motion of a bright red fingernail, flicked right, opened a document and then just as quickly tapped it off again.

"After dinner. Let's not ruin our appetites."

Ruth took the smallest possible sip of wine. She usually loved wine, but it didn't taste right tonight. Nothing had felt right since the fainting spell in the café.

Sophie looked around the restaurant, body rigid with impatience, wine glass and bread basket equally empty, but this time the waiter didn't appear. They both stared at the darkened tablet.

"Fine," Sophie said, giving in by half. "It's a letter she wrote to a friend and never mailed. It references a doubt. That's all."

"About?"

"The feasibility of using a gun for protection in every life circumstance. Based on a single bad day she had." Sophie leaned across the table, whispering. "Man pushed up against her on a New York subway. Not so easy to pull out a shotgun."

A revolver, maybe, Ruth thought. But she understood, because it had happened to her, too. It had happened to every woman.

Ruth said, "That doesn't sound damning."

"In the wrong hands, it could be. And then you've got the immigrant problem. Maybe in a city like New York in 1904, you don't want every person—even every woman—to have their own gun. Annie wondered about that, too. It didn't mean she was a racist."

Before, questions about racism would have grabbed Ruth's attention. But now it was the date—1904—that pricked up her ears.

"Surely, you've been in this situation as a biographer," Sophie said. "You read something that challenges an assumption; it's unclear or unproven, but you know that others will read all the wrong things into it."

Ruth dipped a toe in the water. "Like, for example, the fact that Annie might have spoken to a doctor about her mental state?"

Sophie sat up straight in her chair, eyes wide. "Mental state? When?"

"After the train crash."

"Oh, no no no. Nothing like that. My goodness!" Sophie brought a hand to her mouth and paused there a moment before losing herself in nervous laughter. "Hell's bells, Ruth. You almost had me. That's the first laugh I've had all day."

"I'm glad," Ruth said. "But if we could be serious again—"

Sophie's smile faded. "When you asked me about Lila, you had something in mind. Tell me it's not this."

Ruth plunged ahead. "Did you ever hear of Annie Oakley making a trip to Vienna?"

"For?"

"Psychoanalysis. To discuss a problem that had been haunting her at least since the 1901 train crash, and to discuss earlier trauma, brought back into focus by that accident."

"Psychoanalysis," Sophie repeated, incredulous. "You weren't pulling my leg. Like, on the couch. Talking."

"Is that not possible?"

"Annie wasn't a talker."

"I understand . . ."

"She was a doer."

"Well—"

"She didn't make mountains out of molehills. She wasn't a victim, unlike so many people today."

Ruth started to say something more, but Sophie stopped her with a wagging finger. "Hashtag #NotMe. Or how about, #IdLikeToSeeYouTry. If Annie Oakley had tweeted, that's how she would've done it."

"But the Wolves . . ."

"Precisely. The Wolves. She didn't talk about them."

"She mentioned them in her autobiography."

"Her *unpublished* autobiography."

"Unfinished. Written near the end of her life. If she'd had more time, and maybe more support . . ."

Sophie scowled. "But she didn't name them. She never blamed them specifically for anything that went wrong later in her life— because, in fact, things didn't go wrong. She was a self-made woman. A winner. An undeniable success."

"You can be a success," Ruth said slowly, carefully, "without being invulnerable. I think, just maybe, that Annie was marked by her challenges—by the things that happened to her at a very young age. That doesn't make her a lesser person. Only a more complicated one."

The waiter appeared at their table, two oversize plates in hand. Sophie pretended he wasn't there.

"Ruth, I'm disappointed. If there was one thing I appreciated about your book—your manuscript, rather—it was your restraint. You didn't go on about Annie's supposed victimization in the manuscript."

"I'm not labeling it victimization. But certain things are facts: the Wolves, harassment from Hearst—"

"Name one famous all-American patriot or hero who is best

known for the bad things that happened to him, rather than the path he blazed. Daniel Boone. Kit Carson. George Washington. The point is, only when it's a woman do we emphasize what she suffered rather than what she accomplished."

"I'm not sure suffering and accomplishment are incompatible. You might even say—"

Sophie stood and dropped her napkin onto her chair.

"Ruth, you've done me a favor. Lila tried to tell me and I wouldn't listen. People are always ready to twist things out of perspective. Maybe I misjudged her. Maybe I've misjudged you, too."

For a moment, Ruth thought that Sophie was angry enough to walk out. But she was only going to the ladies' room.

"Steak sauce and a second pinot gris," Sophie said to the waiter before she left the table.

Ruth sat quietly as the waiter set down the steaks and arranged new cutlery, avoiding eye contact. Then he was gone.

The tablet was still there on the white tablecloth, just next to the empty bread basket. At tables all around them, in every direction, couples and families were absorbed in their own meals and conversations or, in a few cases, glued to their phones, ignoring each other and everyone around them.

Ruth hadn't meant to notice the passcode Sophie had used, but her eyes had been drawn to those red fingernails and she'd seen the unmistakable pattern: a straight diagonal, up, double tap on the third digit, and back. Sophie certainly wasn't about to share the text of that restricted letter with her now. She seemed to be rethinking ever sharing it with any researcher.

With one hand, Ruth pulled out her own phone from her jacket pocket. With the other, she pushed her plate of steak out of the way and casually let her arm drift across the table until her fingers reached the screen. 7-5-3-3-5-7. She brought the two screens closer, snapping photos of the letter Sophie thought the world wasn't ready to see, then locked the device and put it back.

A MOMENT LATER, RUTH'S PHONE rang.

It was the home inspector. No problems, all done; a report would be emailed promptly. Ruth finished the call and disconnected just as Sophie was coming back to the table, her face rearranged into a more pleasant expression, ready to tuck into her steak and pretend she'd never raised her voice.

Ruth explained that she was trying to sell her house—a neutral topic, no hashtags.

Sophie was just starting to speak when the phone rang a second time.

"Sorry," Ruth said, and took the call.

"I found him," the voice at the other end said. "Nieman. But it's not Nieman. I've got his number for you."

Ruth pulled the phone away from her cheek. "The home inspector again," she said to Sophie. "Something unexpected. I'll take this outside."

Ruth hurried to the parking lot.

Reece said, "Oh, exciting. You're starting to lie now."

"More than that," Ruth said.

"Good for you. When you hear this next part, you're going think I'm a genius."

"That remains to be seen."

"I kept calling the names on the Antiques Association Directory. 'Nieman' was getting me nowhere, so I started mentioning that the guy we were looking for has throat cancer, and after a dozen more calls, someone knew who I was talking about. '1901 guy,' they call him."

"1901?"

"Because they can't pronounce his last name. Me neither. His last name isn't Nieman. It's like a username, a pseudonym, to get around the problem with the other name,"

"How is it spelled?"

"C-H-something. Maybe 'Cheer-goss'?"

"You spent hours on this and didn't write down his last name?"

"It doesn't matter! I have his phone number!"

"And do we know why he's called 1901 guy?"

There was a pause at the end of the line. "He collects everything related to 1901. Something to do with his family heritage. You're the historian. I figured you'd put together that part."

It was coming to her. Nieman, 1901.

"Czolgosz," she said. "Oh my god. Are you kidding? His name is Czolgosz?"

"That sounds really close."

"Czolgosz is the man who assassinated President McKinley, in 1901. Leon Czolgosz. Who sometimes went by the name Nieman." She should have thought of it before. There were only so many presidential assassins in US history, and he was one of them. "It's just a pseudonym. It means 'nobody' in German."

"And this is the descendant of that original nobody, evidently."

"But what does this have to do with Annie Oakley?"

"Well, she lived around the same time, right? Maybe the 1901 guy got grooving on the train accident, just like you did."

"McKinley's assassination," Ruth thought aloud. It took place in the fall, at the Pan-American Exposition in Buffalo. "September 1901, I think."

"You think?"

"And Annie's accident was in October. Close, but not exactly the same time. And that still wouldn't quite explain it. Sure, they lived in the same time period, but so did a lot of people."

"A time when a lot of people were waving guns around, apparently."

A line was forming outside the restaurant where Ruth had gone to take her call. A woman in a wraparound dress and heels was looking at her.

Ruth put her head down and stepped farther into the parking lot, but families were walking back and forth to their cars. There was nowhere with privacy, and she knew she had to get back to Sophie. The meal would be awkward enough without Ruth arriving back at a half-cleared table, her own steak untouched on the plate.

"Reece?"

He had taken the phone away from his ear. He came back.

"You'll never guess this. October 29, 1901."

"That's the date of Annie's train crash, yes," Ruth said.

"And also the day this Czolgosz guy was electrocuted, seven weeks after the assassination. The *exact* same morning as the train accident. Now our two friends have something in common: a very bad day. Extra grisly for him."

Ruth felt the hairs stand up on the back of her neck.

"It's just a coincidence," she said.

"Maybe. But now we know what attracted Nieman—your guy—to the first journal. It might have been random, at least at first. But he's obsessed with that date. He buys up a bunch of random stuff referencing that year, September and October most of all. And then he gets pulled into more of her story and feels bad for her and wants someone else to understand."

"No," Ruth corrected him. "He made it clear that his primary interest wasn't Annie. But one way or another, the past haunts him. It haunts all of us, but more so if your own ancestor was a notorious killer."

BACK AT THE TABLE, SOPHIE had eaten half of her steak and already requested that the waiter put the rest in a doggie bag. Ruth took the hint and ate a few bites before having hers bagged up as well. Then she picked up the bill.

"I take it the home inspection news wasn't bad," Sophie said.

"You're feeling generous."

Reckless, more like. Ruth said, "Oh, I just think that things will work out."

"Listen. I didn't mean to react so strongly to your questions. At the foundation, we get all kind of people contacting us with their crackpot theories: why Annie Oakley was one of the best sharpshooters in history, why her hair turned bright white after the train accident, all that stuff. Like maybe she wasn't even human. We even had one guy call up a couple years ago, wanting to talk to Lila about aliens, or time travel."

Ruth kept her eyes down, pretending to be lost in figuring the tip.

"My point is, Lila had her hands full," Sophie said. "The crazy stuff made her resistant to the less crazy stuff—the real possibilities, the things she didn't want anyone to know, only because they were too complicated. By the way, thank you for picking up dinner."

"My pleasure."

"You didn't even drink your wine!"

"Long day," Ruth said. "I probably should have ordered coffee instead."

Ruth could tell Sophie felt bad and wanted to leave her with something—not the letter she had originally planned to show her, but a crumb.

Sophie said, "We all know that Annie and Frank were a beautiful couple. But it didn't mean Annie didn't occasionally confide in other people. And you know how much Lila wanted to squelch any talk of even the slightest marital conflict. Well, that letter, in addition to questioning gun ownership as the only thing a woman would ever need to protect herself . . ." Sophie paused for effect. "It was written to a man."

"A man," Ruth repeated. That was it?

"The few of us at the board who have read the unsent letter have all made guesses about his identity. Henry or Hubert or Horatio. I mean, how many first names start with H?

"And to top it off, she signed her name as Z. A pet name, we can only guess."

"But then how did you know it was her?"

"Because it was found with other unmailed letters and personal papers that are undoubtedly hers and written in her hand. One wouldn't need an expert to do a match, but one could, easily. Of course, there was no need, since Lila wanted nothing more than to hide the thing. We never managed to connect the name with anyone in her circle." Sophie stood up and gestured for Ruth to go first. Then she turned back for her forgotten doggie bag, still on the table. "So, he remains forever unknown. Her 1904 crush, I guess. H.D."

H.D.

In the hired car to her motel, Ruth opened the document on her phone.

There was Annie's familiar handwriting. After her disappointment at reading the first journal, written by the analyst, and her long and futile wait to get the next letters, it gave Ruth chills to finally see something in Annie's unmistakable hand: the cursive capital Ts with high, floating crossbars; the varying slope and size of letters and, where Annie's pen had briefly paused, the specks of puddled ink.

Dear H.D.,

If Sophie had been a more willing collaborator, Ruth would have gladly explained. *Herr Doktor.*

The letter continued: *You asked me to send you my thoughts and memories as I have them, given the impossibility of meeting face-to-face.*

Ruth smiled, knowing how Sophie—and Lila—would have misconstrued that line: as if chaste Annie had ventured close to romantic temptation but was now, in line with the self-disciplined personality they all esteemed, turning away from even the appearance of an affair.

Yet I do wish for your counsel, because I am not myself. There was much more I needed to tell you, but it isn't easy to begin, especially when your skepticism is so evident. So, let me start gently.

The other day I was on my way to give a speech in New Jersey to a group of women about the importance of self-defense using firearms, a favorite topic of mine and something in which I believe strongly. Since the train crash and the premature folding of my last theater engagement, I've had even more time to think about how I might contribute to the world, and what I've got to offer is what I know, and what I know is how to shoot—not that it solves everything. Do you see how I go around in circles with this?

But I've started badly. The moment I must share with you was on the subway. I was traveling alone, and a man, a very rude stranger, turned and leaned into me, indecorously and not at all innocently, which aroused in me a familiar rage and also a familiar sense of impotence. I had a revolver on my person. What did it matter? I couldn't get to it quickly, and I wasn't prepared to shoot this man in the stomach, much as I wanted to. A moment later, he backed away. He'd already done what he'd done. And all around me on that New York subway were other people. Women, a Sicilian here, a Chinaman there, and I would have been no happier seeing them pull out a weapon and try to use it in such a sardine can without judgment. It's not the same as being in the middle of the prairie, guarding your home.

Don't misunderstand me. I believe in the deepest part of me that there's a role for protection with firearms, and I continued on my way and gave that speech, and afterward I showed a dozen women how to hit a target, and I had no qualms about that.

What I mean to share, and perhaps this wasn't what you

wanted at all and I will have to start again another day,
was the feeling that rose up in me on the subway train.
It's become stronger lately. Any minor encounter takes me
back, and then I realize that this rage is not new—not new
at all.

Meanwhile, I continue with the practice I described
when we met, the practice you gave me permission to con-
tinue, which doesn't yield its satisfactions easily—a subject
for another day.

But I don't think this is what you wanted from me. I
don't understand your method completely. Yet since we
can't see each other in person, this correspondence must
suffice. I'll set this aside and either mail it or try again in a
more orderly fashion tomorrow. You mentioned an interest
in dreams, and tomorrow I will begin with that. I hope you
will forgive my inadequate form of expression and also my
terrible penmanship. I came to writing later in life than a
girl should.

Very sincerely,
As you would prefer to call me,
Z

THE DRIVER WAS SPEAKING TO her.

"Lady? Motel 6?"

Ruth unpinched the screen, and the fuzzy document jumped
back to its original size. She was breathing fast and shallow now,
disoriented and also thrilled.

"Yes. Sorry. Here, let me pay you."

In the room, locking the door behind her, pulling shut the
cheap orange curtains, Ruth was flooded with all the references
in the letter, the reading that Lila and Sophie had given it, seeing
only what they wanted to see: one tiny doubt about the use of a
weapon on a subway, a confessional tone that could be mistaken

for romance but wasn't. And then there were all the parts they had refused to notice, the very point of the letter. The man who had pushed into Annie, the timeless subway pervert, had made her think again of the past, as everything would until the pressure became intolerable.

Meanwhile, I continue with the practice I described when we met, the practice you gave me permission to continue . . .

The letter was a key, an undeniable bridge to those who could read it alongside Breuer's journal, with its focus on the past and even in its particulars: *your method . . . interest in dreams . . . we can't see each other in person . . . you gave me permission.* Sophie did not doubt, and neither did Ruth, that this letter had been written in Annie's hand. Its relationship to the content of the Breuer journal made that document, too, all the more credible.

Between this and the condolence letter, Ruth had something solid to report to Nieman. And at that same moment, thanks to Reece, Ruth finally knew who Nieman was. Not Nieman at all, but Bert Czolgosz, a man with his own agenda.

3 0

R U T H

Perched on the scratchy edge of her motel bed, Ruth dialed the number Reece had given her. It was 8:20 P.M. in Minnesota, 9:20 P.M. in Vermont. An older woman answered. It was Bert Czolgosz's wife.

"Yes, of course I know who you are," Hetta said with no hostility in her voice. "He's mentioned you. But I'm sorry to say that he can't talk to you."

From the background came the unmistakable news-program sound of pundits interrupting each other.

"He doesn't want to talk to me?"

"No, he *can't*. They operated on his throat. We've tried to get him used to one of those electrolarynx devices, but he refuses to sound like a robot. He won't talk if he doesn't have to. But he can listen. Let me go turn down the news."

"Wait," Ruth said. "Before you get Bert, maybe you can help me understand something first."

She told Hetta what she knew: that Bert was interested in 1901, that she presumed he was fascinated by his ancestor, Leon Czolgosz.

"Yes. The black sheep."

"I'm sorry to bring it up. I'm guessing he wishes it had never happened."

"That's what all his relatives have always said. 'If only.' There are so many stories: the job his great uncle didn't get, the cousin who was bullied in the army once his buddies found out. Even an engagement broken off. That was Bert's mother's story."

"It can't be easy."

"Leon got the letter that told him not to do it a few months before the crime, and that may have spooked him, but it didn't stop him, either. Here, I'll go see if Bert's still awake."

"Wait, a letter?"

"Leon laid low for a while on his parents' farm in Ohio. But he still killed McKinley a few months later. That's how Bert got pulled into the Annie Oakley business. The Leon-Annie letter. Bert got his hands on it in 1983. I figured you knew that was how his interest in Oakley got started."

"I assumed it was because of the fact that Leon was electrocuted on the same day that Annie Oakley had her train accident."

"He discovered that later. The letter came first. Bought it from a private dealer. He sent a copy to an Annie Oakley museum, thinking they'd be amazed and grateful. Never got anything, much less a thank-you."

"You must still have it, then."

"Three years later, we had a fire in the antiques barn, and Bert's original went up in flames. You can bet he contacted the museum at that point, to at least try to get back the copy. They claimed to have never received anything at all."

"That wasn't nice," Ruth said, hoping indignation would keep Hetta on a roll.

"You can imagine how that affected him. He wanted that piece of family history back. So he put out word that he was looking for Annie Oakley letters, especially from 1901, in case she'd ever written Leon again or he'd written back. He started collecting *everything* from 1901. That's when he found out about Annie's train accident. A strange coincidence, but Bert started to think everything about her was strange."

Ruth figured there was no better time to ask the question she knew only Hetta could answer. "You don't think your husband believes he can go back in time and stop the assassination himself, do you?"

There was a pause and a shuffle, the lowered TV volume growing yet more distant as Hetta closed a door in search of privacy. She whispered, "People wouldn't understand."

"But I do. I think he wants to learn because he's still wishing he could change Leon's story. I think your husband wants final proof that Annie Oakley time-traveled, so that he can understand how it all works."

"You shouldn't judge him for it. He's a smart man, and certainly not crazy."

"I don't think he's crazy."

"But you told him the journal, the letters—all of it—are probably fake. I thought it was good news at first. Bert could save his money and put this business behind him. But then I saw the effect it had. He stopped wanting to scribble his notes or visit all those online auction sites. He lost his appetite. He aged ten years overnight."

"I was wrong."

"You were *wrong*?"

Ruth put on her most confident, energetic voice. "I have more information now."

"You were wrong," Hetta repeated.

"And I'm very sorry if I took him off the track he was on. I think changing the past may be possible. But we don't know for sure. Maybe Annie's other letters will tell us."

"Well," Hetta said again, but she sounded happier. "Let me go let Bert know you're wanting to talk to him."

As she waited, something nagged at Ruth. The premature death

of Annie's Wolf probably would have had no great ripple effect
on the world, especially since the farmer was probably halfway to
the grave and had few interactions with anyone outside his limited sphere. But Czolgosz? McKinley? Those were bigger stakes.
McKinley's death made Teddy Roosevelt's presidency possible,
and Roosevelt's policies had long-term effects: a line of dominoes
that ran all the way up to World War I and well beyond.

In any case, it seemed impossible for Bert to interact with Leon.
Aside from the lack of geographical overlap, Bert couldn't have
been born until at least several decades after Leon's execution.
He couldn't temporarily inhabit his own past self and revisit a
moment in which he'd been with Leon. Perhaps that wasn't the
only way to time travel, but it was the only way Ruth knew of,
based on Annie's example.

But maybe there were other ways, Ruth thought. Like some
form of bootstrapping that could allow you to revisit a moment
in your own life, to talk with an older relative perhaps, if that
relative had been alive during an earlier time period and also had
a mind to time-travel for the same purpose. In the case of the
Czolgosz family, they probably all wanted the same thing: to stop
Leon. That level of intergenerational desire must be a rarity.

But the key ingredient was still missing.

In the distance, Hetta called out, "He can hear you, honey!"

Ruth took a breath. She said, "Mr. Czolgosz. First, I need to
apologize."

No answer, of course.

"And second," she said, "I need to ask again if you'll share
anything else you've got—or will get, if we decide to move forward—because I can only help if I know the full story."

When Ruth paused, Hetta spoke up. "He's writing something
for you, honey. I'll read it aloud when he's done."

Ruth waited, but the message was only "Keep going."

"Keep going?"

"That's all he wrote," Hetta said. "And he's nodding."

"I believe," Ruth continued, "that the letter you showed my colleague Joe Grandlouis two years ago is real. I'd very much like to see it in its original handwritten version. I believe the journal is real, too."

Ruth then summarized for Bert what she'd learned in the last couple days: the condolence card from Annie to Breuer's family; another undeniable letter, written in Annie's own hand, that made mention of an H.D., possibly Herr Doktor; new information about Breuer's daughter that could shed light on when and where the documents were found.

"Chain of custody matters if you're concerned about authenticity. This next part could take months or years."

Hetta interrupted. "He's writing, 'I don't have years.'"

"No, of course not. But you asked for possibilities—let's call them scenarios—that were strong enough to justify a continued investment, regardless of whether you make the documents public."

Hetta said, "He's writing another note. I'm sorry, hon, but it's a long one."

"Take your time."

He was still writing when Hetta said to him, "Honey, she doesn't need to know more about Leon."

"It's okay. I do want to know. Please."

When he was done, Hetta read the note aloud.

"Leon felt he had no recourse. He was depressed, lost his job, economy was terrible, immigrants were vilified. He was isolated, holed up on a farm in Ohio right before the shooting. I don't believe most people commit such violence lightly. And I'm not making excuses for him. I just think we should understand. People are pushed to their limits. At the same time, it shouldn't take much to pull a good man back from that limit. The right person at the right time could give him the nudge in the correct direction."

Ruth nodded as she listened, listening for any sign that Bert understood the true mechanisms of Annie's time travel.

He meant well, but he didn't get it.

Ruth struggled to frame the question. "Hetta, Bert. I'm asking both of you, I guess. I know you want to stop Leon, but aside from that family 'stain,' for lack of a better word, would you say you've had a good life?"

There was a pause. Ruth imagined Hetta looking at Bert, and Bert back at his wife. Finally, Hetta spoke up, "He's had a marvelous life. We've been happy. Blessed."

"I'm glad."

Another silence.

Ruth wanted Bert to understand that Annie's fixation on the Wolves was what had sent her skipping and sliding through time. Bert should have understood that already. He'd read the journal and the Sitting Bull letter. He had the same information Ruth did.

"You've had a good life," Ruth said again, fishing. "No major accidents, stresses or surprises."

Hetta said, "His note says, 'We all have our trials and tribulations. Annie Oakley bore a grudge, as many people do."

"A grudge," Ruth recited back.

Hetta read aloud, "She went on to lead a good life, regardless."

Ruth felt like she was in an old argument with Scott, or back in the office of her editor, Laura Boyd. Some people got it, some people didn't. And the ones who didn't were either stubbornly oblivious or simply very, very lucky. Nothing truly damaging had ever happened to them. They'd been spared violence or terror, likely even the deepest kind of remorse or shame. They hadn't suffered nightmares or radically intrusive thoughts.

It didn't matter if Bert Czolgosz knew that time travel was possible. He hadn't experienced what Annie had.

Hetta said, "It's almost a way of honoring his family, to correct this in the time he has left. All his life, Bert's been the most curious person."

Mere curiosity.

Hetta read more of Bert's note. "And then there's the strange coincidence of Leon's electrocution and Oakley's accident. I started a list of such paired occurrences: deaths or mishaps that connect people. Lincoln, Kennedy. Don't get me started. Everything lines up."

Lincoln, Kennedy. Conspiracies, coincidences and corrections. Time travel as a way to make a mostly orderly universe even more orderly. But that wasn't how it worked. Judging from the Annie documents, it wasn't a clear and conscious desire to control destiny that made change possible. It seemed to stem from being *out* of control.

Ruth would waste no time worrying whether Bert might manage to change history.

"In any case," Hetta said, "Bert's smiling here. The moment we hang up, he'll be contacting the seller. He's thrilled you've given your blessing. You *have* done that, right, Miss McClintock?"

"Completely," she said.

A HALF-HOUR AFTER THEIR PHONE call ended, Bert emailed the letter he'd already shared, in part, with Joe Grandlouis.

Dr. McClintock,

You will understand why I didn't show you the Sitting Bull letter before, which the seller showed me to tempt me into the larger investment in the entire collection of nine letters. This letter alone makes Annie Oakley's claims all too plain. My experience with the museum and with your colleague Mr. Grandlouis has shown me what happens when you share something that seems fantastical. They turn on you. I decided at that point to tread more carefully. But it's a bit late for that now, isn't it? Make of this what you will. It was good talking to you finally.

Yours truly,

Bert

P.S. I'll send copies of the rest of the letters as soon as I have them.

Ruth read the full letter, including new and helpful details she hadn't yet seen, like the header—*Dear H.D.* But the most satisfying part was seeing the handwriting, a perfect match to the unmailed letter from Sophie's tablet.

As a form of thanks, Ruth forwarded the note Sophie had been keeping under wraps. After drawing Bert's attention to the matching handwriting, she added a frank postscript: **I took this without permission from the same people who probably never returned your Leon-Annie letter. I trust you won't think less of me.**

At the top of the letter Bert had sent was a light notation: a circled number 4, written in pencil in an unfamiliar hand. Perhaps Breuer's daughter or the collector from whom Bert was now trying to procure all the letters had put it there to keep the undated letters in order.

Ruth took it to mean this was letter number four of nine. Near the midpoint of her letters and perhaps her attempts, Annie had not succeeded in fully confronting the past. It was possible she never would. But Ruth doubted that.

If there was one quality Ruth trusted and admired about Annie Oakley, it was her persistence.

3 1

R U T H

Talked to Bert. He's going to buy the rest of the letters. We
won him over. Also, Sophie gave me letter that adds evidence.
You are amazing.

Ruth sent the text to Reece. Then she changed into sweatpants
and a T-shirt, washed her face, brushed her teeth and stared in the
mirror. The lighting was bad, but that wasn't enough to explain
how strange she looked. Her eyebrows and chin were blurry. They
didn't line up. It was like she was tipsy, looking at herself, even
though she'd had no more than a sip of wine.

She'd already read the Z-to-H.D. letter three times. There was
no point musing on whether Annie ever found the Wolf until Bert
sent the next letters. Ruth had nothing to keep her from turning
back to the harder task, an excavation that was both muddier and
lonelier.

The assignment book.

Coach V. And more V. And then nothing.

It hit Ruth anew. Just months before she'd taken her own life,
Kennidy had had a relationship with her coach, their neighbor.

Ruth started a search of Vorst's name on the Minnesota Public
Criminal History search page. She needed his birth date, which

required ten minutes of Googling and showed her so much more she didn't want to know: that he had a LinkedIn profile, that he'd placed in the top three finishers in his age bracket in the local 10K several years in a row, that he had a YouTube channel with public playlists revealing his interest in aviation and building better calf muscles.

Ruth went to the TV stand, where she had set her book bag, and pulled out her sister's junior-year assignment book again. She crawled into bed with it, pulling up the thin, rough sheets. The last note about V was in April. Kennidy had killed herself in October of her senior year.

Ruth did a search online: "Van Vorst coach Horizon High retirement party." There was an article in their local paper. He'd retired at the end of the 2013 school year, a man in his late fifties in a tight Polo shirt and belted jeans, fit and smiling in the photo, fortunate to have earned such an early retirement—and thus able to afford to sell the house to Gwen's mom at below-market value. A lucky man. A generous man.

Ruth remembered the stack of "while you were out" messages she'd found to Gwen from the school, requesting that she come in for meetings about some disciplinary matter: May.

The drive with Kennidy to the cabin, angry: May.

The coach's retirement: early June.

The house sale date: July.

Ruth retrieved her bookbag and shook out all its contents on the motel bed: nickels and dimes, old gum wrappers, hairbands, and the three sealed envelopes she still hadn't opened.

She opened the overdue notice from the library first. Kennidy had never returned a copy of *Flowers for Algernon*.

The next one was a mass mailing for an upcoming college fair.

That left only one, with Department of Police in the upper left-hand corner.

The motel heater kicked on across the room. She was already

feeling flushed. With the heater going, it was muggy and oppressive. The moment it turned off, Ruth could feel the cold draft blowing under the door. Hot, cold. Noises. A man and a woman had just entered the room next to hers, starting to argue. Anxiety thrummed in Ruth's veins.

Department of Police.

They were parking tickets, most likely, or a reminder of some fee unpaid or community service left unfinished. Ruth remembered Ken, during her fifteenth summer, spending weekends picking up trash. She couldn't remember if that was linked to shoplifting or graffiti.

The letter was addressed to Kennidy McClintock or Parent/Guardian. It was postmarked three days before Kennidy's death.

Ruth unfolded the paper inside. The words at the top read: Destruction of Evidence Notification.

. . . informed that the rape and toxicology kit dated . . .

It was only one short, impersonal paragraph. The rape kit had been collected June 5, 2013. It hadn't been tested. It hadn't been preserved. No one had pressed charges.

It took Ruth a moment to interpret what she was reading. Kennidy wasn't the criminal, she was the victim. Of a crime that had gone unprosecuted.

Ruth's mind went to that warm night when she'd driven her sister to the cabin. But it hadn't been in June, Ruth was sure. She'd still been in school, the semester not yet finished; she'd come home only for the weekend. It had been May.

Kennidy had been angry at the man in the cabin and planned to return. Something had happened later, three or four weeks later at the very most—something Ken hadn't expected and never would have wanted. She only wanted her stuff back.

Ruth had always criticized Kennidy for lacking self-control, but her self-control had been extraordinary. She hadn't killed the bastard.

Ruth pushed the letter back into its envelope, hands shaking. They were her mother's hands, minus the age spots: the same tapered fingers, the same chewed nails. They were Ken's hands, too.

She tried to place them on the keys, but she couldn't even type until she anchored her wrists at the keyboard's bottom edge.

Destruction of Evidence Notification. What did that even mean?

Every county had its own rules about storage and testing of rape kits, and then there were the unintended backlogs—untested rape kits by the thousands—and out-and-out mistakes. She read about kits willfully destroyed while the statutes of limitations were still running, and about women being charged for their own kits. She read about loss and destruction of evidence even in cases where the victim was motivated to pursue prosecution. She read about overfull evidence rooms and poorly trained cops. All par for the course.

Ruth felt she should know and understand more, despite how tired she was of knowing, of searching. It was how she coped. It was a habit, one that was infuriating her at the moment because it didn't help. Ruth didn't want to know the system was so broken, and she didn't want an inside view of Vorst's brain. Her compulsion wouldn't just ebb peacefully, though.

Kennidy had been tested at the hospital. Four or five hours of questioning and swabbing, poking and prodding, and for what?

Come on, let's go home. Haven't you done enough? It was too easy to imagine her mother's plaintive voice.

Ruth let the realization take root, feeling it connect with everything else she had known and wondered. The corners of the room started to darken. But this wasn't one of her attacks. This was just forgetting to breathe.

Oh, Ruthie.

Gwen had constantly complained, and Ruth had accepted the validity of those complaints, never once considering that

Kennidy might be the one being seriously wronged with no one to protect her.

The knowledge was a large, slow-moving ship. One quick flick of the rudder wouldn't be enough to turn it around. *Go easy*, Ruth told herself. Her mother—*their* mother—whom she had always seen as the victim in this scenario, was now a stranger to her.

A thin hiss of static started up in Ruth's ears. Her vision fuzzed.

She stretched out one leg and put her foot on the floor: a trick to cure the drunken spins, supposedly. It didn't work. The darkened television set looked larger now, but also farther away. Ruth changed her strategy, lifting her leg, jamming a pillow toward the foot of the bed as quickly as she could, and elevating her feet. Oxygen to the brain. This was no time to black out. No time to go anywhere else.

Ruth tried to look everywhere but the mirror. She fixed on a corporate-style painting of a blurry tulip next to the door. The bright-orange drapes, closed; the matching bedspread. Focus and breathe.

Gwen had known Kennidy had been tested after being raped.

Gwen had known Kennidy was seeing Van Vorst.

Gwen had known that Vorst wanted it all kept quiet, and that he was willing to pay.

Mom knew.

Ruth thought back to her guesses about Annie Oakley's abusers and now understood why she felt more comfortable pointing the blame at James Rannals or even Abram Boose than at some mysterious man whose last name was literally Wolf. She'd told herself that women always kept secrets about these things.

Kennidy was not a secret keeper. Though Ruth had never known—her own sister hadn't wanted to tell her—their mother had known.

Ruth had to change her theories, not just about Ken and about Annie, but about everything. Why did abuse continue? Not because women didn't talk, not because they didn't always take action. Even when they did, it wasn't enough.

Boose, Rannals, Wolf, Vorst. Whatever. Ruth wanted to see even one of these fuckers pay the price for what he'd done.

ON THAT RIDE HOME FROM the hospital, even if Gwen had opted for silence, Kennidy would have broken down and told her everything. She would have cried. She would have shouted his name.

After Gwen agreed to buy the house, Kennidy would never have wanted to be part of it. She would have wanted to live as far from her Wolf as possible. Tension between mother and daughter must have hung heavy over them, unspoken, all summer. It would have become intolerable in the fall when school started up again. When Kennidy stepped out of the world in October, there wasn't even a note, not that Ruth knew of. Maybe this notice of evidence destruction *was* the note.

Kennidy had received the letter but not opened it, possibly the very day she killed herself. Ruth imagined her sister leaving it on the kitchen counter for their mother to see: *You open it. It's your receipt, isn't it? You can show it to him: proof of compliance. No cops. End of story. You sold your own daughter out.*

Ruth knew that parents sold out their children all the time. It was in practically every history book. Annie Oakley's mother had. Abraham Lincoln's father had. Billie Holiday, pimped out by her own mother. The lovely French ballerinas painted by Degas? Made available to male ballet patrons, as their parents knew they would be.

So much that was beautiful in the world—innocent loveliness, haunting song, virtuosic skill, intellectual brilliance—was mixed up with cruelty and the most egregious breaches of trust. Some people flourished despite what they suffered. Others did not.

3 2

R U T H

Scott answered on the second ring. "Are you all right?"

Ruth had felt strong while dialing, but the moment she heard his voice, she broke down.

"Whoa, whoa," he said. "Let me take this in another room."

She caught her breath between sobs. "You're not alone."

"No. We were watching a movie. It's okay. Just tell me what's going on."

Ruth could picture the moment: Margot on the couch, movie paused, half-empty plates, two beer bottles. The life she would have lived. Obsession had stolen that possibility from her. Ruth now knew that this obsession had a purpose, but she couldn't let her distress about Kennidy obscure the path forward.

She explained the daybook codes and the even more damning evidence-destruction letter. "Now I understand why Gwen was able to buy the house so cheap and why Ken went into a tailspin . . . And I know who it was, Scott. He's still at the school. We've got to do something about it."

"Wait a minute. Stay calm. The only thing you know for sure— the only thing you *think* you know—is that your sister was dating someone named V. And that's just based on scribbled notes."

"V isn't a common letter, Scott. And it came right after several notations for *Coach* V. All the other names dropped away: the other boys, her other girlfriends, too—everything else."

Scott was silent at the other end of the line.

Ruth said, "The other day, I saw Vorst wearing a Toronto Blue Jays jacket. The one with the blue bird and a little red maple leaf, for Canada, obviously."

"Yes, that's where the Blue Jays are from. Everyone but you knows that."

She ignored the taunt. "How many people have anything with that logo in our town?"

"A few dozen?"

"It reminded me. I saw a pennant like that years ago, at the cabin I went to with Kennidy."

"I'm lost now."

"That's not all. Reece told me Vorst is known as a predator. The kids at school talk about it. Reece knows it. He's been getting away with this for years."

"Well . . ."

"Don't do this to me, Scott." Her sinuses were filling, and her throat hurt both from crying and trying to hold in those tears. "It's exactly what I did to her. What my mother did to her."

"Bad things happened to Ken, and they didn't happen to you. It's normal to feel guilt about that. Do you think that's where this overreaction is coming from?"

"Overreaction?"

"You sound a little hysterical."

That word. A century later, and so little had changed. She exhaled slowly. "As for the guilt, you were the one who always thought guilt was pointless. I do feel guilt, but what I'm trying to focus on here is responsibility. It's only fair to Ken to find out what really happened. To be a witness and get some kind of justice, even though it's too late. It's even more important to keep an eye on Vorst, and to think about other students he might be—"

"Stay calm, Ruth."

He'd said that to her twice now. Now that she thought about it, during their two years together, he'd often told her to stay calm, which had always enraged her more.

"It's on us to make sure he's not harming other kids, Scott. Please don't let me down."

"We'll talk."

"Talk?"

"After I ask around discreetly."

"Inform the principal, at a minimum. Reports, even casual ones, have an effect."

"So does gossip."

"But maybe gossip has a function, when people's stories line up. Sometimes gossip needs to be looked into."

"I hear you."

"Stop using your faculty-meeting voice. Please don't be detached about this."

"You're going to tell me what *voice* to use? Ruth, I'm trying to help here."

"Okay, I'm sorry. I take that back. I just can't . . ."

"Let me find a way. I don't want to start slandering a good man based on some confused codes in a teenager's journal from half a decade ago."

"Okay," she said. She wasn't sobbing any more, but she still wasn't satisfied. "Thank you, Scott. But please, don't put it off."

LET IT OUT.

But she couldn't.

She washed her face. She looked in the mirror. Nothing was right anymore.

Ten minutes after hanging up with Scott, Ruth called Joe again, who answered from his home office. It was late, but he was awake and would be for several more hours. He never got any writing done unless the kids were asleep. "What's up?"

"Those American Indians who saw the distant future—did any of them think they could change it?"

"Yes, they believed change was possible and that prophecy wasn't failproof prediction. But I don't have a ready-made story of a specific personal disaster averted, if that's what you're asking for."

"But in general?"

"Well, I'd say if a lot of Indians could have seen the future and easily changed it, North America would have a million more brown faces today. And one less Kevin Costner movie."

"I'm serious, Joe."

"Me too."

At least he was listening. Joe could joke or argue or grow quiet, but he always listened without judgment or a time limit.

"How about traveling to the past? Do they talk about that?"

"Time travel? Not in so many words. Doesn't mean they couldn't." Classic Joe, no absolutes and no surprise at the turn their chat had taken. "I imagine if they had special skills—visions, ways of traveling through time in either direction—they would have used them."

"You'd think they would have done something to avoid a geno-cide."

His pitch dropped. "Blaming the victims, are we?"

"It's not that."

"Isn't it?"

"No. I'm just saying, they could have tried—"

"You don't know they didn't. But geez, Ruth, where would a person even start? It's not like what happened to Native Americans boiled down to one person's mistake on one bad day. It involved millions of people, probably billions of individual actions. Geno-cide is stage IV cancer. You can't come in when the patient's being systemically assaulted and make a few cuts here and there and expect everything to change."

"Sitting Bull knew he was going to die."

"That's right. So he went home for it. Back to the rez."

"Other people could have stopped it."

"Other people *tried*. Didn't need time travel to do it. Sometimes you can't change things."

"What do you think about destiny, Joe?"

"Wow, easy questions tonight. Okay." She heard the squeak of an office chair as he leaned back. "Like the God-given right to expand west and wipe out people and spread capitalism?"

"Not manifest destiny. Just destiny. Fate."

"That sounds like a colonizer's word to me. Justification more than cosmology."

"But what about changing things?"

"In the past again, you mean. Fantasy. Time travel."

"Yeah."

"Sounds iffy. Grandfather paradox, butterfly effect. I don't know the physics. I just know *Terminator* and *Looper* and *Superman*. You remember the late-'70s *Superman* when he flew around the world and made it spin backward to go back in time and save Lois Lane? I rented that in the sixth grade. Man, I fell hard for Lois Lane . . ."

Ruth didn't mean to tune out, but she kept seeing her mother, imagining how she would spend a typical Saturday night: television set on, half-folded laundry on the couch, a mug of whiskey at her side that she would pretend was only soda. No one was ever fooled. Ruth pictured her sister in her own bedroom. She pictured the door, covered with stickers that wouldn't come off, even though at seventeen, Kennidy no longer liked unicorns or the Rugrats. How would Ruth even get to that place, that moment, if she wanted to? She hadn't been there at the time. She was in grad school in Iowa, many miles away.

Ruth tuned back in just in time to hear Joe say, "Why are you thinking about all this? Is it personal?"

"Academic."

"Really?"

"Cultural criticism."

"Well, then. I'd say Americans are obsessed with time travel to the past because they—we—feel guilty, and for good reason. People can't get enough of those time-travel movies: go back and catch the criminal; go back and stop the murder. It's a lot easier than going back to stop slavery, the Holocaust and the slaughter of some ninety million or so indigenous peoples, but the impulse comes from the same place. We're a nation awakening slowly to the truth of the bad things that've been done and wishing there were more reset buttons. Me personally, I don't believe in reset buttons."

Ruth thought of Sitting Bull's own words in the letter Nieman had first sent to Joe. *The future and the past are our two most difficult battles. They are not battles we are always meant to win.*

These lofty phrases annoyed her now, just as they had frustrated Annie.

Ruth thought, *Fuck "not meant to win." Fuck destiny.*

Ruth thought of a young Annie Oakley, stalking through the tall grass, rifle held close to her chest, self-reliant, fearless.

"I have to go, Joe."

"Ruth, you don't sound like yourself."

"I'm totally myself."

Joe was right about one thing: it was justification. The view of the colonist, the missionary, the killer, the rapist: that whatever happened was meant to be so.

"Ruth?"

"I'm fine, Joe. More than fine."

"All right. If you say so."

THEN SHE WAS ALONE AGAIN in the motel room. Its blandness was a balm: at least she wasn't at home, looking out the window at the dark evergreen trees, brown grass speckled with frost, and beyond, to the house of that man—Van Vorst, his stooped silhouette passing within sight of her kitchen window.

But this sterile space also left her feeling untethered, unbound by both place and time, mind spinning.

The more she thought about the past in all its guises—Annie, Sitting Bull, the Wolves, Kennidy—the less she was focusing on Scott, the vision, and anyone else who would be affected by whatever happened. *If* it happened.

She wished, yet another time and with an even more intense longing, for a tranquilizer. If she were home, she would have been scrabbling through drawers, pulling up couch cushions. She could have sworn there were still three Xanax left in her apothecary drawers in the bathroom. She could even see them: the dark wood, the long white bars. Perhaps she had taken them after all. On and off for two years she had taken an uncountable number of pills.

No one had told her to take less. In fact, everyone—including Scott—had counseled her to take more. Her physical pain was real. Her brain damage was documented. Scott had been mad about her going off the clozapine.

Breathe.

The heater ticked on, blowing at the cheap orange drapes.

She was cleaner than she had been in two years. Exceptionally clean for the last few days—not even a Xanax, not a single wine or beer. Yet this week, she'd had the strongest visions yet. Intoxicants couldn't be blamed.

Every time she started to wonder if this was just her own personal history and chemistry, she had to remind herself that she wasn't the only one. Reece had had a vision, too. What he'd seen was different: no Scott in the frame, no clear sense of a shooter. Only panic, Ruth's words to him, and something gone wrong. But it was a vision of something bad happening at the school all the same.

But what high school kid wouldn't have nightmares? They'd watched training videos about active shooters and rehearsed the motions of hiding and fleeing. They'd been primed to have disturbing thoughts and dreams. There was nothing supernatural about that.

She texted Reece.

You there?

Yep.

Everything normal?

He sent a thumbs-up.

She texted: **You got the news before? Talked to Bert.**

Great. Finishing practice.

That was an unusually mellow reply. She'd expected him to be ecstatic.

Still?

It was nearly 11 o'clock.

Guy bailed. Redoing choreography.

She kept staring at the phone, wanting to tell him more—also wanting to make sure that he perceived no signs of trouble. But he would tell her if he knew something.

Good luck.

His reply was swift. **We're going to the diner soon, but after.** After a moment he added, **I'll check in.**

She texted back, **That's okay. I'll see you tomorrow. Holloway's class.**

3 3

REECE

Caleb had ditched practice. Reece was irritated, because they needed him, and also because Reece had wanted to talk to him about Vorst standing behind him in the college-application video.

That night at Rockets, when they'd finished their late practice and squashed eleven people into two cars to go to the Waffle House, he'd asked Raj, Gerald, Justin, Courtney and Vanessa if any of them had ever heard about Vorst's car getting keyed.

"His red Kia Stinger? Are you kidding me?" said Raj, who had grabbed the front passenger seat. "If anything happened to that car, even the smallest scratch, the whole school would hear about it."

"Right," Reece said, steering with one hand and batting away Raj's hand from the radio's volume knob with the other. "Caleb told me he did something to Vorst's car, but I guess he didn't."

"Guy's a liar," said Gerald from the back. "Like when he said I was giving him a hard time."

"He didn't say that," Reece corrected Gerald. "I guessed it. I was just trying to figure out why he looked so miserable."

"Because he *is* miserable. I mean, look at the guy. Wouldn't you be miserable?"

"Oh, come on," Vanessa said. "Give him till next year." When Gerald started hooting, she cut him off. "I remember how *you* looked in eighth grade, Gerald, and I still have our yearbook from junior high. Don't make me bring it to school."

"Let's go talk to Caleb," Reece said. "He used to wash dishes at Bettini's, right?"

"That was in the summer."

"But his house is really close, right? Raj, you carpooled with him last year."

The back seat exploded with groans and pleas, claims of desperate hunger and exhaustion and unfinished homework.

Raj said, "He didn't even bother coming to practice, and you're going to drive around town looking for him? We don't need him. We've got Mikayla, we've got freshmen who want to join. We've got Justin here."

Justin, the smallest of the four people in the rear seat, squashed against the window, was mostly hidden behind Courtney, who was unbuckled and sitting half on Justin's lap and half on Gerald's, whooped at the sound of his name.

"So fuck him," Raj said. "He's done."

Reece didn't want to talk Caleb into being on the team anymore. That wasn't the point.

"But you know where he lives," Reece said again.

"I never went inside his house," Raj said. "You don't want to mess with his stepdad."

"I'm not messing with anyone."

"Then?"

Meanwhile, Courtney started harping on her favorite subject: trying to change the name of the club to something better than Rockets.

Gerald said, "No one cares about the name."

From the back seat came Justin again. "Coach V thinks it's an okay name."

The whole car erupted in laughter.

"I take it back," Gerald said. "If V thinks it's good, it's definitely gotta change."

Reece tried to get everyone's attention. "Anyone seen Caleb get a ride with the coach?"

Courtney made a disgusted noise.

Justin replied, "At least twice. Are you saying . . . ?"

"I'm not saying anything," Reece said. "I was just asking."

"That means you *are* saying," Justin repeated.

"Everyone hold on tight here," Reece said as he made a hard left into the Waffle House's parking lot.

Gerald leaned hard against Justin, punishing him until he squealed.

3 4

R U T H

Midnight, and Ruth couldn't sleep.

She turned on the light and looked in the motel mirror, to one side of the television. Her face still looked strange, her features out of alignment. She lifted a finger toward her eyebrows and noticed her right hand trembling. She dropped her arm and leaned on the desk to still the tremor. She tested the weak arm, leaning forward. She couldn't support her own weight. Of all the body parts injured in the car crash, her right arm had never been a problem. She lifted both hands out in front of her, palms down. The right arm drooped, tired before the left.

Ruth looked at her face again. Then she thought to cover her right eye. Now, her face looked closer to normal. She covered her left eye. This was the blurry side. The image in the mirror stuttered like a weak flame about to go out. Was she having mini strokes?

Aloud, she said, "I am so, so fucked."

She hated hospitals, the ER especially. Doctors had rarely believed her symptoms were real, and what would they make of these latest ones? Yes, she'd had a brain injury from the car accident—already noted. They'd already told her what to do: stay off the computer, avoid screens, don't read too much, don't work too hard, try to get more sleep.

Scott's voice came to her. *You're fine. You're just really tired.*

Whereas Joe would have said, *Damn, woman. What're you gonna do about it?*

She missed Joe. They'd had a good run in those few months together, however long they had been and however exactly they had ended.

"I'm not even sure anymore," she said. And now she was talking to herself.

But at least she wasn't hearing those old phrases from long ago, the ones she hadn't mentioned when Dr. Susan asked with her annoying degree of perceptiveness, "Any voices? Specific words or phrases?"

She hadn't heard or thought lately, for example, *Open the cabin door.* If it had meant only that she should look deeply into not only Annie's past but her sister's, maybe Ruth *had* opened it. Maybe she'd opened it and left it open, rusted hinges squeaking, the door banging in the wind.

Ruth felt the need to get out of bed. She went to the motel door, fingers reassured by the flip of the bolt. Locked. Yet she still had that feeling, as if she'd left a car window open with rain in the forecast.

Her car was back home, undriven, windows closed. In the garage.

Still standing near the foot of the bed, Ruth could sense the image of Scott hovering close to her consciousness, like an optical illusion—faces on either side of a lamp—that invited you to choose how much you were ready to see. She thought of crawling back under the covers, but instead lowered herself to the ground, sitting cross-legged, in a meditative posture. A way to tell her brain, *This is on purpose. This is not panic. This isn't a nightmare, either. I'm not afraid.*

Without resistance, the image appeared more gently, in slow motion. A remembered image, not a lived one. There was Scott's face and the upper half of his body, wearing a white button-down shirt. This was not Scott at his heaviest, the summer before last. This was Scott as he'd looked since beginning to date again. He was wearing the newer eyeglass frames she'd noticed him wearing at her house when he'd come to move his boxes.

Ruth kept her eyes closed. There was nothing to fear and no reason to hurry.

She allowed her inward gaze to sweep across Scott's face and torso in even slower, measured movements, like a lighthouse beam. Her eyes continued around the outline of the frames and over to his left temple, where she noticed for the very first time, a thread of silver. She paused there. If she had noticed this detail two years ago, she would've been able to place the image better as something not belonging to the pre-accident recent past or present, but without a doubt to the future.

Scott Webb, you have gray hair.

Ruth sighed, on the edge of a smile.

And then, maybe because her attention had traveled back to earlier memories—the two of them on Ruth's thirtieth birthday, laughing about the vanity of aging—his image vanished. She tried to recall any part of it: his face, his body, the ground on which he was standing, the sky or grass. Nothing.

She started all over again, but it was as if her shift toward another memory had displaced the entrance to wherever she had been. The way was blocked, but she also felt oddly relaxed, and perhaps it was this very feeling—the sudden, utter lack of anxiety—that made any more visualization impossible.

There was no way to tell when the image, now vanished, was from. It could be a week from now, yes. But it could also be five years away, or ten. Perhaps she'd missed an important lesson in all this: that even if some dark vision in the future were true, we couldn't worry about it every day, throwing away any potential happiness in the process.

For the moment, she believed Scott was safe. She couldn't muster a deep-seated anxiety she didn't feel or head toward a target she couldn't see.

3 5

REECE

Thursday

A t 10:45 A.M., Reece was walking behind two girls on the way out of math class, about to hand a test back to Mr. Webb, when the math teacher put his arm out to stop anyone from leaving.

They'd all heard it: the crackle of the intercom, followed by a storm of heavy footfalls in the hallway. A door slammed. A girl shrieked.

"Get back to your seats," Mr. Webb said, before he pulled the door shut. "Procedures," he barked. Two steps forward, two steps back, sheaf of tests still in his hand. "Lockdown. You know what to do."

But they didn't remember, not at first.

"Blinds," Mr. Webb called out to Tory, a girl who was standing in the back corner of the room, but she didn't move. The school had just replaced the blinds in all the rooms the previous fall, switching from old metal blinds to a solid blackout fabric.

A different student called out, "Locks, lights, out of sight."

Mr. Webb shut off the lights. Now it was dim, with only traces of brightness seeping in from around the windows and doors, as if they were about to watch a movie.

"Everyone down below window level." Still they froze, a third of the class seated at desks and two-thirds standing, backpacks in hands, still fighting the urge to head toward the door. He shouted again. "Down, and I mean all the way. Down and quiet!"

From the hallway, more feet could be heard. Through a vertical slot-shaped window in the door, they saw a gym teacher and a security guard run past. Reece took out his phone, and the action sparked a flurry of imitation as everyone in the room with a phone sent and pulled up texts, took photos and started taking videos, though nothing was happening yet.

"No cell phones," Mr. Webb said.

Reece glanced at his teacher's face to see if he would enforce the rule. He wouldn't.

Good call, Mr. Webb. Who wanted to be the guy who cut people off from getting safety information or sending a final goodbye?

Five minutes. Ten.

"Hey, Mr. Webb."

He didn't answer.

In the drills, there had been a constant stream of PA system announcements. This seemed like a false alarm, but even so, there should be more information. Panic mellowed into suspense, edging toward skepticism.

Guys who had shrunk back into the corners duck-walked toward the center of the room to talk with friends, slapping each other on the back, teasing each other about how they'd looked when they first heard the footsteps and the shriek. Girls who had willingly flattened to the ground under desks without complaint now scooted into cross-legged sitting positions. They started to take selfies and braid each other's hair. *Grooming,* Reece thought. *We're all just a bunch of nervous primates.*

Again, Reece looked at Mr. Webb, who was sitting on the floor with his legs extended in front of him. He still held the stack of papers in his hands, crunching them without noticing, their edges bent between his sweaty fingers.

Reece would feel much better if Mr. Webb didn't look so worried. Maybe "worried" wasn't the right word. He looked heartsick, like someone who couldn't believe this moment was finally happening, that his life had brought him to this: sitting in a dim room, waiting, and not because of a tornado, but because it now seemed normal to assume that someone might be running around with the intention to kill.

A bullhorn in the hallway squawked, and a girl in the class screamed, then covered her mouth with her hands, giggling maniacally. A public announcement echoed down the hallway, "Stay in position. Police are on campus. Stay in your classrooms. Do not open the doors."

Reece closed his eyes and tried to conjure the dream images again, if only to reassure himself none of this had anything to do with what he had seen.

Another half-hour passed. Kids began to complain about needing to use the bathroom and wanting to eat lunch. Mr. Webb took a brief call. Finally, they proceeded in single file down the hall and outside, where they waited in the cold autumn air, leaning against the brick wall, under the POOL sign, while police continued to do a sweep of the building.

Reece closed his eyes and smelled the chlorine wafting from the heavy double doors they'd exited. Nope. That smell wasn't familiar, just as this location wasn't. None of it triggered the déjà-vu feeling.

Gerald leaned into Reece's shoulder to whisper, "I just heard Kale's name."

"What?"

"They were looking for him. Caleb. He left school early. They found a note."

"Where?" They didn't even have lockers anymore. Too dangerous. First, they'd zip-tied them shut, then removed them altogether, replacing them with sports trophy display shelving.

Another guy next to them overheard. "We're fucking freezing out here because of a note?"

Gerald said, "Someone thought he had a bomb or something. A freshman told the police."

"Naw," a senior next to them said. "Bomb scare would have meant evacuating the building, not keeping us holed up inside."

"Unless it was in his car," Gerald said. "Then they'd keep us in here."

Reece said, "Caleb doesn't have a car."

"Anyway. He's a suspect."

"I think you mean 'person of interest,'" Reece said. "But I doubt he's even that."

As soon as Reece had heard Caleb's name, he'd thought of them all crammed into his car last night. He remembered Raj bad-mouthing Caleb and Justin claiming he'd seen Caleb get rides from Vorst. He remembered his own good intention to confront Caleb tactfully—to at least ask about that strange Rockets' rehearsal that had been captured on video. Instead, when Caleb skipped practice, Reece started asking around. That had been a mistake. The rumor mill was starting up again and . . . well, now this.

The facts were few. Caleb had left school early—that was the most solid one. Reece hadn't ever seen Caleb start a fight. Mostly, he walked away from them. He wasn't a conflict-seeker. He was an avoider. Even when he claimed to do something aggressive, like keying a car, it was all in his head.

"Come on," Reece said. "Give the guy a break."

Gerald said, "A break? I'm going to break his legs for making me stand out here all day in the freezing cold."

Reece bummed two cigarettes from a girl who was pacing up and down the edge of the curb like a tightrope walker. He gave one to Gerald. The teachers were standing too close to light up, but he turned his back to them, faced the wall, and put the cigarette in his mouth, unlit. Just for the feel and the flavor. Shit, he really was an addict now. If he didn't stop soon . . .

"When's the last time anyone saw him?" Gerald asked.

"I think it's all fine," Reece said. "He's fine. We're fine. End of story."

"How do you know?"

Reece checked his gut again: no tickles, no whispers. This wasn't the day or the place. He just knew.

The principal got on the bullhorn. "I understand it's chilly, but you're going to have to be patient. We'll let you know the day's schedule as soon as we have permission to open the building again."

No one had sorted out how to deal with the lost lunch period or whether after-school activities would be canceled. The rehearsal for Friday's halftime show was probably not happening. Weeks ago, Reece had thought this performance would be the best thing the Rockets had ever done. Now it would be the worst, especially with the new choreography they'd been forced to sub in, thanks to Caleb's no-shows.

Backing out completely was an option, and Reece played out how that would go, sitting through the first half of the football game knowing the Rockets had given up.

It felt like shit.

"Anyone got anything to eat?" Gerald asked, but no one answered. "Beef jerky in anyone's pocket? Piece of gum?"

Every student had turned to his or her own phone, his or her own thoughts, like they were in the security line at an airport, but worse, because the line wasn't moving.

Reece knew a lot of people who had gone on college tours in the spring or summer. He'd ambled through one college fair, taking home more pencils and bouncy balls than catalogs. What *did* he want to do with his life? He'd decided, based on the disappointment of not getting to transfer to his preferred arts school, that it was too late to take dance seriously. He wasn't a national-caliber dancer. But he wasn't exactly old, either. Whatever his personal best was, he hadn't reached it.

Maybe that was the source of his compulsive searching: because his life felt like it didn't have meaning. No, forget that. Meaning you could find later. He just needed movement and a temporary direction. But he wasn't going to find it doing random Internet searches or reading about Annie Oakley, interesting as that may have been.

Reece thought of Mr. Webb sitting on the floor with legs splayed, looking heartbroken, as if he expected a shooter to explode into the room, ending it for all of them.

He thought of Sergei Polunin saying, "I like imperfections in the world." Reece could think of a lot he wanted to change in his past, but maybe everything that had happened so far would lead him to something more interesting, less predictable. A sideways path to some kind of success he couldn't even imagine yet.

So maybe their Rockets performance wouldn't be great. And maybe Reece would end up at some less competitive arts college and at best, become a big fish in a small pond. Maybe he wouldn't go to college. Hell, maybe he wouldn't be a big fish anywhere. But if he'd died today—if many of them had—what would his regrets be?

He hadn't looked for summer dance intensives. He hadn't looked for a job as an instructor, teaching kids after school. He hadn't borrowed the car to go to Minneapolis for the weekend when good dance and theater acts came to town. Okay, all that was attributable in the last year to depression, but he hadn't always been depressed. At the ripe age of fifteen, he'd scoffed at an invitation to apply for youth representative on the town arts council, even if it meant he might have a say in things like grant making and inviting performers to visit, because he'd assumed that any dancer or singer or painter who would come to their little town's summer jubilee arts week couldn't possibly have any talent. What an arrogant shit!

Reece folded his unlit cigarette in half and pushed it deep into his pocket.

My body is a temple. He took out his phone and texted the phrase to Ruth, because she was nuts herself and he could tell her anything. **Remind me, would you?**

Gerald whispered to Reece, "I'm tempted to cut out of here and go to my car. Mental health day. We barely have two periods left."

Reece said, "I'm pretty sure you don't want to do that." In the distance, at the main exits from the massive parking lots, a half-dozen cop cars were lined up with a news van behind them. "Don't you have stuff in your car you wouldn't want a cop to see if they decided to pull you over and open your glove box?"

"Good point."

The principal's voice boomed again. "Show's over. Let's get back to work now, people."

"She's saying that like we asked to be standing out here," Gerald complained. He scrolled on his phone. "Why does Kale have to be such an asshole? My balls are freezing."

A girl, the one who'd been picking at the bottom of her shoe, said, "I don't want to hear you say the word 'freezing' one more time, and I don't want to hear about your balls. My mom's going to see this on the news and she's going to lose it."

Reece narrowed his eyes against the autumn wind and pushed his hands farther into his pockets. From afar, he would have looked just like the other seniors standing next to him, impatient and indignant. But inside, he felt different.

As they shuffled single-file toward the doors, he pretended to be annoyed and uncomfortable, because that's how his friends were acting, and for good reason. But he couldn't deny it. For no reason at all, he felt invigorated—so suddenly buoyed that instead of passing through the doors, he took over door duty from the shivering kid who was holding one side open.

"My turn. Got it."

Reece took another moment to gaze around the parking lot and beyond in search of a sign or symbol, but nothing appeared. He kept holding the door. He couldn't get enough of the cold, clean air or the view beyond: football field, the encircling track, and behind all that, the dark tangle of green spruces and the clusters of aspens blazing yellow against a bright blue autumn sky.

"Pointless day," Gerald said, ducking into the building.

"The worst," Reece agreed, smiling.

Something had happened or just barely not happened, leaving him feeling oddly at peace and inexplicably refreshed.

3 6

R U T H

When the bus overheated halfway between Rochester and Marshall, Ruth felt it again: a pang of deep and unearned familiarity.

She walked to the front of the bus. "Do you think they'll get a replacement vehicle out here pretty fast?"

The driver looked exasperated. "Honey, I don't know anything except what they tell me."

She returned to her seat. She'd been doing online searches for the first ninety minutes of the trip, looking for any further evidence that Van Vorst had been linked to any arrest, complaint, rumor, anything. Nothing turned up. Her phone's charge was at 37 percent.

She logged in to her email and sent a note to Holloway explaining that, once again, she wouldn't make it in time for either class. In her inbox was a single document combining some forty pages of scanned documents. Hetta had written, **Physical copies in the mail to you, but Bert told me I should send you these. He has not finished reading beyond the first three, but he wanted no further delay and sends you his best wishes.**

On a phone screen, the handwriting was tiny and even harder to read than the journal had been. Ruth held the phone close to her good eye with the intensity of someone looking through a peephole.

At the top right was a lightly sketched number one.

Dear H.D.,

You ask me if these episodes I have recounted might be dreams. I will tell you the difference, because I do have bad dreams.

For example, last night the He-wolf came looking for me, and though I run through the infirmary and then the town and then the woods, I can't stay far enough ahead of him. Sometimes I am not even me but some other young girl, another slave he has caught and kept. I am a mixture of faces, and I know where these faces come from. They are real children from the Darke County Infirmary, other little girls I've helped wash and dress, who might have become slaves loaned out to the same men or other men after I left that place.

In this dream, I can't find my way out of buildings or into them, out of fields or through them. I realize suddenly that I have forgotten my belongings, my warm clothes and my rifle. If I only had my rifle, I would turn and make him stop. Instead he is hunting me. I wake up in a sweat. Frank asks, but I don't say anything except that I've had a nightmare. He presumes, probably, it is about the train crash. He doesn't realize that even now, that Wolf hunting me in the woods is more frightening than any kind of mechanized pain or death.

That, good doctor, is a dream.

Now you will say that I am confused in my time-skipping episodes also, and that they therefore have a dreamlike quality. I am frustrated in these past episodes, but I am not dreaming. You must trust that I know the difference.

The train has pulled into the station.

I will write again soon.

Z

Dear H.D.,

I have made several false starts in our correspondence and wasted both paper and time, but I can wait no more to tell you that I have not only dreamed, not only worried or ruminated, but I have continued the other practice and recently managed to visit my earliest episode yet.

It is May of 1899. I am at a picnic with two friends, visiting an Indian graveyard, a moment that disturbed me. This is the first time I have skipped this far back and been in direct communication with others, able to move and speak at length, rather than simply haunt from the margins, as it were.

Realizing that I have no spectral limitations, I've decided to make use of my capacity for action. I've written a letter to Leon Czolgosz. Surely you know the name? All these assassinations lately and madness everywhere, Europe and America both. I will tell him I know what he is going to do, and that I will be watching him. I intend to go back in time and mail that letter. Then we shall see what he does. I must send this to you before I lose my courage and fail to mail my letter to him.

Sincerely,

Z

Dear H.D.,

I am disheartened. Only a day after completing my plan, while traveling to my next trial (dozens remain) I entered into conversation with a gentleman on the train and mischievously asked him what he thought of McKinley. I hoped and presumed our Ohio president was enjoying the first months of his third term. As soon as the man's face fell, I knew that my letter hadn't had any effect, though I had to ask two more people before I could completely believe. Once I did, the *earlier memory of what I had known (the assassination being in June, in Ohio) began to fade. If I did not write this letter now, a year from now I might not even be able to specify "June" or "Ohio" or any of the other particulars of which I had been so sure, which of course have nothing to do with history as it is now.*

I am halfway between disappointment and feeble hope. My actions have consequences, but outcomes are hard to predict. My mistake was thinking I could influence someone else or change an event of a public nature, something that never involved me in the first place. It is hard enough to direct one's own actions and thoughts.

You can likely see that the shake is making the writing of this letter difficult. The trip made in order to send a letter to a stranger was yet another waste of my energies. I don't look well upon waste. I won't make that mistake again.

Sincerely,

Z

Ruth snapped to attention. The bus driver was ambling down the aisle. "You can get out if you want," he told her.

She'd sunk down in her seat, lost in her reading and her latest realizations: only three letters in, and Bert would have found what he wanted. He knew the outcome of the letter that Annie had written to his ancestor. Annie noted that the assassination was only delayed, not prevented. That kind of meddling was unsuccessful.

But for Ruth—and Annie—the loose ends were still there, frayed and quickly unraveling, given that Annie's failed trip worsened her symptoms.

Ruth opened the fourth letter. It was the one about Sitting Bull, half of which she'd already seen.

The driver cleared his throat. "You don't have to go, but there's a Dairy Queen across the street."

Across the highway, the other passengers were climbing a grassy slope toward a parking lot.

"I'll stay here, at least until my battery runs out."

"Makes no difference to me."

RUTH HAD BEEN TOO ABSORBED in the letters to notice Scott's first text when it arrived.

I'm sorry for not trying longer than we did.

He never texted and had certainly never expressed this kind of plain remorse.

A new message came in before she could compose a response.

Everything fine. I shouldn't have texted.

Ruth checked the time: school had been out for an hour. His first text had come in twenty-one minutes ago.

She texted back: **Sure you're okay?**

She didn't expect an immediate answer. He might not even see this before he got home.

The other new message was from Reece, and just as inexplicable: **My body is a temple. Remind me, will you?**

Was that code, or just a random thought?

Then it hit her. When she'd first met Reece, she'd felt the urge to tell him not only about how to approach history, but also that he should stop smoking in those exact words: "Your body is a temple." She had felt it then, a week ago, a faint outer ring of waves emanating from a pebble dropped into a pond.

But where and when had that pebble dropped?

Something had begun.

She texted Reece: **Are you okay?**

Never better.

Something had happened. But not *the* thing.

And maybe it wouldn't?

Annie hadn't stopped Czolgosz from killing McKinley, but she had made him pause and perhaps reconsider. Czolgosz had been determined. Even after having second thoughts, he'd met an anarchist, Emma Goldman. He'd first heard her speak in May, around when he would have received the letter from Annie. But then he'd visited Goldman in July. Another nudge.

Some dominoes must tip more easily than others. Whoever was prepared to carry out this violent act might not be so motivated.

Ruth tried to imagine the possibilities that might account for a change: Scott had talked to the principal, to the police, to some student, to Vorst himself. He had done something he wouldn't otherwise have done. *Something changed.*

It had to be Scott's actions, based on her call to him last night. It hadn't been a pleasant call, and she winced to think of her own emotional outburst and his apparent lack of concern, which had created another contradiction. For the first time today, he was reopening his heart to her. And for the first time in a long time, she wasn't feeling particularly tender toward him. He'd defended Vorst. He'd shown practically no sympathy for Ken.

But then again, it had been a hurried and difficult discussion. Maybe he'd had time to rethink the ways he hadn't supported Ruth during their relationship. Maybe he wished he'd stepped up earlier and was trying to do so now.

I'm sorry for not trying longer than we did.

Maybe.

She was overthinking it, failing to appreciate the simple good news. Scott was sorry. And more important, he was safe.

Ruth texted him: **On a broken down bus 2 hours from home. Crazy week. Worried about you. Glad you texted. Want to talk more. Miss you.**

A WARNING POPPED UP. RUTH'S phone battery had dropped below ten percent. She tapped the message away and moved on to the fifth letter.

Dear H.D.,

My attempts have continued at the cost of my own physical well-being. You will see that the shake in my hand makes this letter even more unruly, but it can't be helped. At last I arrived to the right place and nearly the right time, and with as much fury in me as I had ever felt. But it didn't go as I'd expected. She was the problem.

I haven't told you much about her, and I didn't expect to because she did not seem to matter, but of course all of it matters.

I hadn't remembered the She-wolf's vulnerability. "I know it isn't easy for you," she told me, "but you're young and stronger than I ever was. You'll be living a better life somewhere, someday. Truth is, he's left me half alone since you've been here."

Sitting at her kitchen table, I felt I had both the ultimate power and none of it. I knew the future, who would live years later and who would die, but in another way, I was still stuck in that period. I would always hear her bawling and begging. I would still feel the He-wolf years from now, leading me to the woodshed. I had to change something—do something— in order not to keep living through it again.

But at the same time, her lament weakened me. The last thing I heard her say was, "It means the world that you don't hate me."

Then I was with Sitting Bull again, only briefly. He said nothing this time. I sensed disappointment in his weathered face. I do not wish to disappoint him or you or myself.

That is the last trip I have made as of this date. But I have exhausted myself in its telling.

Yours truly,
Z

Ruth looked up to see the bus driver coming down the aisle. "Last one off. Your replacement chariot awaits."

She looked down at her phone: two percent. If she'd thought about it, she would have followed the others into the Dairy Queen a half-hour ago, if only to keep her phone plugged in somewhere as she read. It was too late now.

As the driver leaned his hip against a seat, watching her, she gathered all the scattered contents of her book bag, hurried off the broken bus and onto the working one, already rumbling and ready to pull away. Claiming the quietest seat she could find in the back, Ruth pulled out her phone again: one percent.

Dear H.D.,

I have made no visits recently, but that is only because I am gathering my energies for what I hope will be my final attempt, and if it is not successful, I don't know what I will do to enable myself to return to the life I once had, without nightmares or rage, feeling further than ever from the affections of my husband and even my own self-regard. If there was one thing I was certain of prior to these last few years, it was that I was both a moral and disciplined person. I don't fully understand how this certainty has been shaken after so many years. Yes, the trials, the nightmares, my own frustration at being older, injured, newly vulnerable, even financially affected by Hearst's persecution. And yet all that isn't enough to explain why a Wolf, a demon, should regain his ability to haunt me.

I understand you talk with patients who are likewise fixated on disturbing images or memories, and so I came to you. But please understand that my case is both similar and different. Whereas your patients visit their enemies only in nightmares or hallucinations, you must entertain the idea that

I can visit mine on a physical plane, or nearly so, though it has not proven easy.

The hope I cultivated when I first came to you, that if I had a listener and this journey were not made entirely alone, I would not suffer the physical effects as strongly, does not seem to be well founded. Perhaps we are always alone. Frank is good to me, but he doesn't understand. Even if I tried to explain, he would not see things from my side, because his soul is simply too light for it. I have ruined a marriage or come close to it because I can't better control my own darkness.

My hand shakes violently now. When I travel by train overnight, I keep a revolver under my small pillow, but if I had to use it? My aim would be less than perfect. Keeping my appearance tidy with no one to help me is a problem. This sounds like a small thing, but I assure you, with reporters waiting everywhere the train stops, it is not inconsiderable. They surely see my unkempt hair and loose clothing. I try to hide my shaking hand by tightly gripping a closed umbrella or propping the object in my lap with the hand completely hidden in the umbrella's folds.

Even my vision is worsening. Yet I still take hope in what I know of your last patient, that she suffered worse symptoms than mine and those symptoms, bad as they were, vanished as soon as she faced her demons . . .

The phone went dark.

3 7

R U T H

R uth exited the bus station's double doors, looking for a cab. And there was Scott.

He'd been leaning against a post, staring down at his phone, hair rumpled and brow furrowed until he looked up and saw her. The transformation in his expression—relief, anticipation—made her fatigue vanish. It had been months since she'd seen him look irrefutably happy to see her, since she'd seen herself reflected in someone else's eyes as a person anxiously desired.

He rushed forward, ready to take her bookbag and her overnight wheelie. When he was close enough to give her an awkward side hug, she smelled it. He'd been drinking.

"I was waiting for you," he said. "You didn't answer my texts."

"My phone died." She pulled away from the sideways embrace in order to study him better.

"You look a little . . . buzzed."

"Do I?" He laughed. "I guess I was waiting a while. Bar across the street, since school let out. You seem a little worse for wear yourself. You're shivering."

"The bus was drafty."

"Drafty? You're shaking like someone just pulled you out of a hole in the ice."

They put her things in his car and paused at the trunk. She put a hand on his wrist. "Something up with Margot?"

"Nothing like that."

"Are you still together?"

"Actually, as of last night . . . we're not."

"So, it is about Margot."

"Things started changing last weekend after I came to your house to pick up my stuff. That brought some things to the surface. She wanted to move fast. I realized I'd never meant to get that involved in the first place."

"Is she taking it badly?"

He screwed up his face. "A little."

"But this isn't about Margot?"

"To be honest, I didn't think about Margot once today. That's the point."

"What happened today?"

He evaded her glance and walked toward the driver's side. She followed. "Bad afternoon at school. I'll tell you on the way. Come on, let's get you warm."

"Scott." She touched his arm. "I'm not going to let you drive. I'm so grateful you came to get me, but I think you're tipsier than you realize."

His eyebrows went up. "So . . . we're going to sit around drinking coffee somewhere until I sober up?"

She held out her hand. When he didn't surrender the keys, she plunged her hands into her coat pockets, ready to stand there as long as it took.

He shook his head. "You're joking."

"I'm not."

"Why?"

"Because it's time."

"I'm worried you're not ready. What's it been—over a year?"

"Two." She tried not to give away her uncertainty. From the

waist up, she probably looked confident enough, chin up and lips pressed together. From the waist down, she was shaking. To quiet her trembling fingers, she pushed them deeper into her coat pockets. Then she felt it: the hard little corner of something, a broken breath mint or something better. She pinched it between two fingers. She could already imagine with pleasure the chalky feeling of the dry pill in her throat.

"I hope it's like riding a bike," he said. Scott looked up and down the street again, as if another solution might present itself. While his face was turned, she withdrew her hand and popped the half-bar of Xanax in her mouth with a strange sort of glee. So she did have a little bit left. Angels were smiling.

It was supposed to take a full hour to kick in, but that couldn't be true, because she felt immediate relief.

"JUST—DON'T TALK. I'M DYING TO hear about your day. But not yet."

"I can't believe you're driving. That's great."

"Please," she said, checking her blind spot with the purposeful caution of a teenager taking her first driving exam. "Be quiet. Don't jinx it."

Setting the parking brake an hour later, she felt her skin tingle with adrenalized pleasure. Any pharmacological contributions to that sensation were forgotten. They had arrived.

Inside the house, Ruth pulled a half-eaten lasagna out of the fridge and started rewarming it. Scott opened the fridge door, looking for another beer, but there were none in the house.

"Another life change, I see."

He didn't need another, but it was clear he was still on edge. Drinking had been *her* problem in the past, not his.

"Why don't you finish telling me what happened at work," she said, reaching up to a cupboard to pull down two plates.

When she turned, he was directly in front of her, mouth nearly on hers.

"Oh."

"Oh?"

She neither resisted nor fully responded, at least not for that first, infinitesimally small moment. This was why people fought and got back together, to have that first kind of uncertain kiss again—the kind when you didn't know if the other person would pull away or rush ahead. The uncertainty itself was a time-stopping intoxicant. No yesterday, no tomorrow.

She returned the pressure of the kiss. He took the plates out of her hands and set them on the counter.

"So," she said, tasting the beer on his breath and wishing he were one hundred percent sober, wishing he weren't involved with anyone else, even if that entanglement was nearly over. She whispered, "This isn't like you."

He broke off, eyes still closed, and rested his forehead against hers. "I know."

"I don't want you to make a mistake. I don't want *us* . . ."

"I know. But what if everything else in the last year was a mistake? What if this is the first thing that's *not* a mistake?"

LATER, AFTER THEY'D COME OUT of the bedroom and eaten the lasagna, Scott told her what had happened in his classroom. How he'd watched his students tweeting, texting, recording. How he'd waited for the shattering of glass and the spray of bullets.

"And I thought, damn, I'm almost forty years old. I'm a single guy living in a shitty apartment." He stabbed with too much enthusiasm at the last bite of lasagna on his plate. Sauce flew.

"There," she said, "on your sleeve. No, the left one."

He dabbed at the cuff, which only made the stain worse. "It

was like a freeze frame. Like I could see myself from the outside, sitting with my legs out in front of me, this stupid look on my face, utterly incompetent."

"Why incompetent?"

"My private life isn't so great, but worse than that, I'm teaching in a school that can't even keep its kids safe. Because that should be the one . . . the one thing." He looked down, blinking hard. "It's not like I haven't thought it before. When we do those drills? We're inflicting trauma. These kids are training their brains every day: This is how life is. Be afraid, the one time in your life when you have the innate right to be reckless."

Ruth nodded. She had said as much in the past, but he hadn't wanted to hear it.

"Today, I saw a hundred different ways that anyone with the right weapon could kill dozens of kids before anyone knew anything, and no stupid drill is going to change that." He paused. "You're staring at something."

"No." She was trying to avoid seeming distracted. First the sauce on his cuff, now this. But how could she resist staring? "Gray hair. Just a strand." She reached up to touch his temple. "I didn't see it before."

He laughed. "I think I got it today."

"No, really. When did this show up?"

She wanted to pluck it out. She wanted to follow him around, day after day, ready to pluck the next one, too.

Scott reached for her hand and pulled it down, to clasp it between his own.

Ruth thought with effort, *Nothing bad is going to happen.*

"To wrap things up," he said.

"Oh, I thought you'd already wrapped up. I'm sorry."

"Ruth, listen to me."

"I'm listening."

"I thought . . . This is not the life I meant to have. I *had* the life

I wanted to have, or almost, two years ago. I let it—we let it—get away from us."

Ruth shared in his desire to reverse everything and start over. But something nagged at her. Not guilt or sympathy for Margot. Something else was wrong.

From their first kiss in the kitchen to their first full embrace in bed, Scott's body had felt foreign to her. In some ways, it should have. They hadn't slept together for well over a year, and she was heavier than she'd once been, while he'd not only lost the weight he'd gained during their breakup but gone beyond, cycling his way toward extreme fitness. He was more muscular in a few places, dramatically thinner in others. "You never step into the same river twice," said Heraclitus. Scott was a different man.

After they'd finished making love but before they roused themselves to rescue the dry, overheated lasagna, she'd noted the difficulty of finding a comfortable position while nestling into his shoulder. She was imagining a different body, a broader chest, not Scott's; a tickle of hair against her own neckbone, not Scott's. She tried to ignore the associations, because they weren't fair, they weren't right. She had never consciously compared Scott to any other man before, much less to a man she hadn't seen in years. She was thinking of Joe, and it didn't even make her feel guilty, as if she had recently been Joe's partner, as if Joe weren't even married and a father, as if Scott were the interloper. What did Joe have to do with any of this?

Something isn't right.

"Maybe the false alarm at the school was a good thing," Scott said. "Maybe it was the wake-up call I needed." He reached out again to take her hand across the table. "What do you think?"

She'd been distracted, thinking of an image—that narrow-hipped boy, she was sure of that now, propped up by his elbows, the rest of his body mostly hidden in the grass. "Sorry. About what?"

"About us."

She deflected. "Wait, did you tell me what led to the lockdown?"

"Caleb Hill." The name was vaguely familiar to Ruth. "Supposedly, he said something about wanting to hurt someone. But then they questioned another sophomore, and that first kid took it all back. We've got no proof Caleb planned to do anything. The school knew less at four o'clock than it did at two. I expect we'll hear more in the morning. They asked us to come in early for another debrief."

Scott stood up to clear the dishes. The sight of him setting each plate in the sink and filling the crusty lasagna pan with soap and water to soak was such a portrait of normalcy that Ruth was afraid of moving an inch, lest she disrupt it.

She asked, "Do you think this kid actually has violent tendencies?"

"No idea." Then he remembered and brightened. "But the debrief at the end of the day did give me a chance to sit next to John Regatta. You remember him? Phys ed teacher?"

"I think so."

"Great news. Well—it's half great, half sad, but you'll be relieved. I talked to him about Van Vorst."

"You told him our suspicions?"

"*Your* suspicions, and not quite."

"Wait. What?"

"Van Vorst has leukemia." Scott waited as Ruth absorbed the news. "He's had it since Regatta got hired. That means at least six years."

Ruth was on edge. "So?"

"It's the solution to your mystery."

Scott was distracted, looking for the scrubbing sponge, ready to tackle the burnt lasagna dish.

"Leave it. I'll do it in the morning. How does it solve any mystery?"

He turned around, back against the sink. "Well, in a bunch of ways. It explains why he retired so early, which you seemed to find suspicious. Why he felt bad for your mother, who also had cancer, which explains his generosity."

"The timing's still off," she said quietly.

"Whatever the details, he wanted to do a good deed. He saw his own time as limited. He wanted to help. Anyway, the important thing is that he probably won't volunteer again in the spring. He's getting weaker, and his life is busy with hospital appointments. I still think the guy's probably innocent, but either way, it's reason to stop worrying."

"But did you ask John if he'd heard anything about Vorst's reputation? Any stories about him being inappropriate with kids?"

"No, I didn't."

"Did you talk to the principal?"

"Of course not." Scott pulled his chin into his chest. "Ruth. The guy's got leukemia."

"That doesn't affect what he does with his dick!"

Scott looked shocked. "I'm not sure why you always think the worst of people." All the softness in his face, all the normalcy of the previous moment, had evaporated. "Actually, I do. Because you spent years reading and writing and thinking about a woman who was abused as a kid. Thank goodness you've had a break from that. I think your brain needs it, so it can heal and begin to perceive the world as a safe, friendly place again."

"You said yourself: it isn't. I thought that was your great epiphany during this false alarm."

"For one terrible, sad moment."

"Well, take that moment and multiply it by years. That's how I've felt."

"You're exaggerating."

It was the same argument they'd always had.

"I've never wanted to say it, at the risk of making you upset," Scott said. "But I'm going to say it now."

"Please do."

"You think something terrible happened to your sister. I completely get how that led to her substance abuse and whatever came after."

"Suicide." She hated when people avoided that word

"But you've always assured me that nothing happened to *you*. Not directly."

"I was just a witness. And a failed one, at that."

"Listen. Just because something happened to Annie Oakley, and maybe to your kid sister—and we don't know half the facts about that—it doesn't mean everyone is abused as a kid, or that every coach or teacher is an abuser."

"No, of course not."

"And here's the thing about this #MeToo movement. It's caught a lot of bad guys in its web, but it's also caught a few innocent ones. Don't forget that."

"Oh, I haven't forgotten." Ruth was trying her best not to shut down.

"I mean, you're a historian."

"I used to be."

"So you know better than anyone that where there are misdeeds, there's got to be ample evidence, right?"

"One always hopes," Ruth said. "But then again, one has to remember certain near-universals."

"Which are?"

"Some men get away with assault, rape, even murder. And—statistically speaking—women rarely get even with those men."

Scott made a face. "Get even?"

"Yes, take revenge. Women typically don't. Statistically speaking."

She waited, wanting him to ask, which he never had. If he did, she could spell it out: her darkest revenge fantasy, in enough grim detail that perhaps it would purge the desire to finish what Kennidy had started.

Awash in his own relentless positivity, he barely knew Ruth, even after all their time together. He didn't know she hadn't been a good sister to Kennidy. That she hadn't wanted to move back home during those final months when Gwen needed her most. He didn't know the shadows, the rotting corners of her heart, or that her minor acts of bravery—she'd finally driven, to prevent him from driving drunk!—were minor compared to her cowardice. And because he cared for her unquestioningly, blindly, but also shallowly, he could never know her deepest self.

"Garbage night, isn't it?" Scott had turned back to the sink and the glass pan that Ruth had told him not to wash. He filled it with sudsy water. "It's raining. Few more weeks and it could be turning to snow. You want me to pull the can out? I'd hate to see you slip."

"It's fine, I've managed it all these months. But thanks, if you don't mind."

While he was outside, she plugged in her phone and found herself back in the living room, staring at that photograph of Annie Oakley shooting over her shoulder.

She wanted to be here, now, focused on Scott. But she couldn't help imagining their future together, all the secrets she would have to keep. She was still researching Annie's early life. She wasn't taking her antipsychotics. She still had visions, had in fact learned how to prolong them. There was no point in restarting a romance based on delusion.

On the other hand, he had come back. He had kissed her. They had made love, and after that, eaten lasagna. Life should include both those things—love and pasta, in equal measure.

Maybe she could tell him about the journal and letters. Or, she could just relish the pleasures of the last hour or so. Ruth closed her eyes and inhaled. She could smell him—smell *them*. It had been good. It had always been mostly good.

The talk with John Regatta hadn't changed anything. Scott hadn't done anything to stop Vorst.

Scott opened the door again, hair wet from the rain. He came toward her, rubbing his hands together to warm them, and stopped short. His smile faded as he saw her expression.

"What?"

It was exactly like the moment he had stepped into the house last year. Back from his cycling trip, just in time to see the realtor leaving. He had stood there, waiting for the signal: Good news? Bad? It was up to Ruth. The fate of their relationship had always been up to Ruth.

"Nothing," she said. "You look cold, that's all."

3 8

C A L E B

Caleb spent the late morning biking down the old river road and sitting at the picnic shelter until he got cold and bored. His phone was running out of battery. He'd already received a dozen messages from people who rarely texted him—a girl he'd carpooled with briefly forever ago, a science project partner, and Reece, who was definitely still mad at him. They all wanted to know the same thing.

Where are you?

Is it true?

WTF?

He hadn't made a bomb threat. He hadn't brought a weapon to school. He hadn't even made a plan. What he *had* done—stupidly—was tell Justin, a freshman on the Rockets who kept pestering him about why he'd suddenly quit, that he wished Vorst would stop hanging around their practices.

"Guy's a pervert," Caleb had said, staring at his Spanish textbook.

"I guess you would know."

Caleb had held it in—the anger, the embarrassment, the panic that Justin really knew something and would tell the others.

"I hate that asshole," Caleb said.

"Sure you do. But don't worry. He's already got a new pet. I saw him give Mikayla a ride yesterday."

A sheaf of blank quizzes was coming down the row toward Caleb. He took the stack and passed it on without bothering to grab a copy. He didn't have a plan, other than to skip the quiz. A moment later he realized he did have a plan: to leave. So he did.

In his worst moments, Caleb felt that he was to blame for what Vorst had done. He'd accepted the pathetically transparent bribes: twenty dollars when Caleb was broke, a pack of cigarettes, then a carton, then a six-pack of beer. He'd accepted the rides. He'd said nothing when they parked and Vorst put his hand on Caleb's thigh and deep down into his jeans. He'd gone to his cabin once, and since nothing had happened on that particular visit, pretended that the parking lot had been a one-off. But the worst moment that came back to him was the moment he didn't object to Vorst's new game—not until he started to pass out and thought that moment might be his last.

What would it be like to actually die?

Caleb almost asked Reece that once, the day he went over to his house. But the conversation zigged and zagged, and before you knew it, Reece was pressuring him the same way everyone did, asking too many questions. Irritated, Caleb let the question go unspoken. He didn't ask about Reece's suicide attempt, how exactly he had failed. If Caleb ever did it, he didn't want to fail.

Caleb's phone vibrated in his pocket again, almost out of charge.

Lockdown. WTF?

Where are you man? Are you at school? Don't do anything crazy.

You're in such deep shit.

An hour later, when boredom got to him, he pulled everything out of his backpack. Out fell his Spanish textbook, two spiral-bound notebooks, the notebook and papers of Kennidy

McClintock's that he was still carrying around, and a copy of *To Build a Fire*, which he was supposed to have finished but had read only until the middle, where the main character built his first fire. It seemed so easy: *Then he took some matches and proceeded to make a fire. In the bushes, the high water had left a supply of sticks. From here he got wood for his fire. Working carefully from a small beginning, he soon had a roaring fire.*

Caleb had already burned the photos he'd taken from Vorst's cabin, and each one had felt like an itch scratched, a wrong almost set right. How much better it would be to build not just a fire but a *roaring* fire, big enough to burn up *¡Hola, todos!* and notes from history and chemistry and even more than that?

Caleb tried it Jack's way first, gathering little sticks from the bushes around him, but no matter how long he held his lighter to the damp ends of each twig, he couldn't get a single one to remain lit. Giving up, he started tearing pages from books. These flamed up obediently, but they burned too fast. He ripped his Spanish text and his notebooks and the blank pages from Kennidy's notebook and even a few with writing on them, plus all the pages of Jack London. When he was frustrated at the end, he burned Kennidy's essay and the only photo he'd kept of her, too.

Burning those first photos of the other girls and guys had felt right, almost like a purification, but this one didn't. It wasn't just that it was wrong, because she was a person he felt like he knew and these were things her family might have wished they could have back. It was because it wasn't *enough*.

He used up the rest of his lighter fluid and ended up with a charred mess of pages and thick, mostly unburnt bindings, and none of it had given him satisfaction.

Now he had only an old pack of matches and nothing good left to burn. Even arson was something you had to learn how to do right, evidently.

AT 4:15, AN HOUR BEFORE his stepdad was due to get home
and with just enough time to sneak in, get warmer clothes and
some sandwiches, Caleb biked up to his house. Big mistake.

His stepdad's pickup truck was there, next to his mom's
Hyundai, as well as two police cars. One was empty. In the other,
there was a cop behind the steering wheel, a woman looking
down at a clipboard.

He could hear a booming voice even before he stepped into
the house. "Her son's not crazy, and he's not one of those mass
shooters. He's just a fuckup. Remember when there used to be
dropouts and losers, but it wasn't a fucking federal crime?"

Loser. Fuckup. And also, "her son," not "our son." Yep, that
was his stepdad, Roger.

When Caleb pulled open the door to get inside, the cop standing
next to the door swung around and grabbed him by the shoulders.
The next thing he knew, Caleb was on the floor, being frisked. He
wanted to laugh. If he'd wanted to sneak up on his parents or that
cop in his living room, it would've been easy. If he'd actually been
a shooter, he would've aimed through the living room window
and taken out all three of them. *Boom. Boom. Boom.*

The next two hours were hell. Caleb kept thinking they were
going to push him into a cop car, drive him to the station and take
him to one of those rooms with mirrored windows that he'd seen
in movies. Instead, they just hung around his house. Weren't there
crimes happening somewhere?

One of the cops sat down at the kitchen table opposite Caleb
and his parents. Another stood near the door. A third wandered
around the living room and, with Caleb's mom's permission, took
a tour of the upstairs bedrooms. They could hear his footsteps,
which made the floorboards squeak.

The kitchen table interview was like the worst parent-teacher
conference he'd ever attended, multiplied by a hundred.

What did you say to your friend Justin?

How many other friends you got?

Do you like school? What are your favorite subjects?

Do you get high?

Do you get angry?

Do you play video games?

Do you have a girlfriend?

Do you have a boyfriend?

The last question pushed Caleb's stepdad over the edge. He was hungry, no one had made a move to start dinner and he'd already had a shitty day at work before all this. "You're calling my wife's son gay? That's it. That's enough."

Roger stood up, went to the fridge, took out a beer and a container of leftover Chinese food that he pushed into the microwave, slamming its door shut. Caleb's mom had said never to put those containers in the microwave. They had staples and a metal handle. But Caleb's four-year-old half sister, Jessica, loved their flap tops and pagoda pictures on the side. She wouldn't eat the exact same Chinese food in normal Styrofoam containers.

"If my stepson's doing drugs or building pipe bombs or especially screwing around with boys, you won't have to come pay us a visit, because he won't be here—not on this earth, do you got that?"

Caleb kept his eye on the microwave door. There were only twenty seconds left. He heard a zap. He thought he saw a spark. But then again, his whole head felt like it would explode.

Meanwhile, Roger kept yelling, even when the police officer guarding the front door came into the kitchen doorway. The cop at the table stood up. The third guy, walking the rooms above, heard the commotion and came down the stairs as well.

"So, we're about done with this chat, then." Roger set his bottle on the counter so hard, it sent a big splatter flying. He ignored the brown liquid flowing across the counter. His face was purple now. "We've got it covered. She'll see you out."

Caleb's mom hadn't moved.

Caleb's stepdad said it again, louder. "She'll see you out!"

THEY ALL KNEW, AFTER CALEB'S mom walked the three cops to the door, eyes on her feet, that it was going to be a bad night. Roger wasn't a raving drunk, but once he got going, he drank steadily and with purpose. One of the cop cars stayed behind at the curb for an hour after the other cops had left. Roger kept walking between the kitchen and the living room window, staring at the car and cursing. Caleb's mom was so worried she went to a back room and called 911. She was routed to their nonemergency number, and Caleb could hear her trying to put on her best bank teller voice, trying to sound friendly and reasonable, asking why there was still a police car outside her home when her son had done nothing.

As far as Caleb could tell, she got no answer, but ten minutes after she finished the call, the car finally pulled away.

At 11 P.M., Roger was still drinking. Still pacing. It was true that many more lights were flashing down their road—some extra cop cruisers every hour or so, but also normal cars. Curious onlookers? Maybe high school students. Maybe others who'd seen the false-alarm story on the local news or read people's angry comments on Facebook.

"Come on down here," Roger called up the narrow staircase at 11:30, a half hour after Caleb had retreated to his bedroom. "I know you're not asleep."

He was slurring his words. His rifle, which Roger usually kept carefully locked up and well away from Jessica, was on the couch, just sitting there for anyone to see. The drapes were open.

Any time headlights flashed or he heard the sound of an approaching motor, Caleb's stepdad would step toward the couch, pick up the rifle, and not aim it exactly, just hold it, while he walked back and forth in front of the wide windows.

"What'd you do to make them so interested all of a sudden?"

"I didn't do anything."

Caleb took a step toward the stairs.

"You're not going anywhere. Get me another beer."

Pace; pick up rifle; turn off lamp to see through the windows better; turn lamp back on; pace again. An hour passed.

"Get me another." Roger's tone softened. "You want one?"

"No thanks."

But then he turned mean again. "What'd you do to make them think you're a shooter or a faggot?"

"Nothing," Caleb said. "Kids tell rumors. They're, you know, bullies."

"Bully 'em back."

"Yeah, sure," Caleb said.

The cops wanted Caleb to skip school in the morning and asked his mother to bring him to the station for a psychological evaluation, though he was pretty sure she couldn't get time off work. She'd been a single mom for a long time. She knew you couldn't risk losing your job.

"Get me another," Roger said. But his eyelids were heavier now, and for minutes at a time, when he set down the rifle and collapsed into the lounger next to it, he snoozed.

"What you'd do . . . ?"

Caleb waited until he thought he heard a light snore. To test, he asked, "I can get you another beer if you want. Or some potato chips."

Silence.

Caleb got up. He went to the windows and closed the blinds. Through them, he could see the flicker of lights again. Definitely more traffic. When he parted the blinds stealthily from the corner, he saw the glint of a beer can as it sailed through an open window and hit their curb. His mother would have a fit in the morning if people spent the whole night throwing garbage in front of their house. It occurred to Caleb that they might do worse, like TP the hedges or break something.

Just as he was walking away from the window, he heard the clatter of the metal garbage can, then laughter and then the sound of tires peeling out. Caleb went outside to look. They'd spray-painted the garbage in red with the letter C.

Okay, Caleb thought, heart pounding. *Okay. It's not so bad.*

They'd either heard him coming or realized it wasn't so easy to fit big letters on a round garbage can. But he'd scared them off. "C" for Caleb, like they were just letting the world know he lived there. Whatever.

Then Caleb turned around and faced the closed garage door. And there it was, their second draft in large, glowing pinkish-red letters: COCKSUCKER.

"Fuck." He looked back at the street and in through the window. Inside was the rifle on the couch. Inside was his stepdad: mad, drunk, ready to make his own justice. Inside was his mother and his four-year-old sister.

"Fuuuuuuck."

Caleb stepped into the living room. Roger stirred and went slack-jawed again.

When Caleb pictured them bringing Vorst in for questioning, he didn't imagine the coach looking ashamed or repentant. He could hear Vorst's voice, loud and clear, talking about Caleb drinking, Caleb taking pills, Caleb asking to sleep over, Caleb coming on to him. He didn't know how guys like Vorst got away with it, but he knew for sure they always did.

Caleb didn't hate his mom. He didn't even hate Roger. There wasn't a single kid at school he truly detested, even though plenty of them got on his nerves. He wasn't one of those kids they talked about on the news.

The last thing Caleb wanted was attention. If they'd just left him alone and not overreacted—the school lockdown, the questioning—maybe he could've slunk off and disappeared. But they'd shone a spotlight on him that wasn't about to go away.

Two hours later, Caleb grabbed all the cash he could find in his mom's purse—only sixty dollars. He packed an extra pair of jeans, a loaf of sandwich bread, a jar of peanut butter, a gallon of water and the long lighter his stepdad used to light the grill since the starter was broken. Then he grabbed the rifle and put it in the cab of his stepdad's pickup truck, under a tarp. He told himself he was doing it to protect others from harm.

Canada, he thought. It was pretty much the only thing Vorst had talked about at his cabin that didn't drive Caleb up the wall: the Canadian baseball and hockey teams he liked; Boundary Waters, the place he'd gone canoeing; memories from when he was a kid and everyone talked about escaping the draft by going north, if you could believe that.

Caleb would have to ditch the gun somewhere, of course, but far away, so his stepdad wouldn't have it when he woke up or during the questioning that was bound to follow for several more days. No one was going to thank Caleb for taking that precaution, but he was used to it. No one had thanked him for doing anything for as long as he could remember.

3 9

RUTH

Scott was asleep. Ruth lay with the sheets pulled up to her armpits, staring at the place on her bed that had been empty for over a year, trying to feel lucky instead of apprehensive or confused. When she was certain his breathing was deep and even, she rolled toward her nightstand and pulled on her phone hard enough to separate it from the charging cord, then positioned herself comfortably to read.

She had less than a quarter of the scanned document left. She reread the last part of the sixth letter, which had been nearing its sign-off when her phone had died, then moved on to the seventh.

Dear H.D.,

I've received two of your letters, but nothing in the last three weeks. I expected you to question my claim to be able to visit the past, but I didn't anticipate you'd question whether the Wolves existed or acted as they did. Surely you won't pretend these are things that don't happen to young girls or that happen only beyond your own experience, in places like Ohio or Oklahoma.

For fear of further damaging my health, I decided to resist the desire to skip back until I felt stronger, but every day when I checked the mail and saw no reply from you, my resistance weakened. Indignation rose up to take its place. Yet even with that poisonous emotion restored, I have not managed to break out of these cycles of coming and going, of losing my prey to the forces of indecision.

I do worry about Frank and the toll this bitterness has taken on our marriage. For years he has taken on the duty of hiding me from view during my melancholic times, so that my reputation and our income might be preserved. But to think of him and only him is to take my eye off the target.

Dear H.D.,

My mind has worn down the trail so much that at any mere thought, I immediately slip into the past now. I have had to feign illness for fear that a thought will take me and that I will suddenly appear to be in a trance, my mind in some long-ago time while my body remains in the present.
A new trial is in three days, so I must sort out my mind.

I will keep fighting the urge. But already, there have been strange effects of resisting. Dammed water still spills over, and in strong wind, a kite will lift from your hands—or tear—if you don't let it go.

Scott mumbled sleepily into her ear, "What are you looking at?"

Ruth pulled the phone down lower, cloaking the light with the sheets. Only one letter was left. "Nothing. Couldn't sleep."

"Time?"

"I don't know. Past two. Go back to sleep."

She waited for him to settle and kept her phone low, listening to him breathe.

"I keep thinking about the boy," he said in the dark. "The one they thought was going to do something stupid."

"You said it was a false alarm."

"Probably. Caleb will have lots of eyes on him now. Some teachers aren't going to want him to come back. And others will use this to push their own agendas: increased security, more drills . . ."

"I thought the school was slashing budgets."

"This time we have a veterans' group offering to patrol outside, armed, for free."

"For free?"

"They're part of a national . . . group."

Ruth could hear him suppressing any judgmental or political words, anything that would betray bias. This was his faculty meeting voice again. Civility was in such short supply these days, and yet she knew he shared her view that a bunch of wound-up, self-important, politically motivated guys toting guns near the school couldn't possibly be a good idea.

"Go on," she said.

"Everyone thought they were bonkers until last year, and now some of the teachers think it's a lesser evil than arming faculty, because at least vets theoretically know what they're doing. Plus, if they're going to do it anyway—"

"Do what?"

"Patrol just beyond school property."

"But they need permission for that, don't they?"

"Depends on the mood of the troopers and the local police. So if they're going to do it anyway, might be better to have them organized under the school auspices, names and phone numbers written down, proper ID badges. Right? That's going to be the argument at 7 A.M. tomorrow."

"Sounds tricky. You should really try to get some sleep."

He burrowed down under the covers. She waited.

The last thing he said—quietly, more sleepily again—was, "I missed this. Knowing if you wake up with a problem, there's someone right next to you."

"I'm guessing you had someone next to you, at least some of the time."

"Well, yes. But it was never the same, or I wouldn't be here."

SCOTT HAD THROWN AN ARM over her waist in his sleep. Ruth could sense the presence of her phone on the nightstand. She tried to resist, knowing she could read the final scanned pages in the morning.

She thought about the lesson of this last week: that one could assume nothing, that the universe was stranger than we thought, and that even so, it was the smallest, simplest things that mattered most.

Forget the phone. Forget the email.

She lay in the dark under the weight of Scott's arm still, trying to memorize every possible sensation. The rhythmic lift and fall of his chest. The coolness of a twitching toe that happened to brush her calf, making her smile.

They had slept in each other's arms every night in the first weeks of their courtship, when sleep mattered less to her than the electricity of human contact. But following that, they'd migrated, step by step, to their own sides of the bed. He moved a lot and kicked off the covers in his sleep. She was easily awoken and needed a pocket of motionless space, sheet and blanket snugged up to her neck. It made sense to stop intertwining arms and legs—they couldn't simply become insomniacs—but at the same time, she'd forgotten the pleasure of forsaking sleep, the miracle of trust and the joy of simple human touch.

This would be heaven, if she allowed it to be.

Well, it would be more heavenly if she could be just a touch warmer.

The sheet was stuck to her hip by one of Scott's hands, which she tried without success to dislodge. Also, she had to use the bathroom.

Never mind.

She got up and grabbed her phone on the way out.

In the kitchen a moment later, Scott touched her shoulder. She jumped.

"You're up?"

"Couldn't sleep."

"Come back to bed." Scott took her hand and gave it a light, seductive tug.

Dammed water still spills over.

Ruth asked, "You sure that Margot won't be upset to find out we're back together?"

"She might be."

He was still pulling, with a mischievous look on his face.

"Does she ever behave . . . unpredictably when she's upset?"

"I don't know. Doesn't everyone?"

He caught Ruth's expression.

"No, Ruth. She's not someone we need to worry about."

"Okay, you're right." Ruth knew she was sensing danger everywhere, even where it didn't exist. But then again, even paranoid people were right sometimes.

"If it makes you feel any better, she left town to visit her sister this morning and will be there all weekend."

"That's convenient."

"It is. But I'm not surprised. We had a talk last night about our needs and decided amicably—"

"Amicably, you *hope*." Ruth knew Scott wasn't right about Vorst. Why would he be right about Margot?

"I'm certain. We both needed to take a big step back. That happened after your phone call. You remember that call, from the motel? You were crying. With everything that happened yesterday, I realize how much I don't want either of us to have regrets."

One week ago, if Ruth could have written up her dream conversation with Scott, this would have been it. A dose of false terror had helped her win back what she'd thought she most wanted.

He was still holding her hand. Still pulling. But something else had an even stronger pull.

"I agree. Just let me just finish reading this one last thing, then I'll come to bed. Promise."

Scott wasn't wearing his glasses. He looked down his nose with exaggerated incredulity, his eyes large and dark.

"I don't want to wait."

He had never been this playful, not since their first weeks together, and she had never felt so torn. It was all a test. The correct answer seemed obvious. She followed him back to the bedroom, where they still had two hours before his alarm went off. Her phone remained behind, screen darkening.

4 0

C A L E B

Friday

Caleb had stolen his stepdad's pickup, with the rifle under a tarp on the truck bed behind him, hidden next to a pile of junk that his parents kept meaning to drop off at the donation center. He didn't have his license yet, but he'd been practice-driving for six months, and he figured as long as he didn't get pulled over, he could just keep going on 71 to Bemidji, the farthest he'd ever been with his family. He remembered not only ice cream shops, but backyards with docks and canoes just sitting there on mowed lawns, next to ponds and marshy river outlets. Not far beyond that, he knew, there were other, bigger lakes, and probably even less careful cabin and cottage owners. His stepdad talked a lot about Lake of the Woods, which was US on one side, Canada on the other and a whole lot of nothing in between. No one could stop him from getting lost somewhere up there.

He had driven forty miles before he pulled off the road and stopped fast, dust cloud slowly settling as he dug his foot into the brake.

He kept reliving the memory of the first time Vorst had dosed him. He tasted the vodka and Tang; he smelled the old man's aftershave and sweat. He saw stills from that stupid movie on the TV screen beginning to blur in front of his eyes, felt the desire to sleep and the fear of losing control—the sudden desperation to be out of there and an equal desperation to stay, to get it all over with, and also to no longer exist.

It was a black hole, and Caleb knew he would try to claw his way out only to fall back in again and again. The only thing that broke his trance of self-pity and self-contempt was to think of Mikayla. Then he went from queasy to violently nauseated.

He turned the wheel hard and gunned the motor. He was going back to the campus.

41
RUTH

The sun hadn't risen yet when Ruth kissed Scott goodbye in the doorway. They'd lingered long enough over coffee that he didn't have time to go back to his apartment before work. He'd have to wear yesterday's clothes: wrinkled pants and shirt, sleeves rolled up to the elbows to hide the lasagna stain on the cuff.

They hugged again out on the porch, the kind of slow embrace usually reserved for airports. He hadn't bothered to put on a jacket; it was slung over his forearm. She held on to his elbows, under the porchlight. She tried to find that thread of silver again, but in this light, at this hour—his hair tousled, her eyes tired and full of sleep, and that right eye still wonky—she couldn't see anything but chestnut-brown waves.

"See you tonight," he said. "I'll cook. Dinner at eight?"

"I'd rather not wait that long."

That made him smile. "Come to the school, then. Spirit rallies and the year's last football game are at four. The forecast looks good. Bring a blanket, and I'll buy you some junk food. Like old times."

"Okay," she said. "Four o'clock."

Scott had just pulled away when Ruth heard another car pull into her driveway and after a moment, four knocks, rapid-fire.

Margot.

Ruth steeled herself to wait it out. Let her bang or shout. But then Ruth heard a familiar voice.

"It's cold out here. Come on!"

"Oh my god," she said, opening the door to Reece.

"Finally," he said, handing her the newspaper he'd picked up from the driveway. "I thought he'd never leave. I take it you're back with Mr. W."

She let the comment drop. "You've been waiting outside my house?"

"Fifteen minutes. Please tell me there's coffee."

It was 6:40 A.M. No normal teenager was up this early without a damn good reason.

"You must have heard about the false alarm yesterday," he said.

"I did. You know the student, Caleb?"

"He's got problems. I still plan to talk to him, once this all dies down."

"Good. Do that."

"But I don't think he's *the* problem. His house was mobbed by cops, anyway. It sounded like he was practically under house arrest."

"According to whom?"

Reece rolled his eyes. "Facebook-addicted busybodies. Point is, it's not just up to us anymore. The cops and his parents are going to be busy prying the facts out of him, and in the meantime, I don't think he's connected to what we saw. So I guess that's that."

"I guess it is." She searched Reece's face for any signs of anxiety. "But you could have texted me about that. You came by instead?"

"I wanted to check on you. It felt like we made it to the end of something and our team won and we didn't high-five, you know? Just wanted to make sure everything's okay on your end."

"Everything's . . . great, actually."

He pushed his way into the kitchen and opened cupboards until he found a plastic travel mug. "It feels like we stopped it somehow."

"Yes. We must've."

He poured a cup to go, took a sip and sneered. But he didn't toss the coffee down the drain.

Ruth thought of telling him about the latest letters, the Annie Oakley updates. But all that could wait. He was just a teenager, living in the moment, as he should be.

"How have you felt since the lockdown yesterday?" she asked.

"Good. I'm nervous about today's performance, but good." He screwed up his face. "This is gonna sound cheesy, but I feel like I got a second chance. You know?"

"I do."

Reece looked at his phone. "I gotta run."

She followed him to the door. "You're taking my cup?"

"You can come get it from me after the game this afternoon."

"How do you know I'm coming?"

He stopped and stared. "Ruth. Please. You'd miss our performance?"

She smiled. "Okay. I'll get my cup then. See you this afternoon."

At the door, Reece paused one last time. "I need to return something I took from you. It's been bothering me, because I'm not a thief. I can't even blame some dream or voice. I didn't plan to take them. It was just this random one-time compulsion."

She had no idea what he was talking about. He pressed the envelope into her hand. "I took these from the little brown drawers in your bathroom."

"Oh," she said, and smiled. It was a relief, actually, to know she hadn't taken them without remembering. "Maybe you were just looking after my health. Just like me trying to get you to quit cigarettes, right?"

"Exactly."

My body is a temple. But what about the rest of the messages? All those other things he'd said to her—was *supposed* to say to her in the future. Would they all fade from their memories in time? Ruth remembered how Annie had talked about the McKinley assassination that was supposed to happen in June—how once it changed to September, once she *knew* it had changed, the details had begun to fade. Maybe that took time.

"You and Mr. Webb make a good couple," Reece said.

"Gee, thanks."

"No, really. At school, he looks so uptight. When I saw him come out of your house, I thought, 'There's a guy who's finally learned to loosen up.'"

"What do you mean?"

"He looked rumpled, but happy. I'm not saying I know what you spent the last eight or twelve hours doing, but it made a difference."

"Reece!" She winced, laughing. "Is it that obvious?"

"It's all right. It's a good thing."

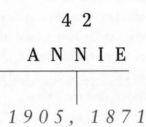

42

ANNIE

1905, 1871

I will him to turn and look over his shoulder. I even dare to push my toe into the snow-dusted roadbed, to make a little scuffling sound, as I hold my breath. But he is engrossed in his task. His collar is turned up. His black-brimmed hat is pulled low over his red ears. He is muttering to himself, "All the luck."

He will turn, and I will say: *"You shouldn't have done it. I hate you for what you've done."* He'll look angry at first, surprised by my presence here, then incredulous at what I'm aiming to do, then afraid. But I can't think about that, because when I imagine too much, my stomach gets weak.

In all my years: so many feathers, so many exploded puffs of fur, so many bloody pawprints in the snow, so many glazed eyes and skinned bodies, the flesh always redder and the body smaller than one would imagine. A rabbit's body: all muscle. When we are flayed, we are all so much smaller than one would think. Dead and skinned, we're all such little, little things. Hardly worth the ground we stand on.

Better to pull the trigger without him looking. Let him turn and look as he falls. But just as I feel the pressure mounting, ready to pull, I slide out of time again. Back to the woodstove, next to Missus, late at night.

"What if he never comes back?" I whisper into the fire and hold my breath, waiting, for the reply.

She slaps me. A flying palm in the near-dark.

"How dare you say such a thing?" she says, tears in her voice.

"I'm sorry. I thought—"

"That I'd be better off? That my sweet boy and I would be better off?"

I hold a hand against my stinging face and lean back, in case there's a second slap coming. "You couldn't be much worse off."

There is an intake of breath. The Missus says, "There is so much you don't know about this world. He was a handsome man, once."

"That isn't saying much."

"He was a good man." The Missus says it defiantly, daring anyone to doubt. "When we married, twenty-seven people came to the wedding, and every one of them said we were the prettiest couple they'd ever seen. We lived in town for a year, did you know that? We used to have three horses. He used to call me his Angel of the Morning." Her voice cracks.

I don't argue with her. I wouldn't dare. But she still goes on.

"He used to smile so much people would ask him what trouble he was brewin', and he wasn't brewin' anything at all. He just was glad to be alive. We once stayed in bed for two days without getting up, and I don't mean that we were sick. I mean we ate our dinner on top of the blankets. I mean we were happy. I mean we were newlyweds."

The Missus catches her breath. Tears stream and drips form at the line of her strong jaw.

"The man you know isn't the man I married, but he's all I got. How dare you come into his house and eat his food and wish upon him bad things, wishing him dead."

But I'm confused. Because if we are sitting here, long after dark, then he is in fact already dead. Or gravely injured. I've done it already. That's why he hasn't come home. But will I get no joy from seeing it? Or is it yet to be done?

The Missus, face glowing in the red firelight, grabs my hands. "You've got me scared, now. You've frightened me with your dark words. Pray with me."

"I don't want to," I whisper, trying to wriggle away.

The Missus squeezes my hands. "Pray with me, if you don't want to see me and my baby and this whole household starve. Pray with me, unless you're a devil yourself."

"I'm no devil."

"Then how come you can do what you do? How come you can shoot a dozen rabbits or birds with the ease of a man shooting one? How come you can make a grown man go weak in the knees? You pray with me, Phoebe Ann Mosey."

And the Missus says the words and makes me repeat them. "Lord Jesus, I am sorry for my sins."

". . . sorry for my sins."

"I renounce Satan and all his works."

". . . Satan and all his works."

"I receive and accept you as my personal Lord and Savior."

". . . Lord and Savior."

"Forgive me my sins."

". . . my sins."

"As I forgive those who sin against me." Then she commands, "Pray for the father of this family." She squeezes my hands harder. "Say the whole thing out loud. Not like you're doing but the whole thing, with your whole heart. Say it again, louder now."

"I won't!"

Suddenly, I am in the Chief's tent. I shout, "I don't want any water!" and fling out an arm. The tin cup goes flying. I hear the gasp of the young woman kneeling next to me.

Sitting Bull's expression does not change. He says, "You are suffering."

"Then let me. I didn't want to come here just now."

"You are free, daughter. We're all free."

"It doesn't feel like freedom. Stop this. I don't want your kindness anymore."

He closes his eyes, and the interruption of that stony glance loosens my bonds to this place. The tent dissolves.

I AM, AGAIN, SOMEWHERE ELSE. Some *when* else. I feel the cold wind again and see his head turn, as his gaze turns from the axle to the sound of my step. Outside again: the pink so faint, the bare trees so black, the entire world bleeding, weeping, just before darkness shrouds everything, a blanket tossed over the carcass to keep the flies out.

The Wolf does not scowl or laugh. His eyes meet mine.

He has frozen in place like an animal knowing it has nowhere to run. I wait for him to beg for mercy. I *want* him to beg. Then I can forgive him, if I so decide. Then the words from my mouth will have meaning. Let him beg. Let *him* say he has a wife he still loves and a baby to feed. Let *him* be the one to cry out about his sins and beg for mercy.

But he doesn't speak or move. His eyes are blurry from the wind and cold.

He says, with a sober dignity that surprises me, "Go ahead, Annie."

I lift the rifle a little higher, narrowing my eyes against the wind. The tremor that curses me in my older woman's form is less pronounced here, but it is not absent. The damage has found its way, finally, to all of my selves. But I can override it.

He says, "You don't have to be afraid, go right on ahead," and closes his eyes.

"Look at me now," I say. But he doesn't.

His face relaxes, the worry about the axle and the pained tooth and not enough money for groceries and the horse going lame just as winter's coming on, all gone in this moment. The guilt for not being a good provider. The sadness for the little girl they lost, the precious little girl before their baby boy. The sadness for what they'd once been and hoped to be. All gone.

"I'm ready, Annie. You just go ahead."

"Unless you want to suffer more than you've got to, open them eyes, I'm telling you."

"I don't have to open 'em. I can see what's coming. I'll sleep good for the first time in ages, better than all the rest of you. I will sleep just fine."

4 3

R U T H

Dear H.D.,

*I was with the Wolf. I had the gun in my hands, his frail
body in my sights.*

*You may insist on calling it a dream or a delusion. Once,
I cared, because I needed you to believe. But I am now past
needing permission or sympathy. What would happen has
happened.*

*I was ready to shoot when I heard him weep. It didn't
make me hate him any less. It didn't make me pity him any
more. He was already about as pitiable as a creature could be.*

The last thing he said was, "Why won't you do it, already."

*He continued to weep, even after I had unhitched his
horse and he had taken off riding, back into town, losing
himself in a night of drink that would leave his wife worrying, but not a widow.*

Dear doctor, that was my last visitation.

The letter continued on another page, but Ruth paused in her
reading.

Her last visitation?

Ruth reread the next-to-last sentence: . . . *that would leave his wife worrying, but not a widow.*

Annie had chosen not to kill the Wolf.

Ruth tried to absorb what she'd just read. She pictured Annie standing there, gun lowered, feet freezing in her tight black boots, eyes narrowed against the stinging wind.

She tried to imagine how Annie must have felt. Tried to see past her own disappointment.

Her own disappointment.

Because Ruth had wanted the Wolf destroyed. How could she possibly want that more than Annie herself?

Ruth scrolled to the next and last page, Annie's final words to Breuer.

I have resisted the desire to return, and it's been no easier than resisting any other kind of strong medicine. But I'm a disciplined woman.

I am writing not so much to establish my innocence with you as to petition for your continued attention and good will. You warned me when we first met that patients become attached to their caregivers. It's true. Even in writing you these letters, I've counted on your audience. I couldn't have put my own experiences into writing if I hadn't had an audience I could trust not only to hear me out, but to keep my story safe.

I could have killed the Wolf. I didn't.

But maybe that wasn't kindness on my part. Maybe if he hadn't wanted to die, I would have killed him. Maybe it was only seeing him so debased and miserable that stopped me, in order that his misery would last. I'm not sure.

As for the tremor, there is no change yet, but I expect that with the urge to go back kept at bay, my own fortitude will step in. I've recovered from many infirmities in my life.

There is no easy answer. One discovers a magic door and
seemingly magic powers, and even so, the puzzle remains:
how to cure a heart that has rotted all these years, eaten
through with the desire for revenge.

According to your method, even telling this story will
help to heal me.

Truly—I must have hope.

Z

WEAK AUTUMN SUNLIGHT FILTERED IN through the half-closed blinds. Ruth had fallen asleep on the couch after Reece had left. It felt like midmorning, but that slant of light told her it was midafternoon. Half a day, gone. Her body and her brain must be trying to recover, taking by force what she hadn't bothered to supply.

She went to pour herself coffee. Even in its stay-warm carafe, it had gone cold. She drank it anyway, impatient and brooding. Then she returned to the living room and read the whole set of scanned letters again, in order. There would never be more.

With effort, she pulled her mind back out of the past, away from Darke County.

Ruth made a guttural sobbing sound. It had come over her quickly after the happy glow from reconciliation sex: this frustration, deep sorrow and something more. Scott seemed to be safe, but the past—Annie, Kennidy—was still all wrong.

The old Ruth would have found ways to extend her research into Annie's life, to consider the possibility that the sharpshooter had lied in her final letter. Perhaps she had killed the Wolf after all. One could check the county records to see if any men of the right age and background had died from a gunshot wound or in a mysterious accident from 1869 through 1871.

The old Ruth might have dedicated herself to researching the

American mythos of the vigilante and why it filled a need for so many. But the old Ruth was gone. She had felt her fading back in that motel room, and now there wasn't a trace left. She didn't want documentation. She was bored—no, offended—by something as passive as academic conjecture.

She got up from her chair and went to the bathroom. In the mirror, her vision was still doubled and fuzzy. She lowered herself into a meditative cross-legged position on the linoleum floor. Thoughts of Scott did not come to her.

Instead: only Vorst, and not the old Vorst, but the younger one, still stooped, moving away from the cabin window, and Kennidy swinging the golf club. Ruth wanted to put herself back there. She wanted to take the club from Ken and break not only the garden gnome, but all the windows.

Open the cabin door.

She hadn't opened it enough: not for Annie, not for Kennidy. The words were back, ready to haunt and punish her. Or maybe just to coax her.

Try harder.

She wanted to start further back, at the house, where Gwen's then-boyfriend had a gun stored. Ruth knew where he kept the key. How hard could it be? Ruth hadn't known how to shoot a gun back then, but thanks to her visits to the range with Scott last year, she knew now.

Thank you, Scott, for teaching me. You were right. I needed to know.

Ruth went through the steps, visualizing the nightstand drawer with the half-broken knob, the tiny bronze key, the gun, the car, the gravel road, the red plastic cups, the cigarettes, the music, the cabin. But it wasn't enough. She was hurrying through it instead of reliving it. She tried to feel the key in her hand, the steering wheel shuddering between her fingers. She tried to smell the cigarette smoke and the dust rising up from the road. She tried to hear the Foo Fighters album they'd been listening to and the other sounds she'd forgotten, like the cicadas screaming when they cut the car's engine, the oak to one side, the cabin in front of them. Ruth had never remembered the cicadas. But these were still only memories. She wasn't time traveling. She wasn't there.

Open the door. Shoot the fucker, once and for all.

"It's our neighbor Van, isn't it?" she'd say to Kennidy if she had the chance to live it all over again. "You stay in the car."

44

CALEB

An hour after turning the truck around, Caleb was idling in a line of cars on a side road headed toward the school parking lot. At first period and again after lunch, the traffic backed up here, but it rarely came to a complete halt unless people were collecting donations. Caleb squinted at a sandwich board on a grassy median, rolling forward when the car in front of him did the same, until he could make out the sign: VETS FOR SCHOOL SAFETY.

Well, he didn't have any quarters—or any patience—for that cause.

All Caleb knew was that he wanted to put himself between Mikayla's body and Vorst's. He knew the next time they'd be in the same place: the game at four o'clock. After that, especially if the halftime show went well, they'd probably all go out to a diner, or the popular kids would break off into their own group and go to someone's house to party, leaving the freshmen and most of the sophomores stranded. Caleb could see exactly how it would go down: Vorst, rubbing his hand across Mikayla's narrow back before the show when she was jittery and giving her one of those annoying sideways hugs at the end, when everyone was celebrating and radiating adrenaline. And then, as the stands thinned out and people headed to their cars, he'd offer her a ride to the diner, or somewhere else if she wasn't up for all that. Whatever she wanted. A beer maybe, in his car? She could have one, and then he could drop her wherever she liked.

That's when it would start. But Caleb wouldn't let it.

Was Caleb even allowed on campus? They hadn't said he *wasn't*, only that he was supposed to come to the police station first, with his mother, for the evaluation. When she came home any minute now, she'd discover he'd taken his stepdad's truck, and she wouldn't be happy. She might even think about telling the police, if she was worried enough. As for his stepdad, he'd be pissed as hell, but there was no way he'd tell the cops. He'd rather find Caleb and wring his neck personally.

A tap on the side mirror startled Caleb. Some guy was motioning for him to roll down his window. Caleb saw no sign of a donation coinbox, a boot or anything else to explain what the guy wanted. The normal security guards at school tended to be younger, clean-cut but not always fit, more like sleepy mall cops in cheap uniform shirts and pleated synthetic pants you could tell they hated. The guy at Caleb's window was different. He was older, for one—maybe his stepdad's age. He had a tanned, deeply lined face. His bright-yellow reflective vest didn't hide the fact that underneath, he had a barrel chest and wide biceps, pulling his long-sleeved T-shirt tight. His baseball cap read, IF YOU LOVE YOUR FREEDOM, THANK A VET.

"You got your school ID, son?" the volunteer asked, once Caleb had his window down.

"In my backpack."

"You look a little young to be driving that truck."

Caleb ignored him.

"You gonna get your identification out for me?"

The man really just wanted to peek into the trunk's cab and look him up and down. Caleb had worried about putting the .22

under the tarp instead of in the extended cab behind the seat, where Roger would have kept it. It only proved how uncomfortable Caleb was even having the gun. He'd shot it before, but never on his own. He should've just hidden it somewhere else. Even considering his concern for his little sister, it had been idiotic to take it.

Except—and here his own mind had generated two incompatible opinions, which either meant he was slowly getting smarter or just going insane—taking the gun had been a bad choice, but it had also been a good one. He *did* need the gun, actually. Without it, he couldn't show it to Vorst and tell him he was in trouble if he ever touched Mikayla, even with just one finger. Otherwise the old pervert wouldn't take him seriously.

With the self-appointed volunteer guard still watching, Caleb reached into his backpack, distracted by the sight of another volunteer coming toward the truck. This man was younger and even buffer, wearing an olive-colored T-shirt and dark sunglasses, plus a rifle slung across his chest and minus the official-looking reflective vest. Caleb followed his progress in the side mirror as the second guard walked along the side of the truck, nodded at clipboard guy, then disappeared into a blind spot, close to the back bumper.

Caleb felt his heart drop down into his stomach even as his fingers stirred the junk at the bottom of his backpack, searching without any help from his eyes, which were still fixed on the mirror. He caught a view of the guy's top half, head tilted downward—maybe looking at Caleb's plates?

"You're holding things up," the first volunteer said. "You got that card or something says you're a student here?"

"Sorry."

The man at the back of the truck said something to the volunteer at the side-window. Caleb couldn't catch the words.

"Someone in your family serve in Afghanistan?"

The bumper stickers.

"My stepdad, yeah."

The guy with the baseball hat seemed to like that.

Caleb finally had his ID between his fingers. The volunteer barely glanced at it. "All right, lunchtime's almost over. Back to class."

He waved him through.

Only after Caleb pulled into the farthest possible space in the student area of the lot and set his forehead down against the steering wheel did his slowing pulse give way to rising indignation. Those guys had no right to ask him for identification or search his truck.

Caleb snapped to attention at the sound of a slamming car door two vehicles down from him and the chatter of two guys walking toward the main building. He had to make sure no one saw him in the truck. He'd have to lay down and pretend to take a nap—or actually take one, if his stomach would settle and his pulse would mellow out, which was doubtful. In truth, he'd barely slept last night between the time he'd made the decision to run away and the moment, around 5 A.M., when he'd finally found the balls to do it.

When he'd slid the rifle under the tarp, he'd spotted the old blanket that his parents used as a liner when they were hauling donation items in the truck. He didn't care that it was a little moldy. Caleb waited until no one else was in the parking lot to get out, go around back, and pull the blanket free, jostling another ripped donation bag, leaking kids' clothing.

He grabbed the blanket, and then he grabbed another donation item: a too-small hockey stick. Just to protect himself in case anyone weird came banging on his window again. Just to help him feel safer.

He left the gun under the tarp in the back.

NOT MUCH LATER, CALEB OPENED his eyes and sat up in time to see a police cruiser pass slowly behind the truck and circle around the student parking lot. His heart was in his throat, key in the ignition even before he could think.

The plates. Vehicle description.

Caleb tried to squelch his panic. He watched two guys walk behind his vehicle toward a small blue sedan. One of them was Gerald from the Rockets. The lunch hour was almost over. Where the hell was he going? Probably where Gerald always went, past the rotary and down a suburban side road to a cul-de-sac to get high with friends until the last possible minute.

The police car passed again, still moving slowly, without any lights or sirens. It came to a halt directly behind Caleb's truck. Caleb was going to be sick. He didn't know if it was better to open the door and start running or to roll down the window and act casual or just sit and stare straight ahead, pretending not to see.

The police car inched forward. It was still behind the truck, blocking Caleb from backing out. He was trapped.

The *whoop* made him jump. One quick strobe of lights.

Oh god.

Another *whoop*.

Okay, okay. He put his hands on the wheel. Then he started rolling down the window, trying to come up with something to say, thinking, *I'm sorry, Mom. I'm sorry.*

He looked up again. The police car had pulled forward. It spun its lights again, and suddenly it was moving fast in pursuit of Gerald's car, which was far ahead, turning out of the student lot.

Someone had told somebody something. Or yesterday's false alarm was just making everybody more careful—except Gerald, apparently. The idiot didn't pull over. He kept going, guaranteeing that not just one car but three took off after him, sirens blaring.

What felt like a burp welled up inside Caleb, and he was too busy starting up the truck to put his hand to his mouth. He vomited, just enough to fill his mouth and drip down his chin. He opened the truck door and spit it out, ashamed.

This was why everything had happened. Because he was a coward, because he didn't think clearly and didn't speak up. And because embarrassment was the first emotion that came to him in any moment of crisis. Not righteous anger, but embarrassment. Like when he'd first seen those photos at Vorst's.

Even now, he was moving too fast.

Spit again. Swallow. Wipe your damn chin. Take a breath. Let the police car pull Gerald over and find the pot he definitely has in his car. Good.

Gerald was finally helping him, and the big stupid guy didn't even know it. That was what Caleb had to do now. Make use of people who weren't even his friends and general commotion wherever he went. He had to make use of confusion itself.

Right now, there were too many eyes everywhere. He'd need to come back here, but without the truck. He'd have to create a distraction, too—something that could keep all the cops away from the football field and anywhere else they could see too much or respond too soon.

Okay. It was starting to come together.

He'd have to come back on foot, just when everyone was looking elsewhere. He'd take the back route, the one that went past Vorst's own house, through the woods. It's what he should have done in the first place.

And there, only when he thought every option had vanished, did Caleb finally see how the plan should go, from the last satisfying moment to the tricky parts that led up to it.

See? Backward.

45

RUTH

Kennidy never had a chance to look Vorst in the eye and decide whether or not to grant him mercy. Ruth's sister should have had that chance.

Ruth was still sitting on her living room floor between the couch and the coffee table, legs folded. The house was cold and perfectly quiet.

Nothing could undo what had happened to Kennidy.

Could it?

There was no need to travel forward, now that Scott was safe. Ruth had never tried to time-travel backward. She was sure that Bert wouldn't be able to do it, but she hadn't dared to consider whether *she* could. Maybe disbelief was the only thing that had stopped her, and that was what Reece had been trying to tell her, what she had really been trying to tell herself, when she told him to draw the figure eight on her wrist. She already knew she could see into the future. She had not accepted that it meant she could see—and travel—back as well. But the two must be connected.

On the one hand, Annie had had to practice dozens of times. On the other hand, Ruth had been practicing as well: going forward, but still. Her blurry vision, tinnitus and tremors bore witness to that fact.

If it were possible, the next thing was to decide what she would try to change. She had already tried—and failed—to bring herself into the scene outside the cabin. She could imagine herself into many encounters with the younger Vorst: she had been not only near his house countless times, but even inside his house as a young girl. That wasn't the problem. The problem was what she would do once she got there. Look for evidence? Threaten him with violence?

There were other moments to consider as well. Ruth wished she'd asked her mom tougher questions on a dozen different occasions, right up to the moment Gwen was dying in hospice care. She wished she'd spent more time with Kennidy during Christmas breaks. There were so many regrets, so much that would have to change, and none of the moments or situations were specific and powerful enough. None seemed linked with a single color or physical sensation or intense emotional experience, anything Ruth could use as a portal.

Ruth closed her eyes and shuffled through hazy images. She was furious at Vorst, but she hadn't been furious when Kennidy was still alive, because she hadn't understood. There were limits to where one could go. Annie had been able to arrive only at moments of strong emotion. That was part of the equation.

Even with practice, even with Annie's dogged determination and willingness to risk her own health, she hadn't been able to go just anywhere. She could go only to a place where she'd once been and where she had already been emotionally aroused—perhaps furious or terrified—and somehow open to visitation by her own future self.

If that were the case, why did certain words keep echoing in Ruth's brain?

Open the cabin door.

But there was an even simpler moment.

Maybe she'd misunderstood it. Maybe it was just *open the door*.

Mom, open the door.

RUTH WAS NO LONGER IN her living room, cross-legged on the floor with her back against the couch. She was in a quiet room with blond wood tables and modern tubular chairs and beige-and-white walls. She recognized the location from a recent dream as well as from her real life. It was a study room in the basement of the main campus library.

Ruth stared across the room at a NO CELL PHONE USE sign even as she held the overheated phone to her cheek. She was talking to Gwen. That explained the mismatch of feelings in Ruth's gut—the knowledge that this was normally a peaceful place, her private refuge, but now it had been invaded with bad feelings. Acid trickled into her stomach.

"You don't know why?" Ruth was saying to her mother. "She's been upset for days, but you haven't even asked?"

"I don't need to ask." Gwen exhaled impatiently. "It's always the same, isn't it?"

"How long has she been in her room, Mom?"

It was 5:50 P.M., the library due to close soon. If she wasn't careful, she might get locked inside. All the lights would go out. But that was less important than finishing this call.

Gwen and Kennidy had been fighting. Gwen hadn't talked to Kennidy since Friday at 11 P.M. when her daughter had come home; that was early for Kennidy. Maybe Gwen had seen her in the kitchen Saturday around noon. It was Sunday evening now. According to Gwen, Kennidy had been in her room all day, and perhaps half of yesterday, too.

"You don't know?"

"I wasn't home the whole time."

"Have you tried talking to her? Have you knocked on the door?"

"Of course I have, Ruthie. Do you think I'm stupid?"

This was a memory, albeit a vivid one. Ruth could still feel her lower back aching, and under her hand, the feeling of living room carpet. She was in her house, still half-anchored to the present, not fully in the past, in the college library.

"But Mom, it's not normal to be in your room all weekend. She doesn't do that. Did you hear her get up to use the bathroom, at least?"

Gwen didn't answer. In the silence that followed, dread flourished.

"Mom," Ruth said, and saying it brought the moment into clearer focus: the feel of the phone against her cheek, her mother's voice replying. Ruth inched farther into the corner so passing library staff wouldn't see her through the study window.

"I've got to get to the store before it closes," Gwen said.

"Not yet, Mom. Wait. You know she takes stuff. What if she did something stupid?"

"I'm sure she's just hungover. She's in a sulk."

"Yes, a dangerous sulk. That's why I'm worried. Are you sure you've heard the toilet flush at all lately?"

"She does this to me on purpose. I'm not going to reward her for that."

"Checking on someone who might hurt herself isn't a reward, Mom. It's the bare minimum."

This was not the conversation Ruth had had with Gwen the first time around. She'd never pressed her mother more than once or twice in a conversation. Ruth was more insistent now. No time for meandering conversation. No patience for Gwen's long-winded complaints. And if this conversation was heading along a different track, it could only mean two things. Either she was remembering incorrectly, out of self-serving desperation. Or she really was back here, choosing to have this phone conversation differently. But only if she could focus. That was the only way she could stay.

Ruth focused hard on what was in front of her: the metal tubes that were the legs of the study table and chair. Heat of the phone against her cheek. Anxiety gripping her throat.

"And what do you mean by that?" Gwen asked. "The bare minimum of what?"

"The bare minimum of supervision you give a child at home under the age of eighteen who isn't doing well."

"Listen."

"No, *you* listen," Ruth said. "Please."

"I told you, she's in her room. She's not coming out. We had a fight."

"Mom."

"Honey, you'll have to call her tomorrow, if you want. Hell, if you want to drive all the way up here tomorrow around lunchtime, I can pretty much guarantee she'll be home watching TV, not even in school."

"Mom. No, listen. This could be serious."

Ruth's mother sighed again, and then pulled the phone away a moment to cough. Neither of those sounds had felt worth treasuring before, but they did now: the sigh, the wet cough, even the slightly labored breath. Because as much as Ruth was angry at her mother, she also missed her. She could hate her and still want her back.

"Mom."

"I have to get going to the grocery store. They're closing in an hour."

In an hour. That meant it was six o'clock. Ruth could remember at the funeral, people asking, her mother refusing to answer, but Ruth had answered with as much cold candor as she could muster. "Mom found Ken in the morning. No, not just a few pills. Several bottles. She was methodical. They said it had probably been at least twelve hours since she'd overdosed. So it might've been around seven or eight P.M. the night before."

"When did you last see her?" Ruth asked Gwen again.

"I told you already. I'm not sure."

"Mom. Go knock on her door."

"Ruth." Gwen's weariness had sharpened into irritation. "If you want to visit, come visit. But I can't make her do anything she doesn't want to do. She goes missing overnight, then she comes back and abuses me, then she holes up, looking for sympathy."

"Mom."

"Did you know she stole twenty dollars out of my purse last week?"

"That doesn't matter right now."

"Maybe not to you."

"*Mom.*"

In real life, Ruth had never said it so many times, not as an adult, never with so much faith in this simple incantation. She had always been *on Gwen's side.*

"Mom. I'm staying on this phone. You're going to go to her room, you're going to knock on her door, and if she doesn't open—"

"I'm not going to piss off the landlord by breaking his door-knob."

The doors were cheap. The knobs were cheaper.

"Mom. You're going to try with a butter knife. You're going to try with your foot. You're going to call 911 if you can't get it open, and not later, when you come back from the store. Now. I'm going to wait here, on the phone. Don't be scared. I'm not going to hang up until you get that door open."

The certainty in Ruth's voice had finally touched a nerve. Gwen's tone changed.

"Did she call you? Did she say she was going to try something?"

"One of her friends called me just before you did." It was a lie. Ruth couldn't name one of Kennidy's friends if her life depended on it. "Disconnect if you need to call 911, but I'll be waiting for you to call me back."

"You don't think I'm a good mother."

"You're going to be a good mother. You're going to get that door open and you're going to get Kennidy help."

The sound of distant sirens brought Ruth back to the present. At first, she felt a sense of accomplishment and blessed relief. Her face was wet with tears. The ambulance and police cars were coming, she must be hearing them through the phone, still connected with Gwen and waiting, and if it had only been six o'clock on that memorable Sunday, it wasn't too late. They'd get Kennidy's door open. She may have taken the pills already, but she was still alive. They could pump her stomach. But how had Gwen called the ambulance? Maybe Ruth was forgetting. Maybe Gwen had hung up and called her back. It didn't matter.

Ruth exhaled, cheek against the carpet. Without knowing it, she had slid onto her front, on the floor. She'd made it to the past and back again, or so she thought, and the difficulty she was having now, unable even to lift her head, was proof of how difficult a trip it had been.

But the sirens didn't stop.

4 6

REECE

Reece was ready with his team, about to run out on the field. The football game had started late due to a problem with parking for many attendees, slowed down by the fascist security volunteers who, without school-district permission, had manned the two public-property rotaries.

On top of that, Gerald had gone missing. From the football field, they'd heard sirens, and Raj told Reece that someone had seen Gerald speeding away from the school lot in his car. But no one was that stupid.

"Well, maybe some people *are* that stupid," Raj admitted. "What do we do now, boss?"

"We make seven people look like eight."

The Rockets spent the first half of the football game on a side field, working out how to change their formations without him. Reece had thought it was hard replacing Caleb with Mikayla and Justin over the course of several days. Now he'd learned he could problem-solve absences or injuries in minutes when it was necessary. High-speed choreographing was a rush, actually, like a complicated three-dimensional puzzle. Maybe he wasn't meant to be a dancer—or not *only* a dancer. Maybe he was meant to be a choreographer or show manager or logistics person, or maybe a little bit of all of them. Fancy that.

Now that the show was ready to start, Reece looked toward the stands and saw his parents. They hadn't come to the school for a long time. When his mom caught him looking, she pumped a fist in the air. He felt an unexpected wave of emotion well up and looked away, swallowing hard. Scanning the stands and the grassy strip along the perimeter of the field, he saw teachers and parents of friends, some standing, others seated on blankets or folding chairs. There was his counselor; there was Mrs. Holloway; there was Mr. Webb, standing, squinting off into the distance, hands on his hips.

Reece scanned the sidelines one more time for Ruth. He expected her to be with Mr. Webb. She was supposed to be here. It was silly to be disappointed, but that's how Reece felt. He'd been wrapped up all week in her Annie Oakley mystery, but he'd also been wrapped up in this performance, rehearsing up to the last minute. Where was she?

He wasn't offended, just disappointed. She was going to *miss* this: the purely exuberant six minutes—that's all they got—where shit could go wrong and they'd simply have to adapt and make it look like it was on purpose. Now, whatever happened, happened. Now, they could have fun.

4 7

R U T H

uth was confused, first by the sirens. Then, as they faded, by the sound of some distant bass beat, palpable even at this distance, causing the very floor she was lying on to vibrate in time to catches of music blaring from the school nearby. She tripped, trying to get up. When she put a hand out to the floor to brace her fall, she saw bright droplets of blood.

She got up more slowly, hands out and ready to catch herself if she fell again, noting as she rose the smear of blood on her inner arm, another small stain on her jeans. But she couldn't see any cuts. Then, finally, she was looking at herself in the mirror. The blood was trickling from her ear, which didn't hurt. It felt only odd, cotton-stuffed.

There was that low bass beat again, accompanied by some higher synthesized riffs coming from far away. It had to be loud to travel this far; is that what the sirens had been for? Police responding to a complaint? But no, they had started up first, the beat after. She couldn't make out a melody. When she clapped a hand over the left ear, the non-bleeding one, she heard only the muffled thud of her pulse and that horrible bass, like a hammer tapping her skull, trying to crack it open like an egg.

Kennidy. It came back to her now.

What happened to Kennidy?

The loss of hearing in one ear, plus the blurry vision in one eye or some kind of damage to one side of her brain, made her feel like she was leaning to one side. She staggered out of the bathroom, down the hall and past a bookshelf, hand out in search of balance, toppling framed photos as she passed.

Ruth bent down to pick up the closest one and turned it over: cracked glass, no other visible damage. In the photo, Gwen looking gaunt but happy. A Mother's Day photo from 2015, five months before Gwen had died. They were at brunch at Gwen's favorite restaurant. In the original photo, only Ruth had been squeezing Gwen. Now both of Gwen's daughters leaned in from either side, their heads rested on Gwen's shoulders.

Kennidy lived.

The phone-call episode hadn't felt like memory or imagination. But it hadn't felt like reality, either. Ruth was ready to believe it was a dream, if not for this: evidence that Kennidy had not died in 2013. And maybe Gwen, less stressed, had lived longer as well? Could she still be alive?

Ruth had kept the memorial card from Gwen's funeral tucked into the bottom of the frame. She got down on her knees, scanning for anything that had fallen. There were three business-size cards, all face down. Three, when there should have been only one. Ruth's blood ran cold.

She turned over the closest, with a plain white backing. It was a floral card with an image of a rose and a handwritten note: *We will meet again. Love you forever, Bob.* Ruth couldn't remember any Bob in any of their lives. She turned over the second card, familiar except for the changed date: Gwen had died December 2, rather than October 10.

Ruth's hand hovered over the final card, hoping it was like the first—just a sweet thought rescued from a flower bouquet. But she could see the back of the card had a religious quote and an address running along the bottom. Ruth flipped the card.

Kennidy Theresa McClintock. In memoriam, June 27, 2015.

Kennidy had made it to nineteen, instead of seventeen. But no further. Something had still gotten to her: her past, her brain chemistry, simple bad luck, maybe tempered with a brief touch of good. *Love you forever, Bob.*

It was Czolgosz over again, Annie's early experiment.

It hadn't worked, except to delay the event. You could change a little. Not a lot.

Ruth was on her feet, unsteady.

Not fair.

She picked another card up off the floor. It was a condolence note from Joe. She kept it because it meant a lot to her, that Joe had written something so personal. They'd dated . . . was it only a few months? No, she could picture their anniversary; they'd lasted more than a year. Both answers seemed correct. Something had shifted there, too. Yet things had ended up in the same place: she'd broken up with Joe. Much later, she'd lived with Scott.

Things had changed and remained the same by unpredictable degrees.

Ruth needed fresh air. She walked slowly to the door and lifted a weak arm but couldn't quite grasp the knob. She tried again, without success.

Her body was fucked. Her mind, even more so. Time-traveling back had sent damaging pulses through her brain. She moved . . . saw . . . heard . . . felt like a stroke victim.

Why don't we hear about more time travel? Why aren't there people having visions all the time? The question she and that boy— the helpful one with the drawing on his arm, had always asked.

Because of this. It kills you.

Ruth got a better grip on the door and yanked. There was the music: louder, repetitive, annoying. A school performance.

Then she remembered. It was already six o'clock. She'd been expected at the school two hours ago.

The sirens. Music. The halftime show.

The bass beat was overtaken by a high-pitched squeal, feedback noise and a voice over a microphone, "One-two." Mechanical shrieking again. Technical difficulties. "One-two. One-two."

Reece. That was his name. *Reece.* Another similar word. Rooks? That seemed right. Alternative, gothic. No, *Rockets.* His group was performing.

The football field, with everyone gathered one last time while the weather was still pleasant.

Scott.

Scott, who had been in her bed just this morning: that hadn't changed. He'd left in a hurry, hair rumpled, white shirt rolled up at the elbows, to hide the stain on his sleeve. Even Reece had noticed. Scott didn't wear wrinkled shirts to work. But that's how he had looked this morning. And that's how he had looked in the vision.

She hadn't made the connection.

Her alarm system, sensitive as it usually was, had malfunctioned. The anxiety of that realization thrummed through her, and she instinctively wanted it—the white bar-shaped pill—because everything that could go wrong was going wrong. But that was a habit she had mostly kicked. Wasn't it?

And now she remembered taking the tiny corner of the Xanax just before getting into the car, to drive Scott home.

It had worked.

Or, it had worked and it hadn't. She had driven him back safely. She had kept her cool when he suddenly kissed her and even later, when they argued and made up.

And she had lost all sense of what was coming. She had lost the signal.

But now it was back, strong and sharp, piercing her bleeding eardrum and thrumming behind her bleary eyes.

The future hadn't changed enough. Scott would be hurt today. The event was coming soon, if it wasn't happening right now.

Ruth's first impulse was to hurry on foot to the school. In her present condition, that could take over thirty minutes. She could call for a ride, but that would take time, too.

She just had to get there early, to do . . . what? Tell Scott? He wouldn't believe her. Stop the shooter? She still didn't know how, and wouldn't know until she could see and assess the situation.

Scott. The field, the sidelines, the green grass, the taller golden grass beyond it. Somewhere in that grass was—or would soon be—a person hidden, watching Scott, watching them all: the performers on the field, the students and teachers on the sidelines, the parents in the bleachers.

She didn't mean to invite the vision to overtake her, but she'd dug a rut for this. It was easier than ever to slide back onto the ever widening, slippery path.

Not again. Her body might not be able to take it.

But there was the deep trail, like a chute, its edges smoothly rounded. And once she was on it, she knew where she'd go, toward the color red or the color of white just before the red. She tried to calm her mind and stop the fast-forward from coming too soon by thinking: *green.* The leafy trees on either side of her, the upper boughs overhead, blocking out part of the sky.

Take a breath. Slow down so you can see.

Ruth knew she had used up her strength by traveling back in time to the call with her mother. And for what? Nothing had changed in the end. The past had only distracted her, as it always had. It was possible she only had one chance left.

She let herself think of him once again, with as much calm as she could muster: Scott, the silver thread in his hair, a worried look on his face. His white shirt with the rolled-up cuffs.

Then she was there.

4 8

R U T H

His mouth was moving and he was saying something, but she couldn't read his lips. He started to turn and look over his shoulder. Then he looked forward again. His arms went out to the sides, with fingers splayed.

Deep breath. Find a way further back.

But Ruth could move back only seconds. She watched him perform the motions again: speak, look over his shoulder, arms out. Scott was protecting someone, while shouting to someone else far away. His mouth formed the word: *Don't.* Now she was sure. The first word was *What?* The second word was *Don't.*

And then he was bleeding, falling, down.

Ruth had to detach herself again from the desire to stare at only him, to lighten her attention, to wish less, to want less, to react less, to be like one of those World War I balloon observers, floating above the trenches. They couldn't stop the massacre; their job was only to watch and report. And yet they were traumatized, too.

She perceived streaks of motion in the background as other people darted away, fell and tried to get up. Several people collapsed on top of each other just behind Scott. Some of them might be injured, others weren't. Some were knotted together into a panicked mass.

Slow it down.

A girl's long hair whipping in the wind. The bottom of a teenager's shoes as he scrambled and tried to get purchase, toes digging into the turf to sprint as far from Scott as the boy could. Kids. Students. Teachers.

Keep looking.

Scott was positioned at the edge of the football field, facing the sidelines.

Just to the right, on the sidelines, stood the Rockets cheerleaders, in their purple shirts. Reece. A small black girl who must be Mikayla. And next to her, with his arm over her shoulder, Vorst.

Behind that group were the bleachers. Too many faces. Metal seats, concrete steps, shadows.

Ruth kept panning, the blur in her mind like the worst case of the drinker's spins she'd ever experienced. She saw, far to her left, behind the football field, the boy lying on the ground, propped up on his elbows like a biathlete or sniper, aiming something long and narrow at Scott's back.

The first spotting of the weapon made her flinch. As if she had pulled back from a parted curtain, she found herself in velvety darkness. She lowered her head and pushed forward again, willing her way through the asphyxiating folds, until she saw the glimmer of green fields again, backed by higher, tawny grass.

Reece, who is he? Reece, are you there?

It's the boy, she thought, *the one who was blamed for making a threat.* She remembered his name: *Caleb.* She struggled to remember the rest of what she'd heard from Scott and Reece. Neither thought Caleb was a problem. So why was he here in the grass with a weapon?

Before, she was only watching. Now, she felt her heavy breathing, the weight of her body and the pain in her knee as she staggered. Ruth felt herself moving toward Scott, but she was on the farthest end of the field, just stepping onto the oval running track around it, still too far to do anything.

Hundreds of feet in the distance, Scott was on his feet, waving his arms, but not at the boy in the grass behind him. He was waving in the opposite direction.

Meanwhile, she could smell a hint of smoke—not pleasant, like burning leaves, but something else that hurt her throat, like chemicals or burning rubber. A brown wisp rose from far behind Scott, outside school property. It was coming from the direction of Ruth's own neighborhood. Those sirens she'd heard—were they police, ambulances, firemen?

These questions and the sensory stimuli threatened to overload her. There was too much to feel and smell and hear, too much to look at. This was harder than the phone call with her mother, in which she had sat and stared ahead and merely focused on the words in that frustrating but controllable conversation. There was too much of everything here: movement, colors, sensations, sound.

Her eye couldn't resist being drawn to the bleachers at which Scott was staring and waving and shouting, though she had trouble deciphering the words due to the white noise fizzing in her ears.

The students in purple shirts—Reece, Mikayla, a half-dozen others—turned as well, to look toward the shadowy place behind the bleachers. Toward the figure who was provoking Scott to shout and wave.

Ruth swung back to see Caleb. He was rising, one hand still on the ground, rear up, legs ready to push off, like a sprinter in the blocks, except his right hand gripped the long weapon, curved at the end. A hockey stick. Caleb was getting ready to charge onto and across the field with a hockey stick.

Not a gun.

But there was a gun, somewhere. She'd seen Scott get shot. She'd seen him fall.

Look harder.

Scott was facing the sidelines and the bleachers. He was shouting at the person—Ruth finally spotted him, only now—with the raised rifle.

The rifle. Another man. It wasn't Caleb.

And then Scott was down. Her vision blurred.

Ruth clapped a hand over her good ear. The shots continued. She opened her eyes, squinting, fighting the urge to stare at the bodies, falling or stumbling. She needed to see the one figure who *wasn't* fleeing. She studied his outline, in fatigues and an orange safety vest. Holding a rifle. At the edge of one of the bleachers, in the shadows, back from the track that encircled the field. Aiming at the boy, Caleb.

The security guard was the shooter.

Spectators continued to panic even after the shots stopped. In the rush to vacate the bleachers, several people had fallen and been kicked or tripped over. Others were trying to help the fallen back up, and the bottlenecks were creating yet other falls as people tried to leap from the sides of the viewing stands and collided with students racing to shelter in the spaces underneath.

Ruth's eyes found Reece, disentangling himself from a group of the trampled, hands on his leg above the ankle, bent over. He took a step, collapsed and rolled onto his back. As soon as she reached him, she tried to create a protective space with her arms as other students continued to stream past. He rolled side to side, moaning. There was a bulge below the knee of his pants-leg, like a snapped bone protruding.

Ruth found her voice. "Help! Someone!"

As she looked up, she saw the volunteer security guard who had shot both Caleb and Scott stumbling forward toward Scott. The guard no longer had his rifle. His face was ashen. He had one hand over his mouth, which was still moving. *Oh my god. Oh my god.*

Even though the guard was no longer armed, a large man

tackled him from behind. The guard fell on his side, arms wrapped around his knees, not resisting.

"Don't hurt him!" someone called out. "It was a mistake. Everyone calm down!"

Two other men had just reached Scott and one was hoisting him onto his shoulder, in a fire-arm carry. *Don't move him. Just wait.* Voices arguing. The mayhem was too much. Some people thought there might be other shooters. And meanwhile, Scott wasn't moving or gripping the neck of the man carrying him. She couldn't tell if he was conscious at all.

Scott. She felt her stomach drop, like she was in a broken elevator plummeting. *Scott.* She wanted to touch him, to make sure he really was alive, to put a hand to his face, to do anything to stop his pain. He wasn't out of danger.

But neither was Reece. Ruth shouted, "There's a boy down over here!"

Go go go, she thought, willing the others to rush Scott to a hospital; searching the crowds also for any sign of paramedics or someone to come attend to Reece. She spotted Caleb, and the two men lifting him: one by the armpits, the other by the calves. It was clear even at a distance. Every part of him was broken.

Ruth turned back to Reece. "I'm too late."

His eyes were slits. "What the fuck happened?"

"A security guard shot Scott and Caleb, too. He must have thought Caleb was aiming a weapon, but it wasn't a gun." She tried to sound calm. "Your leg is broken. But you're going to be okay, Reece."

She was about to say, *Once we get you out of here, I need to go help Scott.* But that wouldn't accomplish anything. She'd only be watching him bleed, shut out of an ambulance and later an operating room, waiting to hear the same terrible news she'd dreaded since the very first vision. She needed to undo all of this—to go back, just one more time, and get it right.

Ruth tried to extract herself from the moment, to breathe, to think of anything—calm green, moving backward—but she still heard Reece groaning. Her heart should have been racing, but instead, it was beating too slowly. The edges of her vision darkened.

Nothing had worked. Not going to the past to help Kennidy, not going to the future to help Scott.

"I'm never going to dance again," Reece said through gritted teeth.

"You will. Better than ever."

"My leg . . ."

"You're young. You'll heal. The paramedics must be coming."

"I can't wait." He opened his eyes, glanced down the length of his leg, saw the blood on his pants and the angle where there should have been a straight shin. His eyes rolled back in his head.

"You're going into shock. Let's keep you here, Reece." She squeezed his shoulder.

"Go to Scott," he moaned. "I'll be okay."

"They're carrying him to the parking lot. I need to make sure you don't get trampled. Let me help you."

He took a deep breath and opened his eyes again. "If you want to help, give me something to take my mind off the pain. A cigarette, at least. Holy fucking Christ."

"You don't need a cigarette. You're going to be a famous dancer someday." She found herself half-laughing, half-crying, so glad that Reece hadn't been shot or injured any worse than he was. "Your body is a temple."

Your body is a temple.

He tried to laugh too, but it came out as a sob. "Why didn't it work?"

"I don't know. I saw this. I *am* seeing this." Was she at home seeing this, predicting it, or just here in normal time, the first and only time it would happen? "I was too slow, Reece. Maybe it

was something I took, a pill that calmed me down too much and
dampened the signal I needed. Or maybe you just can't change
things this way."

What else could she have done?

The loop back. The loop forward. She saw it in her mind. What
came next?

The loop backward again.

But she couldn't go back in time again. She was half-blind,
half-deaf, heart slowing.

*You have to go back to go forward. You have to go forward to
go back.* Were those the only options?

Her mind traced the image on her wrist, following the figure-
eight curves, looking for a sign that one direction was better than
the other, that one entry point was more forgiving of meddling.

For a moment, she had it. But then she lost it again, left with
only a fading sensation, inadequate words, and a certainty that
this imperfect understanding wouldn't be enough.

Looking up, she saw a man running toward them, a woman
just behind him, her face streaming with tears. Reece's parents,
she hoped. But that meant she didn't have much time.

"You've already dreamed this, Reece, what I'm going to tell
you now. But when you dream it, it will seem like the first time.
Draw the infinity loop. Make me figure it out. I can't go back
now, but you will, because you will dream this in the past, and if
you tell me more sooner, I can do better."

"You're talking too fast," he moaned.

"We don't have much time. Don't give up. Just—be honest,
Reece. I'll eventually believe you. But I'm also a skeptic. You'll
have to be firm with me." She started to cry, then laughed at her
own crying. "Just try to remember."

"It's too much."

"Do your best. If you forget some of the words, just draw the
infinity loop. Start with that."

"Why?" He screwed up his face. "I'm going to be sick."

"That's the shock. But you're doing really good. Just stay with me."

"They shot Caleb? He wasn't even *here*."

"He was hiding in the grass," Ruth said.

"No, he wasn't. He left in his dad's truck. Some guys saw him leave. Like he was here and changed his mind or got spooked."

"He must have come back on foot."

"I think he was going after Vorst."

Of course. The coach was the cause of Caleb's fury. She felt a surge of pity for Caleb. First, her kid sister, then this poor kid, and Vorst connected them all. It wasn't just a figure-eight, it was a Gordian knot, one that had to be cut, not loosened. She hated Vorst, and yet she had to stop Caleb from attempting to confront him so the others wouldn't be hurt. But that still wasn't the whole solution.

"I should have . . ." Reece started to say, but another spike of pain overwhelmed him.

"Don't worry. Just breathe."

Ruth smelled the smoke again. Accident or arson.

Reece's father and a second man crouched next to Ruth, preparing to lift Reece. Ruth felt herself outside the circle, no longer needed. She closed her eyes, which had started to burn as the wind shifted, and she pictured Vorst's house going up in flames—perhaps hers, as well. The fire and the mayhem might engulf her.

Instead, the opposite happened. Everything went black and perfectly quiet, and now there was neither screaming nor smoke.

4 9

R U T H

For a moment, Ruth was dreaming peacefully and lucidly. She knew it was a dream, because it was based on a photograph she'd once seen in a museum file and never fully understood. It was labeled ANNIE OAKLEY, but there was no Annie visible and no explanation.

A large group of young women in pale summery calf-length dresses were gathered on the gentle slope of an emerald-colored lawn. They were mingling, laughing, holding small crystal glasses. The only man at the gathering, in a dress shirt and bow tie, was standing behind a cloth-covered table, ladling punch.

They're her daughters, a voice said from behind Ruth. *All eighteen of them.*

I didn't know Annie Oakley had eighteen children.

You didn't? Everyone knows.

I don't think so, Ruth said, still captivated by the loveliness of the scene, the tinkling of soft laughter, the fabrics ruffling: peach, ivory and buttercup yellow. *She was too old by the 1920s to have any daughters.*

Oh, Ruth. You're so literal. But you can see, she's happier now. After those terrible trials. And all that . . . well, you know. She was done with it. Partly because she'd seen it through, she'd faced it. Partly because of Frank. But mostly because of this.

Ruth looked for signs of Annie Oakley, but she must be hidden, enfolded like a bud at the center of this gorgeous arrangement of flowers, these young women who clearly adored her.

The fabrics looked so soft. Ruth wanted to press those cool, pale colors to her hot cheek. She was desperately thirsty. She wanted to walk across the emerald lawn. The liquid in their crystal glasses sparkled.

Not for you, the unseen voice said. *It isn't yours.*

The punch? The beauty? The company? The kindness? Ruth's head ached, and it must be because of the thirst.

It isn't yours to have. It's hers, the voice said. *She earned it, she made it for herself.*

I only want . . . Not just the beverage. But this sense of peace and love. That was what she wanted and could not have.

Ruth felt the image fade, felt herself being pulled back, slow at first and then faster, knowing exactly where she would be deposited: the stillest place. The strongest place. The point at which the two loops converged.

Draw the symbol, Reece.

The only place that was connected to everything else, the only place where change was and would always be possible.

The present.

RUTH WAS AWAKE BUT INCONVENIENTLY positioned, facedown on her own lawn, which was not emerald or lovely, but rather brown, rough and redolent of dog shit.

And yet: there was no smell of smoke.

She heard the crackle of a distant speaker powering up, similar to the one she'd heard—was it hours ago, or only seconds?—before she'd decided to hurry toward the school.

Ruth didn't try to stand yet. She sat still and tried to remember.

She'd been conscious, the Rockets had been starting their show. But there had been that sound system glitch. She'd heard the music stop and start several times. From the time that happened until the end of the Rockets' performance and the moment Caleb was finally positioned, ready to rise out of the grass, it might have been only twenty minutes. That was all she had.

The future and the past are our two most difficult battles. They aren't battles we are always meant to win.

But the present was fair game.

At this moment, Caleb might be in the woods, walking toward the school field.

No. There was no fire yet, and in her vision, someone had started a fire. Unless he had a good friend—and she knew Caleb had few friends—he had done it himself. If she waited here, there was a good chance he'd walk right past her yard and then past Vorst's. But there was also a chance he would see her and start running. In any case, he was close. He had to be, given the timing.

She needed to get to him sooner, and not only that, she needed his full attention. She had only one chance to make him listen.

RUTH JUMPED INTO HER HONDA and pulled out of the driveway fast, scanning up and down the street. He wouldn't be hard to spot: she'd seen him in her vision, even if she didn't remember his exact features.

Reece had told her that Caleb had left the school in his dad's truck. Ruth thought about where she'd ditch a truck: not so far that you couldn't get to the school on foot. On her block alone, she saw two new pickups parked in driveways, but no one walking. The streets and the sidewalks were empty.

Maybe this was a mistake. Minutes were ticking by. Maybe she should have waited at her house, or Vorst's, or the entrance to the trail.

At the first intersection, she had to decide: go straight, past a busy road with fast-food chains; turn left, toward the school and newer houses; or right, toward the older side of town, smaller houses, more weedy lots, places to park and not be immediately seen.

Definitely right.

Just when she had reached a dead-end and was looking over her shoulder to back up and turn around, she saw him: jeans and a cinched hoody, about her height, walking with his head down. And carrying a hockey stick.

Ruth rolled down the window and came up just behind him, rolling slowly to match his pace. She had to choose her words carefully.

"Caleb, don't run away. I want to help you. My name's Ruth McClintock. I'm a friend of Reece's."

He glanced over his shoulder at her without stopping.

"Caleb, I know what Vorst did. I want to punish him, too."

He started walking faster. At any moment, he might duck between houses. She could lose him in an instant.

"Caleb." She had to blow his mind and leave him speechless. "You're going to Vorst's house to light it on fire, and then you're going to go through the woods to the school, where you're planning to run across the field and attack Vorst with that hockey stick. But it's not going to work."

He stopped. He turned and looked at her, through the car window.

"You're Kennidy's sister," he said.

Ruth, it turned out, was the speechless one.

WHEN SHE FOUND HER WORDS again, she said, "Please get in the car."

He was still peering in the window, debating.

"You shouldn't know all that."

"No, I shouldn't. Trust me, I know it sounds crazy. But I want to help you. I just don't want anyone to get hurt."

"Except Vorst."

"Except Vorst, maybe. But nobody else."

"You're bleeding," he said.

"And I can't see very well. It would be safer if you drove, actually."

Ruth hopped out, walked around to the passenger side, and gestured for Caleb to take the driver's seat.

"You're kidding," he said. "I'm a stranger, and you're letting me drive your car?"

"You can go anywhere you want."

"Anywhere?"

"You won't be able to get away in your truck after you do whatever you're going to do. The cops know the plates. But you can take my car."

"I can take your car?"

"I promise."

He narrowed his eyes. "Even if I crack the coach's head open with this stick?"

"Yes."

"Even if I start a fire?"

"Absolutely." She paused. "But let me ask this one thing. Why exactly do you want to start a fire?"

"It's . . ." he paused, sounding less certain. "It's just a diversion. Vorst's got tires leaning up against his house, and I figured if I could roll one out onto the street and get it smoking, I could lure the cops away from the school so they don't spot me right away and stop me."

"Oh," she said. "That's pretty smart, actually."

He looked at her with surprise.

"I live right next to him, you know that?" She could tell from his wide eyes that he'd had no idea. "Don't get me wrong, I'm okay with the fire idea. I'm just wondering. You're sure he has something to light the tire with?"

"Can of gas for the mower, yeah," Caleb said, looking at her suspiciously. "In his carport."

"Good. But there's a problem. There are still way too many armed guards at the school. That's where it goes bad." She corrected herself. "Where it *will* go bad. Turn here if you're going to Vorst's house."

He looked at her like she was still trying to put one over on him.

They'd been creeping down the street since he'd taken the wheel. Now he gunned the motor, testing her. But she didn't tell him to slow down or pull over.

"You're really letting me go to Vorst's house."

"If that's what you need to do. Don't miss the stop sign. Okay, the next left. I think you know the way."

What she wanted most right now was time—a diversion of her own, just until she could figure out the rest.

As long as he didn't make it to the school, the chain of events couldn't start and the accident couldn't happen. If he wanted to play around and make smoke, even if it got out of control, she was willing to risk Vorst's house, the lots across the street, even her own home. Lord knew she had occasionally dreamed of Gwen's house going up in flames, since no one seemed to want to buy it.

"I'm wondering," she said, "maybe we should make it a big fire, not just one they'll come and put out right away."

"It's harder than you think," Caleb said.

"I bet. But maybe we can really get it going. Burn the whole house down. That would send a message, right? Maybe even more than threatening him with a hockey stick."

He mumbled, "What's the point?"

"I don't know. You tell me. Whatever you want to do, we'll do it."

After a moment, Caleb said, "The cabin."

They had just pulled up to Vorst's house.

"What?"

"Everything he cares about is in his cabin."

Ruth turned her head so she could see Caleb better through her only good eye. "You've been to his cabin? You know where it is?"

THEY WERE PULLED UP TO the curb, car still running.

"I need something inside, for our protection," Ruth said. "It'll take only a second."

"You're calling the cops."

"Caleb, if I wanted to call the cops, I already would have. If you're worried about that, hold my phone."

She handed it to him, opened the car door and hurried inside.

Ruth went directly to the bathroom, where the apothecary dresser with its five rows of drawers stood. She knew instantly which drawer held the key. Scott had left it behind.

Just in case you ever need it. I don't like to think of you alone in that house.

In the garage, she rummaged around and found the case that matched the key. She'd always known where it was stored, and even when Scott had come last time for his belongings, she'd neglected to mention it. Neglected, not forgotten. Her subconscious had known even then.

The feel of the handgun, heavy in her jacket pocket, made her feel both excited and sick. She remembered how nervous she'd been the first time Scott tried to hand her a gun. She remembered how upset she'd felt when her mother's boyfriend had brought a gun into their home.

In her subconscious, she must have pictured this, the horrible exciting power it would give her, to have this object in her pocket, in her hand, at the right time.

It wasn't Kennidy who couldn't be trusted with a weapon. It wasn't Caleb, either. It was Ruth.

5 0

C A L E B

It normally took an hour to drive, but Caleb made the trip in forty minutes, head pounding and stomach twisted. On the highway they'd passed a police car, but it was only helping direct traffic around a jackknifed truck. Ruth had been right: he couldn't be seen except like this, in someone else's car. But that didn't mean she was right about everything. He'd listened because she'd appeared like some messed-up, bleeding angel, like the friend he never had, telling him she would help.

Of course, she was probably insane. They were more than halfway to the cabin when he let himself turn and actually look at her, strapped into the car next to him. She'd fallen asleep or passed out with her chin on her shoulder with something that looked like dried blood caking her ear and neck, like she'd been in a bar fight.

So he'd gotten into a car with a crazy woman, injured and high or drunk. But he wasn't nervous about that, exactly. It was his own anger that had scared him most, back at the school.

Then this: Vorst's neighbor. Kennidy's sister.

Caleb looked back at the empty road, watching for police. When he glanced over at Ruth again, her eyes were open, studying him.

"He molested my kid sister," she said.

He nodded.

"You already knew that somehow."

He nodded again.

"He did something to you, too."

Caleb didn't nod this time, didn't speak. He didn't need a heart-to-heart. All he wanted was someone in the car with him, willing to do something big enough to really scare Van Vorst and protect Mikayla.

Ruth asked, "How did he do it? Did he just force you? Or talk you into it, somehow?"

"Does it matter?"

Ruth was quiet for a moment. Then she wiped her nose. "I guess it doesn't. Sorry."

That weakened him just a little. "I can tell you one thing. Your sister thought you were smart, going away to college when you did. She really admired you."

"You're making that up."

He didn't answer. She could believe or not believe him, like the dozens of others who wouldn't believe him about anything that mattered.

Ruth said, "How do you know?'

He left the question hanging there until she said, "Never mind. I believe you. Thanks."

5 1

R U T H

They turned down a long gravel drive past hayfields, passed the oak tree and pulled up to the cabin. Fallen leaves blanketed the ground. The cabin, bathed in the last golden glow of early evening light, looked rustic but not menacing.

Kennidy. Ruth tried to feel her presence but couldn't. Still, she wanted her to know. *We're here.*

"There's got to be stuff in there that proves what he's done to people," Ruth said. "Right? So we need to get in there and take what we can."

"I thought we were burning down his cabin. You were willing to burn down his other house. This is the one he cares about. That's what I told you."

"And you were right. But first, we should get our hands on anything important that's inside."

Caleb looked at her. "But if we break in and steal evidence, isn't that a legal problem?"

Ruth paused. "Maybe."

"Police need warrants."

"You're right. But maybe if we just broke in and brought out something that will show he's guilty, then they'd have to go back inside and do a real search."

"But they won't find anything. It'll all be gone. You said you'd help me burn this place to the ground."

Ruth could tell that something had dawned on Caleb, and it wasn't going to make things easier for her.

"I don't want anything left," he said. "I don't want anyone to see the photos."

So Vorst *did* keep incriminating items here. Photos, at least.

"If he brought you here, he probably brought a lot of kids here. Is that what you saw in the photos?"

Ruth watched Caleb, whose eyes were squeezed shut like he was waiting for a punishment he'd forgotten he'd have to endure.

"I don't want anyone else to see the stuff he has. Not of me, not of any of the other kids. I just want it all gone."

"No one will have to see it except the police and maybe a judge and lawyers."

Ruth had her phone out to dial 911. She'd had weak service a moment ago, but now there were no bars. No way to call in or out, to text Scott or Reece. She paused, watching Caleb step out of the car and go directly to the side of the cabin. He paused next to a grill, bent down and picked up a rectangular white container.

"No, Caleb!"

He was already heading toward the cabin's front door with the lighter fluid tipped and dribbling when she caught up and pushed him from behind. They both sprawled.

He rolled away from her, looking up, incredulous.

Ruth grabbed for the container. Still on her knees, she righted it. There was still fuel inside.

Caleb yelled, "Why'd you *do* that?"

He covered his face with his hands, trying to hold in breathless sobs. "I thought you were going to help."

"I *am* helping."

She sat back on her haunches, waiting for him to get control of himself. "I don't want you to get into even more trouble. Caleb, you need to get out of here. Get home or go anywhere else you feel safe."

"You just needed me to drive you here!"

"I promise you, I'll take care of this."

He glared at her, but his red eyes held more exhaustion than hate.

The sky was already deepening to a cobalt that was still a few shades away from navy, pricked with stars. It would be a clear, cold night. In the far distance, on the highway visible across stubbly fields, the winking headlights of passing cars could be seen.

"You see all those cars? We start a fire while there's still light, and there'll be cop cars turning up here in a couple minutes. They'll find us. They'll find you."

"There's always a reason not to do something. You're just stalling. That's your game."

"It's not. Listen, Caleb. They'll probably put the damn thing out right away. It's not so easy to start a fire. You said it yourself. All those photos you don't want anyone to see. They're still going to be here."

He mumbled something unintelligible.

"But if I wait an hour," Ruth said, "it'll be pitch-black out here, and no one will see the smoke start to rise. Rush hour will be over. The neighbors are far away. The trick is a small, slow burn in the dark, so that it's too big to stop before anyone notices."

Caleb's chin dropped to his chest. He hiccupped like a child, then wiped his mouth with the back of his hand and said, "He comes here every Friday night, so you can't wait too long."

"I'll time it right. Trust me."

"Okay."

"Okay? Promise me," she said, "that you'll drive straight home and stay safe." She didn't mean to lie. But she wouldn't be doing things according to Caleb's plan. And still, the biggest problem was that she couldn't make sure Caleb wouldn't run back to school or make trouble elsewhere.

She looked at her phone. One bar. She started typing a text to Reece. When she was done, she looked at Caleb again.

"Reece knows everything. Go to his house. He'll hide you. That's the most important thing. If the cops find you, you'll be out of options. If you can stay hidden and regroup, with help, you can figure out the rest."

She saw a new flicker in his eyes. Caleb trusted Reece.

5 2

R U T H

Vorst had just fit his key into the knob when Ruth, standing ten feet behind him, grunted. "Hey."

He looked over his shoulder, then cocked his head, registering her shape and the object in her hands.

Given the racket of her chattering teeth, she was amazed he hadn't heard her sooner. She pointed the revolver at him with both hands, trembling from the cold and adrenaline.

She'd been rehearsing this moment in her mind since Caleb had driven away ninety or more minutes ago. Watching more stars appear and the distant traffic increase to its peak, then slowly begin to thin out again, hearing the faint breeze stir the last remaining leaves on the creaky limbs of the oak tree. She'd never had any interest in arson. Too easy.

"Hey," she said again. "Stay where you are."

"Do I know you?"

"Yes," she said, forcing a deep breath into her lungs. She'd had a whole speech planned. Several speeches. But first, she had to suppress her shivering, which was making the heavy gun at the end of her outstretched arms wiggle and dance.

"You're my neighbor," he said in a surprisingly calm voice,

as if this were a normal scene: a woman ready to shoot a man as he was entering his weekend getaway. "What are you doing here?"

"I'm Kennidy's sister," she said.

He nodded.

And now she could say it. The words she had planned for the last hour, and for years.

"Open the cabin door."

THEY SAT AROUND HIS KITCHEN table, forearms resting on sticky placemats opposite each other, bowl of walnuts between them. She kept the gun in her hand, barrel pointed at his face, stock resting on the table's surface.

"Bologna sandwich?" he asked.

"I'm not here to eat."

He'd been offering her things since they'd walked inside: hot tea, cocoa, a beer, potato chips. Bathroom? A heavier jacket? Washcloth for the blood on her cheek and neck?

She did allow him to turn on the space heater. Only that.

Once seated, she had started the trial for which she would be judge, jury and executioner: "You abused my sister. She trusted you as a coach. You molested her. Raped her. And in her misery after all that, she killed herself."

"You left out the part about me helping your mother, by selling her the house at a bargain-basement price," he said, still tranquil, after she'd talked until her words ran dry. "Which helped her tremendously. It was always her dream to own a house. Did you know that?"

When Vorst started to reach forward, she held the gun an inch higher. He slowed his movement but didn't stop, fingers continuing to move toward the nut bowl, sliding the nutcracker out of a slot on the bowl's side.

"Oh, wait," he added. "But that's the only part that's true.

Because everything you said before, about Kennidy, is garbage. You have a dirty mind, darlin'."

Just calling her darlin' almost felt like enough reason to shoot. But she maintained her composure. "I know my mother made a deal with you. To not report the rape in exchange for you cutting the sale price."

He reached for the bowl, extracted a nut and placed it between the jaws of the nutcracker. Ruth would have been more jittery at the DMV than he was now. "You're mistaken. And you're too nice a girl—woman—to be pointing a gun at somebody. Gwen always said so. She said you were the good one, the smart one. Kennidy was the slut."

Ruth flinched. "Leave my mother out of this."

"But we can't. Your mother fully expected your sister to be a single mom someday, poor and with some kid on her hands, unable to support herself, just like Gwen was with you. With both of you, come to think of it. She was pretty disappointed with herself by the end. Which is why," he stopped to pop a piece of walnut into his mouth, "she was actually relieved I'd taken an interest in Ken."

"I wouldn't call it 'an interest,' And don't call her Ken."

"I thought your sister might do well in college. Your mom said she couldn't afford to help her get there once Ken wrecked her sports scholarship chances in her junior year. I asked Gwen, 'But what if you had mortgage payments lower than your rent? Then couldn't you make it work? This was before the cancer, of course."

"If this was some kind of act of kindness, why were you arguing with my mother by email before you agreed on the house price?"

"I was being nice for Ken's sake, not Gwen's. I got irritated with Gwen on occasion. She was weak." A faraway look was in his eyes. "She'd let Ken take off and go to parties, skip her homework. None of that was going to get her into college. Truth was, Gwen also wanted to keep Ken around, not let her develop. Admittedly," he smiled patiently, "it wasn't my job to tell someone how to parent."

None of this was going the way Ruth had planned. She wasn't naïve enough to expect him to admit every detail of his crimes, but she had hoped for some kind of meltdown. She'd expected him to beg for either life or death. She wasn't sure if she would give him what he wanted, but she would let him beg. Let him break.

Only he wasn't breaking. He didn't even look rattled.

Ruth gripped the gun tighter, wondering how she would know the right time to pull the trigger. It was like standing at the edge of a diving board, negotiating with yourself, trying to decide when to jump. Maybe they shouldn't have had this conversation. Maybe she should have just shot him in the back as they were entering the cabin. Her desire to fully know, to ask questions and get answers, had gotten in the way of her primary objective: to erase him from the face of the earth.

"You've done this to lots of kids," she said. "I know about Caleb."

"Caleb?" Vorst's eyebrows lifted. "Yes, I helped him make the transition from soccer to cross-country running—the same transition Ken made, after she got kicked off the team. I took him out for training when his parents wouldn't let him attend the normal after-school sessions."

"That's why he'd love to punch you in the face. And worse."

"I'd drive to a trailhead on the weekend, challenge him to get out there in the fresh air, forget about teammates and anyone else's expectations. To just do his own personal best. He'd shake off the bad week. He'd start running."

An idling car, a young runner heading into the forest—Ruth could see it. She imagined the thin legs moving into ever-deeper woods, legs that could be Kennidy's, or Caleb's or anyone's. She saw feet bounding over logs, the nervous motion of a head checking over a shoulder. She felt the breath of the pursuer, closing on the pursued.

"I'd meet him at the opposite trailhead," Vorst said, "ready with a warm car, Gatorade, and when he'd beaten his previous best time, a hug."

Sometimes we run toward those who hurt us, not away from them. Ruth had understood this, but not fully, because she hadn't wanted to. She couldn't bear to imagine Kennidy, Caleb or anyone else trying to earn this man's warped affections.

"Was that the problem?" Vorst said, looking concerned for the first time since they'd sat down. "The hug? Something he wasn't used to getting at home?"

"A hug," she scoffed.

"I massaged his hamstring once when it was injured. And yes, he may have gotten—sorry—an erection. Which isn't uncommon. I used to do more massages and manipulations on student athletes, but in this climate of mistrust—best to avoid the whole mess, I'd counsel the next generation."

Vorst misinterpreted the look of disgust on Ruth's face.

"That's right. These days, you can't even touch a student athlete—not even to treat an injury—without risking your reputation. When Caleb got excited, I didn't say anything. It would have made him feel even worse. And he didn't say anything, of course. But if it led him to feel ashamed, to imagine scenarios that might provide a cover for that shame, then I can understand his present confusion. Is that what you're talking about?"

Ruth shook her head. She thought of Annie confronting the Wolf. He had been so debased, so miserable. He had wept. He had wanted an end to his misery. He had begged Annie to shoot him.

"You're dying of leukemia," Ruth said.

"True."

"You could be dead soon."

"There was a one in four chance I'd make it to five years, and I've done that, but how much longer? The odds aren't great. But I still have good days."

"Why don't you just admit it, then."

Vorst stared at her: lids heavy, eyes dry.

Ruth said, "Admit that you've molested children."

"I have helped hundreds—no, thousands—of children. I have dated a few young women who probably shouldn't have been hanging around with someone as old as me—it's true. I've molested no one."

Ruth remembered the night driving, the music and the smokes and the whiskey, the sight of Kennidy in front of the headlights, swinging the golf club.

"I came to this cabin with my sister, back when you and she . . ."

He was focusing now, squinting, nodding almost imperceptibly—and that felt good to Ruth, because he seemed to be listening and trying to remember. He couldn't deny something she had been part of. He couldn't weave a whole new fable around something she had experienced.

"She broke your garden gnome," Ruth continued. "Because she was pissed off at something you'd done."

Vorst's face relaxed. "Oh, yes."

"And?"

"Your sister had a big heart—easily moved to romantic notions and easily broken. Not because of something I'd done, but because of something I wouldn't do. Are you getting my drift?" A whisper of a grin crossed his face. "Your sister had a crush on me. You spend a lot of time with students as a coach or a mentor. You fill an empty space. Young people get the wrong idea. It happens."

"But somehow an unrequited 'crush' led to a visit to a hospital emergency room just weeks later?"

"Poor girl." Vorst shook his head yet again. "Nothing to do with me."

"She came back here because you had something of hers. My sister was no pushover. She probably put up more resistance than some of your other victims."

"She came back," he said, "because she needed a real adult to help her. You know what we used to talk about? College. Scholarships. If none of that panned out, maybe finding work up north."

"But only if she'd do the other things you wanted."

"You've got no reason to be assuming that, and neither will anyone else."

"Let me make this clearer," Ruth said, feeling her jaw stiffen. "I am going to shoot you in the head, whether you admit it or not. So this is your chance to come clean."

He stared at her again. Slowly, apologetically, he began to shake his head. "You've got the wrong idea, darlin'."

The pressure sat on her chest. Nothing was going the way she'd pictured it. "I want you to imagine yourself dying."

"That's why I'm not afraid of you. That's why I'm not going to lie to you. Because I'm going to my grave with a clean conscience. Because I never did anything wrong to a single boy or girl, and in fact, I have a record so clean that the moment I tell police about this night, you are going to be looking at some real problems. You have a made a very big mistake coming here, Miss McClintock."

IT WAS LATE. SHE'D LET him get up once, to make them coffee and bring out a bag of Oreos. Then they'd sat back down at the table. After a while, he'd gestured to a folded newspaper on a sideboard, and she'd let him take it and spread it out on the table to read to buy more time as she continued to sit, watching him eat as he read, the cookie crumbs falling into the grout between the table's white tiles. The gun was still in her hand.

Ruth wasn't sure how to extract herself from this situation. Vorst had a story and a way of telling it that might persuade any judge or jury. If she let him go, he wouldn't run, he'd stand tall. People would believe him.

She thought she heard the wind picking up outside, but it was hard to tell with her messed-up ear and the rising and falling static that sizzled even in the good one. Looking out the window, she thought she saw a faint glimmer. She covered her good eye: no glimmer. She covered her bad one: a spark or flash, a bright white light, then blackness again.

Caleb wasn't one to talk. He'd be a terrible witness, if it came to that. Kennidy's rape kit had been destroyed long ago. Ruth felt increasingly certain that Van Vorst would never pay for anything he'd done.

And now, after two cups of coffee, she desperately had to piss.

"I really need to go." Somehow, he knew she didn't mean *leave*.

"As do I," Vorst said, folding the newspaper.

"You first," she said.

She stood and followed him to the bathroom, waiting outside the closed door, just to send him the message that he still wasn't off the hook.

He stayed in there long enough to make her anxious. She wandered a few steps away toward his bookcases, wondering what kind of books a man like Van Vorst read. *Think and Grow Rich. Build a Better Birdfeeder.* On the next shelf: *The Next Person You Meet in Heaven.*

She ran a finger across the clamshell cases of old videotapes, mostly from the 1990s and early 2000s: Disney, Americana, football movies, Christmas classics. *The Patriot, Remember the Titans*; *Elf, The Santa Clause.*

She thought of Caleb and his mention of photos. She looked for a scrapbook or box of some kind, but saw only more old movies, more books about investing or church. She idly pulled one of the videos out of its slot, opening one clamshell case, and then another.

Below the cassettes was a drawer. She pulled it open: empty. No one had an empty drawer unless he was reorganizing.

She opened the deeper drawer beneath it. On the top was a shallow tray, full of flash drives: maybe a hundred. She flicked one aside with her fingers and saw through the bottom of the mesh tray what looked like an outline of a human figure, like a young model posing for an old-fashioned Sears catalog.

She lifted the tray up. There was a larger space beneath, full of printed photos. The eyes in the top photo seemed to be staring straight at Ruth. The girl was in white underwear and a training bra. Twelve or thirteen at most, with glazed eyes and a woeful expression. Beneath that, the same girl, in a progression of poses, some with minimal clothes and some without. This was no Sears catalog.

Ruth swiftly inhaled, and then she felt the sharp pinch at the side of her throat.

"You're an intruder," Vorst said softly, breathing into her neck. "and based on that spilled fluid I smelled outside, an arsonist. With a gun. I'm defending my cabin."

Ruth still had the gun in her hand. But she didn't know what to do with it. Whatever he had in his hand—a box cutter, scissors, maybe just a pencil—it was sharp and pressing hard on the side of her throat.

"You fucking monster," she whispered.

"No," he said. "Everyone has their weaknesses. I've helped a ton of kids, and they love me. You wouldn't understand that kind of love."

He grabbed onto her right elbow, trying to pull her arm back to take the gun. She pushed free, hard, and aimed the only direction she could: straight up, firing into the ceiling.

Even as she twisted, she felt the sharp tug of something tearing at her neck, but she focused only on trying to empty the gun so there wouldn't be any ammunition left by the time he pulled it out of her hands.

Two.

She would rather those bullets enter his body, pierce his flesh, make him suffer. But the position was wrong, the timing was wrong and there was only this one chance to empty the rounds before he tore the gun away.

Three-four.

Much as she'd wanted to. Burned to.

Her hand was slipping. He had her elbow up so high she cried out in pain and squeezed the trigger one last time. Ruth knew that not all revolvers were six-shot.

Five.

Some held six cartridges. Some, like Annie's favorite 1881 Smith and Wesson, seven. Others eight or even nine.

With the last tug, Vorst had managed to spin her around. Now he pushed her backward so she fell onto her back, hands trying to protect her face, just as the door opened and Scott rushed inside, with Reece and Caleb behind him.

They had been outside—that was the sound, the glimmer— waiting as long as they could, calling for emergency help that hadn't yet arrived.

Vorst spun toward the sound of the door opening, lifted the revolver and aimed.

FOR A MOMENT, RUTH THOUGHT she understood. This was how Scott would die—a fatal shot, no matter all that she had done to try to save him.

But when Vorst squeezed, nothing happened.

A five-shot. .44 Magnum. It could have been a six-, but it was a five-, and she'd known it. Being right felt good. Being alive felt even better.

Then it was over. Reece tackled Vorst. Caleb piled on as well. Scott was trying to pull Ruth to her feet while shouting instructions to Reece, to pin Vorst's arms behind him and to look for the X-Acto blade he'd plunged into her neck.

"Is that what it was?" she asked before passing out.

5 3
R U T H

Saturday

She was in a hospital bed with tubes taped to her arm. All signs were good.

"How do you feel?"

She thought about it, knowing what answer they—Scott, the nurse and doctor—all wanted:

Fine.

Okay.

Better.

Relieved.

Happy.

Safe.

She opened her parched lips, ignored the burn in her throat and pushed out the first word anyone had heard her say all day:

"Angry."

5 4

R U T H

"Still," she said six months later, when she and Scott had their last argument—a quiet one—and he began to pack his belongings into boxes again. "Yes. Still angry."

"But why? He's being prosecuted. Reece is doing great. Caleb is safe."

"I just am, that's all."

They were in the kitchen of her mother's house. Someone had just made a low-ball cash offer that Ruth was going to accept. All the cabinet doors and half of the drawers were open. The table was covered with his share of utensils, glassware, small appliances. It was a mess, but a mess that suggested change, at least—a final, belated end to the pretense of some unsustainable status quo.

"You've got a good lawyer."

"It's not about that." Yes, she had some legal troubles, not that they weren't worth all that had followed, opening the door to an investigation of Vorst.

"I don't get it. Your health is better, your work prospects are better," Scott said. "You've even got a publisher."

"Fiction. They're insisting I write it as fiction."

"Well," Scott said sensibly, as always, "how else could they publish that sort of book?"

She'd told him everything. His reactions to the full story of Annie's abilities and Ruth's visions had been . . . mixed. It was like two people of different religions marrying each other, agreeing on certain moral principles but not on the nitty-gritty details that simply demand faith.

And there were unignorable timeline differences. In the version of life that he recognized and relied upon, which for her was only one of several possible versions, many events, from Kennidy's death to the beginning and also first ending of their relationship, had all happened later. Yet they had happened. Which didn't mean they were celestially predetermined, but rather *over*determined, caused by more than one factor or circumstance, so that removing or rearranging life's dominoes didn't stop their final cascade.

It was off-putting for one person to remember a spring courtship or a certain fall moving day that for another person never existed.

But that wasn't their main problem, not by far.

Scott was still trying to convince Ruth of all that had gone right. He was an optimist to the end, or at least a contrarian. "You'll certainly get more people interested in Annie Oakley."

"True."

Ruth had already published an excerpt of the manuscript online, summarizing just one aspect of her forthcoming book—that Annie had been analyzed in Vienna—and even without the full paranormal revelations that would be made in Ruth's "novel," the new angle had ignited interest.

At the same time, Ruth had taken to writing opinion pieces about gun control and sexual abuse for newspapers and web-sites. The editors who knew Ruth's topics of interest would keep coming back to ask her to write short-notice opinion pieces. Because shootings kept happening. And abusers and assaulters kept being yanked out of the shadows.

"You're finally making use of your expertise. You're produc-tive and delusion-free. I don't get it," Scott said, holding up to the light a juice glass with a hairline crack. One less thing to pack. He slam-dunked it into the trash.

"I'm not angry about my work. Or my health."

"Then about *what*?"

"About the world. About nothing changing."

Scott sat down on the nearest kitchen chair. "If everyone stopped living just because of things that don't seem to change . . ."

"No," she countered, still standing. "I didn't say I'd stop living. Or speaking. Or writing. Or reading the news. Or pursuing justice in the courts. Or doing all the things we have to do to fight men like Vorst—because no one thing works. We have to do all of it. What I said is that I'm still *angry*. Doesn't someone have to be?"

"I don't know . . ."

They'd had this conversation many times already, about righteous rage, the pendulum swinging too far, people using topical issues as an excuse for impulsivity and incivility, the problems of noise and hate, the magnifying effects of social media, what exactly was or wasn't productive. Ruth didn't claim to be an expert. All she knew for sure was how she felt. On top of it all, she'd learned something from Annie: *There's no one answer. You have to try everything.* The courts, telling your story, therapy, taking back power, facing your enemies squarely. Annie had done it all. Ruth wasn't obsessed with Annie as a person anymore. She was simply determined to learn from her.

Ruth said, "You used to be upset because my mind was always in the past. But now it's in the present. I'm focused on today."

"A today that pisses you off."

"Sometimes."

Scott was still rubbing his forehead in frustration, eyes hidden.

She said, "That's the part you get to choose, whether you mind being with a woman who is angry. At least some days. At least this year." She tried to smile and lighten her tone. "Or this decade."

He lowered his hands and met her gaze. "I do mind, actually."

5 5

A N N I E

1 9 2 5

It wasn't so easy as I made it seem in the final letter I mailed to Vienna. I told Herr Breuer I had left the Wolf alone. I suppose I wanted the good doctor to think I was not only healthier, but also a moral person. The fear of being judged leads us to strange choices, as does the desire to flatter the person who is helping us. Furthermore, it is true that I never killed or even maimed my abuser. I did continue to hunt him, to haunt him—whatever you'd prefer to call it. To keep an eye on him, at least.

This was in 1906. I had shown up for a normal trip to Greenville and the neighboring counties on another pretext, to see family and friends, when I discovered to my astonishment that the Wolf was still alive. He'd seemed so old to me when I was a child, in the early 1870s. But he must have been only forty or so. In 1906, he was in his middle seventies and still thriving, the damned fool.

I didn't expect the matter to be properly ended until he died of natural causes. I was no longer anywhere near as tormented as I'd been, but I wasn't content, either. I considered, one last time, writing to Herr Breuer. Instead I did something unusual. I found the address for Miss Bertha Pappenheim.

Feeling not entirely cured myself, I wrote asking her—with utmost temerity—if she had remained cured, following her

sessions with Herr Breuer. I thought she might deny it, because
her past travails were not something she advertised. Instead, she
replied with the most delightful candor:

*Cured? No doctor cured me. Herr Breuer? He saw me
only until 1882, and I went through even deeper turmoil
in the months to follow and did not emerge from that tortured state for eight more years. The doctor himself once
remarked that he wished I would die and be put out of my
misery. That is how much he believed in my own powers of
recovery, which is to say, not at all.*

*I experienced institutionalization and went through
many dark phases, but in the end I must insist that the most
important cure was the one I effected by myself—and no,
my friend—if I might call you a friend and wish you will call
me the same—I will go further and say it wasn't I who did
it. It was the world of work which deserves the credit: hard
and necessary work outside of the home or salon, raising
my voice and dirtying my hands, taking on the causes that
most invigorated me. After 1890, I immersed myself in the
world of women's rights, I stayed busy, I concerned myself
with helping others, I challenged myself to learn new things
for practical reasons, I allowed myself to feel deep emotions
without fearing them.*

*Please allow me to give you one piece of advice. Rest if
you need rest and talk if you need talk, and if using words
to describe the horrors in your mind gives you peace, then
write and speak and do what you must. Certainly. But do
not expect mere bedrest and talking for talking's sake to
heal you. Find yourself a challenging new task to embrace
and immerse yourself in the problems of others so that you
might forget—however briefly—your own dark past, as
well as your present-day problems. Forgive me for being so*

*blunt, but I know you are a woman of action, and I trust
you will understand and not be offended.*

That letter from Bertha was priceless to me. Of course, I'd
already been active in helping women before I read her advice,
but I'd always questioned whether that was enough, not understanding that it could be enough for a few women and enough for
me, and that was how the world sometimes works, a woman or
ten or one hundred at a time. We do what we can. Most important, I hadn't truly credited those activities for all the healing they
might impart. She'd told me something that fitted well with my
own constitution, for I was never a talker or a writer to begin
with.

Even so, I did send the Breuer family a condolence letter when
he passed away. Perhaps he would never have cured me entirely,
but he did listen that day I burst into his waiting room, a strange
woman he didn't know with an even stranger story to tell. That
was a kindness I'll never forget.

5 6

R U T H

Two and a half years later, Ruth ran into Joe at a bookstore in Seattle, though it wasn't really so random as all that. Her book launch was well publicized, and she'd posted about it on social media knowing that he'd moved to the city and hoping he would come.

He invited her to stay at his house for the weekend before she moved on to other events in Portland and northern California. It didn't sound like a romantic invitation, especially since his sister Justine was also visiting, from Spokane.

"You sure it won't be too crowded?"

Ruth had to remind herself often not to mention his wife Christine, because he had no wife. They'd never married. He hadn't even met her, because he'd been dating Ruth at the time he and Christine were supposed to have met, in one of the alternate past timelines that she still remembered faintly and about which he understood nothing at all.

As soon as she arrived, Ruth took turns holding baby Thomas and chasing three-year-old Reka in and around the blanket-and-chair-forts the toddler had constructed in Joe's basement. Ruth did the dishes whenever she could and, as the first one up, walked Custer, the rescued beagle with a morose face, because it was the

best way to be helpful in this busy house where she was the out-
sider.

Only on the final night, after everyone else had gone to bed,
did she and Joe stay up drinking a high-quality port from Trader
Joe's in place of the cheap red wine they'd drunk in grad school.
They listened to a windstorm building outside, thrashing at the
tall cedar trees in Joe's yard. Joe had lit a candle on the table and
had a flashlight nearby, ready in case the electrical lines went
down.

"So, I have to tell you," she said after he poured them both a
second glass. "I wanted to kill him. Vorst, I mean. Not Scott."

"I figured."

"And it scared me, Joe. If I could have controlled the gun better,
if he hadn't overpowered me . . ."

"But you had time before he got his hands on you. You were
adamant about that. You spent a long time at that kitchen table,
pointing the gun without using it."

"Because I wanted more answers."

"Which you didn't get."

"You've always been straight with me, and I need to be straight
with you."

"Okay."

"I just need someone else to know what I was capable of. I
don't want you thinking I'm a better person than I am."

He leaned in close. "Listen," he said. "As far as I'm concerned, you never have to be anyone other than the real Ruth
McClintock."

She felt a lump in her throat.

The wind gusts got stronger, rattling the house. "That's gonna
wake up the baby." He got up and opened the kitchen windows
to let in the air that was making the panes shake. "Sometimes it's
better to just let the storm do what it wants to do."

When he returned to the table, Ruth served them both more

port. "I'm not getting us drunk, I promise. These are just really small glasses."

"They're delicate. We're high-class now."

Ruth took another breath, inhaling the fresh green smells from outside: bark, resin and even the tides, even though the ocean was a mile away.

"I learned so much from Annie, and I believe she found a better way to heal. She seemed gratified with the work she continued in her fifties and early sixties with Frank. Midlife was the low point. After that, she seemed less haunted."

"And would you say that you're less haunted?"

"Me?"

"About Kennidy."

Ruth chose her words carefully. The truth was, her own interpretation kept shifting. The extra time that Kennidy lived had seemed inconsequential at first. Not so now.

"She was loved. Bob was a good man." Ruth could remember more, day by day. She alone had two timelines, two sets of staggered memories that were equally real, clear in her mind. In both timelines, Ruth was still away at graduate school when Kennidy died. They hadn't had much more time together, only the occasional visit, but Kennidy had graduated high school, and now, Ruth could remember that happy occasion.

"So. That's good."

"But . . ." It was a wound she couldn't stop picking at. "When I was sitting in Vorst's cabin, I was scared of my own anger. I wanted to see him suffer. I wanted him dead."

"But since you confronted him, you're doing other things. That conference you're keynoting is pretty exciting—"

"Joe, I'm not talking about speeches and books. I'm trying to understand something about history here. If it's so full of lessons, why do we still have to go back into the trenches and keep reliving the worst parts and repeating everyone else's mistakes?"

"Santayana. You know the quote."

"But it's incomplete. 'Those who don't read history are doomed to repeat it.' Sure. But even those who *do* read history are *still* doomed to repeat it."

"I guess that's why it's even more important to know it. I mean, if we have to repeat it whether we read it or not, then we might as well read it so we know what we're up against."

She pondered that, nodding.

"Pretty good, right?" Joe said. "I'd better stop while I'm ahead."

He stood up and cocked his head, listening for something. "That's Thomas. I promised Justine I'd let her get at least one night's sleep while she's visiting."

Thomas—and Reka, too—were Justine's kids, not Joe's, named after their parents. Ruth knew it, but for brief moments, she forgot.

She often wanted to tell him that in another life, he'd married and had his own children—his very own little Reka and even littler Thomas—but Joe had said he wasn't ready to know anything about the him she'd known before. "It's not a life I lost, because I never had it to begin with, from my point of view. Maybe when I'm eighty. You can tell me then." Which meant, at least, that he believed her.

Joe stood in the doorway of the kitchen, looking back at Ruth. "What?"

"Nothing."

His hair was mussed, with flecks of leaves in it. His flannel shirt was damp with rain. Ruth was unquestionably attracted to him and kept forgetting there was nothing wrong with that. She wasn't engaged anymore. He wasn't married. They had more in common now than they'd once had. The last few years had at once calmed him down and riled her up.

He said, "I can tell you were about to tell me something."

"No, you were about to tell *me* something."

"I already told you: baby's crying."

"That's it?"

"That's all there is. I just heard the future calling, and he's hungry."

The lights went out at that moment, but she had a candle and her phone.

"You take the flashlight," Ruth said. "I can't help?"

"You're not on duty. Relax."

"Joe . . ." She knew she shouldn't delay him, but it felt important to tell him before she lost her nerve. "You'd be great with kids."

"You kidding me? No way I could be this patient if they were mine."

"Trust me."

"I'm not even the marrying type."

"You're wrong about that." She had a vision then, too, not at all supernatural. They should have been together. They could *still* be together. It was up to both of them now, and nothing stood in their way.

He held the flashlight under his chin, which made his broad face look ghoulish. "This crystal ball thing is giving me the creeps."

"Sorry," she said, laughing. Then he was off to tend to more important things.

For now, Ruth tries to make no big moves, but only to stay in the present, as Annie did after her final visitations to the past—and her trials against Hearst—were over.

For one of her upcoming conferences, she plans to talk about Annie Oakley's later-in-life philanthropy, about which relatively little is known. Ruth is determined to find out more about how much money Annie donated in her later life. Maybe she can locate the names of particular women she supported, track down their descendants.

In the meantime, Ruth allows herself the pleasure of day-dreaming, replacing old dark images she'd dwelled upon for so long with these new ones: eighteen or twenty young women gathered on a vast green lawn. It is the late '10s or early '20s. They are wearing thin, summery dresses. They are holding glasses, laughing and talking.

The orphans' lives haven't been easy, which is how they have come to Miss Oakley's attention. But the women are happy at this moment—relaxed and cared for, sheltered and nourished and educated.

These details are mere speculation, but it's speculation that will see Ruth through months of looking through grainy photos. It will lead her to ancient postcards, orphanage and school records, family trees, census notes. This was the contented phase that Annie had earned, that she had made by turning from bitterness to kindness and generosity, which is not to say she could have done this earlier in her life. She wasn't ready for it. She had to face her own orphaned years and come as close to extinguishing her adversary as she would dare.

But the Wolf is not here in this frame. One can tell by the fearlessness of the women as they stand tall and comfortable. In the distance, a waiter drops a dish, but no one cringes. The sound of a distant car pulling up on the gravel drive makes none of these girls peer worriedly over a shoulder.

When the image starts to fade and Ruth longs to bring it back, to be sustained by it, she only has to focus on the smell of the lawn, the sounds of tinkling laughter, and most of all, the colors:

peach,

pale yellow,

ivory,

white.

ACKNOWLEDGMENTS ───

This book consumed more than a decade, on and off, and was written in the form of many drafts, including ones that bear no resemblance to the book in your hands. I may have forgotten some of my earliest peer readers, but I am still grateful for the time you spent. My extra appreciation to those who provided substantial feedback and encouraged me to grapple with this strange story that wouldn't leave me alone, including Brian Lax, Tziporah Lax, Kate Maruyama, Karen Ferguson, Jennifer Ettelson Besmehn, Bill Sherwonit, Ellen Bielawski, Lee Goodman, Kathleen Tarr, Leonard Chang, Susan Taylor Chehak, Ana Veciana-Suarez, Honoree Cress, Gail Hochman and Rebecca Johnson. At Soho Press, Amara Hoshijo made this a much better book on many levels, working tirelessly even during the most tumultuous year any of us will ever collectively experience (I hope). For all they've done to help with this book and the ones preceding it, I am eternally gratefully to Bronwen Hruska, Juliet Grames, Paul Oliver, Rachel Kowal, Alexa Wejko, Rudy Martinez, Janine Agro and Steven Tran. Additional huge thanks to Gary Stimeling for his sharp eye and Kimberly Glyder for her cover art. Finally, I am grateful to booksellers in both the US and Canada, the latter my new home since 2017, a refuge found after a decades-long search.

ABOUT THE AUTHOR

ANDROMEDA ROMANO-LAX is the author of five novels translated into eleven languages, including *The Spanish Bow*, a *New York Times* Editors' Choice, and *Annie and the Wolves*, selected by *Booklist* as a Top Ten Historical Novel of 2021. Her novels reflect her interest in topics as varied as art acquisition during the Nazi era (*The Detour*), psychological scandals of the 1920s (*Behave*), and artificial intelligence and the future of elder-care (*Plum Rains*). Born in Chicago, she lived in Alaska, Taiwan and Mexico before settling on a small island in British Columbia, Canada. In addition to writing her own books and blogging for 49 Writers, a statewide literary nonprofit she co-founded over a decade ago, she works as a private book coach.

BEHIND THE BOOK

I.
The real story of Annie Oakley and Frank Butler

II.
Discussion Questions

THE REAL STORY OF ANNIE OAKLEY AND FRANK BUTLER

By Andromeda Romano-Lax

C lose to 150 years ago, a fifteen-year-old girl was invited to participate in a private shooting match with a famous marksman and vaudevillian named Frank Butler—ten years older and amused to be in a face-off with a scrappy Ohio teenager.

Reports vary on whether Annie Oakley shot perfectly or missed one in twenty-five shots, but in any case, she beat Butler fair and square. He lost not only the match, but a $100 side bet, worth over $2400 today.

By all reliable accounts, Butler took the loss well. As proof of his regard, he gave Annie and her family free tickets for his upcoming show. Annie, for her part, showed more interest in Frank's French poodle. The real courtship began when Frank sent follow-up letters to Annie signed with the performing poodle's name, "George."

The couple later wed, though Annie kept her professional sur-name. When Frank Butler realized his wife was the more talented and beloved performer, he stepped back, out of the spotlight, becoming Annie's manager, publicist, and most loyal supporter, protecting her good name from the haters of her day, including a certain newspaper publisher, William Randolph Hearst.

I left the Annie and Frank "meet-cute" and other details of their early marriage out of the novel you now hold in your hands, by the way. Maybe I shouldn't have. But this new paperback edition gives me the opportunity to correct the record.

Most Americans who know anything about Annie Oakley's life remember the details that are completely false: like the idea that Annie lost that famous match with Frank. Or that they tied. Or that Frank heckled Annie or stomped off, fuming. Wouldn't that make sense? These were the 1800s, when men were surely more backward than they are now. Annie was a fatherless, poorly educated waif; Frank was famous, though not wealthy. He needed the money and he had a reputation at stake. Wouldn't it be normal for a man to smart over such a humiliating loss?

Well, no. But we're forgiven for having few public images of men losing honorably. We learn a lot from movies and television, not to mention politicians.

Broadway and Hollywood couldn't stomach the true Annie and Frank story—one of complete female competence and talent, and of graceful male acceptance and humility. In a 1935 film starring Barbara Stanwyck, Annie is shown throwing the match in order to save her rival from losing his job—a nod to the concerns of the Depression era, but also the first step in eroding our cultural memory of a feisty girl who wouldn't have done any such thing.

In the 1946 Broadway musical, Ethel Merman's smitten Annie sings "You Can't Get a Man with a Gun" and loses the match on purpose. In the 1950 movie starring Betty Hutton, the character representing Frank quits the Wild West show in a snit, unwilling to be outgunned by a woman. In these versions, Annie has become not just feminine but silly, a girlish caricature—and Frank, even when he is called by another name, is unlikable as ever.

Even in recent revivals, the story stays the same. Annie either loses or can't win without suffering negative consequences. Frank is an egotistical buffoon.

To the frustration of Annie Oakley's descendants, the idea of a bratty Frank and a trivial and lovelorn Annie has outlasted what we know about the real couple. And that's a shame. In every era, we could use more role models of successful marriages in which a man fully supports his wife's career, taking pride in her accomplishments.

My novel, *Annie and the Wolves*, is about more than Annie Oakley, as you already know or will soon find out. It's only partly historical fiction. The rest of the novel is a thriller, concerning a modern-day historian named Ruth who is fighting her own demons, as well as other characters dealing with human "wolves" and the possibility of violence in their Minnesota community.

But part of the pleasure of writing this book, admittedly, was learning about the real Annie Oakley. I promise you that she was much more interesting than her screen and stage portrayals. I enjoy thinking that this book might challenge your preconceptions of Annie Oakley and perhaps even send you along your own research journey—filling in the blanks and discovering, as Ruth does, why Annie's story still matters today.

DISCUSSION QUESTIONS

1. In this novel, which combines an accurate historical foundation with an undeniably fantastical plot, time travel is key. Why do you think the author added this element, and how does time travel as a trope relate to issues like trauma and memory?

2. How does this version of Annie Oakley compare with what you knew about the American icon before, whether fromz Hollywood movies, musicals like *Annie Get Your Gun*, or other popular sources? Why do you think characterizations of Annie Oakley have varied so much over the last century?

3. Some historical tragedies are more easily popularized than others. As Ruth and Joe Grandlouis discuss, the Holocaust is frequently depicted in movies and novels, while other tragedies—including ones closer to home—remain off the public radar. Do we turn toward some difficult public subjects and away from others for predictable reasons?

4. Reece and Ruth bond quickly. What do you think each one gets from the other, and why—aside from any supernatural connection—do they work well together?

5. Ruth's love life is a mess. Which of her romantic relationships were you rooting for, if either? What were some of the biggest differences between Scott's and Joe's attitudes or personalities during times of crisis?

6. One of the most famous time travel stories, by H.G. Wells, was published in 1895. Around the world during this same decade, standardized time zones were being imposed. What connections do you draw between new ideas about time, fascination with time travel, the development of "talk therapy," and concerns about mental health in this time period?

7. Is there something you'd change about your past, if you could? If you could return to one particular day and re-live it, which day would that be?

8. Psychologists claim that the fantasies of revenge are nearly universal—yet rarely acted upon—in western culture. What does "vengeance" mean to you? Do you believe that imagining vengeance has the power to heal or do you think it's harmful?

9. The issue of gun control, as well as the historic role of guns in American society, becomes critical as the story progresses. Characters bring differing perspectives to the table. Did any of the events or opinions resonate or conflict with your own views? Would Annie's 19th-century views be in step, or out of step, with contemporary attitudes and priorities?

10. The novel is a braid of two historical timelines, a structure also used in Romano-Lax's *Plum Rains*, as well as many other novels, from A.S. Byatt's *Possession* to Erika Swyler's *The Book of Speculation*. Have you read other books that adopt this structure for particular thematic reasons? What challenges and opportunities does it pose for the reader?